ALSO BY DARNELL ARNOULT

What Travels With Us: Poems

Sufficient Grace

A NOVEL

DARNELL ARNOULT

FREE PRESS

New York London Toronto Sydney

FREE PRESS
A Division of Simon & Schuster, Inc.
1230 Avenue of the Americas
New York, NY 10020

First Free Press trade paperback edition 2007

FREE PRESS and colophon are trademarks of Simon & Schuster, Inc.

For information about special discounts for bulk purchases,
please contact Simon & Schuster Special Sales:
1-800-456-6798 or business@simonandschuster.com.

Designed by Helene Berinsky

Manufactured in the United States of America

2   4   6   8   10   9   7   5   3   1

The Library of Congress has cataloged the hardcover edition as follows:

Arnoult, Darnell
Sufficient grace: a novel / Darnell Arnoult.
p. cm.
1. Schizophrenics—Fiction. 2. Middle-aged women—Fiction. 3. Missing persons—Fiction.
4. Southern States—Fiction.
I. Title.
PS3601.R586 S84 2006
813'.6—dc22 2005058001

ISBN-13: 978-0-7432-8447-9

ISBN-13: 978-0-7432-8448-6 (Pbk)

First, for William.

Finally, for Juanita.

CONTENTS

Sufficient Grace

INVITATION

And when you turn to the right or when you turn to the left,

your ears shall hear a word behind you, saying,

"This is the way; walk in it."

—Isaiah 30:21

RACIE FOUND the church fans in Martelli's Trash and Treasure on Manchester Boulevard. They stuck up out of a brass spittoon like a clutch of flowers. *Take up the fan*, a voice whispered. She turned around, but no one was there. *Take up the fan*, the voice said again, this time a little louder. At first she was uneasy. She listened for a full minute and heard nothing. She touched an edge of one of the dusty cardboard pictures. *Take the lot of them*, the voice said. *We can use them all.* She brought the fans home and hid them in the top of the coat closet and waited. She waited for over a month and a half. When the voice spoke again she was relieved. *Draw the body of Jesus*, the voice said. *Draw the body of Jesus*, it insisted. *Draw it larger than life.* The voice has since become a comfort.

Gracie stands on a step stool, a broad plastic rectangle of cream-colored Rubbermaid plastic. Her copper-red hair is twirled and knotted at the nape of her neck, the way she always wears it when she is working. She is still a slight woman at middle age, still has elegant limbs, radiant skin, but now her body carries the artful curves that so often come with menopause. What was once hard muscle is now fleshy solidness.

In her left hand Gracie holds a Wilcox Funeral Home fan with Jesus printed on it. Jesus wears white and red robes and his hands are extended, as if offering sanctuary. In her right hand Gracie holds a newly sharpened standard yellow number-two pencil with an unused eraser at the top.

She stretches her arm as far as she can toward the crown molding and draws the first light strokes of hair. With those first feathery lines she begins what will become a larger-than-life-size Jesus on the bedroom wall, the wall at the foot of the bed. Ed can see it every morning when he wakes up and every night before he pulls the chain to turn out the lamp. Jesus will have to watch over Ed because she won't be there to do it. As she stands on the stool softly striking the pencil lead against the freshly dried white latex paint, Gracie asks Jesus to look after her, too, to give her the gift of art so that she might do Him justice. She will take the fans with her. Leave the big Jesuses for Ed.

Ed needs volume. You need portability, says a voice.

She sketches Jesus' jaw line, then begins the eyes. Their intensity, the way they first pierced her with their compassion, is hard to translate onto the Sheetrock wall, but then she feels a tremble go through her body, that jellylike shock that happens when you touch something electrical and un-grounded. Gracie jerks slightly to the left, catches her balance with her pencil hand extended. The eyes improve with a few short strokes of the pencil and take on a vision of their own. Gracie knows the unfinished Jesus is watching her.

The top and sides of His hair take shape. Gracie draws His beard and His mouth. The upper lip is almost invisible. The rounded bottom lip curls out as if to speak. She listens. Nothing. She draws His nose, His cheekbones, the lobe of each ear. She moves as she draws. A line here, smudge there. High. Low. The image pulses forth with her heartbeat. Locks of His long hair fall to His shoulders and keep her from having to draw the ears in their entirety—a blessing. Ears are the hardest things to draw next to hands and feet.

A breeze blows through the open window and Gracie glances out to see the daffodils in bloom along the driveway. Their heads already bend toward the ground. The bright flowers have burst forth in an unseasonably warm February; now, so close to Easter, they will soon be spent. Dashes of yellow fleck the bare woods and leaf-covered ground up to twenty or so yards from the driveway, then raggedly trail off into a buffer of trees be-tween the house and a small city park. The sky is overcast. The gray light makes the waning daffodils appear translucent. Gracie decides to draw daffodils at Jesus' feet.

Ed wasn't pleased when she painted just three walls white in the whole house. "Why not all the walls?" he said. "Why random walls?" She didn't tell him she was making canvases. It wasn't going to help, so she didn't bother. He wants a room all one color. He has become so boring, so shortsighted, so out of touch.

By lunchtime she hopes to have Jesus drawn on all of the white walls: Jesus with open arms in the bedroom, Jesus praying in the garden at Gethsemane in the kitchen over the sideboard, Jesus knocking in the foyer on the white wall beside the front door. She has a fan to go by for each drawing, a full package of sharpened number-two pencils, and a fat white eraser for mistakes and shading, at His cheekbones for example. She never noticed before how high and sharp His cheekbones are.

Gracie is pleased with the drawing of Jesus with open hands. Good proportion, accurate perspective, the illusion of three dimensions. Her childhood art lessons flood back to her. She remembers that young art teacher she had in college. She puts off drawing the hands. She shades the hair around His ears, then steps down to have a sip of iced tea. The stool slips on the hardwood floor as she dismounts, and she lands with a little jump, her hand reaching for the pine cone–topped bedpost just behind her. The bed was her Aunt Claire Bailey's on her mother's side. Aunt Claire never married.

Gracie bends to draw the hems of the robes and notices the baseboards are dirty. She doesn't want dirty baseboards to take away from her drawings. She'll make time to wash them before she leaves.

His sandaled feet are easy. Only the tips of His toes protrude from the ripples in the full hemline. She shades the sandals with the side of the pencil lead. She finesses the toenails, tries to make up for the lack of visible feet by doing a particularly good job on the tips of His toes. She sharpens the pencil to get that crisp edge of the nails as they curve over at the sides and tuck into the flesh.

The feet of Christ, the voice says. *You are at the feet of Christ.* Silence. *Now, the hands.*

Gracie ignores the voice at first. She stands up straight and shades the folds of His sleeves. She widens His lips. It occurs to her that she has never seen a picture of Jesus laughing. She will draw a laughing Jesus when she's had more practice, when she's good enough to draw without a picture to go by. She climbs back onto the stool and adjusts the outer edge of one eye. She uses the eraser to soften some of the lines, to fill in the darker quality of His lips. Gracie fine-tunes everything until there is nothing left to do but the hands.

She looks at the fan for guidance, but the illustrator has taken the easy road, made the hands generic. She wants the palms and fingers of Jesus to be as detailed and perfectly drawn as the tips of His toes. But she was never good at drawing hands. The fingers never looked right. Gracie makes several attempts, then the voice says, Look at your own hands, Gracie. And she does. Gracie looks at her own hands and sees the hands of Jesus.

She moves the dressing mirror closer to her so she can get the right perspective. She begins to draw each wrinkle, each fold, each bend. She takes off her wedding ring and tosses it onto the bed. She extends her hands as if calling all those who need God to come to her. She looks at the way her hands drape down from her wrists, the way her fingers extend and curve back.

When she finishes the drawing, she collects the stool, the pencils, and the eraser. She walks across the room to the doorway and turns to look back at the completed Christ figure. Gracie realizes with joy that it is the best pair of hands she has ever done.

As Toot makes her tenth circle of the backyard, having already mowed the front and sides, a sharp pain shoots up her left leg and through her hip like someone has stuck a wire in there and flipped on a circuit breaker to her backside. She winces and adjusts her position in the cushioned seat.

The seat was damp when she sat down, so now the skirt of her butter-yellow cotton dress, the one she made spring before last, is a soggy mess. Toot wears her broad-brimmed straw hat with the faded green sateen band. She has been doing yard work in that hat for at least ten years. It is a comfortable hat, been wet from rain enough times that it fits her head just right. No point in getting a new one, not for yard work.

In natural repose, Toot's mouth is always a birdish circle. Her lips are beaklike, the upper lip coming over the bottom in a little point at the center. When she is mad or determined, her mouth tightens into a small hard neb that pushes out even with her nose if you look at her in silhouette. Now, despite the pain in her hip, her face is calm. Her lips are gathered in firm concentration. She is praying. She always prays while she mows the huge backyard, one trip round for this person, the next go-round for somebody else. She devotes the circumference of the backyard to her husband Homer who's been dead nigh on thirty years. Then she proceeds through the members of her family in order of their closeness to her. When Toot thinks of her son Arty who's been gone only two years, and his widow Mattie who's taking it all so hard, she simply meditates on the word *peace*. Then she prays for her twenty-seven-year-old grandson, Sammy, a veterinarian, and his girlfriend, Doristeen, who's thirty, unmarried, and the mother of a small child. And she prays for Tyrone, Doristeen's little boy, who's come to stay with Sammy for a while, which means he's also come to stay with Toot and Mattie. Toot has recently elevated Tyrone to family status in her prayer ritual.

Mattie's too deep in her grief to want a child in the house, but she tries to talk to the boy on occasion. Toot was reluctant to take on a child to raise at her advanced age. But Sammy wants this woman bad, and wants to be a good daddy to the boy, even though his work keeps him gone from the house most of the time. So Toot prays especially hard for Tyrone, who spends most of his time in a book.

Once the family is prayed for, Toot's prayers shift to a litany of friends and neighbors who share her circles of mowed grass. As each circuit of the yard becomes smaller and smaller toward center, Toot prays faster and faster to get them all in, all the many folks she prays for on a regular basis. Toot closes out her praying as she moves back and forth to chew away the heart of the yard, that thick box of grass too small and square to get at any way but in straight lines up and back. As always, in the last prayer, this straight-line prayer, this chewing prayer, Toot requests mercy for the soul of a white man she used to work for. She prays for his soul often, because he was a good man who met a sad end, and she saw its results. It lives with her, and in times of prayer, the picture of him rises up. Before she can get that last prayer all the way said, the lawnmower commences a familiar and unwelcome sound.

"I'm gon' finish this whole yard, I'm telling you." Toot's mouth has now pulled into a hard pooch. "I know it's your will and you just teasing me." She looks directly up at blue sky for confirmation and ignores the heavy gray clouds coming over the horizon. "I'm gon' finish that last little bit beyond the garage and down the sides of the road. You'll see."

Mattie fussed at her all morning, saying Toot is too old to be out mowing the grass, even on a riding lawnmower. But Toot's age seldom hits strong enough for her to feel it. At seventy, she has survived things most people never have to face. She raised her child and the white children of the women she worked for, and she has made it to the place where she doesn't have to work for anybody but herself. She wiped babies' butts in other folks' nurseries, cooked meals in other folks' kitchens, swept dust bunnies out from under other folks' beds and settees, and wiped the dirt out from behind other folks' toilets. She ironed shirts on the balconies of the Bible college dormitories for fifty cents a shirt every Friday and Saturday for ten years until the boys got smart and bought permanent press. After years of saving every penny she could and listening to the money conversations of the white men she served dinner to at the country club, one day she didn't have to work for other people anymore. All of a sudden, she got to do what she pleased. And she isn't going to quit mowing grass just because she has another birthday.

There's a chug and another chug and then the riding mower jerks to a stop, leaving a two-foot square of uncut grass dead center of Toot's backyard.

"You just trying to make a point, I see," Toot says to no one visible. "You know good and well I ain't got no more gas for this contraption."

Toot climbs off the mower and limps across the yard, her leathery hand firmly smoothing out her damp dress over her hip with each step she takes. She winces as she climbs the two deep, wide concrete steps at the back of the house.

"You finished, Miz Stubborn?" Mattie asks from the kitchen as Toot stops on the screen porch long enough to slide her grass-covered sneakers off her feet. She is careful of the corn on her little toe. The good thing about wearing her yard shoes is she has cut a little hole in the canvas and the corn never bothers her till she eases the shoe off her foot. The aroma of baking pound cakes and frying apple pies hits Toot's nose and goes straight to her empty stomach.

"I'm out of gas," she answers, coming into the kitchen. She sits at the dinette table and pours lemonade into a glass of ice Mattie put there for her when the lawnmower stopped running.

"You're out of gas, or the lawnmower's out of gas?" Mattie asks. Mattie stands tall with her hands on her hips. A flour-dusted apron covers her T-shirt and relaxed-fit jeans, a dish towel hangs over her shoulder, a spatula dangles from one hand.

Toot ignores the question and instead notices a new heaviness about Mattie's hips. Not fat, just the thickness that can't be fought off. It shows more in the blue jeans than in a skirt. But Toot's not going to tell Mattie how to dress. Mattie is tall enough to carry her age well and wear just about anything she wants.

"You got any pies cool enough to eat?" Toot asks. "If I can't mow, I might as well have pie with my lemonade."

"Yes, ma'am. You want apple or cherry?"

"Ooowee! Cherry pie with lemonade could turn a body inside out." Toot gets up and breaks off a piece of fried apple pie from one of the couple dozen cooling on the brown paper sacks spread across the countertop.

"Where Sammy?" Toot asks.

"He just got back from pulling a calf for Harvey Rodey. Said he was heading to the garage to finish up your houses."

"You finish up the pies," Toot says, "and get the cakes out. I need you to take me to Rodey's Store for more gas. I got to get this yard done today 'cause we 'pose to do the churchyard tomorrow. And I know the Lord gon' hold off on that rain till I get done."

"You do?"

"I do."

"And what about tomorrow?" Fried pies shaped like half-moons sizzle in three large cast-iron skillets. Mattie flips the pies in the pan closest to her.

"He just gon' let it rain a little tonight." Toot takes a long drink of lemonade.

"Humph," Mattie says and turns the pies in the second skillet.

"You'll see." Toot puts the empty glass on the table and looks around the room. Her body moves slow. "Where the boy?"

"What's hurting you?"

"Ain't nothing hurting me. I just waited too long and got to pee, that's all. Ain't a thing wrong with me."

"Tyrone's in the front room reading a book. And it looks like you already peed."

"That boy read too much. It ain't natural for a boy that young to read all the time. And the front room for company."

"Well, he's almost company, and he sure likes that room, and he sure likes to read." Mattie watches Toot head toward the hallway. "Are you limping?"

"No, I ain't limping. I ain't limping. Nothing hurts me. And it ain't gon' rain tomorrow. I just need me a ride to Rodey's Store."

"The BP is closer."

"I ain't spending my money at no new gas station. Clyde Rodey's store been good enough for me for years. I expect it'll keep being good enough for gas, too, as long as they keep having gas pumps."

Toot limps to the bathroom for aspirin or something stronger if she can find it.

Mattie grabs the third skillet handle with the dish towel and turns the last of the pies, then slings her dish towel back over her right shoulder. She's been frying pies all morning. When she cooks for the farmers' market she gets in a rhythm. She sets cooling racks on the table for the cakes and makes room on the counter for the batch of pies fixing to come out of the skillets. She lays out fresh paper bags along the countertop in place of the first ones that have soaked up all the grease they can hold.

Mattie loves to cook and is glad to make money at it. The days she cooks for the farmers' market, Toot gives her space and the kitchen feels like it's hers alone. Her fried pies and pound cakes are well known in

Coats and all its contiguous counties. Only last week a woman from Roanoke came up to Mattie's table and asked her about making rolls and desserts for a restaurant. Said they'd send someone to get their order every few days.

Mattie absently wipes her fingers on the end of the dish towel. She is regular as a clock about some things. She always keeps a towel on her shoulder when she cooks, she always listens to Sam Cooke before supper, and she always knows a lie when she hears one. She knows Mama Toot is lying.

"Tyrone! Tyrone!" Mattie calls toward the living room.

A young boy's voice answers back, "Yes, ma'am?" Mattie hears his little stocking feet come across the hall and stop in the center of the family room beside the kitchen. She knows he is standing there on the other side of the wall with his skinny legs bent slightly and his big eyes open wide, waiting to hear what she'll say next. "Yes, ma'am?" he repeats.

"Get your shoes on, Tyrone. We fixing to go to the store."

"Yes, ma'am, Miss Mattie."

"Get you some change out the jar on my dresser. You can get you one of those chocolate Easter bunnies with marshmallow inside."

"Yes, ma'am," the small voice says, and Mattie hears him scamper back toward her bedroom.

"Get enough for two," she hollers back to the bedroom. "If I eat one with you, I won't be wanting to eat my cakes and pies before I can get them sold." Mattie reckons Tyrone might be the closest thing to a grandchild she's going to get. She might as well warm up to him.

She checks to see if there's any liniment under the sink, then carries the bottle to Toot's bedroom and sets it on the bedside table. She checks her hair in Toot's dresser mirror and hurries back to the kitchen. Using her dish towel again for a pot holder, she grabs each cast-iron handle in turn and lifts pies out of the skillets and places them carefully on the fresh brown paper. When all the pies are lined up in rows on the counter and the burners are turned off, Mattie hangs her apron on the hook by the kitchen door. She keeps her towel on her shoulder and goes out to the garage to tell Sammy she's taking his old truck to Rodey's.

Sammy has spent years learning to be a veterinarian, and where is he?

Out in the garage building birdhouses for the farmers' market. Toot's painted birdhouses are in high demand from just before Easter weekend right on up to Labor Day. Every year he helps her get ahead. But no one paints a birdhouse but Toot. Nobody is allowed in her paints.

The timer on the oven is going off when Mattie comes back to the kitchen. Each cake goes on a cooling rack. By the end of the day, the kitchen will be full of cakes cooled and wrapped in stretch-tite. Some will be sliced in individual portions, some halved, some whole. There will be two coconut, two caramel, two plain yellow with milk chocolate icing, two German chocolate, two Italian Cream, and three carrot cakes, one for the lady who comes every week to buy a carrot cake for her mother. By the end of Saturday afternoon, her table at the market will be bare, all the cakes, pies, and breads gone. This week the table will probably clear early, since it's Holy Week. Folks buy for their Easter dinner and Easter company and Easter trips to see relatives.

She inventories the table and countertop: two plain pound cakes, lemon pound cake, almond pound cake, Arty's favorite, chocolate pound cake. She makes most of the pound cakes in loaf pans, but the chocolate she bakes in the tube pan, the way Arty liked it. All afternoon and evening she will bake bread: oat, sourdough, rye, whole wheat, whole wheat and honey, and cinnamon swirl. Then there are the rolls: dill, potato, orange glazed, and cinnamon. The woman in Roanoke wants to offer Mattie's dill rolls and chocolate pound cake on her restaurant's menu.

"What you put this liniment in here for?" Toot hollers from the bedroom. In a few minutes, Toot comes out with her black oxfords on her feet, her black pocketbook on her arm, and smelling of horse liniment. "I don't know what you put that bottle in there for. Ain't nothing wrong with me."

Mattie breaks off a piece of the apple pie Toot sampled earlier and puts it in her mouth to keep from laughing. Once she laughs, Mama Toot will get mad and the day will be oh so hard.

Tyrone appears in the doorway. His safari shorts droop with all the pennies in his pockets. "I'm ready," he says in a small voice.

"Couldn't you find no quarters?" Mattie asks.

"No, ma'am."

"All right then, let's go."

Mattie takes the towel from her shoulder and tucks it in the handle of the oven door. The three of them—the old woman, the widow, and the child—march out the back door one after the other. The sweet aroma of cakes and pies fills the vacant space left in their wake.

Drizzling rain dampens Gracie's clothes as she walks away from the Victorian house on Starling Avenue, her black trench coat with a ten-dollar bill forgotten in the left pocket hangs on the hall tree by the front door, a hall tree that once belonged to her grandmother Betsy on her father's side. Gracie doesn't think of the pinto beans cooking in the Crock-Pot on the counter by the sink. The house smells of the fresh corn bread she baked and left wrapped in foil, but she is taking flight from the insatiable desires and demands of domesticity. She is rising above a mortal's need to hover and nurture. She knows Ed will eat the beans and corn bread for supper. He will grumble over cold bread, but he can put it in the oven. He can't cook it, but he can heat it up. Gracie can't be concerned with what he does when the beans and bread are gone.

She leaves behind her wedding ring, too, resting at the center of the bed where she tossed it, a golden ring floating in a sea of white-on-white Martha Washington loops and stitches. She has cut her credit cards and checkbook into little pieces and piled them in the center of a serving platter on the kitchen table. *They can follow you with those*, the voices said. The baseboards gleam. She has washed her cleaning clothes, and they toss rhythmically in the dryer. The snap and zipper clink against the speckled drum. The tinny sound echoes through the kitchen and into the empty hallway. Ginger will find them later, probably still warm, and fold them and put them away. Gracie lets go of the beans and the corn bread. They slide away with the coat and the ring and the hall tree, the empty fern stands and white rockers that line the veranda, and so much more. Her last willing memory of that day is of daffodils against the brown leaf-packed ground along the drive.

Gracie slides into her champagne Olds Ninety-Eight. Out of habit, she places her purse on the seat beside her, along with the fans, then cranks the engine, and turns on the radio. Her fingers tap lightly across the top of the steering wheel to Schumann's "Happy Farmer." She stops the car for a moment at the edge of the driveway, then backs out onto Starling Avenue, shifts the Ninety-Eight to the little *d*, presses the sole of her red espadrille firmly against the accelerator, and speeds off. At Brewster Street, Gracie ignores the red light at the empty intersection and the Olds careens to the left. One of the fans, Jesus with the open hands, slides across the ecru leather seat and watches from near the passenger door.

Gracie maintains her light touch on the wheel and drives on into the dreary day. She feels light. Her fingers play the wheel as if it is a keyboard. She makes various rest stops along the way, and, after leaving I-85, visits three roadside hamburger stands in search of safe food.

I wouldn't eat that if I were you, the voices say at Top's Barbecue Shack on Highway 86, and then again farther up the road at Bill's Dairy Bar. As Gracie backs out of her parking spot at the second drive-in, a soft voice says, *I'd get rid of the purse, too. They can keep track of you with it.* Gracie pulls alongside the Dumpster. *It gives off a homing signal*, another voice says. *Toss it*, says another. Gracie extends one leg out of the open car door and, with her right hand still on the steering wheel, she raises up enough to fling her Coach shoulder bag up and over the roof of the car and into the Dumpster. *Two points*, says another voice. *Two! Two! Two!* the voices cheer in unison.

Just before she passes the WELCOME TO VIRGINIA sign, Gracie pays for an approved cheeseburger and fries at Wimpy's Hamburger Hut with the emergency twenty Ed keeps in her glove compartment. She uses the change from the twenty to buy gas at a small store after she turns onto Highway 58. North Carolina is behind her and soon she loses track of road numbers. She drives only by instinct, turns on one country road after another because it feels right, and passes places she only vaguely recognizes.

The sky is streaked in orange and purple. The rain clouds move in the opposite direction from the Oldsmobile as it barrels north by northwest. The late afternoon sun lights a remnant of watery glaze, causing everything in sight to sparkle. As the sun drops low and blinding toward the horizon, the big car lurches and then again and again. Gracie's playful grip tightens and she instinctively pulls the car off the curving two-lane. Rain-drops from tree branches overhanging the road's shoulder hit the car with a barrage of splatters that bleed across the newly waxed champagne hood. The motor dies, making the car nearly impossible to steer. Momentum pushes it a little further as it struggles and slides around in the mud and tall grass off the road's low shoulder. For a brief moment the car is still and silent. Even the music from the radio pauses. Then, with the first notes of Chopin's Nocturne in E Minor, the mud beneath the right rear tire gives way, and the car's rear end begins a slow swing to the right and descent down the embankment. It slides magically through larger trees, crushing small volunteers and underbrush.

When the Olds drops, for a brief instant Gracie hangs as if in flight. Then the bottom of the steering wheel grabs her and knocks her sharply back against the seat while her stomach remains aloft. As she has so often done in recent months, she gives herself up to the lift and pull. She says nothing, makes no sound. She and the car drop from sight without a strug-gle. The car comes to an abrupt stop when the center of the rear bumper lodges against a large hackberry tree. Gracie's head gives a little bounce away from and back to the headrest, flight and alight, then the headrest cradles her head like a hand. Her fingers still lightly hold the steering wheel. Stunned but not hurt, she looks straight ahead, up really, and stares through the arch of the scalloped wheel and across the shimmering dash-board into the liturgically colored sky. She watches the upper rim of a glowing orange ball drop beyond the right corner of the hood, down past the lip of blue-gray mountains she knows to be just out of her sight— mountains not so distant, but indistinct in the sun's burning light.

When dark comes, she closes her eyes to rest. The radio plays Debussy's Arabesque no. 1 in E. Gracie opens her mouth and feels the round full musical notes float from the radio over her tongue and pop like bubbles, spilling silent words behind her lips. Gracie swallows them and drifts off to sleep. In the darkness of early night, with the car off the road and poised to take flight like a rocket, Liszt's Hungarian Rhapsody no. 2 laces the moistening air and masks Gracie's mellow snoring. At the last notes of the rhapsody, as if it has waited for the music to end, the battery gives up its final pulse of power. An occasional hoot of an owl is the only other sound as Gracie's snoring tapers into quiet, shallow breathing. By midnight the owl has taken flight and the faint ping of raindrops once again filters through the budding tree branches and speckles the ground and the vertical Oldsmobile.

In a dream Gracie hears winged women laughing and clapping their hands. Through her closed lids she sees their great shadows hovering over her, their shadowy hands waving, their wings opening and closing. She hears them singing hosannas. In the way of dreams, she can see and not see. Her body rises and rises until, in the dream, she floats over a river, not much more than a creek. Beyond the river is a plush green field, mowed close. She comes to rest on the smooth grass-covered ground, and it wraps her in its green blanket of earth.

In the narrow space between what is real and what is not, what is of this world and what is not, a new voice, tender and deep, thick as syrup and resonant as music itself, says to Gracie, *Whoever welcomes you welcomes me*. And the winged beings chant in sweet unison, *Wade in the water, children. Wade in the water. God's gonna trouble the water.*

Gracie grows lighter and lighter until she feels nothing and hears nothing. She only faintly sees shadows moving, shadows of winged creatures waving their hands over her closed eyes. After a time, Gracie's body rises to float again, and the single deep sweet voice, more distant sounding than before, more powerful than the others, says to her, *Because you are empty, I will fill you up*. Gracie becomes nothing but white heat.

Ed wades through a dry sea of noise. Shania Twain's voice swells and ebbs at ten decibels in tandem with the eruptive rush and hum of air compressors. The boys in the bays pierce the waves with the cadent zip-zip-zip of their impact wrenches pulling and replacing lug nuts around various vehicles from one wheel to another. Tires hiss and expire, give up their rims. Tire tools drop in harsh thuds. Metal clangs against metal. A white '95 Caddy's engine cranks, and Charlie Ensrud backs it out of bay four. A primer-covered El Camino's starter clicks in vain. It all echoes across the concrete floor, back and forth off what little cement block wall is left exposed between tools and parts and tires. Thank God for the small acoustic reprieve of the insulated tin roof.

After years amid such cacophony, and before that, the orchestral sounds of residential construction, Ed has significant high-frequency hearing loss. He knows that these days occupational therapists and industrial psychologists recommend ear covers. But nobody who's supposed to wear them likes them. Most men won't wear them until it's too late, if ever. As Ed sees it, there are only three crucial differences between now and the old days. The music used to be a whole lot better. The prices were way cheaper. And he had hair on top of his head—even had a ponytail. What Ed doesn't realize is that he still has those nice cheekbones and the hazel eyes women notice when they check their cars in, never mind the slight paunch riding above his belt. He still has the hands of a working-man, even though now, as owner of Tire Man, he is more accustomed to the relative quiet of his office just off the showroom, where Estelle prefers to play talk radio. She says the customers don't notice their wait as much when they're listening to talk radio. His tools have become ballpoint pens, catalogs, NCR purchase orders, ledger books, balance sheets, a Rolodex, and an adding machine.

Ed has to run the front desk until somebody gets back. Ordinarily, this is Estelle's job, but she's at the dentist. And Wally, Ed's assistant manager and pseudo son-in-law, has gone to pick up a cycling switch for a GMC Dually. They go out two or three times a season and Ed knows the part number by heart, like so many other letters and numbers that clutter his brain. He clips a work order for two low-profile tires for a Miata to the message strip in the third bay.

The phone rings, and Ed picks up the receiver in the first bay while fumbling with the volume on the radio controls. He pushes the button for line one, presses the receiver hard against his right ear, and sticks a finger in his left.

"Tire Man. Ed speaking." Nobody answers at first. He peers over his reading glasses to watch Charlie Ensrud balance a tire. He's just out of high school, but Ed figures to have him doing alignments in a couple of months. A voice comes over the wire.

"Daddy, where's Mama? And why don't you buy a new phone cord? This one is so damn twisted you could hang yourself trying to talk on the phone."

All Ed hears is a muffle of words coming from the receiver. "What? Can you talk a little louder?"

"Daddy, where is Mama?" Ginger shouts into the phone just as an air compressor shuts off. She sounds peeved. Lately her ass is on her shoulders about something nearly every time he talks to her. It's bad enough Gracie's going through the change, now Ginger's having sympathetic mood swings and she's only twenty-eight. The two of them have always been unpredictable, but Ginger can be so hard, so harsh. He's learned to be grateful in both cases when it isn't something he's done to set one of them off.

"She's home I reckon. Have you tried her there?"

"I am there. She's supposed to meet me here at four to go pick out uniforms for the doughnut shop."

Good. It's not him she's mad at. "Four? What about supper?" It's been a long time since lunch and Ed is looking forward to walking in and sitting down to a nice hot meal.

"Well, there's pintos in the slow cooker."

"Is her car there?" Ed asks.

"No, but her coat's still in the hall. Don't you think that's strange? Her car's gone, it's been raining off and on all day, and her raincoat's still there on the hall tree? She ought to at least have her coat. Did you have a fight with her over money or something?"

"No," Ed runs his fingers over his scalp where hair used to be. "Why?"

"She's cut up all her credit cards and the checkbook. They're in a little mountain of pieces on a plate in the kitchen."

"Maybe they're just out of date."

"Checks don't go out of date, Daddy. I think it's strange."

"I don't know. Strange is a relative thing," Ed says cautiously. He doesn't want to talk to her right now about how strange her mother is getting. Gracie's always been a little different, but it's getting annoying. She won't let him listen to anything but classical music, and she's never liked classical music before. Gracie says he needs culture, awareness. She tells him to look closely, be quiet, listen. But there's never anything to see or to hear. He figures it's her hormones.

"And another thing," Ginger yells in the receiver, "speaking of strange. What's the idea of drawing Jesus on the wall in the kitchen?"

"You can quit yelling right now. The compressor went off. What did you just say about Jesus?"

"On that white wall in the kitchen," she says, still a little too loud. "The Jesus."

"What Jesus?"

"The one kneeling at the rock praying over the sideboard. Hell, Daddy, he's big as the sideboard. How could you miss it?"

"There wasn't any Jesus over the sideboard when I left this morning. That's how I could miss it. What rock?"

"The one drawn on the wall in front of Jesus. He's kneeling at a rock praying. I have to say, the drawing's pretty good. Who did it?"

"I don't have any idea who drew it," Ed says, but he does. What in the world is Gracie doing drawing Jesus on the kitchen wall? She's never even been religious. Those white walls. Ed breathes deep to remain calm, something he heard on talk radio about stress control.

"If you got the time," Ed tells Ginger, "wait there for fifteen or twenty minutes and see if she turns up. I don't have a clue where she is, but I'm sure she'll be back in a little bit."

"I don't have all day. Wally and I are supposed to go to Home Depot and pick out countertops, if I get home in time. I don't see why she can't just be here like she's supposed to be. Bye." The dial tone sounds before Ed can say *bye* back to her. He hates that. People ought to wait for someone to say good-bye back. He and Gracie surely raised her better than that. If she's going to open a doughnut shop, she had better learn that subtle things, like hanging up before a person can say good-bye back for instance, will lose a customer. And that cussing. People don't want to do business with a cussing woman. There isn't much difference between a tire and a doughnut. Business is business. She'll have to do more than make a good doughnut to succeed. There's always somebody else who can make as good a doughnut as you. That's the most important concept to grasp in working for yourself. Product is only as good as the service that comes with it. He needs to write that down. He'll use it to start out his sales meeting next week.

After giving Charlie a few tips, Ed returns to the service desk and does a search on the computer. He's one tire shy of a set for the Dually. He doesn't give another thought to Ginger or Gracie until later that night when he's eating cold corn bread from a piece of torn aluminum foil and hot pintos from the Crock-Pot.

Ed doesn't like eating alone. And he doesn't like looking at giant pictures of Jesus while he eats. They're bound to give him heartburn. What's that woman thinking about, drawing Jesus over the sideboard? Jesus at the front door, too. A door only used for UPS deliveries and to fend off encyclopedia salesmen and missionaries. And he can't begin to bring himself to deal with the Jesus at the foot of their bed. How's he going to sleep with Jesus looking at them all night? How's he going to get it up the next time a little loving comes to mind? They're married and all, for twenty-nine years, but it isn't normal to have Jesus watch a man have sex with his wife. There's going to be a fight probably, but Ed's going to paint over that bedroom Jesus.

Ginger's buying a doughnut shop, not IBM. And just how long can two women shop for uniforms? Ed wants things to be like they're supposed to be—employees answering the phones, wives serving up the dinner and keeping a man company while he relaxes from a hard day at the office, rooms painted just one color, pictures on the walls small and framed and plain enough so that no one notices them. Is that asking so much?

At ten o'clock Ed goes for seconds on beans, this time using a bowl. He crumbles in a piece of corn bread and adds some chopped onion, a little Texas Pete. He flicks off the Crock-Pot, then takes his second round of supper and a fresh glass of tea into the den to catch *Andy Griffith*, which usually makes him feel better about everything. There's no Jesus in the den. Ed feels lucky Gracie didn't decide to paint the heart of pine paneling.

Ed wakes up at eleven-thirty, turns off the television, and goes to see if Gracie is in bed. No Gracie. He calls her name out loud to make sure she isn't down the hall or in the bathroom. No answer at all. He tries Ginger's number. No answer there either. It's Wally's bowling night, but Ginger should be home by now. *An accident? Could that be it?* After wrestling with the phone book Ed finally finds numbers for the emergency room and the highway patrol.

"Hello. My name is Ed Hollaman and my wife is missing . . ."

After almost two hours of phone calls, several frustrating conversations, and being put on hold numerous times, Ed puts the phone receiver in its cradle for the night. No Grace Hollaman admitted to any ER and no accidents reported involving an Oldsmobile, or any other kind of car, in the last forty-eight hours in four counties.

Ed walks into the bedroom and looks at the Jesus with open hands. The flood of light from the lamp he turns on reflects off a small gold ring in the center of the white bedspread. Something he'd missed earlier, in the room's natural light.

There it is, he thinks. *She's run off. She's left me.*

He should have seen it coming. People say men have midlife crises, but it's the women. No wonder they call it *the change.* He hears stories like this at the Moose all the time. Women leave their husbands for no reason, with no warning, when they hit the hot flashes and the night sweats. At poker a few weeks ago, one of the guys was talking about his sister-in-law running off with a parking lot attendant. Now it's Ed's turn to be left.

In almost thirty years of marriage, Ed has never known Gracie to take off her wedding ring, but here it lies, cast among the nubby loops of the spread, the ones that make pockmarks on his face when he takes his Sunday nap.

"She's gone," Ed says just loud enough to make sound in the empty room. *We'll see how long she stays gone with no plastic in her pocketbooks.* Hurt makes him shrink just a little. He looks to the giant Jesus with the open arms and involuntarily mirrors him. Ed's eyebrows go up, his mouth hangs open, and he extends his hands as if to ask, *What in the world?* But

Jesus has his poker face on. Jesus with the open arms isn't giving any answers.

Ed reaches for Gracie's wedding band and puts it on the bedside table. As he turns back the covers, he thinks of calling Landry, his lodge brother, down at the police station. One of the people at the highway patrol station suggested calling the police if Gracie didn't come home. But now Ed understands this is personal, private business. Not something to have in the paper in the morning. It's only Gracie and one of her hare-brained ideas coming between them. He used to think those ideas were entertaining, made her interesting to live with. But the ideas have gotten stranger, more difficult to swallow, like all that classical music and three Jesuses on the walls. Now those ideas wear him out.

She'll be back tomorrow. After she's scared me a little, made me pay attention. That is, if there's no parking lot attendant or grocery boy in the picture. Ed thinks of calling Ginger again, but he knows it won't do any good. *If Gracie was over there, Ginger would have called by now. No sense waking her up so she can worry.*

Ed climbs in bed and takes a deep breath in an effort to remain rational, logical. Kidnappers would have taken the credit cards, maybe even the checkbooks. Gracie never carries cash. Says she doesn't need it. Ed always makes sure there's twenty dollars in her glove compartment so she has something in an emergency. And Gracie usually has some little problem here and there that eats away at that small reserve. A tip for the grocery boy, not wanting to write a check for a pack of gum, donating to a deaf man who hands her a printed card in the Wal-Mart parking lot.

Tomorrow he'll know what to do. In the meantime, he situates himself in the middle of the bed, pulls up the covers, and closes his eyes. He tries to think about tires, about fan belts, about alternators for El Caminos. But it isn't working. He wants to sleep on his side of the bed like he always does, and wants Gracie on her side pulling at his covers, her rump pushed up against his. He wants to forget that Gracie's ring is on the table by the lamp and not on her finger where it belongs. And, perhaps most of all, he wants to forget that Jesus is looking at him through the dark.

J EZEREEL HOLINESS can only be called small. But then Rockrun is small, standing in the shadow of the big mountains, a tiny mostly black community on the banks of a medium-sized creek, tucked between two mostly white townships. To Mattie, walking to Jezereel Holiness is as natural as breathing. The Rileys have worn a thin ribbon through the woods between Toot's farm and this small white church with its simple steeple and its bright red doors. First a footpath, then a cart path, now it is a narrow road for the riding lawnmower and the cart full of lawn equipment it pulls from the house to the church every week. And it is an artery between Mattie and Arty.

In the past few months, Mattie has become a one-woman Jezereel gardening committee. Today she has used her mattock to break up the hard ground in the stone-bordered flower bed she has built between the front of the church and the highway, and now she pushes the spade deep into the turned soil to work in the sand and fine gravel, the seasoned manure and compost. The sad old sign and lifeless junipers that once squatted in front of the church have been dug up and hauled away. Mattie works hard in the late April sunshine to amend the soil. In the middle of the bed is the beautiful new sign Brother Hairston made, based on Mattie's drawing.

Anything that keeps her near the church is welcome work. Not so much because she wants to be close to God, but because she wants to be near Arty and the life they had together.

After an hour of toil, the enriched dirt begins to take on a mealy texture. Mattie pushes and pulls the garden rake through it until the top of the dirt is smooth and evenly distributed within the circle of large layered creek rocks. Then she kneels down and pushes her hands deep into the loose earth. She imagines herself beneath it, pulls her arms out of the ground and smells the clay and organic matter on her skin. She shapes a mound of dirt into a firm hill that she pretends is a leg, a beautiful strong black leg. She smooths away the leg and begins to plant as she cries. One Carissa holly goes on each end of the new sign, then white dwarf azaleas beneath the sign, both front and back. Out from the foundation plants, as she sobs with abandon, she situates a triangle of Homestead verbena. Next month, she'll fill in with Purple Wave petunias. White and purple flowers near the sign, bright yellow forsythia on either side of the red doors, and assorted colors of daylilies alongside the walkway. Mattie wants this church that she and Arty attended to be a glorious hallelujah of color. Next year she will plant a tiered perennial garden against the hillside, lots of bulbs and tubers. With the last verbena in the ground, everything watered, and her cry over, Mattie goes inside to wash up and get her vase of daffodils to take to the grave.

Her face now dry but puffy, Mattie stands in the open doorway of the sanctuary and tries to take in all the details—the earth, the stone walls, the new gravel in the parking lot, the sound of Toot's mower buzzing on the other side of the church, the hard blue cloudless sky that comes after days of rain. She wonders if that is the color Noah looked into when he saw the dove fly back at him with an olive branch, when God decided to make peace, make a new covenant. *God, you need to make a new covenant with me.*

Mattie fights to stay in the present. Only work saves her. Baking, for instance: the measuring, the kneading, the spooning, the checking. And the vegetable garden at home: all that planting, weeding, picking, canning, preserving, pickling. And quilting: the sitting and piecing her squares and strips. And the silent and diligent partnership she and Toot make as they sit across from each other at the quilting frame, each of them stitching their perfect path. And at the church: the landscaping and gardening, carrying the rocks from the creek to the cart, getting them to the flower bed, her regular assistance to Toot in the upkeep of the sanctuary and the cemetery. Time is nothing more than a schedule in widowhood, what has to get done in the next little bit and what has to get done after that—what day to make the cakes and what day to piece the quilts and what day to plant the spring peas and what day to put in the Purple Wave petunias—all in an effort not to cry too much or sleep all day. One day ticks off into the next, one chore ticks off into the next, one washed dish in the drainer and then the next. In the spring you plant petunias, in the fall you plant pansies, and set out the mums. Getting through an hour is as hard as a week. That is widowtime.

For Toot, on the other hand, this work at the church is her tithing. She did these things and more for white ladies all her early womanhood, and now, in her domestic liberation, as Sammy refers to it, she does those same things for the house of the Lord. For Mattie, though, it has become a working-off, a purging.

As she walks to the cemetery, Mattie thinks of Sammy. He's pushing her to move past her grief. A son losing his father, that is part of the natural cycle, and the son moves on. But a woman losing her husband? That is not so easy to reconcile. Mattie understands too that Tyrone is part of Sammy's plan to bring her back to life. Sweet as he is, Mattie is too tired to want to love anyone new, even a quiet, awkward child.

"That girl has a five-year-old boy and never even been married. That baby's daddy is MIA, no more than a leaf in the wind," Mattie had barked at Sammy a few months ago, when he first mentioned Tyrone coming to the farm for an extended stay.

"I love this woman," Sammy had said to her. "I want to give her and Tyrone a family, and I need you and Mama Toot to help me. I want to help her make a better way for herself and the boy. Surely, you can understand that."

"What if she's hard to pin down like her own mama?" Mattie asked the pillow beside hers in the middle of the night. "What if she up and disappears without nothing but a little note, like she says her mama did?"

"Tyrone needs a father and a family," Sammy refrained for days.

"Give the boy and his mother a chance," said the pillow on the other side of the bed, its voice a vibration in Mattie's chest.

So now Doristeen works on a special teaching certificate in Charlottesville, and Tyrone hides and scurries around a strange house.

Mattie moves down from the stoop, lets her fingertips slide along the black iron rail like it's another body part—an arm, a dark arm. But it is a railing. Her body calls to her at night sometimes. *Remember me, sweet thing*, it sings. *Remember me*. She wakes up thinking Arty is singing to her.

In the daytime she knows it's her own voice crying out from some mouth deep inside her that longs to be fed.

She hears Toot come around the corner of the church on her last pass at the side yard by the parking lot. Toot presses the clutch, shifts up into fourth, and lifts the blades.

"You go on down in front of me," she shouts, "or you be eating my exhaust till next week."

Mattie picks up speed and heads through the cemetery entrance, two concrete pillars decorated with glass and stone and shells that she and Arty brought from the coast. The population in the cemetery now outnumbers the head count inside the church on any given Sunday morning or Wednesday night. She straightens flowerpots as she walks, sets some on top of headstones as she passes. She's going to mow around the headstones with the push mower, if she can get the thing cranked. People in the Jezereel congregation are all the time donating to the church what they need to donate to the dump, like that old push mower.

Toot engages the blades of the riding lawnmower and the hum of the machine climbs to a roar at the edge of the cemetery fence. Mattie knows from many such workdays that Toot will make three full laps to cut the narrow strip of grass outside the cemetery fence. Then she'll park the riding mower and come inside to move and shift the rest of the pots and vases and statues of Jesus and little baby angels as Mattie pushes the smaller mower around the cemetery markers and over and between the graves, always aware she is walking on the dead. Sammy will come by this evening, after he makes his rounds to the farms, and he'll weed-eat whatever grass or weeds have escaped the women. The women save that for him so he is a part of it. All this work at the church is like a symphony. Tyrone will need a part, Mattie decides. He can help with the petunias to start. The boy doesn't touch enough dirt.

Mattie draws closer to the tree line. Arty's grave is near the edge of the cemetery, on the side closest to their farm. She sees the double marker situated beneath the giant poplar. She can't read it yet, but knows Arty's name is etched in black letters, his date of birth and his date of death beneath it, and the words Soul Searcher. Mattie's name is beside Arty's, her date of birth in the same crisp block letters. But a blank space for her date of passing makes the polished granite marker look unbalanced, like an unmade bed.

Death makes the world uneven. Just ask Louise Redd, her baby's grave still fresh as Mattie's flower bed. A wreath with an Easter Bunny and a pink ribbon coming across yellow silk roses stands at the head of the small mound of earth, and a ceramic cherub prays beside the bunny. *Now, how uneven is that? To lose a child, to be a mother with full breasts and empty arms.* Mattie sinks deep into the idea of all the sad people who have stood in this place and looked for somebody who cannot come back. As she turns toward Arty's grave, Mattie focuses on something that does not belong in a cemetery, the shape of a body on top of the dirt, a woman's body sprawled on the ground in front of Arty's double marker.

For God to work through Mattie, even in her grief-stricken fog, even with her need for a new covenant, is not so unbelievable as some might think. It is a gift like any other gift, an act of love.

Mattie knows this to be a gift and a charge almost immediately because a wife doesn't just walk out of church every Friday and find another woman, white at that, lying across her husband's grave. That is how she first knows it as a sign, because of the unusual nature of it, and then because, after a few days, she won't be able to see it any other way.

"Lord, Mama Toot, come quick!" Mattie calls. "Toot!" she screams, her voice urgently rising over the din of the lawnmower. She begins to run to the woman, to Arty. Her breath is short as her knees hit the soft spring grass beside the woman's body. Grass stains press into her skirt. Mattie rolls the woman over on her back. The woman is breathing. She is still breathing.

"Mama, that's a white woman you found, not a stray dog." Toot knows Sammy says this louder than he means to. She doesn't even need to cut her eyes at him. He checks himself and speaks a little softer. "We got to call DuRon and tell him what happened before somebody comes looking for her. Mama Toot, you know I'm right." Sammy looks at Toot for help that she doesn't give him. His chin drops and he looks at Toot as if to say, *I can't believe you're not helping with this.* He looks back at his mother and sets his jaw. "Some of her people's bound to have filed a missing person report, Mama. The police probably already know all about this woman. You've got to go to the police. Hell, she needs a doctor. Have you thought about that?"

"Don't you blaspheme in this house," Toot says.

First they take in the child. Of course they did that for Sammy. Now they have a middle-aged white woman. Toot wonders who's going to come to them next. She thought she was done taking care of white folk.

Toot knows Sammy's right. So does Mattie, deep down. He isn't saying anything new. She and Mattie both thought all this already, talked about calling the police, having a full house, folk looking for a white woman and finding her with them and them not saying the first word about her being there. They talked about it while they were loading the strange woman into the little cart Toot pulls behind the riding lawnmower. But Mattie doesn't reveal what they've already talked about, and Toot plans to see where the Lord takes this chat Mattie and Sammy are having.

Mattie keeps right on stitching her appliqué. Sammy stomps off to the kitchen, probably to get him some pie. Mattie's working on a tulip quilt that's so pretty, they plan to hang it behind the cake table at the market when she gets done. They aren't selling it for a dime less than five hundred dollars. Toot told Mattie if she believes she'll get five hundred, then she'll get five hundred.

Sammy comes back in holding a piece of sweet potato pie. That was his daddy's favorite pie. He just stands there leaning on the doorjamb looking at Mama Toot, then at his mama. He's clearly wondering what's come over them both to bring that woman home. He starts to say something, then he stays quiet and takes another bite of pie. Of course they had to do something with her, Toot thinks, because there was no phone at the church. *That woman riding in that trailer behind the riding mower wont any worse than her working her way through woods full of saw briars in the night rain like she'd already done and sleeping on that grave ever how long till they found her.*

"Mama, will you please talk to me about this?" Sammy says, licking the last of the pie off his fingers. Mattie pushes her reading glasses up on her nose and pricks one thread from the white backcloth with a single-thread needle and catches the rolled edge of the red calico tulip. She does pretty work. Toot has always admired Mattie's quilting. *You'd have to look and look to find a stitch that wont perfect.* She says next she's going to do a memory quilt, one to hand down to Sammy. But right now, Mattie refuses to look at Sammy, keeping her eyes on her needle and thread as she moves it out and away from her, cinching the cloth together, tiny stitch after tiny stitch. "Yes, sir," Toot says quietly, "your mama can sure enough sew."

Sammy looks at Toot as if to say, *Don't change the subject.* "Look at me, Mama," he says and sits down in the chair beside her, his torso pitched slightly forward. "I am going to call DuRon. I have to. Daddy is dead. I'm the man of the house now, and I say we need to call the police. You hear?"

Toot thinks, *Oh Lord.*

Mattie, she looks up from her sewing, stares at Sammy over her gold-framed Walgreen's reading spectacles, and says in a voice solid as a rock, "That woman was sent to me by God. Rachel stays right where she is. Nobody is going to call no police to be taking her away. That is that. I'll take care of the doctor."

Yes, Lord, Toot says to herself. It's no wonder Arty brought her into that house. She's something, that Mattie. If Toot had doubts before, she knows now the Lord is moving in her. *Yes, He's moving right now.* Toot can almost see Him in her living room, can feel Him in Mattie's talk, solid as a rock. But Sammy, he's not ready to give up yet.

"Mama, you've gone and named that woman?" Sammy's whole body leans closer, showing he can't believe it, his old talk coming back on him. Then he gets back to his proper self. "Mama, I am a respected member of this community. I have white farmers paying me to doctor their animals. You think they're going to want to do that when they think I might have kidnapped a white woman?" He runs his hands along the fronts of his legs. "Mama, I can't let you keep her. You don't name people you find. You call the police!"

Toot knows he just went too far, raising his voice, saying what he said, and she can't help him now. *You gon' to have to get out of this one your own lonesome self.* Mattie keeps her head down, her fingers moving, sewing, never missing a stitch. Sammy leans back in the club chair and slaps his hand on the top of the end table.

"Am I the only one aware that we are black people and the woman in the laundry room is white?"

Toot wants to say, *You fool, you pushing your luck.* But she just keeps listening and watching, ready to put her face back to her Bible if anybody looks to see if she has something to say. She's turned to Genesis 48, where Rachel is buried away from her people. That's how they came up with the name. Toot is the one who named the woman. They had to call her something. They couldn't have her there for who knows how long and call her *white woman* or *stranger*. If anyone asks Toot what she's reading, she can quote it without looking. Mattie's about to finished her tulip. Her jaw is twitching. That means she's going to let loose. *Oh Lord.*

"Now you listen to me, Samuel Riley," Mattie starts, and Toot thinks, *Oh Lord.* "And don't you 'But, Mama' me," she says, leaning back at him so strong and sudden that he backs off. "You are not your daddy. You do not tell me what I can and can't do. Your daddy, bless his soul, didn't even try that. Therefore, you don't *let* me anything. That woman, black, white, purple, or green, came out of nowhere and was laying on my sweet Arty's grave. Now, *that* man could be the head of my house. You, on the other hand, are still a boy and will always be a boy to me. Especially if you don't respect your mother anymore than you are showing me tonight." She stands up and takes a step at Sammy and he sits all the way back in the club chair like he used to do when he was ten and Toot was on his case for throwing rocks at the chickens. He can't get back any farther. "Now, Rachel laying on your daddy's grave may not be a sign to you or your educated highfaluten friends you been hanging around with, so that you don't go to church except to trim the weeds and the shrubs, and it may not be a sign to DuRon and the rest of them down at the sheriff's office, or to Harvey Rodey and some of his lily-white friends with their sick cows. But that don't concern me. I can see for myself and that's all the sign I need."

Amen, Toot thinks. Mattie holds her eyes on Sammy's face for just the right amount of time. Toot might have held it a little longer, was it her, but Mattie did it long enough. Then Mattie sets back down and goes right on with her appliqué, starting another tulip, like she expects him to move on to some other subject. And he does.

"Mama," Sammy says, struggling to be calm, looking back toward the kitchen at the swirls in the linoleum, hunting him a good comeback in those layers of vinyl and Aerowax. "Mama, I am almost thirty years old."

She cuts him right off. "You are twenty-seven years and six months old come next Tuesday and I don't care if you are fixing to turn sixty-two and can retire early. I got business with this woman. God's business. Now you go tend to some business of your own. Some horse, or somebody else's cow, or something. I do thank you for getting her in the house this afternoon and in the little bed. Now go on."

"Mama," he says again, this time a little impatient.

"You go chase some woman or something. That's what you're usually about when you're not out giving shots to dumb animals. You leave Rachel to me."

"What is that suppose to mean?" he wants to know, meaning about the women, and Toot sees him look around to see if Tyrone is close by. "And will you stop calling her Rachel? You don't know her name." Toot sees from his face that he knows he has lost the battle.

"For now, her name is Rachel. We got to call her something. Now go on, I tell you. Get on out of this living room."

Sammy stands up and in a minute the screen door at the back of the house screeches and slams, but not before his feet hit the dirt past the back steps. His truck door slams, too, in quick time and with a whole lot of noise. There's the racing motor and gravel thrown up underneath his truck and out from under it. He peels out the drive onto the road like he used to when he first learned to drive. In Toot's experience, when a man wants to show off or show he's mad, he's almost always going to do it in a car or some vehicle—unless he's the type to hit. Toot doesn't allow any man around her to hit. He'll be a dead man, weighted to the bottom of the river, if a man ever hits her or one of hers, as long as she's able to pick up a two-by-four or a 12 gauge. But Sammy doesn't seem the kind to hit. Just to leave rubber, throw gravel, throw down his hat maybe, let the door slam. Not much more than that. Maybe say something he shouldn't say, something he'll wish he hadn't said later on. *Now we all gon' do that from time to time.*

Mattie, she picks up her stitch, makes her a nice knot that will hold till that quilt's long in a rag bag, and she bites the thread loose with her teeth. Toot keeps telling her not to use her teeth. Mattie weaves the end of the needle into the folded edge of the drape beside her chair, extra thread spun around the needle top like a little turban. It's ready now to sew on the next button or do a little bit of quilting or mending. Toot knows this part without even needing to watch. There's an army of threaded and unthreaded needles there on the backside of the curtain. That's one of the things Mattie and Toot agreed on from the beginning. You've got to know where your tools are, and needles go in the backs of curtains. It's important to keep them in reach and ready for what little job might come next.

Gracie wakes up in a narrow bed in a small room with a cabinet full of jellies, chow chow, pickles, and creamed corn among other things she can't quite make out behind the lead-glass doors. The doorknobs on the cabinet are large diamonds. She hears music and singing coming from another room. Sam Cooke. She has been hearing many things recently, sometimes words, sometimes music, sometimes singing, but she cannot always see the source. In fact, she initially questioned the source. Now she has faith in it. Sometimes she starts to see it, but it doesn't quite happen.

Soon, the voice says. And there are other voices. *Soon,* they all say. For now, they are invisible, or shadows at best.

Gracie has always played the radio during the day while she cleaned house or hooked a rug or cooked supper or made the beds. If she was alone, she sang with the radio and danced a little as she dusted tabletops or chopped onions or slipped oatmeal raisin cookies from the cookie jar. It was almost always rock and roll, something to sing along with, something to make you move like you're young and life is still ahead of you. She particularly liked to vacuum to Aretha Franklin turned way up loud, garden to Bob Seger, iron to Neil Diamond. She listened while Ed was at work because he always wanted the music off and the TV on when he came home. Ed wanted quiet or a good rerun when he came home.

More recently though, when Ed has been out of the house or she has been alone in the car, Gracie has listened to classical music and jazz. Sometimes, she's insisted they listen to the classical station while eating supper. If Ed made noise about her turning it off, she just ignored him. And for some reason, he never got up to turn the dial.

She particularly likes Tchaikovsky and Coltrane. Rock and roll make her want to sing. The instrumental music makes her listen, pay attention to things she didn't notice before. It doesn't muffle the voices that are there beyond the music. She can hear what they say without the lyrics confusing her. Sometimes that's how they say things. The music floats into her mouth and pops and the words explode into her head. Sometimes what she hears is not so distant at all but inside her, vibrating in her lungs or her belly or her brain or her tongue or her eyelids or her nipples. Who would think a nipple could talk? It's as if pieces of a puzzle float around her and in her, and if she tries to grab one piece she has to let go of another. Sometimes there's so much sound inside her, she flicks the extra from the ends of her fingers. Sometimes the sound is right next to her, like the person next to her on the bus. But there is no bus and no person.

The last thing she heard from her voices was the singing, and the wings beating in the shadows above her, and the single deep voice promising to fill her up. Gracie has always felt so empty.

The voices are quiet now. But she knows the chorus will return, will come to her at the simplest or the strangest moments. When she is grocery shopping they come to tell her what food is poison and what isn't.

Rub the poison off the cabbage and flick it on the eggplant, one voice had said. *No one ever really buys eggplant.*

Gracie watched the eggplant for weeks and it got old and was discarded and new eggplant took its place.

One voice tells her when to drive her car and when to walk. One tells her that Ed's screwing his secretary of twenty years, blond-headed Estelle. Of course she isn't a real blonde. Gracie doesn't need voices to tell her that. Gracie has given Ed the benefit of the doubt when it came to Estelle. Men don't usually go for women who are so obvious, and Ed isn't the kind to fool around at work, if he fools around at all. But one voice seems convinced he is screwing Estelle, or if he isn't screwing Estelle now, he soon will be. Another voice sometimes defends Ed and says it isn't true. Honestly, the idea doesn't bother Gracie. She hasn't liked sex with Ed for a long time. *If Estelle is happy with that job, maybe she should have it. I've had it longer than I need.*

One of the voices told Gracie to leave home. *There's nothing left for you here now,* it said. *Go left at the light!* the voice told her without much notice at Starling and Brewster. She remembers the tires squalled. And what happened? Here she is in a little room with jelly and pickles and canned corn. Light green cotton sheets rest cool against her legs, old cotton sheets worn slick from washing and ironing, like the ones she had as a child. She sees the sharp creases from the iron at regular intervals across the sheet where it covers her chest and arms. Everything in the room comforts her, even the washer and dryer.

The sun is going down and rays of light come in over her head and strike a row of jellies turning them to jars of emeralds, rubies, amber. Things look different to her now, as if she sees beyond what is ordinary, into a world that exists beside the one everyone else knows about. She sees more than the thing itself. She sees what lives inside it.

There is a small window beside her bed. For a few minutes her room is bright with the light coming from the west, but then the sun drops, perhaps behind a row of hemlock trees. She likes the idea of hemlock trees. *Hemlock.*

Gracie opens her mouth and lets the word float in. She decides to bite into it and it squirts at the back of her throat and burns like bitter mint. But the word is not poisonous. It doesn't bite back.

How long has she been sleeping? She remembers another sun dropping over the hood of her car. Her room grows dim. The door beside the jelly cabinet leads into a kitchen. She sees a slice of vinyl floor with orange and gold swirls, the corner of a yellow Formica table across the room and two of its matching chairs. Gracie hears someone in the kitchen. Her body is limp, like she has no bones. Only her eyes dart from one new thing to the next. Thoughts come like lightning now, until she feels the need to rest her eyes and let her thoughts slip into the quiet clouds that float at the back of her brain.

It feels good to rest in the little bed. A beautiful mint green camp spread with white flowers woven into the green lies atop the sheets. She knows if she turns it over the spread will have mint green flowers on white. Her pillow is filled with feathers. Not too round, not too flat. Her mattress is on the soft side. She thinks perhaps she is in a fairy tale again, a fairy tale where she is a child. Not a princess of the wood, like when she first met Ed all those years ago, but a child. The dream comes to her again, the dream of the grass, winged women, floating. Gracie doesn't mind that she can't move. She couldn't breathe where she was before. She would rather be still and breathe than move and have no air.

A small round head peeks out from behind the kitchen wall. Big brown eyes look at her from the top half of a brown face. The big bright eyes blink.

A black woman in a dark blue dress, her hair up in a twist, comes into the kitchen and flips a light switch by the door. Yellow fills the doorway of Gracie's room and casts a magic glow in the kitchen.

"You're going to go blind working in the dark," the woman says to someone Gracie can't see. "What do you think lights are for?" Then, in a raspy whisper she says, "Tyrone, stop looking at that woman. Go color a picture for your mama."

The big eyes and the top of the brown head disappear and a small shadow moves quickly toward the yellow tabletop and out of sight.

Gracie hears women talking. The woman in the blue dress is speaking more quietly. Only mumbles. Words too far from Gracie's mouth or her ears. Gracie can't taste them, can't swallow them, can't make them out.

Gracie is content that the little room smells like Tide and Downy and hyacinth. The hyacinths are above and behind Gracie's head.

Fairy houses often have window boxes, one of the voices says. Gracie is relieved to know the voices are with her in this new place.

Perhaps someone will come soon and feed her jelly jewels and pickle gems. Her stomach growls and then she drifts back to sleep. In her dreams she sees only colors, and the colors are dancing.

"You are going to go blind working in the dark," Mattie says as she turns on the overhead light in the kitchen. The sun is going down and there stands Mama Toot working at the countertop. "What do you think lights are for?"

"She still sleeping," Toot says.

Mattie's neck is sore from lying bent on that old hard pillow. She fell asleep in the front room again. Seems like all she does is work and sleep and try to stay in her dream. She looks over at Tyrone peeping around the corner into the laundry room.

"Tyrone," she says with sleep in her voice, "Stop looking at that woman. Go color a picture for your mama." He obediently goes back to the table and takes up his Crayolas with his long fingers. He is a mixture of cautious wobble and balance that sometimes makes Mattie nervous, like a long-legged baby animal not yet used to his limbs. It is his head and hands that he uses well. He must have a hundred colors in that box of crayons. Sammy and Tyrone are going to Charlottesville for Easter to be with Doristeen, and Tyrone is busy making Easter cards for his mama and Sammy. The boy hardly makes a sound. Mattie wants him to create some disturbance. Little boys aren't supposed to be that fragile. She doesn't mean just now, while the woman is sleeping, but in general, he needs to make some noise like little boys do. Instead, he colors and reads and carefully scurries around the house. Even when he talks, it's more like a peep. Mattie doesn't know what to do with a boy like that.

"What do you want me to do?" she asks Mama Toot. Mattie has lived with Mama Toot all her grown life. They share the house and all that's in it. But they do it in shifts. Right now it's Mama Toot's kitchen.

"Cut up a piece of that roast in the icebox," Toot says without looking up. "We can make that woman a fine chopped soup. Put the bone and all in the pot. She needs red-meat strengthening."

Mattie first stretches out the kink in her back from lying on the living room couch, a couch for sitting and not lying, then she starts doing as she's told.

"She ain't moved a bit since you and Sammy got her in the bed and I fed her that little bit a corn mush," Toot says as she turns half to Mattie, only half because of arthritis in her back. She tries to hide it, but Mattie sees it. "You gon' feel that in the morning," Toot says, nodding her head toward Mattie like she's the one in bad shape. "You gon' be wishing you hadn't lifted that woman into the cart all by yourself. I ain't no invalid. I could've helped you."

Most of Mattie's life with Mama Toot has been one pot calling the other kettle black.

"You think I should have called the police?" Mattie said. "With her being laid out on Arty's grave like that?"

"I ain't saying no more than I already said about that yet. I'm saying you gon' keep up thinking you a mule and dragging heavy things around, you gon' end up in the bed like that white woman in the washroom. Laid out and can't get up. That's all I'm saying just yet. That, and I don't see no harm in calling DuRon after we sleep on it a night. DuRon gon' leave her here with us anyway. What he gon' do with that woman at the jailhouse?"

"He could send her to the hospital."

"The hospital won't take her with no money, no insurance card, no address, and no people. Besides, DuRon know you can take care of her good as some hospital nurse." Toot hunts the salt shaker. "And she already woke up and ate a little something. She just don't want to talk. That's all."

Toot puts her vegetable pans on the back eyes of the stove and opens a jar of sweet corn and a jar of string beans. Toot knows it's a sign too. Mattie hears it behind what Toot is saying. That woman lying right there on that grave, so sound asleep that dragging her among those headstones to get her to the cart didn't even wake her up. Mattie has nursed a lot of people in her time and she knew the stranger wasn't in a coma. She was sleeping so hard she couldn't wake up, that's all. She's wore herself out walking through all those woods, Mattie supposes. She's cut up from saw briars and tussled up from tree limbs, those red shoes ruined from wading through the creek. It's no wonder she can't help but sleep. And when she's not asleep, she won't say the first word. Not one.

"You checked her good and made sure she ain't sick?" Toot asks Mattie.

"Yes," Mattie says, pouring the contents of the jars Toot hands her into the small saucepans. Mattie listens for that little sizzle of something cold hitting the hot pan. "I guess she could be in shock," Mattie says, "but I don't think so. She could have been there for days. I hadn't been to the grave since Tuesday. I think she's just plain wore out."

Mattie used to go every day, sometimes twice a day. But some days she'd rather think about Arty alive than be reminded he's dead. Some days she doesn't feel like he's in that grave at all. She just waits for him to show himself.

"What's her signs?" Toot asks while she washes what's dirty and puts it in the dish drainer, like Mattie doesn't know Toot hasn't been in there checking her out while Mattie was napping.

"No fever. Blood pressure, respiration, pulse all normal. She's just sleeping."

"She'll wake up again soon then," Toot says satisfied.

Toot puts the big pot with the meat and the broth on the front eye. When steam starts rising from it they begin to take out spoonfuls of each solid ingredient and cut each bean, each bite of meat, each kernel of corn into tiny pieces, far too tiny to choke on. Mattie and Mama Toot know this routine. They did it enough for Arty. They fed him little chopped-up pieces of meat in soup broth by the teaspoon full when he got so he couldn't swallow anything else. He had a cancer in his throat, on his esophagus. Too many Chesterfields and a little too much toddy, the doctor said. Arty was a big ole man, and when Mattie was in his arms, she knew somebody good had hold of her. But when he died he was a few big ole long brown strings held together by almost nothing. If they had held him up to a window they could have seen right through him to what was out-side. Mattie has nursed folks for a long time, but it's not the same when the person is yours. When you have kissed every inch of that sweet velvet skin that in no long time is shrunk and draped over nothing more substantial than a coat hanger, like the limp clothes in your closet. So Mattie and

Mama Toot know how to stand there and do their parts. Many's the time they have stood in quiet, working and praying to help the one thing they most had in common, working and praying to keep him among them.

Arty had the sweetest baritone voice you ever heard, a founding member of the Soul Searchers. They cut a few gospel records with Duke and then Peacock. But Arty didn't want to travel like they needed to do to sell the records. So the quartet stayed home and just traveled around Virginia and North Carolina on Sundays. Mattie has every record he ever made and she keeps them like new.

He was always where he said he was. Never lied to her. She never really worried about him a day he was living until he said those words. *Come here, baby. We got to talk*, he said. *We got to talk, now*. He told her he was sick, and in no time at all he was gone.

She didn't even worry much about him in Vietnam. He wrote her letters, sweet letters telling her that if she worried about him it would make him worry, too. That would make him think about her when he needed to think about what he was doing. *Then my ass'll get blown away*, he wrote. He also wrote to her in those letters, and to Mama Toot in her letters, too, to dwell on the sight of him coming home. To close their eyes and see him walking in and surprising them while they were snapping beans. And don't you know, that's just what he did. It happened exactly like they pictured it. Mattie looked up and saw him coming through the yard. When she got so she could breathe, she stood up and put her hands to her mouth, and snapped and unsnapped beans fell out of her lap and went everywhere. The pan she was snapping the beans into made an awful clanging sound when it hit the porch. But you couldn't hear it because she was hollering and bawling like a baby. *"You shaking like somebody plugged you in, girl. Come here and give your husband some sugar."*

She tried picturing him well and strong and his tumor shrinking from the radiation. But it didn't work that time. God had a different vision for Arty. And His vision is always stronger. That's the only way Mattie's mind can take in Arty's sickness and his dying. Is to think that God wants him more than she does, or Mama Toot.

They have been raised up to believe anything of God, to believe He can say your time is out no matter who loves you or how much. She doesn't see herself loving anybody like that again. Enough to nurse them, enough to see them fade from her like fabric in the sun. Fade until you can only think you know the colors that used to be.

She looks at Arty's picture for a long time every night. She can't see him clear anymore unless she thinks of him moving. She looks for him everywhere, but moving. Maybe she'll see him singing and stepping around on a stage when he was young, his low voice coming to her, his hips swaying and hands waving the motions the Soul Searchers used to do. She sees him working on a car, his head in profile, his cap on backward, his hands moving just out of her sight beneath the hood. She can see him coming toward her like he has something to say to her. She can see his right shoulder when she thinks of the two of them dancing slow and knows what his cheek felt like against hers. But just to sit and remember his face, that's getting harder and harder to do. Even when those other things are happening, his face sometime gets too dark to see plain. She only feels his eyes and sometimes his smile on her. So she stares at his picture every night. Even then, sometimes Mattie looks at it too long, and she can't see it whole anymore. She only sees it in little pieces, one blue eye at a time. She wants his face to come back to her in the light and hold her in its sweetness until she too is gone from this place. But it can't hold her any better than a sieve can hold water.

Toot is taking the meat and broth from the pot. Mattie has slipped away again and Toot has worked on, waiting for Mattie to return to herself. Toot hands Mattie the bowl with some of the chopped-up corn and beans in it. Mattie mashes them up real fine with the back of a fork and scrapes them into the broth. They end up being more like a thickening. Toot doesn't say anything to Mattie but lets her go through the motions she knows so well. Toot blows across the top of the broth. It's in a shallow bowl so it will cool fast. They go into the laundry room. The woman's eyes open.

"Hello," they say. The stranger doesn't say anything. "She's right where we put her," Mattie says.

"Told you," says Toot. "She ain't ready to talk. Let's see is she ready to eat."

Mattie lifts Rachel up at the shoulders, feeling the stiffness in her own shoulders from lifting the woman earlier, and she sits down on the bed behind the woman, lets the stranger rest against her like one spoon into another. Mama Toot pulls over a little stool and sits down close. She puts the broth on the night table and lifts a half a spoon up to the woman's lips. She pinches the woman's mouth open and her own mouth opens too. She pours the broth in and gently closes the woman's mouth again, while Toot's stays open in a perfect O until the woman swallows. Toot and Mattie together feed the stranger this way until almost all the soup is gone. Something they can do blindfolded. Something they can do without talking at all. This act is more prayer than feeding. And in the absence of the man they both love, the prayer is feeding them.

"CENTERTOWN POLICE DEPARTMENT," a woman's voice says. "May I help you?"

"Hershel Landry, please. Tell him Ed Hollaman's calling."

Ed leans back against the kitchen counter and tries to unwind the phone cord while he waits. Every day it gets more and more tangled, no matter what he does to free it of its ropy fix. A recorded man's voice is explaining to Ed the importance of keeping children properly restrained in a moving vehicle when he hears a click and then Hershel Landry is telling someone in the background he'll get back to them when he knows more.

"Just the man I wanted to talk to. We missed you last night."

"I wasn't up for poker."

"It happens. Listen, can the lodge count on you to donate tires for the Senior Citizen's van again? I been meaning to check with you about that for a week."

"I do it every year."

"Just crossing my t's, that's all. What can I do you for, buddy?"

"Hershel, Gracie's disappeared."

"What do you mean, *disappeared?*"

"She took off a couple of days ago. Left me. But it isn't like her not to call me, or at least get in touch with Ginger, so I thought maybe I'd better tell you about it. To be honest, I thought she'd be back by now."

"Are you at home?"

Thirty minutes later Hershel is at Ed's drinking coffee and staring at the platter of torn checks garnished with minced credit cards, still the centerpiece on Ed's kitchen table.

"Have you two been having troubles? She been acting funny or anything?"

"No troubles. Just her listening to classical music is all. And these big Jesuses."

"What's that about?" Hershel asks.

"Beats me."

"She didn't leave a note?"

"Nope. Just the ring on the bed and the plate and the Jesuses. Oh, and my supper in the Crock-Pot."

"That was nice of her." Hershel takes a ballpoint pen from his breast pocket and stirs the tiny mound of paper on the platter. "She join a church lately?"

"Not that I know of. Look, I've called everybody I could think of. I've driven around town I don't know how many times looking for her car. Nobody's heard from her. I talked to the neighbors again yesterday, and the only thing I've come up with is the lady across the street who said she saw her get in her car all by herself around three-thirty in the afternoon and drive off."

"And that was Thursday afternoon?"

Ed nods. Hershel Landry puts his pen back in his pocket and downs the last of his coffee, then pushes the mug across the table.

"Bank accounts?"

"She hasn't touched a dime."

"Have you moved anything since she left?"

"Just the bed covers to go to bed. Hell, I'm still wearing the same clothes I came home in the other night. At first I thought she'd left me, but I figured she'd call Ginger. Now, with neither of us hearing from her, I'm worried something's happened, something bad."

"Is the car in her name, or yours?"

"Hers."

Hershel stares at the platter of paper and plastic for a minute.

"Ed, I'll tell you. I'll take some pictures and send somebody over here to dust for fingerprints to see if we come up with anything other than the prints that belong here. I'll ask around and put out a verbal alert about the car locally, maybe contact a few nearby law enforcement folks I know, but I've got to be honest with you. There's not much I can do. The ring and the credit cards and an eyewitness saying she wasn't abducted—it's pretty clear. The car's in her name, so I can't file a stolen vehicle report. I see she didn't cut up her driver's license. I can run a trace on that easy enough, see if she's using it for identification to cash some checks she didn't chop up. But all evidence says she left of her own volition, and nothing points to foul play. I don't have much cause to hunt her down."

"I understand."

"Taxpayers don't like paying their policemen to chase down runaway wives anymore than they want to pay firemen to save kittens up a tree when there's a house burning down across town. You know what I mean? Unless, of course, it's their kitten."

"I figured as much."

"Look, buddy, no offense, but she's always been a little, how do I say this, different. Nervous. I've heard you say it yourself. Maybe it's just midlife power surges. She'll go off for a few days, then, when she calms down and her money runs out, she'll come on home. You know how they get at this age."

"I've been thinking it might be that."

"Her leaving without any money seems strange though, regardless of hormones. You have any reason to think she's fooling around? I hate to ask, but, you know, it happens."

"Hell, I didn't even know she could draw. What I don't know right now, Hershel, could fill a pretty damn big hole."

At the curb Hershel turns back to Ed. "Do you want me to pick up the ticket rolls for the Burn Center raffle?"

"I'll get Estelle to drop them off this week."

"I'll get up with you when I know more."

Ed wonders how many times a day Hershel says that or something close to it. If he's even aware he's saying it. He watches Hershel wave as the unmarked Ford pulls away from the curb.

Ed goes back inside to call Ginger, only to get her answering machine. He hears the beep but doesn't leave a message. He's too busy pulling the phone cord as hard as he can until just a short part of it is a taut line. When he stops pulling, the cord hangs in an awkward arc, no longer curled in its tight spiral, but still tangled as much as before. Ed gently places the receiver back on the wall and makes a mental note: Tell Estelle to pick up a cordless phone next time she's in Wal-Mart.

TYRONE ISN'T COMFORTABLE in his own skin when he tries to play like other children. Long spindly arms and legs in an almost constant bend at his elbows and knees make him always appear sharply crooked. In a pleasant contrast to his angular body, the boy's head is a series of round shapes. A round crown and forehead with two smaller circular cheeks below large bright brown circles for eyes, a clover-leaf nose, beautifully rounded lips with a perfect bow in the upper center, a delicate dimple in the middle of his chin. His forehead is long with a high hairline of toffee-colored fuzz cut close to his head. When Tyrone's hands are near his face it is a natural study in geometry—the soothing circles of his head and face against the sticklike arms and long elastic fingers.

Tyrone has heard the story of his birth so many times it seems like it is his memory and not his mother's. She has told him over and over how when he was only a few days old, old women rubbed his head with cupped hands and talked about it in hushed and confident tones. "Oh, what a pretty head he has!" And, "His head is so lovely, so perfect in the hand." And, "Law, this child has a regal head. He'll be special, very very smart." And, "This here head is a sign of intelligence."

When the old women finished remarking on his baby head, they started in on his hands. They held up his little fists and they placed their fingers in his instinctive grasp, his long fingers draped around their own life-worn digits. "This child is going to play music. Just look at these fingers." And, "Missy, this boy must take piano from an early age. Then guitar." Then, "Yes. Oh yes. Keep these long fingers busy with music."

Only Tyrone's great-grandmother, known to be a conjure woman, turned the tiny hand over and spread back the cluster of long miniature fingers to peer at his pale palm. "Hmm," she said. Everyone listened. They stopped their comments and deferred to her vision. She ran her short fingernail on her pointer finger around in his tiny open hand, looked at his mother and said, "He will be five years old when one of the great events of his life occurs. It will change him and put him on a new path." Since coming to Mama Toot's and Miss Mattie's farm, Tyrone worries that he will miss his life-changing event. How could his life be changed here, in the middle of nowhere?

Tyrone's mother has taken the old women's comments to heart. Already, at just five years old, Tyrone is in his second year of piano. His music teacher tells him he plays like someone with two years more experience. The old women had been right about his intellect, too. Tyrone reads at a fifth-grade level and he hasn't even started school. He prefers to read a book in the evenings after supper rather than watch television like most children his age. In the city, where he ordinarily lives with his mother, he would rather read than play at the park or on the playground at preschool. His flyaway appearance often draws jibes and jokes from youngsters on the jungle gym who have normal compact bodies. They play easily and fluidly from merry-go-round to tunneled slide, from tag to kickball. But Tyrone has to fold himself in first one direction and then another to play with the other children. He is, however, a hot commodity in Red Rover. Because of his long fingers, it is a challenge for opponents to break through at some link where Tyrone stands. Unfortunately, they don't play Red Rover often, and most days in the city Tyrone prefers his books and his drawings, and his sometimes playmates prefer their more coordinated peers.

Even though Tyrone initially felt isolated and a little abandoned in the country, he is willing to admit to several benefits, now that he has been in Rockrun for a while. First, Tyrone likes Sammy better than his mother's previous boyfriends. He is funny and he talks to Tyrone like he is a real person. He doesn't just do things for show—pat Tyrone on the head and give him some cheap toy he bought in a convenience store, then look around and ask if the babysitter has arrived yet. Sammy always asks Tyrone about his day, about what he is reading. Sometimes Sammy buys Tyrone a present, and it is always a book, usually about science, Sammy's favorite subject. Second, Tyrone has never eaten so well in his whole life. And third, Tyrone likes looking at the horses and cows and chickens and the yellow dog named Buttercup. He looks at them from a distance and records them in the pictures he draws every day. Then he colors them with his crayons and markers. Tyrone wishes his great-grandmother had mentioned art in her prediction, or some of the old women had said something about it. He wants more than anything to be an artist. Without a piano to practice on at Mama Toot's and Miss Mattie's, he is able to devote all that practice time to drawing and coloring.

With so many subjects at hand, Tyrone draws almost as much as he reads: pictures of horses running, or drinking from the trough, or lying in the warm sun, pages of spotted cows grazing in pastures or lying down beneath trees in the cool mud by the creek, sketches of chickens pecking for seeds in the dirt and of the chicken house with chickens sitting on nests, overflowing wooden crates stuffed with straw and full of pale brown and beautiful aquamarine eggs. He draws the house they all live in, the barn, the garage, the sheds, and the feedlot. His eyes fall on some new subject every day. At quiet time, Mama Toot's nice way of saying nap, and at night after supper, he sits in silence reading one of the many books Sammy has given him or one his mother packed with his things.

After several weeks of watching Tyrone draw and read, Granny Toot has pushed him out the door without his drawing pad and pencils. "Go run and play," she tells him.

"But I don't like to run and play," he says under his breath. She closes the screen door between them anyway.

"You know how to run, don't you?" she asks.

"Yes, ma'am," he says.

"Then go do some of it. See won't Buttercup run and play with you. You know how to throw a stick to a dog, don't you?"

"No, ma'am. I haven't ever had a dog before," Tyrone replies from the circle of swept dirt surrounding the back steps. His eyes are cast down.

"Humph," says Toot. "A boy need to know how to throw a stick to a dog. That's what being a boy is. Now you do this," she says. The screen door creaks open, and she steps out and lets the door pop shut behind her. She walks over to Buttercup and takes a big stick from in front of her. Buttercup wags her tail and begins her dance of anticipation. "You just hold it back and let it fly." With those words the stick sails through the bright sky toward the fence line at the edge of the yard.

Buttercup launches across the yard in a blond streak and returns with the stick in her mouth and her tail still wagging.

"Now, I got to warn you, she don't always bring the stick back. Sometime she want you to come for it. Here you try."

Tyrone takes the stick, which is now slick with dog spit, and throws it. It doesn't go very far. Buttercup is on it in seconds.

"You don't throw too good, do you?"

"No, ma'am. People laugh at me when I throw balls. I guess it's the same thing with sticks."

"Did I laugh at you?"

"No, ma'am."

"Well, nothing gon' fix that throw of yours like doing it time and time again. I'm gon' go inside and not watch. Now you throw all you want till you get good. Buttercup gon' help you. She gon' like to help you longer than your arm gon' hold out." Tyrone looks forlorn, helpless. "You be throwing good in no time. You try some running and jumping and skipping too. No boy need to read and draw all the time." Toot bends to take the stick and says, "Here, I give you two pointers about throwing anything—be it balls, sticks, rocks, whatever. But don't be throwing no rocks at the house or at people or at my chickens. You break one of my windows, I'm gon' have to show you how to fix windows."

"Yes, ma'am."

"Just throw rocks into the creek or out the garden or something like that."

"Yes, ma'am."

Toot pulls the stick back behind her shoulder. "Always look where you wanting to throw, and always let go when it feels right to hit that spot. But let your arm keep going like that." Toot's body stretches into her throw and then her old slightly humped shoulders follow her arm over and beyond her center of gravity in a perfect motion. "That's what you call follow through. Look where you throw and follow through. You do it enough, you be good at it."

Tyrone looks up at Toot like she is punishing him.

"You out here in this yard all by yourself. Nobody gon' be watching 'cept Buttercup and the Lord. You try things you ain't never tried before. This the best chance you gon' ever have. You might surprise yourself."

"But the stick is icky," Tyrone says in a whiny voice.

"Don't whine, boy. I ain't never liked to hear no child whine. You stronger than that, I know. I ain't never met no boy who minded a little dog spit. Just get used to it. Get some dirt on them hands too. I want to see some dirt under those fingernails by supper time. Then you can use my little brush to scrub it out again. You hear?"

"Yes, ma'am."

Toot goes in the back door, once again lets it slap shut, then marches in the kitchen like she is no longer concerned about what takes place in the backyard.

Tyrone looks at the stick, looks at Buttercup, and he cries. He doesn't see the kitchen curtain move a little to one side, doesn't feel Toot's protective eyes on him. Buttercup jumps on his chest, knocks him down on the swept ground. She licks at Tyrone's wet face. At first Tyrone is frightened, but can't make any sound of alarm. Then the dog's paws on his belly begin to tickle, and the dog jumps over Tyrone and runs around and lands on him again. Before long the tears turn to welcome grunts and then unrestrained laughter—a baptism of laughter in the religion of a boy and his dog.

On the sixth day of running and jumping and throwing, Tyrone bends to pick up the stick without thinking of dog slobber. He waves it in the air and Buttercup jumps and wags her tail as if to say, *The stick. The stick. I want the stick. Oh, please, please! The stick!* Tyrone waves the stick behind his head and fakes a throw, which Buttercup obligingly lunges for and jumps back. Then Tyrone lets the stick fly into the warm fresh air. His eyes focus on the weedy spot beyond the old garage. The stick arches higher and higher and then begins its descent toward the target. Buttercup leaps once, twice, a dozen long but rapid leaps. The stick hits the ground and Buttercup immediately snags it and overruns it, tumbling and rising, the stick clinched between her teeth. She shakes her head from side to side and Tyrone runs to her.

As Toot has warned, while Buttercup likes to chase the stick over and over, her return rate is only about fifty percent. Buttercup wags her tail in an illusion of cooperation, then, as Tyrone reaches the short shadow growing from the garage in the postnoon sun, Buttercup turns and runs into the cool dark cavelike outbuilding.

Tyrone peers in after her. The light from outside makes the garage a dim room of shadows and shapes with a dirt floor. Tyrone's eyes adjust to the dark and he can make out shelves upon shelves that hang over an L-shaped worktable, the upper shelves loaded with paint cans and brushes. An infinite variety of tools hangs from nails on the ends of the shelves and from the bare walls facing the tabletops. Beneath the work-tables are deeper shelves laden with jars of beans and beets and corn. Tyrone steps into the cool garage and looks for Buttercup. A shadow moves in the far dark corner to the left, and at almost the same time Buttercup brushes beside Tyrone from the right. Tyrone feels a strange chill go down his spine. At that moment, a wind comes out of the garage, blows up through the treetops, and comes back around the house behind him. He turns to see Buttercup sitting still, her stick on the ground, her manners much improved. Tyrone throws the stick a few more times. He's running and skipping toward the house when Toot calls him in to wash up for lunch, the usual tomato soup and Spam sandwich. After his good lunch and his quiet time that follows, he takes his drawing tablet and his box of crayons, pencils, and markers and sits on the back steps to draw. He can feel his muscles move, a sensation he has not been aware of before. The running and playing and throwing make him sore in a good way.

Tyrone sits looking at the garage, thinking about the dark corner and the movement he saw there. Movement that couldn't have been Buttercup. He begins to draw the garage. He draws Buttercup holding the stick in her mouth. She is taking it to someone. As Tyrone draws the picture, the figure beside Buttercup is not a little boy. It is not Tyrone. It is a tall black man with blue eyes. He is someone Tyrone has never seen, but someone he imagines standing in the dark corner of the garage, the man Buttercup saw even when Tyrone could not. Tyrone knows something he can't know, feels a presence he can't touch. His muscles ache. For the first time Tyrone more than wants to draw. He needs to draw.

SISTER REBA RENFRO lifts the rear glass, then lowers the tailgate of her pale green 1960 Ford Galaxie station wagon, and pulls her tent poles out of the cargo area hand over hand until they all lay stacked behind the car. She is baptized in the blood and traveling for Christ.

"Thank you, Lord, for this good-running automobile, Lord," she prays, "even if it is the ugliest station wagon ever made. Thank you, Lord. Just goes to show ugly can still count for something. It does what I need it to do. Amen."

The previously owned funeral tent she carries with her everywhere she goes isn't big enough to shelter her usual congregations accumulated by a revival's end, but it is large enough to get attention from the road and shade or shelter the early comers—part of their earthly reward for skipping lunch or dinner to praise the Lord.

Sister Reba keeps the backseat folded down and travels light in every personal way. She can pack tent poles, canvas cover, and ten folding benches in the cargo area and still see out the back. The ice chest has its special place in the front passenger seat and her duffel bag sits on the front floorboard along with a nylon sleeping bag and a three-man dome tent that is only large enough to sleep two, which is still one more person than she needs room for. She keeps her mind and heart on the future, but sometimes she feels the need to look back and see where she's been. At those times, God takes hold and pulls her forward with a strong hand.

A nice brother-in-faith made the benches for her before she left Meridian in '92. Because of him she almost stayed in Mississippi. A close call, that's how she thinks of it. If he knew better, he'd think of it that way too. Next to a baby, he came closest to causing her to stay put and have a life outside of preaching. That good-looking soul made her think twice about her traveling life. She likes to hit her spots at least once a year, and every few years she makes a little adjustment to cover some new territory.

Many's the man that tells her she looks like Lena Horne. She does. She also looks ten years younger than she is. What she doesn't look like right now is a preacher, as she bends over in her blue jeans, stretches up into the cargo area to reach that last folding bench from up near the front seat. She turns heads on a regular basis, and in turn, they try to turn hers with talk of the flesh. She knows what that kind of talk can get you. Only, that sweet handsome brother in Meridian, he had more to say than that. It was a bona fide temptation. The serious kind of temptation that can suck you in and, next thing you know, hold you down. You'll be kicking, screaming, and trying your best to get away, but your life, the life you're supposed to have, will be just out of reach. Sister Reba is a saved woman, saved from many things by the voice and spirit of God. She plans to stay saved, too. Foolishness such as men delays her only so long. She expects after her hot flashes ease up a bit, such foolishness won't delay her at all.

With the tent standing and the benches in place, Sister Reba pulls out the painted plywood sandwich sign and drags it to the edge of the road. That's where she sets up mostly, on the roadside near filling stations, country stores, and hot dog and hamburger joints. As a rule, it guarantees a steady flow of revival goers, and the business proprietors understand the mutual benefit of playing off each other's clientele. Sister Reba has proven to them over the years that their business picks up when she's preaching nearby. Her gift is to draw a crowd and keep their attention until they hear God in their hearts. It starts out being her words, but then they hear way more than she can say. They come to hear and understand so much more than she can impart on her own.

On this particular day Sister Reba has set up between the Red Hot Dog and Johnny's Shell Station on a narrow well-traveled Georgia road running from Lithonia to Loganville. She sets up her sign near the road's edge and walks to Red Hot's order window. Leaning in to the smell of good greasy food, she sees a familiar face. Hazel has worked at the Red Hot for ten years. Hazel always comes to Sister's evening meeting when the revival's in town. Sister Reba pulls a paper napkin from the dispenser at the order window and wipes her brow and neck. Setting up that tent can bring on a powerful sweat.

"Hazel, sweetheart, give me two all the way with a little Texas Pete." Reba knows Hazel can hear the tired in her voice.

"Reba! How you been?" Hazel scoops ice into a waxed paper cup and starts filling it from the drink fountain. At the same time she pulls a small tin of Bayer aspirin out of her apron pocket. "I saw you setting up over there. I don't know how you get all that stuff to fit in your wagon. You want fries with those dogs, honey?"

Hazel comes to the window and passes Reba a drink, then pops the tin open and flips two aspirin into her hand and slides them toward Reba. "I know you want a Dr Pepper." Hazel turns to extract two bright pink wieners from the pot of warm water and places them in two open buns on the wooden board before the fixings. "What're you preaching on this year?"

"Leftovers. I got a *good* sermon on leftovers. You come hear it."

"I will. You know I will. You need a place to stay?"

"Thank the Lord. I knew I could count on you."

"Always."

"You got to *LOVE* God. You know *THAT.*"

"I do, honey. You know I do. Why, I pray for you all year till I see your face again and know you're doing all right. You need to learn how to drop folks a postcard. Let them do a little advertising when you're coming to town."

"Jesus is my advertising executive. He lets folk know I'm rolling into town. Now, tell me, didn't you have a feeling you'd be seeing me today, or at least this week?" Reba takes the two aspirin and swallows them down with the cold Dr Pepper.

"Now that you mention it," Hazel says, "you have been on my mind lately."

"See, you knew I was coming."

Hazel deftly wraps the hot dogs. Her hands fast, familiar with the filmy paper, the dog, the small white paper bags always to the left of the butcher board. It is a seamless motion. Fold, tuck, fold, roll, reach, flap, insert, add napkins, fold, and crease to close. Almost like music, no louder than a brush on a cymbal. Hazel can do it with her eyes closed.

Reba reaches in her pocket.

"Now, Reba, you know that's on me."

Reba sits at one of the middle picnic tables under the long metal awning that stretches from the boxy little building almost to the highway. She enjoys each bite of her supper, just out of conversing distance from Hazel. She needs to contemplate her sermon for the evening. Each year she has a theme. She's learned over the years that women preachers are most effective when they use the things of women for their sermons. The men get moved too because what is of interest to women usually has something to do with taking care of men, or the men's children. Men always work themselves into the center of everything. But if the sermons hit home with the sisters first, they keep coming back and bringing their menfolk with them.

Before long Reba will go in the restroom over at the Shell station and put on one of her good dresses. She'll fix her hair a little bit, pinch her cheeks, put on enough mascara to make her eyes show up at a distance, but not enough to look like she's wearing makeup. Then she'll read some from the Bible. The spirit will put the words in her mouth if she'll take the time to get her mind right. A few regulars will drop in before six o'clock for some private prayer. It's true. They'll know she's come. God lets them know. For some reason they'll decide to go a certain way, maybe a way they only take once a month or once a year, and there Sister Reba will be, waiting for them. From her seat under the awning, Reba studies her sign, made for her by a nice man that lives outside Lilburn. Maybe she'll set up over there next week, beside Curly's Sunoco and the car wash. If the energy is right, if the hot flashes aren't too bad, if he's still single, maybe he'll offer to take her to dinner.

What she wants most tonight is rest. Hazel has a good mattress in her guest room and Reba can always count on a good night's sleep when she stops here. But she has a long way to go before sleep. She eats her hot dogs and thinks about her sign and her sermon. She'll start with a good song to get them going. Maybe "Rock of Ages." Something everybody's going to know, at least the chorus. Then she'll open saying, "God LOVES leftovers. Don't *tell* me you don't love *left*overs," she'll say. From there straight into Matthew, the loaves and the fishes. She'll make it corn bread and catfish. Put the disciples and Jesus on the banks of the Chatahoochee River. They were really on the banks of Galilee, Jesus and the disciples, traveling often out into the desert, but these folks don't know a thing about Galilee or the desert. They need to know what they have in common with Jesus. So many carpenters under her tent, so many fishermen. So for tonight, Jesus will be blessing catfish and hushpuppies on the banks of the Chatahoochee and feeding them that needs feeding. That's something the people who come to her tent will understand. Something they can taste. If you put them there with Jesus, put Jesus where they can find Him, meeting on level ground, make them think they are beside Him, seeing what He's seeing, tasting what He's tasting, eating out of His very hand, they'll go with you to that deeper place. Even the biggest skeptic will fall out with the Spirit and flail his arms and legs for the Lord, if you go at it right.

Reba spins her sermon like a love web as she watches the road. A baby-blue pickup comes over the hill and slows down in front of her sign. She can see the driver, a middle-aged man. She can already feel his sorrow, feel his heavy heart. She can tell she'll see him again. It is revealed to her. He slows even more and reads the words on her hand-painted plywood marquee.

Sister Reba Renfro's
Traveling Gospel Crusade.
GET GOD'S MESSAGE.
Right here!
Right now!
Services daily at
Noon and 6 P.M.
All week long
Spiritual counseling anytime.
JESUS IS CALLING YOU!

OFFERTORY

We are shaped and fashioned by what we love.

—Goethe

"WHO DO YOU RECKON SHE IS?" DuRon says with his mouth half full of the piece of chocolate pound cake he grabbed while coming through the kitchen to the laundry room.

"Now, if we knew that, why'd we call you?" Toot says.

"She's a woman of few words. I'll say that."

"You telling us something we already know."

Dudley Ronald is his real name but he's DuRon to everybody in Coats County. Even the election posters say DuRon. If not, no one in the county would know who was running for reelection to the office of high sheriff. DuRon is a tall man, not as broad in the shoulders as Arty, but bigger around the middle by a few inches. A bit of belly hangs over his gun belt. *Ain't no beer belly,* Toot thinks, *just too much cake.* There's enough drinking in his family already. His mother spent most of DuRon's childhood dead drunk. His skin is pale and loaded down with freckles, a white blond halo on top of his head. He and Arty were like salt and pepper. His mama was always more interested in drinking than feeding her children, so DuRon took up with Arty and was home to eat supper with him most every night. DuRon slept in Toot's house or out in the woods beyond the fields in a tent most of his boyhood. Toot wonders if his mama ever even asked where he was. His mama and daddy were sharecroppers with a bad way about them, and they must have stayed drunk sure enough, because they weren't the type to let their boy practically live with black folks. The funny thing was, DuRon stuck to Arty because Arty never judged him by his family. By the time DuRon finished high school and went to Vietnam, his mama was dead from liver disease and his daddy had left one day and not ever bothered to come back home. Nobody in particular wanted to look for him, not even DuRon.

Toot saw DuRon's body go through all the changes from boy to man. All the stages of doing and not doing. Of running too much, then sitting too much. That boy was a trial to her at first. He followed Arty home from Rodey's store when they were both about six years old and was a constant presence from then on. Always hungry. Always asking questions she didn't have answers to. Getting Arty into the only little bit of trouble he ever had. But she came to have a deep affection for DuRon in a short time. He could have held on to some of those examples his family set, but as far as Toot knows, he has, in the end, turned out to be honorable. Her sweet boy is deader than dead, and here stands DuRon in her kitchen with a mouth full of chocolate pound cake and a sheriff's badge on his shirt. *God has a strange way of doing.* But Toot has learned to trust the Almighty, even when it is hard to do. She has learned to be His vessel even when she's worn out. She knows deep down Arty isn't gone at all, but more alive than any of them. Still, it is hard to see DuRon stuffing his face, asking stupid questions, when Arty is dead too young.

"Where you reckon she come from?" he says just after taking another bite of cake.

"DuRon, didn't your mama tell you don't eat and talk at the same time?" Toot says, and takes away his cake.

"Oh, sorry, Miss Toot." He looks like a boy being chastised and he wipes his mouth with the handkerchief from his back pocket. "That is some mighty good cake though." He looks longingly at what she has taken from him.

"It ought to be good. We sell them, you know. You ever think about buying one?" Toot looks at the man with fake aggravation. "You'll get more cake when we finish looking at this here woman and get back to the table."

"Yes, ma'am."

Mattie steps into the small laundry room from the kitchen. She'd grudgingly agreed to call DuRon, but only because he was Arty's friend since childhood and she knows him almost as well as he knows himself.

"She came down from heaven and landed in the cemetery," Mattie says and squeezes in between Toot and the washer.

"I suspect she come from some place closer than that," DuRon says.

"She didn't have no pocketbook, no name tag, nothing," Toot reports. "We didn't see no car, and we rode all around. She don't look like the kind to be riding a motorcycle. Do you think?"

Mattie winks at DuRon. The kind of wink that says he is outmatched by Mama Toot and just as well needs to get on with his business because there isn't room for foolishness in the laundry room today.

"Well," he says as he puts his handkerchief back in his pocket, "I'll take her fingerprints and put out an APB on her. That's an All Points Bulletin."

"We know that, fool," says Toot. "We watch *Dragnet* reruns like everybody else. How in the world did you get to be a sheriff?"

"Ma'am?"

"Have you ever found a criminal?" Toot asks as she turns away. "Have you ever found out who somebody was you didn't know all your life? This whole thing may have happened so you can prove yourself. Lordy. Why do me and mine have to help with that? I wonder. I'm too old for it." Toot walks into the kitchen and DuRon looks sheepishly at Mattie.

"Now, Miss Toot, I ain't that bad. I just like to think out loud is all. And sometimes my mouth is full while I'm thinking." DuRon follows Toot into the kitchen and Mattie follows DuRon.

"Well, think between bites in this house." Toot fixes him a plate with a fresh piece of cake and what is left of his other one. She pours him a cup of coffee. DuRon starts to sit down.

"Not that one," Toot says, and DuRon realizes he has pulled at Arty's chair.

"Yes, ma'am." He moves to one of the side chairs facing the windows.

Toot puts the cake and the coffee in front of him, pours a little bit of Pet canned milk in his cup, and hands him a fork, a spoon, and the sugar bowl.

"Now when did you say she showed up?" DuRon asks, and then puts two heaping spoons of sugar in his coffee.

"Do you still have all your own teeth?" Toot asks him.

"Yes, ma'am. Why do you ask?"

"Nothing. It ain't nothing."

"When did she show up?" DuRon repeats.

Mattie clears her throat. "Thursday," she says.

"This past Thursday?"

"Well, no," Mattie confesses. "The Thursday before Easter."

"I see. Why did you wait three weeks to call me? I'm just curious."

"Well, for one thing," Mattie continues, "we thought she would be talking by now and telling us who she is."

"If that's one thing," said DuRon, "what other numbers do you have?"

"The second thing is that Sammy was going to call you if we didn't and I thought it would be better if it was us."

"And for a third," Toot adds, looking straight at DuRon's eyes, "we believe the good Lord wants her here with us for some reason. We found her on his grave, you know."

"Yep. Well. Does she get up and walk around?" DuRon scratches his head.

"Some," both women lie at the same time.

"But she doesn't talk at all?"

They both shake their heads.

"And you want to keep her?"

Toot looks at Mattie, and Mattie looks at DuRon. "If we can, we want to take care of her. She'll talk when she's ready. And neither of us wants Rachel in a hospital or jailhouse."

"I thought you didn't know her name."

"We got to call her something, DuRon," Mattie says.

"Yeah. I guess you do." DuRon sits back and takes a few sips of his coffee while Toot and Mattie sit in silence and watch him. He is in a power position with these two women for the first time in his life. He wants to handle it correctly. He knows they have been through a hard few years.

"Well, I don't see as we have a crime," DuRon says between sips of coffee, "so there isn't any reason to take her to jail. And if she's awake and walking around and eating and doesn't show any signs of being sick or a danger to herself, I don't see much point in taking her to the hospital."

"That is exactly what I told Sammy, but he wouldn't listen," Mattie says, relieved.

"But," DuRon adds, "if she starts to do anything suspicious or starts to talk, I want you to give me a call. You don't know who she is or what she's been up to. She could be a criminal. Remember that."

"We will," says Mattie.

Toot holds her tongue. It isn't her way to pay too many compliments, but she is proud of DuRon for being such a reasonable man.

While DuRon finishes what is left of his first piece of cake, Toot picks up a glass from the dish drainer, wipes it dry with her dishcloth, and places it beside DuRon's coffee cup.

"Oh, I don't care for anything but the cake and coffee, Miss Toot."

Toot closes her eyes for a moment, then opens them again. "Where'd you get that badge? From the back of a comic book? That glass ain't for you to drink out of. It's for you to get fingerprints with. Maybe you ought to watch a little *Dragnet,* too. Weekdays from five to five-thirty on Channel 6."

"Yes, ma'am," DuRon says.

Mattie can't help but laugh. This kind of exchange has gone on since DuRon was six years old. Arty used to laugh about it too because DuRon never figures out what he does to aggravate Toot so, and he never gets out of what seems like a circular argument with the old woman. Yet he keeps coming back and she keeps putting plates of food in front of him.

Toot shakes her head and picks up the glass with her dish towel.

"Where you going with that?" DuRon asks, this time without cake muffling his words.

"Gon' get you some fingerprints. You still got your second piece of cake to eat and your coffee gon' get cold."

"Yes, ma'am." DuRon presses his fork into the new extra-thick slice Toot cut him, cuts the front corner off and slides the moist bite into his mouth.

"Don't you have a fingerprint kit or something?" Mattie asks as she tops off his coffee.

"That glass'll work fine," he says. "It'll do just fine." DuRon takes a swig of hot coffee and another bite of cake and shakes his head. "Lord have mercy, you make a good chocolate pound cake, Mattie Riley."

"You just cake crazy. Come to think of it, you're just plain crazy."

Sitting there looking at Mattie smooth the tablecloth, it occurs to DuRon that Mattie Riley will never see him without seeing Arty beside him and that Arty will never really be dead to her. DuRon also realizes, with some surprise, that this makes him a little sad.

E D COMES IN through the mudroom, what used to be the back porch. Ginger's been there. The dirty clothes are gone from the top of the dryer. The washer lid is open and the inside bare. Ed walks a circle through the first floor of the house where he sees signs of her activity in almost every room. The bed in the master bedroom is made, probably with clean sheets. Every throw pillow is in its place. He checks the downstairs guest room. She made that bed too. When Ed has insomnia, he gets up and moves to the guest room. At least he knows it isn't a Jesus looking at him that's keeping him awake. Ed thinks of moving to the guest room permanently, but that doesn't suit him either. And he doesn't want to sleep in Ginger's old room. Too frilly. He has decided not to paint over the Jesuses until Gracie lets someone know where she is, what she's doing, who she's with. It is almost Mother's Day. Surely she'll call Ginger then.

Ed didn't seriously consider Gracie being with someone else at first. But the police are convinced the evidence points in that direction. While there were no fingerprints other than family, her taste seems to have changed. Landry thinks the wedding ring on the bed might have been a symbolic gesture. He's informally put the word out about Gracie and the Olds, but the car hasn't been found or even spotted in North Carolina. "It's like I said before," Landry said, "she's an adult and she's got a right to leave home if she wants."

Every day Ed tries to tell Ginger that this is a low priority when she insists they call the police again and again. But Ginger has a point. Maybe Gracie ran out for something and was kidnapped. They have no way of knowing until Gracie calls to let them know or the police, by some miracle, come up with something. Ed hates to face the obvious, but after so many weeks without word, no activity in the bank account, no note, no ransom, no car, he too is beginning to think there's someone else, someone taking care of her. The thought that she might be dead, well, he never entertains that one.

This week's newspapers are no longer scattered semifolded beside the recliner. The big bathroom off the bedroom is Gracie's territory. His bathroom is the small one off the downstairs hallway. Sports sections are no longer fanned out in front of his toilet. His toilet paper is in the holder on the wall, not on the floor beside the missing sports sections or on the back of the commode, where he usually sets it. Back in the kitchen, the TV dinner tins are in the garbage and the forks and glasses are washed and drip-dried in the dish drainer beside the sink. Ed opens the fridge to a full gallon pitcher of fresh sweet tea on the top shelf, a shelf that's been wiped clean, and a Ziploc sandwich bag full of lemon slices cut in full circles, the way Ed likes them. In the five weeks since Gracie's disappearance, Ginger has learned how to offer him what he needs and keep her presence to a minimum. The ice is in the big green plastic bowl and the trays have been rinsed clean, refilled, and put back in the freezer for when the bowl gets empty again. The kitchen smells of Comet and Top Job. He appreciates her little invasions, but when the remodeling is finished at the doughnut shop, she won't have time to be his caretaker.

Ed fixes himself a glass of tea, not bothering with the lemon slices, and sits down at the kitchen table.

"Where are you, Gracie?" he says aloud. "It looks like you could at least make a phone call." He takes a long cold wet swallow and sets the glass on the oak table top, ignoring Gracie's instruction to always put a napkin under his glass. A collection of pale circles have formed on the polished tabletop. Ed doesn't notice. What he does notice is that this house has always been more Gracie's than his. The thought hadn't occurred to him before, but now, with Gracie gone, he sees that everything about the house is the way she wants it—wanted it. From where the furniture sits to the pictures of Jesus, it's all her doing. Ed simply has places for his things, and even that is not by his choice. His dirty clothes go in the clothes basket on top of the dryer. His belongings go in either the right-hand side of the walk-in closet, the bottom two drawers of the dresser, or in his tiny bathroom off the downstairs hallway. Everything else is at Tire Man. If he sits in the recliner in the manly den, if he falls back onto the bed with his head landing on his feather pillow, if he shaves his face with Barbasol, if he drinks a glass of tea, it is somehow part of Gracie's design. When did he stop making his own decisions? When did he stop defining his own life? Ed taps his fingers on the table and when he reaches again for his glass of tea, he notices the pale wax circles lacing the oak tabletop. Ed sees that he is getting careless, and knows he's good and hungry.

After another Hungry Man TV dinner and a Popsicle for dessert, Ed calls Wally to come over and help him.

"Watch your fingers," Ed tells him as they carry the upended kitchen table through the door and out to the garage.

"Are you getting a new table?" Wally asks.

"No. I'm going to sand this one down and polyurethane it. I've been wanting to do that for years."

"Ed, you might want to check with an antiques dealer. People on *Antiques Roadshow* get real disappointed when the appraisers tell him what their furniture would be worth if they hadn't refinished it."

"I don't give a damn about any antiques appraiser. If Gracie can paint Jesus on any blamed wall she pleases, I can polyurethane the top of a table. Hell, I might polyurethane every tabletop in the whole blasted house and see how she likes it."

"What if she never sees it, Ed?"

"She will. She'll feel it the second that brush puts the first streak of high gloss on this baby. It'll send a shock through her."

"If you say so."

"I say so. I might even do the floors."

"Then you better go for low luster. If you don't, you're going to have light ricocheting off the floors and the furniture and blinding you when you walk in and turn on the lights."

"Well, there won't be any rings on the table, will there?"

"No, sir."

"Not a damn one. I'm going to need a fan out here."

"Yes, sir."

"Speaking of antiques," Wally turns to run his hand over a canvas tarp covering a large object, "when's the last time you took the Dodge to a car show?"

"I don't know. Maybe ten years, eight."

"Seems like such a waste. You wouldn't polyurethane this baby, would you?"

"That's different. It's a truck."

"A awful pretty one, at that." Wally lifts the canvas to reveal a sea foam green fender and door with a strip of chrome running along the bottom. "It's kind of sad, really."

"What's sad?"

"She never had a life."

"Who never had a life?" For a second Ed thinks Wally is talking about Gracie.

"The Dodge. A thirty-year-old truck with a name like the Adventurer, and she's only got thirty thousand miles on her clock."

"Thirty-two thousand, and she's thirty-one years old. I'd say she's had an easy life. That Dodge has made it to old age in mint condition. Who can say that?"

"I'd say she's had a boring life. If you ever want to get rid of this truck, Ed . . ."

"Marry my daughter and then maybe you'll inherit it. Now cover that thing back up."

After Wally leaves, Ed heads for the den, turns on the TV, and goes straight to the satellite program guide. He scrolls down to TV Land and clicks on an early *Andy Griffith Show*, then reaches in the drawer in the side table for a pad of paper and a pen. At the top of the page he writes, TO DO. He draws a line, and under it he writes: sandpaper, polyurethane.

Mattie sits at the edge of the little bed and spoons up small bits of Cream of Wheat. It's a curiosity to Mattie that Rachel can stay in bed twenty-four hours a day, barely moving except to turn over or raise up enough to eat. The covers are always undisturbed whenever Mattie or Toot come in to check on Rachel in the mornings. She'll allow herself to be helped to the bathroom, and she's making more eye contact and smiling when someone comes in her room. Toot occasionally sings to her in the old-lady remnant of what was once a beautiful alto while she does the laundry. Tyrone reads to her, mostly Bible stories and Dr. Seuss. He likes the sound of Dr. Seuss when read aloud, and Rachel closes her eyes and smiles while he reads.

Mattie and Toot take turns talking to her. Mattie approaches the task as a coach, trying to get her to try words, to answer simple questions. Toot's method is to talk to Rachel as if she is normal; Toot goes on faith one day soon she'll talk back.

After giving it some thought, DuRon had recommended having Dr. Brock come out and give Rachel a once-over, to make sure she wasn't injured in some way that wasn't obvious. The only community doctor who still makes house calls confirmed there's no physical explanation for her silence. "She may have a condition not so readily diagnosed," he said, "but she seems as physically sound as you and me. She's not talking, but she certainly seems happy where she is. When I asked her if she wanted to go to the hospital for more tests, she shook her head no."

Dr. Brock was getting old, and Toot and Mattie thought for certain he had imagined this, but they didn't argue. If he thought Rachel could make a decision and communicate it to him, all the better.

Mattie hears shoving of furniture and an odd noise coming from the front room. Toot is saying something but Mattie is too far away to make it out.

"What is that woman saying? She knows I can't hear good anymore." Mattie puts Rachel's bowl of cereal on the little table by the bed and goes to see what Toot is mumbling about. When she gets closer to the living room, Mattie realizes Toot is talking to herself.

"Where my pencil?" Toot says as she moves things around on the end table beside the couch. She lifts Sammy's college graduation picture, the brass praying hands, the unused ashtray that says NEW YORK CITY under a likeness of the Empire State Building. The ashtray is a souvenir from Mattie and Arty's honeymoon. Toot picks up the doily and runs her hand under it, then checks her hand.

"Humph, time to dust. If I had my pencil I be making me a list of what I need to be doing. Where that dang pencil?"

She runs her knotty fingers into the back of the sofa and down the sides of the cushions, lifting each to peek beneath. She moves to the matching chair and pokes and pulls and makes noises, dissatisfied with what she finds. Nothing but some little scrap of Christmas ribbon, a Mr. Goodbar wrapper, and two nickels. No pencil.

"What are you looking for?" Mattie says as she steps into the living room.

"My pencil. I always keep a pencil on this here table, and it's gone. You had my pencil?"

"No, ma'am. I have my own pencil, thank you. You leave it in the kitchen maybe?"

"You know as well as me that I got a kitchen pencil. I'm looking for my living room pencil. They two different pencils."

"Have you looked under the couch cushions?"

"Under couch cushions, chair cushions, table doilies, picture frames. By the way, Sammy been letting Tyrone eat Mr. Goodbars in my living room?"

"Sammy's so busy trying to impress that little boy so his mama will marry him he's liable to let him do anything. He's liable to let Tyrone eat a Mr. Goodbar on the lap of St. Peter."

"St. Peter got his rules and I got mine," Toot says as she shoves the chair cushion back into place. "No candy in my living room unless I offer it. He gon' get all bedeviled over that tall wavy woman and start kowtowing to her and her little boy, and I'm gon' get big old chocolate stains on the good sides of my couch cushions." Toot points to the couch cushions, now on their everyday side. "I'm gon' flip those pillows over for company one day and there be a big old brown circle of chocolate and a couple little peanuts stuck to it. And it won't be Tyrone's little behind I be switching. You tell that to Sammy for me. You hear?"

"What you want to say that for? About Doristeen bedeviling Sammy."

"You think I'm making it up?" Toot laughs.

"No. I just don't want to be ugly about her."

"I ain't being ugly about nothing. That's a fact of nature. A man, any man, good or bad, get that thing on his mind and he just might as well put a collar round his neck and hand the woman the leash. Specially a woman that keep it to herself—make men work for it. That ain't bad. That's good, if she good."

Mattie retraces Toot's searching fingers, feeling for the pencil on the mantel. "I just hate to think of my Sammy being under some spell."

"We don't always get what we like," Toot says without looking at Mattie.

Mattie's hands slide under the white cotton scarf that Toot puts on the mantel during the spring and summer. She thinks about her son and that tall woman and looks at her hand for dust. "Humph. Need to dust good in here."

"Exactly. But first I need to write something down."

"What do you need to write?"

"That fool Henry Morehouse on the radio. Every Sunday I listen to him running his mouth and I make a list of all the things I got to say to him should I ever decide to say it. I got several things today to add to my list."

"Mama Toot, why do you listen to ole Henry if you think he's a fool?"

"When the man play a song by, say the Five Blind Boys, like the fool he is, he burst in all through that beautiful song dedicating it to different people. They be starting the second line of the first verse and here come ole stupid Henry saying over the song, *And I ESPECIALLY want to dedicate this song to Mosetta and Tiny Ray in their time of trouble.* Then, before those sweet singing men can get to the chorus, here he come again. *And I also want to ESPECIALLY dedicate this song to Sister Maybelle Wright who is in the midst of her bereavement. Sister Maybelle, may these words comfort you in your time of SORrow.*"

Mattie starts to laugh as Toot throws back her head and mimics Brother Morehouse.

"The boys starting in on the second verse and here that joker come, *And for those other of you whom* SO EVER *are also be*REA*ved, I hope you will remember our* SPON*sor, Alston Funeral Home. We have the* FINE*st in suits, dresses, and caskets for your loved ones and the* FINE*st accommodations for them, whom so ever they may be.* That man get on my last nerve."

"Mama Toot, then why do you listen to him every Sunday?"

"'Cause it's a sight easier to get news from that jackass of a preacher about people in this community than it is by reading that thing this town call a newspaper. I may have to put up with Henry Morehouse, but the fool tell me where I'm needed. I listen to him for that. They gon' come a day when I'm too old to help anybody. And that's the day I'm gon' tell him what I think of his ignorant interrupting ways. Don't nobody listen to him 'cause they want to. They listen 'cause they need to."

Mattie is now on her hands and knees looking under the sofa and then the chair for the lost pencil. "Well, I don't see a pencil. You want mine?"

"No. I got one in the kitchen I can use. That ain't the point."

Mattie starts to laugh again. She rocks up from the floor and sits back into the chair behind her, crossing her long legs and letting her arms and hands rest on the high arms of the chair. Even in grief she is graceful and easy. Toot remembers what she saw in Mattie when Arty brought her home that first time. Toot knew right away what had caught hold of him. She still approves. A hard thing for a boy's mama, even when the boy's a man, even when the man is dead.

Toot scrunches up her already wrinkled face and pokes her finger in the air as if she is making a period to punctuate the conversation. Then she turns and goes to her room.

Mattie puts her head on the back of the chair and tries to think of nothing, but the image of a bowl of half-eaten Cream of Wheat comes to mind and she gets up to go finish feeding Rachel. When she gets back to the laundry room, the bowl seems more empty than she remembers and the mush is a little too crusty to give the sick woman anymore of it. Mattie pats Rachel's leg and Rachel smiles at Mattie, then looks straight ahead as if Mattie has disrupted her conversation with some invisible somebody.

Toot gives up on her living room pencil long enough to get ready for church and she, Mattie, and Tyrone leave Rachel to Sammy for a few hours. Reverend Love is guest preaching this morning, a stark contrast to Brother Henry's gossipy accusations and salesmanship. In Mattie's way of thinking, Brother Henry has reduced his preaching to something close to selling cars, while Reverend Love has elevated his to art.

By late afternoon, everybody is home again and the smells of Sunday dinner are everywhere, drifting through the windows and the screen door and settling on the porch and in the swept yard and the big green lawn beyond the dirt circle. Webbed lawn chairs wait in the circle for the Sunday eaters to come out one by one and take a place in the shade to talk off their dinner and comment on the morning's sermon. Buttercup has come to rest at the back steps in readiness for the scraps she will receive when the big dinner is over. Butter beans, creamed corn, mashed potatoes, fried chicken, gravy, biscuits, cucumbers in vinegar, sliced tomatoes. Buttercup even eats tomatoes. And the sight of Mattie's sweet potato pie can make a dead man hungry.

Mmm, baby, you made my favorite pie.

"Don't you just love sweet potato pie?" Rachel says softly from the laundry room, apparently to no one.

I certainly do.

ED LOOKS UP through the plate glass window at the big clock in the showroom. The minute hand of the clock moves up and over the twelve and the other hand rests on the seven. He likes the longer daylight of spring, the change in time both natural and artificial. His fingers click over the adding machine keypad as he taps out the tallies for the day's business. He goes over Estelle's figures, ever since she went and got some of those long fake fingernails about a month ago and they make her totals come out wrong. He's going to tell her to cut those claws back to a manageable size if she wants to keep using the adding machine at Tire Man.

Ed had wanted to name his business Tire King, but that name was taken. In the end he came to like the sound of Tire Man. *Sounds like a superhero*, Gracie said. *And who will people want when they have troubles but a superhero?* She used to look on the bright side of everything.

Not long after he opened Tire Man, he had nailed a good contract with Jessie Burgess's towing service. They bring in the motorists stranded on the interstate, the ones always glad to find a real garage open on the weekends. From the beginning, everyone in town has known that Tire Man goes far beyond tires. Practically everything related to auto mechanics is possible in the bays of Tire Man except transmission and body work. Ed's fingers fly over the adding machine. Lots of oil changes and tire rotations for people planning to travel on Memorial Day weekend. Holidays always mean oil changes and tire rotations, brake checks and tune-ups, front-end alignments. Everyone wants the best mileage on a long trip. Good steady business from reliable old customers and the new advertising campaign is doing a good job of bringing in a steady stream of newcomers. He hates to admit it, but Estelle's idea about putting a coupon in the Welcome Wagon packet was a good one. He'd be more receptive to her ideas if she wasn't so pushy, always trying to shove them down his throat.

As he finishes his paperwork for the day, he sees Estelle glide across the other side of the window and hears her gently turn the doorknob. She glides everywhere lately, acting strange and giggly. It annoys the daylights out of him when she gets like that. Her head pops in the door.

"Firestones were the big seller this month," Estelle says in her best flirtatious voice. "Did you notice? I wanted to be sure you caught that."

"Well, we do have a sale," Ed says without looking up. "It'd be hard for me to be in this business for twenty-three years if I didn't notice things like that, don't you think?" Ed hears her giggle and he throws his pencil down on the desk, his totals complete. He reaches back and rubs his neck.

"Kink?" Estelle asks.

"Little one." *Mistake.* "It'll go away by the time I get to the car."

"Here, let me help." She rounds the desk before he can protest.

"It'll be all right," he says, suddenly nervous. "You don't have to bother. It's past time for you to go home." He tries to mean it. Tries to mean it in spite of the burn between his shoulders, the spot he can't reach on his own. It feels like concrete.

"I'm not one to pay overtime, Estelle. You know that. Now, get on out of here and go home." He used to mean it. He used to know what Estelle was up to and say what needed to be said to keep her at bay. It isn't like he doesn't know what all the giggling is about, all the sly watchfulness, the readiness to take advantage of the situation. He just prefers to pretend it isn't there. He always meant it. For years he meant it. *Estelle, go on home. Estelle, get off my desk. Estelle, button the top of your blouse. People will think I'm running a whorehouse instead of a tire service.* He has come right out and said it all, and she has seldom, if ever, in the twenty years she's worked for him, been daunted. But now, with Gracie gone, it's getting harder and harder not to take Estelle up on her offers of help and support, even if she does get on his nerves so bad sometimes he wants to lock her in her office and throw away the key. He wants to mean it. *Estelle, go on home.*

Gracie was acting so strange and now she's been gone for two months. No idea what's happened to her. "No coat or nothing, I'm telling you, I saw her leave with no coat or nothing," Mrs. McDaniel says to him every time she catches him outside. "It's a wonder she don't get pneumonia. My brother died of pneumonia back in 1919. It's nothing to mess around with." The old woman says this to him like he can do something about it. But Ed doesn't know where Gracie is, doesn't know if she has pneumonia, doesn't know if she has a boyfriend, doesn't even know if she's still in one piece. The police don't have a clue either. *Estelle, go the hell home.*

She is standing behind him, gripping his shoulders in her strong smooth hands. He can feel those long crazy-looking nails against his collarbone. It's hard not to notice those things. Dark pink fingernails like the ones in the magazine ads, only longer, way longer. She massages his shoulders hard, pushing and kneading, then scratches her nails over his back through his shirt. She cups her hands around the sides of his neck and pushes her thumbs around on either side of his spine, his head moving from side to side as she works out the heaviness and makes the concrete muscle limber muscle once again. He groans before he can catch himself. She steps closer to his chair and her breasts brush against the back of his head. He feels something lift between his legs.

"Man, that felt great. Thanks." Ed reaches around for Estelle's hand, pats it, abruptly stands, rolling his chair back and forcing Estelle to step away. "You ought to get on home now. You work too much."

"That's a funny thing for a boss to say." She is trying to look deep into his eyes, but he won't look back. She searches for a sign. Searches for the thing Ed knows she waits patiently for year after year.

"You need a good home-cooked meal. Come on home with me and I'll fix you some supper," Estelle says, walking out the door as if Ed is going to follow her. He almost does. He comes so close. She stops and looks back over her shoulder, the twist of her body showing off her small waist and round firm hiney packed into a tight black skirt. Estelle looks good at forty-two years old. She takes good care of herself and she wants to take good care of Ed, too.

"I need to get home. Ginger's coming by with supper," he lies.

"Well, maybe next time," Estelle says. Ed wishes he could hear discouragement in her voice, but he doesn't. She meant what she said, and if anything, she probably senses a little headway. Maybe she's right. Maybe next time. He'll have to be careful. Not let down his guard. Not let her corner him like she's just done. If something doesn't happen soon it might be next time. *Estelle, go the hell on home.* All her years of waiting might pay off. His dick pushes at the wall of his jeans. He grabs his Windbreaker, the one that says "Tire Man" across the back, and holds it in front of him. He scoops his keys from the desk.

"Come on, Estelle. I'll walk you to your car."

By the time Ed gets home he's starving. But he decides going to sleep is easier than fixing something to eat. He's tired of fast food, tired of eating in restaurants, tired of TV dinners, tired of being prey to attractive women bearing invitations to dinner.

The next morning Ed's eyes open to the dusty grayness of first light. In his dream Estelle was a big spider with long blood-red fingernails at the end of all those legs. She was trying to seduce him with chocolate chess pie and a baked ham. He's wet with sweat, exhausted, and, for the first time since Gracie left, he really needs a drink. He reaches for the bottle of bourbon in the bottom drawer of the bedside table. When the sun comes up, Ed leaves a message for Estelle and Wally on the answering machine at Tire Man. "I got things to do today," he says to the machine. But that is a lie. He has nothing to do but wait for Gracie, and in the meantime, learn to feed his own damn self.

Along about six o'clock in the evening, after a good helping of Maker's Mark for breakfast and a peanut butter and jelly sandwich for lunch, Ed dials Ginger's number from the wall phone in the kitchen. The cord is twisted into a series of spurs and knots, so he lets the receiver dangle in space for a few seconds, then checks to see if she's answered. Finally Wally picks up at the other end.

"Hello," Wally says, a little out of breath.

"Wally, Ginger there?" Ed asks, trying his best to sound happy. Happy people are less vulnerable. Why hasn't that occurred to him before?

"Oh, hey, Ed. No, she just went to the Harris Teeter for coffee. You want her to call you back?"

"No need to call back," Ed says. He's frustrated. His stomach growls. "Say, Wally, you don't know how long to boil eggs, do you? Hard-boil them?"

"Let's see. Seems like ten, fifteen minutes maybe," Wally says with semiconfidence.

"Ten minutes after they start boiling or from the time the water goes on the stove?" Ed reaches into the refrigerator and takes out the egg box. He wonders if the eggs are still good. Seems like they must be at least a month old. Some Ginger brought over saying, "Anybody can cook an egg, Daddy."

"Boiling, I think," Wally says pensively.

"Do you put the eggs in when the water boils, or from the beginning?" Ed breaks open an egg into a cup and takes a whiff. Smells okay.

"Beginning," Wally says, now becoming more confident. "You sprinkle some salt or vinegar in the water too to keep the eggs from cracking. I've seen my mother do that. Are you deviling the eggs or just eating them as is?"

"Just eating, I guess. Unless you know how to devil them. Deviled eggs sound pretty good." Ed gets excited at the thought of deviled eggs.

"They're actually pretty easy, if you cook the eggs right. You cut them in half, flip the yolk in a bowl, mix in some mayo, some mustard—just a little mustard—some sweet pickle juice. You only want to use sweet pickle juice. If you don't have sweet, leave out the pickle juice."

"Wait, let me see if I got everything." Ed rummages through the fridge and comes out with everything he needs including Vlasic Sweet Baby Gherkins.

"Okay, what do I do then?"

"Then you mash all that up with a fork."

"Wait. How much of all that stuff do I put in the bowl?"

"Just enough to look right. I don't know amounts. I'd do a spoon full at a time till it tastes right. Anyway, you mix all that up good and spoon it into the egg white halves. Sprinkle with paprika and you're done."

"Well," Ed says with an edge, "you're just a regular Betty Crocker. How the hell do you know how to make deviled eggs? Since when did you learn to cook?" Ed is getting mad and he doesn't know why.

"They're cheap and I like them. My mother used to fix deviled eggs all the time for covered dish suppers and on Sundays. You got a problem with that? Hey, man. I'm just trying to help you. What are you getting so sore about?"

"Aw, nothing. I'm just tired and don't want to cook my own supper. You say ten minutes boiling?"

"Maybe fifteen. You might want to cook a bunch and put them in the fridge. That's what my mother does. Then you can devil a few at the time or just peel one and eat it with salt. If you do a bunch you can also crack one at ten minutes and see if they're done enough. That's what I'd do. I'd cook a bunch and crack one at ten minutes and see if they're done."

"How come you're not this smart at selling tires?"

"Because I learned deviling eggs from my mother. I learned selling tires from you."

"You know what? Have Ginger call me."

"You going to tell her to ask me to marry her?"

"No, dimwit. I want her to teach me to fry chicken by Sunday. You can't fry chicken, can you?" Ed hates being helpless. He believes if he tries hard enough, he can remember a time when he wasn't.

"I'll tell her to call you. And frying chicken is out of my league, man. If you want to try gravy though, I'm pretty fair on that and biscuits."

"What kind of gravy?" Ed asks.

"Oh, sawmill, red-eye, brown beef, cream gravy. I can do the chicken gravy, too, once Ginger fries the chicken. You know fried chicken's hard, Ed. You might want to start simple, say hamburger steak and tossed salad. A little garlic toast."

"Wally, any fool can cook a hamburger."

"Well, you can't boil an egg, can you? How am I supposed to know you can cook a hamburger? You sound pretty undomestic to me."

Ed hangs up the phone and counts out his eggs. Six ought to be enough. He might as well learn to cook. He'll do it one thing at a time. But he's not putting any paprika on his deviled eggs. The least he can do is slice green olives and put them on top like his mama used to do.

Ed finds the olives and a pot. He stares at the smooth surface of the water as he waits for it to boil and wonders how good a cook Estelle is. *You need a good home-cooked meal. Come on home with me, and I'll fix you some supper.* He knows she makes a good chocolate chess pie. Brings a couple in every Friday. Where there's chess pie there might be roast beef and that baked ham he dreamed about, chicken casserole, or salmon patties and creamed potatoes.

Ed takes his mind in another direction. He looks around the kitchen and spies the bright red *Betty Crocker Cookbook* on the shelf near the breakfast nook. When he opens it, Ed is glad to see all the pictures. He flips to the index and looks up eggs. Further down the indented column he sees the word *deviled*.

T OOT SITS ON the back step beside Tyrone. Tyrone has his pad open and is coloring a picture of Buttercup. He has drawn the dog, the garage, and a tall dark man with blue eyes holding a bone.

"Who's that?" Toot asks, pointing to the man.

"I don't know."

"He in a bunch of your pictures, ain't he?"

"Yes, I guess so."

"Well, he is or he ain't? You drawing him. You shouldn't have to guess about it."

"He just gets in my head, in the picture I see. So I put him in the pictures I draw. He's nobody I know or anything." Tyrone looks up at Toot for approval. "He's a nice man."

"How come he got blue eyes?"

"Because that's the color eyes he has."

"If you made him up, how you know that?"

"I don't know how I know."

"Humph," Toot says. What she thinks is, *This child need a daddy. I hope Sammy up to it. I hope that Doristeen know a good man when he in front of her.* Still, Toot thinks about the blue eyes and wonders.

"How come you don't sit in a chair instead of on the back steps?" Toot asks.

"The steps fit me better."

Toot looks at the swept circle full of lawn chairs. A big white glider, like the one on the front porch, sits to one side of the back door. Green plants and flowers of all kinds circle the porches. Big pots painted white and full of geraniums stand around the edge of the dirt. Green houseplants rest on little painted tables and on pieces of fat tree trunks cut the height of tables, all the plants destined to bloom or hang full of foliage before the summer is out. The little circle around the yard is a summer sitting jungle. The green yard fans out from it, clear for running and playing, except for the three big white oaks near the house and the pin oak and walnut that stand farther out, nearer to the barn. Off to the right is a small orchard

with apple and peach trees, a few plum and a cherry. Toot's big flower garden and vegetable garden are out past the garage. The only other trees in
the yard proper are two mimosas between the front porch and the dirt
road that comes down by the house from the hardtop. They're good trees
for climbing, if you're a beginner. But here sits Tyrone on the steps. Not
even in a chair. Toot stops beating around the bush and decides to broach
the conversation she came over to have with him.

"Tyrone, I'm gon' ask you something and I want you to tell me the
truth, even if you think you might get in trouble. Understand?" She rests
her hand on Tyrone's knobby knee.

"Yes, ma'am." Tyrone looks at Toot's mouth to see if it is drawn up
tight. It isn't.

"Did you go in the garage and get in my paints? The paints I use for
birdhouses?"

"No, ma'am."

Toot looks hard at the boy. He looks back with his big brown saucer
eyes.

"You sure? 'Cause somebody been in my paints and tried to make it
look like they hadn't been. And on top of that, they's a bunch of little boy
footprints all over the garage floor." Toot has found signs of Tyrone's tennis shoes and Buttercup's paw prints covering the dirt floor. She can't
make out any other prints beside theirs and hers and Sammy's, and she
and Sammy had come in the garage together. The clincher is a spot of
green paint on Buttercup's ear. "Now, being truthful and taking the medicine beats lying to keep out of trouble. You know what a lie is?"

"Yes, ma'am." Tyrone's eyes begin to fill with water. He tries to hold
them open, to keep the tears in place. He wants his mama. He wants
Sammy. He's almost his daddy. He would do. Tyrone wants Toot to believe
him, but he can see that isn't likely.

"Yes, ma'am, you messed in my paints?"

"Yes, ma'am, I know what a lie is. But I didn't touch any paints. I
have my own paints in my box. I went in the garage this morning for
Buttercup because she took the stick in there and left it and I had to go
get it out."

"I looked at your paints, Tyrone. They empty. All used up."

"But I haven't even used my paints yet!" Tyrone's surprise is genuine. His peepish voice has become big and disappointment looms large on his face. Toot knows the boy is telling the truth. Her own memory tells her that. She has not seen a single painting by Tyrone since he's come to Rockrun. Only drawings, and only made with his pencils and markers and crayons. His paints, she realizes, ought to be like new.

When the conversation began, Toot was convinced she had her culprit. Now she knows he's innocent. Tyrone is a good child, except for that Mr. Goodbar on her sofa cushion. But somebody has used Toot's paints. If not Tyrone, then who?

"What about my living room pencil? Have you had my living room pencil?"

"Granny Toot, I have my own box of pencils." Tyrone now sounds irritated.

"Who said you could call me Granny?" Toot asks in a voice that surprises even her. "I mean to say, I'm not old enough to be no granny."

Tyrone is both surprised and hurt. Surprised because he thinks Toot is as old as God, and hurt because he thought she would like him to call her Granny. He blinks and two large round tears run down his round face and land on his drawing. They make the paper pucker and the marker colors bleed.

"Tyrone, you too tired if you crying over this here conversation. Go take you a nap. You getting nervous." Toot takes the pad and markers away from Tyrone and stands up so he can go in the back door.

"I'm not tired."

"You go have you some quiet time anyway. We got to do the market tomorrow and you gon' need some extra rest. I'm expecting to sell a lot of birdhouses and you gon' have to work hard to take all that money from people. You gon' earn your allowance tomorrow."

Tyrone goes inside with his head hanging low. When he has gone through the kitchen and back to the bedroom where he stays, Toot looks up and asks, "Don't let it be him that used my paint. I don't know who's doing it, but I don't want it to be that Tyrone." She opens the screen door and goes inside to do housework. Her birdhouses are drying and she needs to change the beds to keep herself out of the kitchen. Today it's Mattie's kitchen.

"Okay, here we go. One. Two. Three." Toot pivots Rachel around and puts her in the rocking chair beside the bed. She tugs at Rachel's nightgown until it's straight and adjusts her pink sweater.

DuRon has been coming by every few days to check on Mattie and Toot and see how Rachel is doing. Since they don't know who she is or how she got here or who she might be associated with, DuRon feels it's important to keep abreast of things. The first trip he made back to see Rachel, he walked up with a sack of clothes from the thrift store in Martinsville. Just about everything fit, including the pink sweater. Of course, he got a piece of pecan pie for his effort.

Rachel puts her arms on the armrests and laughs, seemingly at nothing.

The windows and door are open. An oscillating fan rotates on its axis from the top of the dryer and a nice breeze keeps the room comfortable.

"Here, I might just as well strip this bed while you sit there. You got to get up out this bed some," Toot says as she tugs the fitted sheet out of its grip on the mattress. "If you don't start getting around a little better, we gon' pull Arty's wheelchair out the shed. You got to get outside. Start to walk and talk. Tell us your name. Things like that."

Toot finally pulls the edges of the sheets from under the mattress and lets the dirty sheets fall in a pile on the middle of the bed. She grabs the end of each pillowcase in turn and shakes it vigorously until each naked pillow spills out onto the pile of sheets.

Toot drapes the sheets around the agitator, drops in the pillowcases, and then adds a scoop of Tide. "Don't use no washing powder but Tide. I been using it since I don't know when. Only thing'll get dirt out. Smell good too. Here, smell that." Toot waves the laundry soap scoop under Rachel's nose. "Don't you think that smell good and fresh? I wonder what you use at your house." Toot looks to see if there is any response. Rachel smiles briefly and sits staring at the box of Tide until her eyes start looking funny and she lets out a big sneeze.

Toot goes to the linen closet and brings back a stack of fresh white bed linens, which she sets in Rachel's lap.

"Hand me a bottom sheet," Toot asks in a firm voice. This is what she used to do with the little girls who followed her around all day while she cleaned their mamas' houses and made their families' beds. "You know what that is?" Toot points. "A bottom sheet? Hand it to me now," she coaches.

Rachel pulls the sheet from the bottom of the stack and hands it to Toot.

"Well, now we getting somewhere." Toot takes the clean white sheet from Rachel's hands and unfolds it to get a grip on the side. With a hard snap that makes Rachel jump, Toot unfurls the sheet and drapes it across the little bed. When she reaches across the mattress to hook the elastic corner around the far upper edge, she stops before she gets it completely hooked. Toot shifts her weight and rests part of it on the hand by the wall. Her eyes focus on a small spot of dark green, a smudge on the pale mint laundry room wall.

"What you got here?" Toot eyes the green smudge more closely and sees that it is a leaf. She scoots the bed back from the wall a little bit more and sees that the leaf is attached to a tree. Further down, on the floor next to the baseboard, is Toot's living room pencil whittled to a rough point, probably with the steak knife on the floor beside it. Drawn along the bottom of the wall behind the bed just above the baseboard is the Garden of Eden. There stands blond Adam and a redheaded Eve, their bodies small and naked, their heads big. They are painted in the same colors as Toot's birdhouses. The snake is drawn in pencil, but not yet painted. Beneath the green tree of knowledge, Eve's pink fat hand offers a tempting blue fish to Adam.

"Hmph," Toot says. She climbs off the mattress and sits on the edge of Rachel's bed. "Well, I'll be," she says low. She stares at Rachel, who is now holding up the top sheet, waiting for Toot to take it from her. "Hmph," Toot says again.

"Hmph," says Rachel. Then she drops the top sheet in Toot's open hands.

PASSION

Oh, love is a journey with water and stars,
with drowning air and storms of flour;
love is a clash of lightnings,
two bodies subdued by one honey.

—Pablo Neruda

translation by Stephen Tapscott

SISTER REBA SITS on a brick wall near the entrance to the North Carolina State Fair in Raleigh. She always stops and buys her ticket at any fair—the little bazaars with rides set up in a parking lot, the county fairs with livestock and jars of preserves, and the state fairs with exhibits and competitions, the looping roller coasters and the rodeos—the bigger, the better. Reba is drawn to these chaotic carnivals where she can survey a perfect cross section of people, stare at their faces while they are occupied with other things—crying children, cotton candy and candy apple hands, trying to carry too many stuffed animals, or looking for the restrooms. She tries to ferret out their hearts, their troubles, their hopes, and she prays for them without them knowing it, without them even being aware of her presence. She keeps a low profile, first nibbling on a ham biscuit and sipping Coke, then pinching off pieces of funnel cake and washing it down with black coffee. She appears to be minding her own business, and in a way she is, imagining the lives she might have had— nurse, teacher, bank teller, farmer's wife, aunt, sister, grandmother, mother. Mother.

Sister Reba always finds a perch near the kiddie rides—the duck-shaped boats that float in a circle, carried along by some unseen metal arm beneath the water's surface, the little cars and planes that rise and dip endlessly around and around. *Mama! Mama!* she hears the children call. *Ma, see me flying!* She watches parents and children on the Ferris wheel and the merry-go-round and she thinks of her own daughter, frozen in her mind as an eight-year-old child, braids and barrettes all over her head, a lollypop in her hand. For a little while Reba allows the memory to hiss up like steam from a kettle. She hears the little voice calling her to watch her cartwheel, watch her jump rope, look at some picture she's drawn. Reba sits on the brick wall and imagines it is Doristeen on the merry-go-round, and it is Reba holding her hand as she rises and falls to the tinny sound of the calliope. She imagines it is Reba who takes the picture as the little girl comes around the corner in the bullet-shaped airplane, the little girl ecstatic at the combination of her new independence and her reassurance at the sight of her mother, who puts the ever-present camera to her face and clicks, then waits for the child at the metal gate.

Don't call here if you ain't coming home, now. I done told you. Reba hears her mother's voice hiss across time and into the pay phone receiver. *I ain't accepting this call if you ain't coming home, 'cause it just gets her hopes up.* Reba eventually gave up on phone calls and the Christmas presents that retuned unopened. The call that mattered most had to be the one Reba heard from God. But her mother didn't see it that way. Didn't see anything good about a woman, unmarried and traveling with men—even preachers, even gospel singers. *A woman needs to stay and raise the child she done gone and got. Your baby needs you. God has aplenty in his army.*

But God said, *Give up all you have and follow me through the eye of the needle.* He didn't say it out loud, but in her heart. God didn't make Abraham slay Isaac, but Abraham had to be willing to do it. And Reba had to be willing to leave everything behind and travel for God. She knew she was called to the life she needed, and somehow Doristeen was left with the life that was meant to be hers. In Reba's heart, Doristeen will always be eight years old, big eyes, long limbs, licking on that lollypop, holding her grandmother's hand at the end of the driveway. Doristeen will always be waving to Reba, when Reba takes the time to look back.

Sister Reba walks away from the kiddie rides and finds a nice barbecue shack on the midway. She gets her sandwich and her sweet tea and goes to find another place to sit, one away from children, down near the deformed animals and fake shrunken heads and the real live dragon. She goes to find a seat where the people in front of her will give her someone new to pray for, someone whose story she doesn't want or need.

E D SITS IN HIS burgundy Toyota Tacoma pickup in the almost empty parking lot of Three Star Mall, better known among the residents of Centertown as Three Store Mall. It was a struggle for developers to attract anchor stores—well, any stores. A few downtown merchants, who opposed the mall from the get-go, nicknamed it Three Store Mall. The ringleaders, Arnold Schulman and Willard Brewer, encourage people to use the name as a joke. Schulman owns the oldest department store in Centertown, Schulman and Schulman, and Willard Brewer owns and operates Brewer Appliance Sales and Service. In the end, the best the mall developers could do was recruit three chain stores—Dillard's, Sears, and Goody's. All the other stores are small, most of them privately owned, and prone to going out of business only to be replaced by someone else trying their hand at shopkeeping.

Arnold and Willard are still in business, but nobody knows for how long. Ed almost went to Schulman's to find a fish poacher. "Every good cook needs a fish poacher," Chef Bernard says on his Food Network show Ed has taken to watching in the evenings. Ginger said Schulman's would have it, and Ed, as the proprietor of a Centertown business himself and a fellow lodge member, feels an allegiance to Schulman. But Schulman might see him and strike up a conversation. Ed doesn't want to feel foolish in the heart of town, a tire specialist buying a fish poacher. Particularly since he doesn't even know what to look for in a good fish poacher. What if he buys a crappy one? What will Schulman say then? What will happen when he runs into Schulman at the lodge and Schulman thinks about Ed and a fish poacher? No, Ed needs to be at the mall, whether he wants to be or not. If this experience goes okay, he'll buy something from Schulman later and make it up to him.

Ed is not one to frequent department stores. In fact, he has never been to Schulman's or the mall. Never needed to. His knowledge of the mall and its controversies comes from his faithful daily reading of the *Centertown Reporter*. Ed always fetched the morning paper and Gracie always did the shopping. She bought almost everything: his Levi's 505 dungarees, thirty-six thirty-two, his heavy-gauge knit sport shirts and his boxer shorts and undervests and padded work socks, the heavy-duty steel-toed work boots he's worn for twenty-five years, size ten and a half Ds, his few pairs of khaki trousers, and the Sunday suits he needed for weddings, funerals, and regular church attendance, the latter ending years ago. She bought his yearly allowance of cologne each Christmas, his razors, his shaving cream, his deodorant, his toothpaste, his toothbrushes, his dental floss. Gracie had made all these purchases since the day they got married, since before they got married.

Everything else comes from a uniform catalog, and Estelle orders that. She does it for Ed and all the boys at Tire Man. It's in her job description. She orders the dark blue work pants and the light gray shirts with names embroidered in red letters on white patches sewn over the breast pocket, quilted navy coveralls for winter.

Ginger has been in charge of Gracie's Christmas and birthday presents and all-important cards since she was old enough to drive a car. Before that, Estelle handled it and even took Ginger to buy presents for her mother. He knew the nightgowns and housecoats and perfumes and hand-bags and fancy bowls and earrings came either from Schulman's, Three Store Mall, or the outlet mall up the interstate in Burlington.

Ed and Gracie started out with used everything: couch, stove, refriger-ator. Her grandfather didn't approve of her marrying a non-Catholic, and her mother was afraid of her grandfather, so neither of them assisted the young couple setting up housekeeping. The used furniture they started with wasn't like the family antiques they have now. It was stuff they rum-maged through junk shops for when they were still infatuated and every-thing was fun, even poverty. What Gracie wanted when Ginger was little was to replace the old with the new. So one time he had Estelle order a side-by-side refrigerator when Ginger was in kindergarten, and Gracie had boys from the store move the old Frigidaire into the garage for extra cold storage when she needed it. When she canned or before a Tupper-ware or bridge club party, she wiped out the old fridge, shut the door, and plugged it in. She wanted to make use of what little life it had left. *Gracie was like that, is like that*, he corrects himself, *making the best out of what is left.* When her mother died, Gracie inherited the nice antiques. She got the family pieces when there was no family left. Now they seem to be Ed's. *One day they'll be Ginger's. Maybe one day they will be Gracie's again.* He catches himself like that all the time, thinking or talking about Gracie in the past tense. Then he tries to retract it by projecting her back into his future.

So, as far as shopping goes, Ed doesn't know how to shop. Well, only at the auto parts store. That's easy. He knows the make and model of the car he's working on, knows what part is broken, and a book can easily tell him what he needs to buy in the way of windshield wiper arms, oil pumps, water hoses, fuses, or fan belts. It's sensible, scientific, and alphabetical. There is a science to men's shopping, leaving only a little margin for creative thinking and decision making. Most of the decisions have been made at a factory long before Ed ever has a shopping quest to fulfill.

Here, in the mall parking lot, it is a sight different. He parks the truck at 9:30 A.M. on Wednesday morning, before the crowd begins to gather for a day of browsing and buying and lunching and socializing. Ed moves beyond what is familiar. He is about to cover new ground. He is about to go in search of Dillard's kitchenware department.

Ginger told him to go there, if he wouldn't go to Schulman's. "Find what you need at the mall, for heaven's sake," she said. She told him to make a list. He did that. She told him to park at the entrance to Dillard's that faced the bank. He did that. She told him to be one of the first ones there because she knew he didn't want to look foolish in front of anyone who might know him. He is ready for that. He arrives thirty minutes before the store opens to be sure he's ahead of the crowd. She told him to go on a Wednesday because the postweekend shoppers will be done by Tuesday and the sales won't start until Thursday. "There's more downtime in the mall on Wednesday, less customer traffic. Clerks are usually stocking shelves and doing busy work they can't get to during the peak shopping times." Ginger knows this because she worked at Big John's Pet World all through high school.

Ed is to walk up to the doors across from the bank at 10 A.M., when they are unlocked for the public. He is to pass through men's sportswear on either side of the doors and follow the uncarpeted section of the floor around to the right, between ladies' accessories and the shoe department. He'll make another right, going between perfume and cosmetics. He is then to walk through an archway with sheets and towels stapled to the wall. Then, staying on the tiled walkway, turn right again into kitchenware. Three rights to get in. Three lefts to get out. He can handle that.

Ed reaches in the pocket of his Windbreaker to check for his list. At one minute to ten a young man with dark wet-looking curly hair wearing a yellow shirt and baggy black trousers comes through the inner doors of the air lock and unlocks the outer doors. At one minute to ten no other vehicles have pulled into Ed's end of the parking lot.

Most of the parking lot activity is near the main entrance, far from Dillard's, just as Ginger predicted. Walkers. Lots of people come to the mall early in the morning to walk. It is part of Dr. McKinney's heart rehab program. The walkers go in the main entrance, and they don't usually stay to shop. According to Ginger, a nurse is in there to take blood pressures, check heart rates, and give general advice, and there's a nutritionist to counsel patients on their diet. The patients, and anyone else who wants to participate, walk themselves toward better health and go home before the shoppers get in their way.

Ed steps out of the truck, pushes the lock button, and shuts the door behind him. His heart beats faster. He doesn't want to ask for help. He doesn't want to call attention to himself. He doesn't want to do his own shopping. He doesn't want Estelle to do anymore of his personal shopping, and Ginger's too busy with the doughnut shop. But he really wants to poach a salmon, dammit, and there isn't a fish poacher in his whole big kitchen, so there is nothing left to do but go where they sell fish poachers.

Ed pushes through the first set of doors, then boldly pushes through the second set into the cool air of the big mall. Only, he pushes a little harder than he needs to and trips, ever so slightly, over the threshold into a new world.

When he makes the turn into kitchenware he meets a surprise, so much so that in the end there is nothing left for him to do but let go and relax. There, directly in front of Ed, between the main aisle and the cashier's station, is a woman's broad butt sticking up in the air. Cream-colored fabric with large navy blue daisies is spread tightly across her rear. The flowery bottom is suspended over the soles of a pair of well-worn low-heeled shoes, sensible shoes as best he can tell. Ed leans forward and sees the woman's red face turned out toward the aisle with the right side pressed hard against the tile floor. Her lips pooch out like a blowfish and her eyes are squeezed shut. She is straining. She is holding her breath. Her right arm is jammed backward under the floor display. A grunting noise issues from somewhere in her body, but it is hard to say exactly where it emanates from.

"I'll be right with you," she groans. The words are hard to understand through her fishlike mouth. "Just . . . one . . . second. Got it!" She extracts her arm from beneath the base of the display case and raises her shoulders from the floor. Ed bends down to offer her a hand up, which she accepts. When she stands, Ed finds she is an attractive woman, despite the red face and dust bunnies in her hair. She is short and round, but in a sexy kind of way. She has bold blue marblelike eyes. She's no longer fishlike but friendly and slightly crooked. Her bottom teeth are slightly crooked too, a few white dominoes leaning in the wrong direction. Her smile is pretty nonetheless.

"Oh, thank you." She lets go his hand. "This darn register tape got away from me and rolled under the display. As if I don't hate replacing register tape enough." She takes a deep breath and lets it out. She hands him the register tape while she brushes the dust off her ample round bosom, her knees, and her arm. Two light gray smudges remain on the front of her white sweater, right over the tip of each breast.

"Now," she says, taking back the register tape, "may I help you?" The woman runs her hands through her frosted hair, cut chin-length. It makes her face look as round as a basketball. She fluffs her hair up a little from the bottom and looks down in the direction of her left breast, making a little double chin as she adjusts her name tag, which reads in black letters on a gold background, PARVA WILSON.

"I need to buy a fish poacher," Ed says, shoving his hands into his pants pockets.

"Oh well. Electric or range-top?" she says as she continues to straighten her clothes and pat at herself, repeatedly trying to brush away the gray circles from the front of her sweater. Ed contemplates this question as Parva Wilson pulls at a chain around her neck and retrieves a pair of apple-red reading glasses she had slung around to her back before going after the register tape. With the glasses on the end of her nose, she tilts her head back and eyes the inner mechanics of the register.

"Well, I don't exactly know," Ed says. Honesty is the best approach, he decides. Plead ignorance. "I didn't know there was more than one kind."

"Heavens yes," she says, slapping the door shut on the register and dropping the reading glasses from her face to rest at her gray-tipped bosom. She has nice breasts. Ed tries not to keep looking at them, but she keeps doing things to draw his attention there. *Late forties*, he thinks.

"Just about any small cooking appliance they make these days can be electric or range-top," Parva Wilson says in the polished sales speak of an experienced retailer. "It's a yuppie's market, you know."

"I'm not a yuppie," Ed says defensively.

"Oh no, of course not." She reaches out and touches his arm as she blinks her eyes and pinches her cute crooked mouth together. "We're both a little too old to be called that."

He notices her nice smooth hands, the short nails with clear polish.

"Matter of fact, I don't know too many yuppies around here, do you?" She never stops smiling and prattles on. "Well, that young cardiologist, Dr. McKinney, the one that's got everybody walking everywhere. I'd have to say the McKinneys can be considered yuppies. Mrs. McKinney is one of my best customers in the small appliance line, you know. Well, in every line I carry, actually. Even special orders sometimes, particularly her cookware. But I was really just referring to the larger marketplace and its impact on manufacturers. In general, the marketplace wants options and extras these days. As retailers, we have to be aware of that." Parva brushes dust from the countertop beside the register.

She sounds smart and Ed is out of his element. He does what he prefers his ignorant customers to do when they need tires—rely on the salesman's expertise. "Which kind of fish poacher would you suggest?"

"There are a lot of advantages to a free-standing electric fish poacher. More even heat, better temperature control, and now they are so easy to clean. Tell me, do you have a gas or electric range?"

"Gas. All right, I'll take one."

"Take one what?"

"Electric fish poacher."

"Oh, well, we don't carry those." She turns and walks toward the end of the display aisle.

"What about your responsibility as a retailer?" *Why in the world did she just go through all that speech for then?* He wants to get in and get out as quickly as possible and he has already been here fifteen minutes. Other people are going to come in any minute.

"Oh well, like I said, we don't have many yuppies around here. We stock according to our clientele, of course. If we were in a more cosmopolitan area, I'd stock a greater number of options."

"What do you have then in the way of fish poachers, for the kind of people that live in Centertown?" Ed asks, trying to sound even, not frustrated.

"We have this nice stainless steel number that works quite well across two burners, particularly with a gas range." She reaches the end of the aisle and holds up a long narrow pan with a lid to match. "It's ample sized so you have some flexibility in the size fish you can poach, you see." She walks back to the register holding the pan and removes the lid to reveal the stainless interior and removable tray with holes in it. It looks exactly like the one Chef Bernard used last Thursday night.

"That's good. I'll take it." Ed reaches to his back pocket for his wallet.

"Wonderful." She smiles. "Excellent choice. Cash, check, or charge?"

"Cash."

Her fingers nimbly dance over the register keys. Ed doesn't see how he has made an excellent choice when there isn't much of a choice to make. She only has one fish poacher to sell him in the first place.

"Is this a gift for your wife?"

"No. I live alone." *Where did that come from?* Well, it is true. He does live alone at the moment.

"So you like to cook, do you?" She hands him his Dillard's bag.

"I'm learning." He says it before he can catch himself.

"Oh well, I love to cook. I find it very relaxing. To me there is nothing more soothing when I'm stressed than to bake a cake or make a big pot roast. All the beating of batter and cutting and chopping is quite cathartic. It's my creative outlet, really."

What kind of cake are we talking about here? Ed would love to have a big slice of homemade yellow cake with milk chocolate icing and a glass of cold milk. He doesn't care how early it is. Once he gets this fish poaching thing down, he'll try cake baking. His biscuits are improving. They are now soft enough to eat and don't taste like baking soda. He can probably move on to cakes without much trouble. Chef Bernard pointed out just the other night that baking is the most scientific aspect of cooking. "You can be creative when you cook; but when you bake, you better follow the formula," Chef Bernard is fond of saying.

"Come on back if I can help you in any way," Parva Wilson says.

"Thank you . . ." Ed looks at her bosom one last time, then her name tag, "Mrs. Wilson."

"Miss. Miss Wilson. Parva, please just call me Parva. Enjoy your fish."

Parva Wilson shoves her hip against the register drawer to make sure it is closed and turns toward a stack of boxed merchandise near one of the shelves.

Ed starts backtracking through handbags and the shoe department, wondering how hard it will be to bake a cake from scratch. Making his third left toward the exit sign and his pickup truck, he brushes aside the obvious question. *Just how good a cook is this Parva Wilson?*

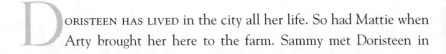

DORISTEEN HAS LIVED in the city all her life. So had Mattie when Arty brought her here to the farm. Sammy met Doristeen in

Raleigh when he was finishing his veterinary degree and she was dating a friend of his. Tyrone was a baby. He remembers thinking his friend was crazy dating a woman with a child. Over the past few years he's lost touch with that friend.

Sammy went back to Raleigh six months ago for a five-year reunion. His friend couldn't make it. When Sammy walked in Harris Teeter to pick up some beer, there stood Doristeen, working a second job to save money for graduate school. She remembered him. Called him by name. Sammy went back two hours later to buy chips and dip just so he could ask her out.

"My mother is a preacher," Doristeen says, mostly to Reverend Love. This is news to Sammy. He is sitting on the porch with Mama Toot, Mattie, Doristeen, Tyrone, and the reverend, who is running a revival in Rockrun. When the reverend's in town, Mama Toot always invites him to Sunday dinner. Mattie, Mama Toot, and the reverend sit in the metal chairs. Mama Toot bounces her chair easylike on its L-shaped frame. Mattie sits still and stares off into space. Doristeen and Tyrone are in the glider. Sammy is sitting on a crate with his back against a porch post. Reverend Love loosens his belt a notch and stretches his legs out long to make room for all he has eaten, so it can move on down past his impending heartburn. Sammy's eaten a good bit, too, and it's hard for it to get settled when he's bent up like a baby sitting on a box. But Reverend Love has Sammy's usual seat, and Sammy knows none of these women will let the good reverend sit on a box.

"The Bible speaks against women in the pulpit," the reverend says to Doristeen.

"It speaks for it too, Reverend. Like most things, it just depends on where you look. Believe me. I've heard this argument more times than I can count. I know it backwards and forwards. Paul said this, Joel said that, and on and on it goes. God can make His demands on anyone, no matter what the sex, no matter what the personal cost."

"I think Scripture is quite clear. Women should be silent in church," counters the reverend.

"And their daughters shall prophesy," quotes Doristeen.

"Prophesy doesn't mean preach, Miss Washington." The reverend shifts in his chair slightly.

Mama Toot gives Doristeen a look, not a bad look, but a kind of look that means, *You wasting your time on him.*

Doristeen's legs are crossed, and they are some fine legs. Sammy sees the reverend has noticed those fine legs, too. Obviously, being a man of the cloth doesn't keep you from being a man under the cloth. Reverend Love crosses his legs and folds his hands in his lap.

Doristeen's bottom leg pushes the glider one way then pulls it the other. Sammy watches the muscles in her foot and calf change with each motion. Her high heels are plain black pumps, polished. She is a nice-dressing woman. Tasteful.

Tyrone sits beside Doristeen, his round head resting against her chest, his eyes closed. He is transported by his mother's presence, lulled into an afternoon nap by the smooth rhythmic motion of the glider, the warmth of his mother's body, her familiar smell. Sammy is lulled by those things, too. Doristeen's calf muscle works the glider just as steady, all the while she lightly rubs her hands over Tyrone's legs and talks to Mattie and Toot and Reverend Love, having devoted her full attention to Sammy the night before.

"How long will you be preaching your revival, Reverend?" Sammy asks, trying to draw his gaze away from Doristeen.

"As long as it takes, Samuel. Maybe one week, maybe two. But as long as it takes for me to feel like I've made a difference. You got to preach till you know they love church."

"I thought you preached for them to love God," Doristeen says. Sammy can hear the challenge in her voice. She can't resist. He knows this much about her.

"God *is* His Church." The reverend is close to taking offense. Sammy can tell Doristeen wants to pull the preacher over the edge. But she holds back out of respect for Mattie and Toot, or out of fear of them. She told Sammy that she's convinced Mattie doesn't like her. He tries to tell her his mother is just grief-stricken about his father, but Doristeen doesn't think it's only his father Mattie's grieving for.

Doristeen will leave on the afternoon bus and won't be back for a couple of weeks. Sammy hates to see her go, but women fall for Reverend Love like young girls fall for movie stars, even if he is a chauvinist. For once, Sammy will be glad for Doristeen to get on back to Charlottesville and to her schoolwork.

Reverend Love has been holding revivals in Rockrun since Sammy was a boy. He can work a congregation, work it up good. Even Sammy's cried tears and gone to the altar. But he was a boy then, and his only sins were stealing a piece of peppermint from his mother and daddy's dresser and lying about washing the back of his neck and behind his ears. Now, as a man, he finds God in a different way. While Sammy respects the ways of others and believes church has its role to play in society, if not always for the best, Sammy sees God in and through science. He doesn't say that out loud, of course, at least not in this particular company, because then there would be a long discussion he doesn't want to have again. The reverend will be forced to witness, and Mama Toot will take Sammy by the ear later when they are alone, if not take after him with a hickory stick. He is a grown man, but it hurts like crazy when she grabs his ear if he's not expecting it. Right now he wants to be left alone to pay close attention to the woman in the glider. He's happy to keep his heretical beliefs to himself.

Everything about Doristeen is fine to Sammy, and he wants all his womenfolk to get along. It was his idea for Tyrone to come here. When Doristeen mentioned the program in Charlottesville, Sammy saw a good opportunity to build a relationship with Tyrone, make him part of the family, and help Doristeen at the same time. He and Tyrone could try each other on for size. If these women can get along, and he and Tyrone can have something special, then Sammy can have the life he wants where he wants it. Peaceful. Easy. A nice family and his veterinary practice in the place he feels most at home.

Sammy is the first black vet in the five-county area, working in a practice with a white vet named Calvin Prater. Calvin is progressive in many ways, but has lived here so long he can hide his new thinking by talking like it's old thinking. His clients are getting used to Sammy. He and Prater talk about it, how Sammy will take over the practice slowly, winning the white men over as well as the black. Just because he's black, that doesn't mean the black farmers automatically accept him without his proving himself. Their cows are their livelihood.

"Miss Doristeen, what do you study at the university?" the reverend is saying.

"Education, Reverend Love. I want to be a teacher. I have a degree in mathematics, but I have to finish a program in education in order to receive a teaching certificate."

"It must be very hard to pursue your education with a small child. Do you have family in Charlottesville?"

"No, sir. But I manage. And Miz Toot and Miz Mattie have kindly offered to let Tyrone stay here until I can finish my studies." Doristeen looks down at Tyrone. Reverend Love turns to give Mama Toot a look of admonishment, but she ignores him.

Doristeen looks at Mattie and Mama Toot. "I think this boy has gained five pounds in pure muscle from all the running he's been doing."

Living out here in the country, married to a nice animal doctor, teaching in a country school, having a good strong ready-made family for Tyrone, all that will be good for Doristeen, Sammy is sure. Tyrone's head slides down his mother's side and settles in her lap. She pulls his legs around and tucks his feet in at the end of the glider. Her hand rests on his hip. Doristeen seldom mentions any family other than Tyrone. And her one mention of her mother didn't make the woman sound like a preacher.

"Family is important, the most important thing, Miss Washington," Reverend Love says. Sammy hears the reverend's self-righteous tone creep in. He's a nice enough preacher, but they all talk like they don't live in the same world the rest of the people do. That's why Sammy looks for God in science, not in the pulpit. "Do you really think it is in Tyrone's best interest for him to be separated from his mother?" Reverend Love goes on.

Doristeen instinctively rests her hand over Tyrone's ear. Sammy is ready to say something he knows he'll catch hell for later, but he gets cut off before he can take a breath to get started.

"Excuse me, Reverend," Mama Toot says, and Sammy can tell she's loaded for bear. "I say this with all respect, but I'm surprised to hear such a comment as that from you to this young girl."

Reverend Love bristles a bit, but he knows not to challenge Toot. She has a lot of sway in this small town. "Miss Washington has a child. She is a woman with woman's responsibilities, wouldn't you say, Tallulah? Hardly a girl."

"Hardly a girl, barely a woman. Far as I can tell, you don't have no first-hand experience being neither." Toot can make anyone as uncomfortable as she wants to make them, even Reverend Love.

"It is true, Reverend. I worry about leaving Tyrone," Doristeen says quietly. "Not that I think he isn't taken care of here. It's obvious from his stay on the farm he is well cared for and quite happy. Even so, I worry that he doesn't understand why I'm asking him to live somewhere other than with me. But Sammy and his family have kindly offered to be his extended family, and if I can just finish this one-year master's program, I will have my certification and can get a teaching job. Then we'll be together again and I'll be able to better provide for him in the long run." Now that Doristeen has defended her position and talked herself into feeling guiltier than she was already, Mama Toot finishes where she started for.

"How many children do you have, Reverend?"

"Well, Tallulah, you know I've never married. I don't have any children. But I know what the Lord has to say about women and family."

"You ever look at a child and seen you couldn't feed him? Or not send him to school for a month 'cause you need him to work in a tobacco patch?"

"I assure you I grew up with hardship, if that's what you're asking." The reverend sits up and tightens his belt.

"That ain't what I'm asking at all. I'm asking if you ever look into a child's face, your own child, and seen your own life coming back at you too fast. You ever look at a child and know you was all he had, and what you decide to do and not do gon' change his life for the rest of his days? You ever done that?"

"No, I can't say as I have done that, exactly."

"I didn't think so. Then you keep your preaching on my porch to what you know and you let this young woman do what she need to do for her boy, which is leave him with me. Now if you want to stay for ice cream, take the conversation some other kind of way."

Sammy sees Doristeen look down at Tyrone and rub her hand over his head. She's trying not to let her delight take over her face. She'll like Toot, and by Toot's defense of her, Sammy sees she already likes Doristeen. Mattie stares now at Reverend Love, looks like she wants to smack him into next week. But she doesn't say a word. What makes her angry is the reverend's ignorance, not any defense of Doristeen. Doristeen is right. Mattie doesn't like her. But Sammy doesn't see his mother liking anything lately except work and dreaming—and maybe, just maybe, Tyrone.

"Where that Rachel?" Toot asks no one in particular.

"Where do you think?" Sammy answers. "Out by the garage, painting tractor parts, I was hoping to have hauled off."

Mattie looks up and gives Sammy a hard look.

"What make you think I want to get rid of any of that?" Toot asks.

"Do you want to keep it?"

"I don't have no need to get rid of it. It's been there for I don't know how long. Rachel, she doing good at making use of it, now that I got her her own paints and brushes."

"Working on the Sabbath?" Reverend Love interjects, trying to reassume the authority of his collar. "I'm surprised you would let a guest work on Sunday."

"This gal's had a string of Sundays. If she's up walking around and doing something, I don't care what day of the week it is. And I don't think God cares neither."

"What are you going to do with painted car parts?" Sammy says. "Fill the yard up with them?" He toes at the dirt by the porch and thinks of Rachel standing in front of a rusted car hood this morning painting it silver with rust retardant. Now she's spraying a coat of dark brown paint over the silver.

"I don't mind yard art." Toot talks as she bounces in her chair. "Look around. I got lots of it." She talks to Sammy as if he is trying to sell her a vacuum cleaner and she already has one she likes fine. "You getting uppity in your taste," she says, not looking up. "My taste ain't changed. You my grandbaby and I love you, but this here my yard and I like painted car parts as good as birdhouses. Besides, you don't never know what somebody gon' pay for in the end."

Reverend Love looks at Sammy, obviously taking comfort that he's not the only one outdone by Toot.

"It's not enough to paint Jesus and all these Bible characters on fenders and hoods and steering wheels," Sammy says. "She's painting fairies all over them, too. I think she's crazy as a bat."

"Sammy, we all crazy," says Toot. "You, me, your mama, the reverend, even Tyrone. We all got something make us crazy. You ever go in to doctor a bull and wonder if you crazy?"

"I'd say so," Sammy says and smiles. He can't win with Toot or his mama. He wonders why he even tries. He used to think his father was too passive with these women. Now, he understands what the man was up against. Even Reverend Love won't tangle with them beyond a certain point.

"You see?" Toot says, driving home her point. "Getting up in a pen with a bull to give him a shot's crazy too. A lot crazier, in my opinion, than painting Jesus on a car hood or Daniel in the lion's den on a rusty trunk lid. And fairies are all right. They Christian just like angels."

"I beg to differ here, Tallulah," the reverend throws in. "Fairies are creatures of the devil."

"Then how come they cried when Jesus died?" Toot says. "Ain't you never seen no fairy stones?"

"What on earth are you talking about, Tallulah?"

"I'm talking about fairy stones. Sammy, fetch our jar."

Sammy goes into the house and Toot pulls from inside her collar what looks at first like a small wooden cross on the end of a chain. Mattie sits quietly and smiles.

Toot holds it out for the reverend to see. "This here a polished fairy stone. Can't find 'em hardly nowhere 'cept in around Fairy Stone Park and up along the river over in Patrick County."

Sammy comes out with a gallon jar of rough stones, and each one seems to have a cross buried in it. "It's brown staurolite," Sammy explains as he hands one to Reverend Love. "A combination of silica, iron, and aluminum. The minerals crystallize in twins, and the ones at a ninety-degree angle look like crosses. If you sand them down and oil them, they look like wood."

The reverend turns the little rock in his fingers, then looks at the cross Toot holds out for him to see.

"Can't find 'em nowhere but round here."

"Actually," Sammy says, "this is a rare area where there are a lot of the ninety-degree stones. But they can be found in other places. People collect them around here like arrowheads."

"How, may I ask, does this prove fairies are Christian?" Reverend Love says to Toot, as he lets go of her necklace.

"These here crosses come about when the fairies heard about Jesus being crucified. They cried like babies and they tears fell down in the dirt and made these stones. Now, don't that sound Christian to you?"

Reverend Love shakes his head in disbelief and Toot takes the opportunity to wink at Mattie. Mattie chuckles.

"You might as well give up, Reverend," Mattie says. "You've met your match."

"Humph," says Reverend Love, as he lets the stone drop back in the jar Sammy still holds out to him.

Sammy extracts a stone and hands it to Doristeen. "It's good luck," he says. "Take it back to school with you." Doristeen smiles at Sammy, then takes the conversation in a new direction, as if she knows she has precious little time to make some headway with what may be her future mother-in-law.

"Miz Mattie, that pound cake you sent back with me last time was delicious. I'm not very good in the kitchen, and I had a little piece of toasted pound cake with my morning coffee for the entire week. It was a treat, I'm telling you."

"I'm glad you liked it. I'll send you back with another one." Sammy isn't clear if the emphasis of Mattie's statement is on giving away cake or sending Doristeen back. "I'll go get the ice cream freezer," Mattie says.

"We've got frozen strawberries, so how about strawberry ice cream?"
Everybody nods.

"I had to leave Arty once," Mama Toot says to Doristeen. "My sister,
Brenda, had a good day job in Martinsville. The lady next door to the
woman she worked for, she need a maid. But she only want a live-in.
Homer and me had just managed to buy this place and the first growing
season wont so good. He went to work at the loading docks at the towel
mill. A black man couldn't work on the inside back then. And I went to
Martinsville and worked for the family Brenda told me about. Only I got
so homesick and missed Arty so much I took to crying. The white woman
I worked for, she'd come in and find me crying in the soup pot. I cried over
the pork roast. I cried into the laundry basket. I cried over just about every
job I done." Toot tells this story, all the while bouncing her chair in the
same easy way. "At first the woman got aggravated and said she didn't
want to eat my cooking if I was going to cry into everything I made. Then,
when she seen I hurt so bad I couldn't stop, the woman took pity on me, I
reckon. I had me a little apartment over the garage behind the big house,
and she told me, since I was living out there on my own, I could bring Arty
with me if he didn't cause any trouble. Her little girl was about the same
age, three I think they was, and most of what I was doing was looking after
the little girl anyway.

"When I come home to get Arty, Homer 'bout died when he seen we'd
both be gone. But he seen too it was the best way to keep what we worked
so hard for. We just had to keep on working and sacrificing. Now that"—
she points at the reverend who has sulled up—"that's how strong
families do."

"How did it work out?" Doristeen leans toward Toot so she can hear
better. "When you went to work in town?"

"Oh, it wont the first time I had to go work in town. But it was the first
time I had to stay there overnight every night. I did all I could for as long
as I could. But everybody's life has its own path to take. After a time,
things got better for us, and me and Arty come home. Later on, I got day
work with a Catholic family. Leaving a child be hard, even for a day, and I
know leaving your own boy with somebody else, don't matter who it is,
don't matter what the reason, can break your heart. Even if it his own

daddy you leaving him with." Again Toot looks straight at Reverend Love as she speaks. "You doing the right thing, Doristeen. Tyrone a good smart little boy. He know his mama love him and she gon' come back to get him soon. He gon' be fine."

Sammy sees Doristeen's satisfaction. Tyrone nuzzles to try to stay asleep with all the talk around him. He has run all day with Buttercup and thrown stick after stick to show Doristeen what he can do. Sammy sits quietly on his crate and imagines Tyrone is his son. That he and Doristeen have been together for years. That they are just sitting here on this porch visiting with his family on a Sunday afternoon. He imagines that when Tyrone wakes up they'll all have strawberry ice cream and then he and Doristeen and Tyrone will drive back to their house on the other side of Toot and Mattie's farm. He pretends the three of them are already a family.

———————

E D SETS HIS GLASS of peppermint iced tea on the end table, then thinks better of it and grabs a coaster off the coffee table. He gets comfortable in the old blue recliner that used to be his spot for watching college football. But college football has given way to a new pastime. He pulls his notebook and mechanical pencil from the drawer of the end table and finds the remote stuffed in the crack along the side of his chair cushion. He clicks first the satellite box and then the TV with one hand and takes a sip of mint tea with the other. He works the remote without looking. The jazzy theme music starts and Chef Bernard's name spins into focus in the middle of the twenty-five-inch screen.

"Come on, Barney. Give us a gadget today. I need a gadget, baby."

Ed watches Chef Bernard every evening when he gets home from work. This week Frank Otis is on vacation and Ed is helping out in the back, but Ed leaves jobs half done at the end of the day if staying to finish means missing Chef Bernard. Wednesday he left a blue GMC pickup on the rack, no oil change and no front-end alignment. *It can wait till Thurs-*

day, he had thought without hesitation. Now here he sits in his pine-paneled den, surrounded by hunting pictures and old sports trophies, ready to watch a chef on Food Network prepare artful cuisine that Ed means to try in the evenings to come. His other favorite show is *Betty Bakes*. Betty comes on at eight o'clock on Saturday mornings. Ed is making Saturday his day to bake desserts he eats during the following week. He gives Ginger and Wally enough samples to keep them in desserts from Sunday through Wednesday. Wally is a sugar freak. Ed is hoping Wally will fill out some between Ed's desserts and the doughnuts.

Chef Bernard marches down the steps waving at the studio audience and shaking hands with folks in some of the aisle seats. Women in the audience try to kiss him. He has a nice little move that keeps them away from a smack right in the kisser. It's a skillful side maneuver, a fake left then right, like football, and the closest any woman gets is the corner of his mouth. Usually he manages to orchestrate a landing of lips square on his round rosy cheek.

Chef Bernard is American but is supposed to be of French descent. With those rosy cheeks and that head of red hair, he looks more Irish than French. He is also supposed to be from the South, somewhere around Savannah, but he sounds like someone off a network news broadcast. Ed thinks Chef B—Ed has taken to calling Chef Bernard either Chef B or Barney—will have more stage appeal if he gets his Southern accent back. Maybe he can take voice lessons to undo what damage the voice lessons he must have already taken have done.

Ed is beginning to think of Chef Bernard as a son, or a nephew. He admires Chef B but feels he needs some guidance in matters other than cooking. Ed wonders if he changes his oil often enough, or rotates his tires regularly. Really smart talented people often forget such things and it ends up costing them in the long run. Ed sees this all the time. He wonders if Gracie has had her tires rotated, checked her transmission fluid.

The opening commercial break is over and Bernard is back in his studio kitchen raring to go on the first recipe of the day, homemade strawberry short cake.

"All right, Barney. I need a gadget. Come on, give me a gadget," Ed says as he sets his tea down on the bass-fishing coaster and takes up his mechanical pencil. Ed begins writing in his spiral-bound notebook as Chef Bernard goes over the premeasured ingredients and holds them up in those nice little tiny Pyrex bowls. The camera cuts in close to the countertop and all you see are Chef Bernard's hands and the ingredients. It reminds Ed of auto repair training videos.

"I need a gadget, Barney," Ed chants as if for a magic seven in a crap game. "Come on, now. Come on, Barney. Don't let me down."

"Now, before we get started," Chef Bernard is saying to Ed, "I want to suggest that all of you have one of these in your kitchen. A pastry blender. Very handy gadget, this is."

"Yes!" Ed writes *pastry blender* in the upper right-hand corner of the page. It is as if Chef Bernard talks directly to him, gives him exactly what he asks for.

"Shortcake is essentially sweet biscuit dough," Chef Bernard is saying, "so to make good shortcake, you must make good biscuits." Good, Ed needs to work a little more on his biscuits. "And there is no better aid in good biscuit making—or piecrust making, for that matter—than a good pastry blender."

"Yes! Thank you, Barney."

Every night as Ed watches *Cooking with Bernard* he pays strict attention to the ingredients and the techniques Chef Bernard is noted for demonstrating, but he also tries his best to spot a kitchen gadget sufficiently special to send him on a quest to Three Star Mall. While Ed suspects pastry blenders can be found at Kmart, he also wants to order Chef Bernard's new line of cookware. Now he has two reasons to go to Dillard's—the pastry blender and a cookware consultation. The more questions he has, the longer he can stay without being too obvious.

Parva Wilson is his equipment consultant and is full of good cooking tips. Ed's short-term goal is to buy a gadget from Parva Wilson every few days. The only thing occupying Ed's thoughts these last few weeks—more than cooking—is Parva Wilson and the two little smudges of dirt she had on the front of her round plump breasts the first day he laid eyes on her. Ed calculates that after the purchase of at least two more gadgets he and

Parva will be familiar enough for Ed to ask her to lunch. His purchase of Chef Bernard's full line of cookware will be a sizable commission for Parva, so perhaps Ed can use that opportunity to segue into a lunchtime celebration in the mall's food court. A few days after that, he'll take her a lunch he makes himself. Fried chicken and Dijon potato salad. That's nice and portable.

Ed is developing a passion for cooking, and he enjoys giving away much of what he cooks. Last week he took chocolate chip pecan cookies to work and Estelle was downright jealous. She is used to getting praise from the guys when she brings in those pies on Fridays, but the fellows made so much over Ed's cookies that she got mad and said she had to go to the drugstore to get some Tylenol. The trick to those cookies, Ed has learned, is to let your butter and eggs get room temperature.

What would Gracie think of Ed cooking like this? In the old days, she would have laughed. But Gracie doesn't know Ed anymore, and Ed doesn't know Gracie. Sometimes he worries about her. But then he thinks about the way she drove away of her own free will, how she is taking great care not to be found. He thinks about her wedding ring left lost in the middle of that big lonely bed. Then he stops out-and-out worrying and only hopes she is safe.

"Waxed dental floss," Chef Bernard is saying, "is the best way to slice through the middle of a cake layer, say for Boston cream pie, or, in this case, a giant biscuit for shortcake. You can also use thread or fishing line. But it needs to be thin. The thinner the better. Just place it so." He carefully encircles the warm shortcake with a strand of dental floss. The camera closes in on the way he crosses the ends from one hand to the other. "Now, like so." He pauses for the cameraman. "And then pull the ends in opposite directions, thusly." Slowly his hands move out from the shortcake until the floss comes out of the bread and his hands stretch the floss taut well above his worktable. *"Voilà!"* Chef Bernard's hands go up in a V for victory, the dental floss now dangles from his right hand. "You see? You have two perfectly even pieces where before you had one!"

THE CRANE LOWERS a twenty-foot beige plastic doughnut onto the flat roof of the little building. Three men stand on the roof and guide the giant doughnut onto two iron poles that stick up into the sky from the tarpaper top of Dixie Donuts. It is a spectacular sight. The shop's large windows are framed in Pepto-Bismol pink stucco, making the building look like a really big gift box.

The doughnut is Wally's idea. He thinks it will catch the eye of folks coming down the exit ramp from the interstate. Truckers often pull off at the exit to gas up at the truck stop, which is within walking distance of Dixie Donuts. The idea is to get truckers to buy doughnuts for the road. Ginger has a Trucker's Dozen entry on the menu. It's the same as a baker's dozen, thirteen doughnuts. It comes with a thermos refill on coffee.

Ginger stands in the parking lot beside Wally, his arm around her. She looks a lot like Gracie—small, fragile, dainty. Only her hair is more blond, like Ed's, and she has Ed's hazel eyes. She and Wally both have blond ponytails that hang down the backs of their T-shirts. They wear the same size jeans, too, except Ginger's are shorter.

About fifty people stand around to watch the event despite the early August heat. You can see the thermal waves rise from the tarred roof. The three men on the rooftop wipe their faces regularly with handkerchiefs. Some folks have pulled off the road to witness the mounting of the giant doughnut. It isn't every day you get to see something like this. The sky is bright blue overhead, but a black line forms behind the DAYS INN sign up the interstate. The workmen are anxious to fit the big doughnut on its moorings before the dark clouds on the horizon roll into striking distance. Suddenly a heavy gust of wind blows the doughnut too far back. The huge plastic circle catches one of the workmen off guard and knocks him over. Fortunately, he isn't standing near the edge of the roof, and in a few seconds he is up, standing, hands on knees. He's a little shook up, but fine. Ginger wipes a tear from her face. It's almost time for her period and everything makes her cry. Even seeing this giant doughnut set in place is an emotional upheaval.

Ed stands closer to the building. Ginger knows he's fighting the urge to get up on the roof and help the three men place the doughnut. Ginger is totally surprised by how helpful her father is with the new business. Last week he gave her the idea to offer beignets, deep-fried New Orleans doughnutlike things that you serve hot with confectioners' sugar sprinkled on them. She made them at home in her Fry Daddy and they were delicious. That will be the Mardi Gras Weekend Special. Wally came up with that title, since Mardi Gras usually makes people think of New Orleans. It will come with a choice of coffee or hot chocolate with real whipped cream.

A goodly number of tourists see the blue sign for the Centertown Historical Museum and stop off the highway to visit. Ginger has designed a museum coupon for one dollar off a dozen doughnuts. She can pick them up at the printer tomorrow. The museum director is happy to display the coupons near the front door with the brochures of other tourist attractions in that area of the state.

Ginger isn't happy with the pink walls and wants the building painted a reddish orange. But the second order of business, after gutting the inside and getting the kitchen ready, was to get the doughnut mounted. Next weekend will be the grand opening under new ownership. Ginger lets a few more tears run down her cheeks. She wants her mother to see this. To see Ginger's accomplishment. But she doesn't even know where her mother is. The police are kind, but not particularly helpful. Maybe her mother has left her father for someone else. Women leave their husbands all the time. But Gracie has left her daughter, too, without a word. And that isn't so common. That isn't easy to understand. It certainly isn't easy to forgive. Not with any yardstick Ginger can find to measure by.

There is a heavy thud as the big doughnut drops that last foot and slides snugly into place. The men on the roof immediately raise their hands to signal to the crane driver. At the same moment, a cheer goes up from the onlookers. Everyone is clapping, happy to witness the event and happy to head back into the air conditioning. Wally tightens his grip around Ginger's shoulder, sweat or no sweat. Ed looks over at them and gives them a big thumbs-up. Ginger bursts headlong into the biggest cry-ing jag she's ever had, her period notwithstanding. Wally does what he does best—stands there knowingly, lets her cry into his chest while he holds her close and rubs his hand slowly up and down the back of her moist Dixie Donuts T-shirt. Most important, he never utters a single word of comfort. He knows as well as Ginger that it would be useless.

THE FOOD COURT at Three Store Mall is teeming with Saturday shoppers. Small children, hungry and restless, noisily wait for their Happy Meals and the prizes inside. "Give it to me," they beg, or whine, or demand of their mothers. Mothers struggle to keep their little ones under control until they get seated and get their packages, purses, and lunches situated. *Look at me,* the little ones all plead. *Answer me.*

Teenagers stand around the edges of the food court and the outer door of the adjoining arcade. Some of the girls are clean and primped. Others have big hair and cigarettes hanging from the tips of their fingers. The boys need to pull their pants up to their waists, but they don't because it isn't cool. Their large-legged blue jeans drag the floor like dust rags, col-lecting and wearing away at the same time. If they have hats, they wear them indoors. If they wear hats, they wear them backward. Some kids have leather jackets and no hats at all. Some wear blue and white Car-olina football jerseys. Some dress like they are color blind. Despite what side of the fashion fence they come down on, the teenagers look at each other with hostile yearning—too good to speak, too cool to touch, too hot to handle. All the while their hormones scream, *Come to me. Take me. Look at me. Speak to me. Pick me.*

Ed spots a clean empty table for two and takes long strides to get there before anyone else does. He puts down his tray and steps around to pull out a white-coated wire chair for Parva Wilson. She puts her tray on the table and slides into the chair gracefully, then inches forward toward the table, her breasts bouncing with each little hop of the chair.

"So you've never taken cooking lessons?" Parva asks Ed as she opens the cellophane container of knife, spork, napkin, salt, and pepper. She arranges everything around her plate of China Wok No. 6, Garlic Chicken.

"Not exactly," Ed says as he takes his seat across from her. He wanted to take her to a nice place for lunch, maybe Spinners or Applebee's, but she said she only had thirty minutes. Dillard's is conducting a storewide inventory in preparation for the back-to-school shopping frenzy. The entire staff is busy rearranging displays to accommodate the second wave of fall merchandise. Ed stares down at his China Wok No. 10, Beef and Broccoli. "I've been watching Food Network on satellite TV. Chef Bernard mostly."

"Oh, Barney! He's quite a good cook. A good teacher too."

"You know Chef Bernard?" Ed's eyes are wide, his face open and innocent.

"Well, I wouldn't say I know him exactly. I've met him. He came to the Nashville store for a book signing a couple of years ago. I was department manager there at the time. We chatted some when there were no customers."

Parva's way of talking, the way words flow from her lips in her Mississippi accent makes everything she says sound like music. Ed thinks he detects something foreign embedded in something very Southern.

"You call him Barney?" Ed is a little disappointed he isn't the only one who calls him Barney. He doesn't care for the familiarity with which Parva speaks about Barney either.

"Oh yes. He said to call him that. But it doesn't quite suit him, does it? I only met him the one time. He was a nice enough fellow."

"Well, that's good to know. I hate to find out TV personalities I like are assholes in real life. Excuse me, I mean jerks." Ed is embarrassed at his crude language. He takes a bite of his beef and broccoli.

"Don't be silly. Everyone's an asshole at some time or another, even Barney, I'd say." Parva looks up at Ed and smiles. "And speaking of names, what does Ed stand for? Edward?"

"No. It's short for Edgar."

"Edgar. I like that. Do you mind if I call you Edgar then? It has a bit of a ring to it. You don't look like an Edward."

"Everybody calls me Ed. But if you like Edgar, I'll answer to it." Parva clearly isn't like everybody. "Your name is unusual. Is it foreign?"

"Heavens, no. It's a rather funny tale, really. My mother's sister is named Marva and my mother always wanted to name a child after her. They were very close. Six minutes after my mother had her first daughter, she had me. My mother was a big woman and I was a surprise. She named my older sister Marva, as planned, and thought it would be cute if our names rhymed. So she went down the alphabet and decided on P for Parva."

"Are you identical twins?"

"As different as night and day. And what about you? How did you get your name?"

There in the midst of tired mothers, whining hungry children, and the futile arrogance of adolescence, Edgar Hollaman and Parva Wilson laugh and talk about cooking and all the little innocuous subjects and questions that they can safely bring into the conversation, things that do not call too much attention to their desire. They sit in the white-coated wire chairs, each looking for any sign from the other of something more than curiosity. They are not arrogant, like the teenagers, not tired like the children, and thankfully not frazzled and weary like the mothers scattered throughout the food court. Ed and Parva are balanced in a space all their own. They sit amid the shoppers' mayhem, but Ed and Parva are laughing. *Look at me. See me.* In their own quiet way, with their own brand of urgency, they say *Come to me. Ask me. Take me. Want me. Pick me.*

What they talk about would sound so boring to the teenagers hanging at the edges of the room. To someone eavesdropping, they are chatting about the advantages of electric frying pans and steel-belted radials. They laugh. They laugh and they laugh until forty-five minutes goes by and Parva reluctantly glances at her watch.

"Oh, I'm so sorry. I'm very late." Parva slides her chair back. "I really must go."

"You go ahead," Ed says, shocked that their time is more than gone. "I'll clean up."

"Thank you, Edgar," she says. She runs a few steps forward, then runs back.

"We have a sale next week on reusable coffee filters. Just thought I'd let you know."

Ed nods and waves, and Parva runs down the mall toward Dillard's. He watches her go through Dillard's doorway, watches her move deeper and deeper into the store, watches her grow smaller as she enters women's perfume and cosmetics, watches her until she disappears.

TOOT GETS UP early to read from her Bible in the new light. If the weather is rainy or cold, she sits at the kitchen table. If the weather is warm and dry, like today, she goes outside and sits in a yard chair to read. She starts when the light is too dim to see and all she can make out is the open book and the colors of the ink on the paper. While she waits to see the words become words, she picks up a page from one side or the other and feels the words between her fingers. The page is filmy and soft and trimmed in gold. And when the light gets stronger, she sees the shadows of her fingers on the other side.

The long boxy columns in black and red ink begin to take shape. She sees lines coming in, lines of words that don't yet look like words. They're not quite talking, they're whispering too low for her to hear. Then the sun's rays hit the back of clouds riding over the edge of the earth and she begins to discern shapes of the alphabet. When true daylight rises up from behind the Earth and over the tree line, it shines bright on the page, and the words, they bloom like flowers. Toot feels like she is part of a revelation.

This morning she's outside in her yard chair looking through the dim light at the shape of the columns. When the light gets stronger she sees she is looking at the Book of John. Soon she makes out the words and her eyes fall to the footnote at the bottom of the page. When those small letters, too, become clear, she reads, *for an angel of the Lord went down at certain seasons into the pool, and stirred up the water; whoever stepped in first after the stirring of the water was made well from whatever disease that person had.*

She has just read that small block of words when she looks up and sees a figure moving through the hollyhocks. Now, Toot can grow her some hollyhocks. Can't nobody deny that. And she always cuts back so she will get a good fall blooming, like she will soon have to do. There's nothing in that one patch of garden by the garage except hollyhocks and she keeps good care of those flowers. She's got every color God makes and some He helped her to make. So by the garage there is wall after wall of those tall ladies blooming their fool heads off. And Toot looks up from John and sees a figure. Toot is a saved woman, mind you, washed in the blood of the Lamb. But she also knows about the old ways. She first thinks it is a revenant, or some other kind of harbinger. Then she sees that it's Rachel.

Now, Rachel, she's just a woman. Toot doesn't think she's anymore than that, nor any less. But she imagines her with wings right now, sees a picture in her head of Rachel descending on the graveyard like the angel into the waters of Bethesda. That, she'd say, is her own mind playing out the sight of Rachel in the garden coupled with the Word she's been reading. But for a bit, she sees a shadow following behind Rachel. A real thing by her guess, not of her imagining. While it lasts, Toot sees it isn't quite right, doesn't quite fit, because it doesn't have a match like a shadow to the light or the woman, or anything else she sees. The shadow fades without any help from the sun. *Bless my soul.* She sees Rachel good right then and sees she's naked as a jaybird and grinning. With her carrot-top hair, it's almost like one of Toot's hollyhocks has come to life. Rachel walks out of the tall stalks and all those pink- and yellow- and peach-colored flower balls, like so many heads looking every which way—looking up at the house and out at the pasture and down at that naked Rachel, who looks for all the world like she is walking out from the walls of a cool bright fire. Then Toot gets confused. She thinks the light must be playing with her old eyes. Was that Rachel or not? But Rachel walks right up to her, and she is real enough, standing bare as the day she was born, wet with dew, and so covered in chill bumps her skin looks like a plucked chicken's. Tiny pieces of grass and mud from the garden cling to the tops and sides of her feet. Her little breasts hang, sway back and forth the least little bit when she walks. Toot doesn't even take her eyes away, and she doesn't scold her either. Rachel's stomach is starting that drop through its own time, down to the plumb of a woman's body where it goes. Part of Toot wants to fuss her out good for walking around the yard with no clothes on, but something catches Toot's voice in her throat. She doesn't jump up to cover Rachel with her sweater. Doesn't get her in the house and dress her before somebody sees her like that. Instead, Toot thinks of those pretty pictures in the laundry room of naked Adam and Eve, what pretty bodies they likely had, how all bodies are pretty. Something holds her words back in her throat, holds them from down below her ribs someplace, maybe at the small of her back. *Be still. Be quiet*, it says. So she sits quiet. *Quiet*. And she lets Rachel walk right at her, past her.

Then it's over. Toot wonders if it was a dream, a dream while she was wide awake. But it wasn't a dream. Later she'll find mud on the floor, grass in the little bed, and hollyhocks in the chair where she sits to tell Rachel Bible stories.

For the moment, after Rachel goes in the house and gets in the bed, Toot's eyes fall back on the page, and she starts again, this time at John 1:5. *After this there was a festival of the Jews, and Jesus went up to Jerusalem.* Toot thinks to herself, and not for the first time, *God works in mysterious ways.*

The next time Toot sees Rachel, it is before breakfast. These days, Rachel gets up and eats at the table. No talking, mind you, but eating on her own. This morning she comes in for breakfast dressed in some of the clothes DuRon brought her, just like always: dress, sweater, tennis shoes. *Tennis shoes. Tennis shoes. Something about tennis shoes.* That's when it hits her. The funniest thing. It hits Toot while she's looking at Rachel with all her clothes on. The familiar birthmark she saw this morning, right there under Rachel's breast. She saw it the whole time Rachel came at her in that morning light. But her mind wouldn't have any of it at the time, not in the bright light of morning when Toot's mind was on the Word.

Mattie is the one who gives Rachel a bath most of the time. Says it's too hard on Toot's back to pull her over. *That ain't so. Ain't a thing wrong with me.* But Toot gives the job over to Mattie because Mattie needs it. On the days Toot gets Rachel dressed, she does it quick, and she's never noticed the mark. But Toot saw the thing when Rachel walked naked up through the yard, even if it didn't come on her until now, at breakfast. A little little handprint.

Toot knows that mark. That little caramel-colored hand the size of a dime there on Rachel's side, below her left breast, over her rib bone, like it's reaching for her heart. There they stand in the kitchen, Rachel with all her clothes on, and it hits Toot what she saw when Rachel was naked. Toot knows now that Rachel is no stranger to her after all, that her name isn't Rachel, and her being here is no mishap.

———————

DuRon sits at the table like always. His hat is on the seat beside him. He has a bad case of hat head.

"DuRon, you need a haircut," Toot says. "You eat lunch yet?"

"No, ma'am." DuRon runs his hands through his hair.

"Want a ham sandwich and a Coke?"

"That sounds mighty good." He doesn't know what it is, but he loves being fed by this woman. Always has. Even if it is nothing but a bowl of beans with onions and a piece of light bread.

"I fix it while I'm talking."

Mattie sits quietly at the table across from DuRon. Rachel is some woman named Gracie, who Toot knew as a child. Mattie was so sure Rachel had been sent here for a purpose. Yet that purpose has not been revealed to Mattie. She is part sad and part angry. She had been so sure. Is she just a foolish woman? Her head feels heavy, her arms are tired. There is no sign to read. No connection with Arty to make. No reason to have fought Sammy so hard to keep her here. Sammy is right. She is a foolish woman hanging on to a dead man while the rest of the world keeps on living.

"So you worked for her mother?" DuRon says.

"The woman swung from one place to another," Toot says, as she pulls bread out of the bread box and takes the ham out of the refrigerator. "She be sweet one minute, mean as a snake the next.

"One time she got short with me and told me hateful like to clean Gracie up and take her for a walk downtown. I was young and mad. Law, I was mad. So I took and gave Gracie her bath and greased her hair and put it in little plaits all over her head and put her in the stroller. Mrs. Price come out on the porch and seen her child looking like a black baby for all the world except her skin and she started to say something. I wont but twenty-two, maybe twenty-three, at that time. But she knew I'd be gone, and she knew she need me, and she went on and let me walk right down the sidewalk with that child all greased up. It liked to killed her. And she wont going to say nothing to Mr. Price, 'cause he know then she treated me bad." Toot laughs for a minute, then her face draws up serious again.

"She stay home for a spell and be friendly enough, then she take to driving off in her big car and not coming back sometime for days. Mr. Price, he come home for lunch one day. I forgot about not serving meat on Friday. They was Catholic. I heated him up some leftover pork roast and potatoes and dished him up some coleslaw and started to take it to the dining room. 'I'll eat it here, if that's all right,' he said and sat down in the kitchen. He never notice he eating meat, and I didn't think nothing about it till I done washed his dishes. Mrs. Price wouldn't have allowed that, the meat on Friday, or Mr. Price eating in the kitchen, neither one. And if she heard him ask me if I mind, Lord, I hate to think what she'd have to say about that. But I said, 'It's your house, Mr. Price.'

"He was the saddest-looking man by that time. I been working there maybe two years. Gracie be about two years old. I was 'pose to leave that day at four o'clock. I need to get my beans in and canned, so I gon' take off a little early on a Friday and get started before the sun go down.

" 'Toot,' he said, 'can you stay the weekend? Mrs. Price, she's not here this afternoon and I might have to go looking for her.' He was pitiful. Not just 'cause he need help, but because he love her no matter how she act.

"I said I didn't have no way to let my husband know. But if he let me, I'd take Gracie home with me. She'd like being on the farm for a few days. See all the chickens and cows and horses. I didn't expect him to let her come home with me, but I guess he was in a fix. So from then on, when Mrs. Price run off for a few days, Gracie come home with me, come here to the farm. It went on that way for as long as I worked for the Prices. That's why I never envy rich folks. Seeing those people every day made me know rich don't mean nothing by itself."

Toot slices a big red tomato and goes to the refrigerator for lettuce and mayonnaise.

"How long did you work for the Prices?" DuRon asks and takes a napkin from the holder in the middle of the table.

"I work there till Gracie was eight. Then something bad happen. Made everything come to a head." She puts DuRon's sandwich in front of him and sits down at the table.

"What happened?" DuRon takes a bite and wipes his mouth, his mind trained on Toot's words. It is like the weekend days when he was a kid and Toot would tell him and Arty the scariest stories while they ate their lunch.

"Mr. Price a nice man. Kind man. His heart was so broke, couldn't nobody help him. One day, after Mrs. Price come home from being gone for days, she shut herself up in the bedroom and wouldn't come out and wouldn't let nobody in and wouldn't quit crying. Mr. Price, he went to the cellar and shot hisself in the head with his German pistol."

"Were you there when that happened?"

"DuRon, don't talk with your mouth full. How many years I been telling you that?"

DuRon nods. Mattie sits quietly watching him eat his sandwich and listens to the story. She keeps thinking about how empty the laundry room will be.

"I was there, all right. 'Bout drove me crazy, myself. A dead man with the back of his head blowed out in the cellar and a crazy woman locked in her bedroom on the second floor. And it almost time for school to be out. I called the sheriff. I called the doctor. Then I walked to the school to meet the child. By nighttime, Homer come looking for me. Wanted to know was I all right."

"So you quit after that?" DuRon starts on the second half of his sandwich. Mattie realizes he doesn't have anything to drink and gets up and fixes him a Coke just to be doing something.

"Mrs. Price's daddy, he still alive at the time. He owned some kind of factory in Burlington. He come to Martinsville and asked me would I stay there in the house with them until the funeral was over. Give him time to make some arrangements. Homer and me agreed it was the only thing to do. I'd got right attached to Gracie. She'd been with me so much here and there. DuRon, you probably played with the child your own self as much as you was down here. She was a sweet child in spite of all that mess going on in the family."

"What finally happened?" Mattie asks.

"The daddy, he buried Mr. Price in a couple of days. Then he got Doc Fitts to find a 'rest cure' he called it, a sanitarium, for Mrs. Price. Said she had 'delicate temperament.' That's what rich white folks call it when a woman willful, spoiled, and got the blues so bad half the time she can't live."

"What about Gracie?" Mattie asked.

"He found her a school to go to in Lynchburg. One of them boarding schools, a Catholic school just for girls.

"Asked me was there anything from the house I wanted. I thought about it. There was lots of things I would like to had. Mr. and Mrs. Price was always giving me what they didn't want no more. But I was afraid of taking anything more from that house. We packed up what we thought Mrs. Price might want when she got to feeling better, and some things for Gracie to have one day when she grown, things belonging to her daddy's family. His people lived far off somewhere the other side of Arkansas and hadn't seen him since he went in the Army. They didn't even speak. Something about him becoming Catholic so he could marry Mrs. Price. Then Mrs. Price's daddy sold everything else that was in the house and the house too. He gave me some extra money for staying there in the house till time for Gracie to go off to school. He stayed there too, but he was always off taking care of business or shut up in the study.

Toot spreads her hands across the yellow Formica table. "All the girl did was cry. Her grandaddy wanted her to dress up all the time. Wouldn't let her wear her tennis shoes. She had a pair of red tennis shoes she always wanted to wear. She wear those shoes with any color clothes she had on. She sneak and put them things on when the granddaddy made her dress up. Finally he burned them shoes. Then she just cried and cried. I thought then, she was gon' be a crying woman just like her mama. Sweet one minute, mean the next, crying the next. But turns out she don't cry much. Just when I call her name this morning and she look back at me and said 'Tootsie Mae. Tootsie Mae.' That's what the white folks call me back then. She said my name so soft and big tears come out her eyes. But that the only time I seen her cry since she show up on Arty's grave. She just paint pictures on everything. That's all. And, as I see it, that beat crying."

"So her name is Grace Price?" DuRon says, pulling out his pad and pencil.

"I got a feeling her name something else besides Price. When she got here she had a place on her finger, looked like a wedding ring been there. 'Course you can't tell it now."

"It'll take me a while to track down who she is, what her name is now." DuRon makes more notes on his pad, then puts it in the breast pocket. "We'll have to track down where she lived before she took off and all. I just wonder how she got here in the first place."

"Mattie, fix this man a piece of cake. I got to go to the garage." Toot pats DuRon's shoulder. "You up to it." Then she leaves out the back door.

DuRon looks at Mattie. "That is the nicest thing that woman has ever said to me."

"What kind of cake you want?" Mattie says and pushes herself up from the table.

"What kind you got?" DuRon asks, pretending he doesn't see how hurt she is.

E D HAS NEVER understood why Wally and Ginger don't have central heat and air. It's 2000, for Pete's sake. Even though they set up the box fans to draw the air in a deliberate circle through the house, and the house stays pretty cool most of the summer, it seems uncivilized. When it's cold they heat with a wood stove. Ed grew up without air conditioning and central heat. He didn't choose that way of life and neither did his parents. But Wally and Ginger have a choice. And it befuddles Ed that they choose wood heat and box fans.

It is the third Saturday in August and Ed tries to sit near a fan, even though the only chair in that vicinity of the living room is the most uncomfortable one in the room. He's come by to visit for a few minutes and drop off some food for Ginger and Wally. Ed spends less and less time at Tire Man and Wally spends more time there to make up the difference. He says he doesn't mind because Ginger is tied up with Dixie Donuts. Partly out of guilt and partly out of genuine generosity, Ed makes good reheatable dinners and brings them over on the weekends so Ginger and Wally can heat them up through the week and don't have to worry about cooking supper. Ed brings by a sampler of desserts for Wally and Ginger every week, along with the make-ahead suppers. This week the assortment includes a few recipes he tried from the Food Network Web site and a few recipes he has been experimenting with on his own. He hopes by giving Ginger and Wally this little bit of help, Ginger won't cry quite so much. Won't get angry quite as often. Ginger has quit asking if the police know anything new about Gracie. The answer is always the same and it only seems to make her feel bad to hear it said out loud yet again.

Ed can only stay a few minutes. He wants to get home in time to catch *Good Eats*. It reminds him of *Watch Mr. Wizard*, the TV show he liked as a kid where the guy did all kinds of experiments. He made an egg go into a Coke bottle and not break, kept air in a glass under water, all sorts of good stuff. *Good Eats* makes Ed's kitchen activities seem more scientific, more challenging. The show on mayonnaise was amazing. Tonight's show is on the soufflé. Between *Good Eats* and *Betty Bakes*, Ed has taken off in the baking department. *Betty Bakes* taught him the importance of exactitude in baking. It makes all the difference. And *Good Eats* demonstrated the strategic mixing of dry and wet ingredients. Ed's buttermilk biscuits are now heavenly.

Ginger and Wally come back into the living room with saucers of mocha java cheesecake and some iced coffee. Wally went to college up north and they drink coffee over ice up there. Ed thinks overall that's not such a good idea, but it is hot as blazes outside and anything over ice sounds good to him today.

"Ed, man, this cheesecake is out of this world," Wally reports when he sits down on the comfortable sofa away from the box fan.

"You haven't eaten any yet," Ed says, noticing Wally's wedge of cake is intact.

"That's his second piece," Ginger says. "He ate one while I fixed the coffee. I think we're going to start serving iced coffee at the DD. What do you think?"

"Good idea. You must get a lot of Yankee truck drivers coming through there. They'll probably appreciate it."

Ginger and Wally look at each other and Ginger rolls her eyes.

"Daddy, you can cook, but you certainly don't make the cut for being cosmopolitan."

"Why would I want to be that? It's a women's magazine. Right?"

"Right," Wally and Ginger say together.

"Daddy, this cake is so good. I can't believe you can cook like this. You couldn't make a sandwich before Mama left." Ginger takes a big bite of mocha java cheesecake.

"I could so make a sandwich."

"Well."

"Ed, you did have to call me to find out how to boil eggs. Remember?"

"Well." Ed takes a sip of his iced coffee. Not that bad, really.

"You know, Ed," Wally says after swallowing the last bite of his second piece of cake, "you ought to enter Chef Bernard's dessert contest."

"How do you know about that?"

"I watch a little satellite TV now and then. And I have to say, you have me wondering what kind of magic they work on Food Network. Ginger's right. Last Easter you couldn't boil an Easter egg. Now you can make cheesecake."

Ed looks down in an effort to be humble. Then he just looks at Wally.

"So you really think I ought to enter The Sinfully Chocolate Sweepstakes?"

"Absolutely," Ginger and Wally say together.

"I'll think about it." Ed takes out his handkerchief and wipes perspiration off his forehead and then from the back of his neck. He hopes Ginger or Wally put the cheesecake in the refrigerator when they finish eating. It won't do to leave a cheesecake sitting out in that unairconditioned kitchen.

———————

WOULD YOU LIKE some more wine?" Ed holds the bottle up toward Parva's glass. At Chef Bernard's suggestion, he has picked a subtle Oregon Pinot Noir to accompany the grilled salmon.

"I'm not used to drinking wine with lunch. If I have anymore, I'll get a little tipsy." Parva glances up at Jesus praying at the rock. "Well, maybe just a little more."

Parva blushes. Perhaps it's the wine, or being alone with Ed in his house in the middle of the day. Or maybe it's the big Jesus on the wall. For the first time, Parva is nervous about being with Ed. She had not figured him for a person who would draw a big praying Jesus on the kitchen wall, clearly a room he spends a great deal of time in. Parva doesn't have a thing against Jesus. But she surmises Ed must be quite religious. Religion isn't a bad thing at all, but it can be complicated if someone is, well, a zealot.

Since that first day when he came looking for a fish poacher, she has fantasized about him. He was so gracious to help her from the floor after she retrieved the register tape, and he called her by name when he thanked her for his package. She watched him walk away, noticed the way he carried himself, his broad shoulders, the sound of his walk on the uncarpeted aisle floor. When he turned to go through the arches back into clothing she noticed the roundness of his stomach and thought how comfortable it would be to lean into a man like that. Now she gets excited when she sees him come down the aisle from linens. If she's busy putting up merchandise or dusting shelves, she listens for the sound of his walk, the way his heels hit the floor in their distinctive slide and click. Sometimes she makes displays on the center aisle with things she knows he might be interested in. She casually walks with him in that direction after he checks out, hoping he will linger beyond his purchase and talk with her about what she has displayed. He always does. Cooking gadgets are his most frequent purchases. She plans a Christmas display with gadgets as ornaments on the tree and pots and pans with big red bows underneath the tree as presents. She sent a copy of Barney's book, *Cooking with Bernard,* to the network to get it autographed for Ed, and she received the nicest note from Barney saying he remembers her quite well and has a new book coming out around the holidays. He wants to do another signing at her store. Of course, he doesn't understand what a small store she works in now. She is saving the book for Ed's birthday, which she knows is a long way off.

"Another dill roll, Parva? More salad?" Ed is so thoughtful. Quite a good host.

"Another roll would be nice. Did you make these?"

"I'm glad you like them." Ed gives her the ins and outs of making Parker House rolls as Parva ruminates on the situation.

She's also surprised that Ed lives in such a large well-decorated old house. Lots of nice antiques, large rag rugs, and Persian carpets imply a woman's touch. It's a nice combination of the old and new, the formal and informal. The kitchen is so large. The shiny old oak dining table with ball-and-claw feet sits by a double window that looks out on roses along a split rail fence. Ed says the formal dining room is just for show. And she agrees the kitchen is much more comfortable. But the praying Jesus above the sideboard is a little unusual, like the proverbial elephant in the room that no one mentions, so Parva decides there is only one thing to do.

"That's quite a lovely Jesus there on the wall," she says. "Did you draw it, Edgar?"

"That? No. My wife fancied herself an artist. There are several Jesuses in the house, I'm afraid."

"Are they all this large?"

"Larger."

"My goodness." Parva decides not to push Ed for more about his wife. She will learn what she needs to know soon enough.

Ed knows he should have painted over the Jesuses. It isn't that Ed doesn't like Jesus. He grew up going to church and Sunday school. He likes Jesus fine. But to have Jesus so big, and in so many places, and his eyes following Ed, always watching is unnerving. He wonders why Gracie stopped before painting Jesus over the bathtub and the washing machine. He never used the front door or the living room, but now he takes fits of standing in the living room and looking at the foyer wall. He tries to get some message from Jesus at the door, but like Jesus with the open arms there is nothing. He used to read the Sunday paper in the living room, but now he reads it at the kitchen table. To be honest, he is used to the Jesus in the kitchen. That Jesus is busy praying, he's trying to do something about the situation. Sometimes Ed looks up and asks for a little help with a difficult recipe, a fragile soufflé. He has become so used to the praying Jesus, that it only occurred to him while he was frosting the cake that He might overwhelm Parva. He thought about eating in the dining room and avoiding the kitchen, but the dining room furniture, which once belonged to Gracie's grandfather on her mother's side, is so intimidating. Besides, Ed loves the kitchen. He wants to share it with Parva, maybe in part because of this particular Jesus. Perhaps Parva is the answer to Ed's prayers. Ed does pray, but not with words. He doesn't know what to pray for, so he prays with an open mind.

Ed resists painting over the Jesuses because he can't bring himself to put a brush to the wall until he hears from Gracie, until what hangs in the air all around him settles. As a child, Ed believed Jesus had a sense of humor. Surely he does, surely God does. Why else would Ed find himself in this situation? Why else would Ed find himself in a house he bought for his wife, while he eats lunch with another woman, and Jesus looks on from every side?

"Would you like to see the other Jesuses before or after dessert?" Ed says.

"Dessert? I hope it's chocolate."

"Chocolate Kahlúa cake with pecans?" Ed looks for Parva's approval.

"Where did you get a marvelous recipe like that? It sounds delicious."

"I made it up myself. I've been experimenting."

"By all means then," Parva says, "let's have dessert."

An hour later, in Ed's bedroom, his hand eases up Parva's silk stockings. Her calf is slender, but her knees and thighs are ample. His body half covers her. She smells sweet. Her skin is soft compared to his rough workman's hands. So why is nothing happening? *Nothing* is happening where it should definitely be happening. He pulls back. Sits up. He thinks of Gracie. He's even on her side of the bed.

"I'm sorry. I don't know what's wrong. I've been thinking about this for weeks now. I just can't seem to focus."

Parva sits up as well, her pink linen dress hanging loosely from her shoulders. Ed had unzipped the back of her dress and unhooked her bra before his severe doubt set in.

"It could be the wine," Parva offers.

"I suppose. Or it could be a lack of practice."

"Or . . . it could be . . . Jesus, Edgar."

"Don't get upset. I'm sure it will be all right."

"No. I mean Jesus." Parva points to the wall. "He's looking right at us. Don't you find it a bit distracting?"

Parva gazes up at the Jesus with open hands. The only white wall in the mauve room. The room is soothing for the most part—clean lines except for the pine cone tops of the bedposts, a simple antique dresser and side table, hooked white bedspread. But the seven-foot Christ making an altar call from the foot of the bed isn't soothing. Parva doesn't need to know much about Ed's situation to know Ed's wife knew what she was doing, leaving a big ole Jesus at the foot of Edgar's bed. Any woman would hesitate before taking off her clothes in this room. His eyes are so penetrating, and his hands so loving, offering, authentic. Yet, there is something odd about the hands.

"Maybe we should stare at Him and get good and used to Him," Parva suggests. She wriggles around and sits against the headboard. "Then it won't matter so much."

"I don't think it will help me. I've been staring at Him for a little over four months now. He just stares back and we never get anywhere."

"It's really a very good drawing. Your wife is talented, or is she your ex-wife?"

"She defies definition at the moment. It's safe to say we are separated, though. Does that make you too uncomfortable?"

"Well, I wouldn't say uncomfortable, if you are separated."

"It surprised me, about her being talented in that way," Ed says, trying to find that place where they could ignore what needed to be ignored for at least a few hours. "I didn't even know she could draw. Something bothers me about it though." Ed sits back against the headboard beside Parva. "I mean more than the usual bother of a big Jesus at the foot of the bed. It's something about the hands." Ed takes Parva's hand in his. "I can't figure it out, but I keep staring at them. I can't stop looking at them at night before I turn out the light. Do they look normal to you?"

"They're awfully delicate for a man's hands, and maybe a little small, now that I think about it. But then he was probably a delicate sort of person."

"He was a carpenter," Ed says. "The last thing he'd have is delicate hands. Those hands there look almost girly." It comes like a flash of light—the ring in the center of the bed, the ring Gracie cast off her finger and flung to the center of the antique Martha Washington. He looks again at the hands, the familiar hands, as he feels Parva's moist palm against his own and lets it go.

"I don't want to sound forward Edgar, but do you by chance have a guest room without a Jesus in it?"

"Yes! I do!" he says, taking heart. "I have several. One right down the hall." Ed scoots off the bed and reaches for Parva to help her up. "Good idea, Miss Wilson."

Parva takes his hand and does a hip walk to the edge of the bed. Once up, she turns to straighten the spread. She smooths the wrinkles, tucks her hand briskly under the edge of the pillows, checks to see that the hem is level at the floor. She is graceful about it, too, for a woman partially disrobed and slightly tipsy.

Parva's stocking feet slip from under her on the slick waxed floor in the hallway, but Ed catches her and gives her his arm for balance. After making their way to the next bedroom, he kisses her hand in an effort to remedy their clumsy start.

Parva looks around the room. Unlike the other bedroom, this one is busy. The wallpaper is covered with a lattice burdened by wisteria. The purple vine, heavy with flowers, runs and climbs and droops and loops and takes over in the room as it does in nature. The drapes are a purplish blue stripe. Creamy hydrangeas spread across the plump down comforter and rows of pillows are propped against the high ornate iron bedstead. Green ivy runs along the bed skirt. The hem, deliberately too long, lies gracefully against a mint rug. Thankfully, the oak armoire is the only focal point. Not a Jesus in sight.

Ed moves close to Parva and touches his lips to hers. They taste of wine, Kahlúa, and chocolate. Ed and Parva sink into the down comforter, and with a few more well placed kisses, the positive tension of desire and curiosity returns, their breathing becomes deep once again. Parva reclines against the array of thick soft pillows and pulls Ed toward her. It has been so long since her breasts have felt the touch of a hand other than her own. And then, there are the touches Parva has never experienced from another human being. Parva expects to shortly cover new territory. After all these years, after thinking she might never know what it's like, after praying to be loved like this at least once in her life, Parva knows she will not move away from it, only toward it. Ed's hand once again slides up her stockinged leg. She buries her face in his neck. He smells of Mennen Skin Bracer and Ivory soap. Parva takes in a deep breath for courage and slides her foot up his trousers. *Want me. Pick me. Take me.* Ed's hand is at the top of her panties, his fingers linger at her smooth puffy midriff. She is lost in the scent of Ivory soap and his warm breath in her ear. "Parva. Parva," he says. Parva feels like a flower about to open, about to unfold its petals, expose its heart, its center. "Oh

God," she says. "Parva, Parva," Ed says again, his hand now flat on her round belly.

Just then a woman's voice pierces their foggy wine-enhanced passion and the back screen door springs shut on its hinges. "Yoohoo. Hello." The words move through the house like arrows meant to strike a deadly blow to all within earshot—Ed, Parva, and the three Jesuses.

Ed hears footsteps in the kitchen. "Daddy, are you here?" Ed's entire body goes rigid, except for the part that was finally getting stiff. It loses its starch.

"Daddy?" the voice calls again.

"Dammit!" Ed whispers in Parva's ear, where only moments before he was moaning her name. "It's my daughter." He sits up and looks around. "Quick. This was her room. She comes here first thing when no one's home. She always does." Ed knows this because of all the times he has pretended not to be here when she comes to check on him.

Ed silently scrambles from the bed and hauls Parva up after him. Her round, usually friendly face is full of disappointment and confusion.

"God. What'll we do?" Ed whispers again. He looks at the armoire but knows it is full of Ginger's things. An avalanche of clothes, stuffed animals, and high school memorabilia will fall out all over them if they open it. "Quick," he says, grasping at the next obvious option. "Under the bed. Hurry." He pulls up the dust ruffle. "Just climb under the bed for a few minutes while I get rid of her. Do you mind?" Her new expression breaks his heart. "Of course you mind. What am I thinking? Don't do that. Of course you're not going to do that."

He drops the dust ruffle, but in the next instant Parva reaches to pick it up. She drops to her knees and slides all the way to the rug. The bedsprings are thankfully high off the floor, and Parva rolls halfway under the bed.

"Go! Go!" she whispers. She shoos Ed away with her hand as she slides from the mint rug onto the polished wooden floor beneath the bed and her face disappears behind the ivy-covered chintz. She puffs out the fabric from behind and it falls gracefully into position as if no one was ever there.

Parva hears Ed greet Ginger when he catches her at the end of the hall.

"Boy, have I got news for you," Parva hears her say. Then the voices move farther away. She can't make out any words, but she detects excitement in Ginger's voice. Ed's voice offers deep, even tones in response. They talk for half an hour. Parva is almost asleep when she hears intelligible words.

"I'll call you later and we'll decide what to do next," Ed says.

"Okay. I'll try to get hold of Hershel and see if he's found out anything else," Ginger replies.

The door slams with the same loud whack as when Ginger entered, and Parva rolls on her side and slides and pushes and works herself back out from under the bed, throwing the bed skirt up as she emerges. The light from the lifted ruffle reveals large round shapes under the bed. They are pushed back against the far side, next to the wall. There must be thirty of them, all the size of a two-pound coffee can. Rocks. She slides back under the bed and touches one of the yellowish red rocks. It has been washed clean. Then Ed's hand is under the bed, fishing for her. He's there trying to help her out from under the bed. He offers to help her up, just like the first day they met. Only it is not like the first day they met at all.

"I'm so, so sorry," he says, as she gets to her feet.

"Edgar, I'm not ashamed to say to you that I'm happy to get *in* a bed *with* you, but this is the last time I'll get *under* one *for* you." Parva kisses his cheek and turns around to face the bed.

"I think you might as well close me up. I don't know about you," she spits a little dust out of her mouth, "but I'm not in the mood anymore."

Ed hooks Parva's bra like they have been intimate for years. He zips her dress and tries to get as much dust off of her back as he can. *Someone needs to vacuum under the beds*, they both think. He plucks some big dust motes out of her hair and turns her around to check her front.

"Your daughter seemed very excited. Did she have some good news?" Parva is brushing herself off, smoothing her dress, moving toward the door. When no answer comes, she stops and looks at him dead-on for a reply.

"A member of the family has been missing for some time and she's finally turned up."

"Oh? A close relative?"

There is a moment of quiet. Their potential love affair hangs in the silence like the scent of wisteria. It fills the space between them—full, potent. But the promise dissolves with the first note of regret in Ed's voice.

"My wife. It's my wife they've found."

In a twinkling, the only remnants of possibility are the balls of dust scattered over the floor and stuck to Parva's rumpled clothes. Ed, confused and defeated, turns and walks past her. He walks back to the kitchen, back to the praying Jesus, while Parva holds back tears and brushes again and again at the dust clinging to her pale pink dress.

COMMITMENT

Now, women forget all those things they don't want to remember, and remember everything they don't want to forget. The dream is the truth. Then they act and do things accordingly.

—Zora Neale Hurston

GINGER USED TO PLAY with Weebles all the time when she was little. Every now and then she runs across one rolling around loose in the bottom of a cardboard box in the attic. The big purple plastic chairs in Centertown Memorial Hospital emergency room look like they should have depressions in the middle shaped to cradle the large rounded end of a giant egg, a giant teetering Weeble. But instead they're molded to hold human bottoms, at this moment Gracie's and Ginger's, and not very comfortably, either.

Gracie is staring off into space, refusing to acknowledge where they are or who Ginger is, and Ginger's getting good and tired of it, not to mention getting claustrophobic in the little room. The wallpaper is vinyl, if you can believe that, and smells like disinfectant. Ginger may throw up in the ER without a trash can to upchuck into.

Ginger hates hospitals. It is funny to her that along with these two Weeble chairs they also have a Weeble love seat. The unnatural construction of these molded seats is counterproductive to scooting up close to someone and pitching woo, which is of course where the love seat got its name. But here it sits in the emergency room, in a holding area designed for crazy people, just waiting for two giant crazy Weebles. One's thoughts go wild waiting forever in a room like this. There's no telling what will creep into your mind. Ginger thinks of Gracie and herself as Weebles and she wants to cry.

The sheriff from Coats County called her at Dixie Donuts. Said they tried Ed at work and couldn't reach him. Estelle suggested they call Ginger and gave them the number. Ed was supposed to be home today. Ginger had told her daddy the sheriff's office would be calling to make arrangements to bring her mama back. One parent disappears and then finally shows up, and then the other one disappears. It's like trying to hit those gophers on the midway at the state fair, here one minute and gone the next. Ginger understands when parents have a hard time keeping up with a child, but a child ought to be able to keep up with parents.

Ginger got to the hospital as quick as she could, once she realized Ed wasn't going to show up at the shop, and she brought the policemen the Stakeout Special. Just a little thank-you present for bringing her mama home. Hershel Landry, a regular at Dixie Donuts, suggested the Stakeout Special. Ginger asked him if the local police did a lot of stakeouts. He said no, but they ate a lot of doughnuts, and the policemen in the movies ate doughnuts on stakeouts. Sounded good to Ginger. The Stakeout Special is three jelly-filled, three powdered, three cake, and three plain glazed, plus two large coffees. The policemen who brought Gracie back to Centertown seemed grateful when Ginger handed them the doughnuts. They were off duty and did it as a favor to Hershel, since no one could find Ed to send him after her. Typically law enforcement won't cross county lines for something like this, much less a state line. But it pays to be connected, and Ed, with all his lodge brothers and civic service, is well connected.

The officers are standing at the nurses' station, and the door is slightly ajar. They're quite familiar with the folks behind the desk.

"How was she?" Ginger hears a woman say.

"Heavy as lead," the short pudgy policeman answers, with his mouth full of one of Ginger's doughnuts. "Why in the world these nut cases always want to go limp on us is beyond me."

"Now, Larry," the woman says, "you mean to tell me when they come to fetch you, 'cause they will, you crazy son of a gun, you intend to cooperate?" Ginger hears laughing, lots of laughing. The handsome blond policeman is actually snorting. *God, a man who snorts. His poor wife. Thank God Wally doesn't snort.*

Who knows what her mama's been through, shut up for months with strangers and sleeping in a laundry room, no less, not knowing how ill she is. And now the officers and nurses are out there laughing at her—and by extension, Ginger. She's ready to take back her doughnuts when the door swings full open and a man with longish blond hair, a white coat, and black suede clogs, comes into the room. He has a clipboard and a pen in his hands and little wire rimmed glasses resting on his nose. Since Ginger met Wally, she has decided that little wire rimmed glasses are sexy, but the clogs make her wonder. The man writes something down and looks over his reading glasses at her. Then they both look at Gracie because she has started laughing, giggling really. Ginger doesn't know what to do exactly. Gracie is giggling so hard her eyes are closed, and Ginger, of course, assumes she's laughing at the man's clogs. *I mean, come on. Clogs?*

"What are you laughing at, Mama?" she says, hoping like all the world her mama won't tell the truth and offend the doctor. After all, Ginger's counting on him to commit Gracie. If Gracie pisses the man off, they could be here all day and not get anywhere. Gracie just keeps laughing and shaking her head. When the doctor speaks, Ginger detects a faint accent, maybe German. Not so you would notice really if it wasn't for the clogs.

"Are you Mrs. Hollaman?" he asks Gracie. Gracie looks him directly in the eyes, her own green eyes moist from laughing so hard, and then she closes her eyes again and shakes her head no.

"Well, you are, too," Ginger says.

The doctor turns to Ginger. "And you are her daughter, I presume?" Ginger sees his name badge on his breast pocket: HOWARD WARNER, M.D.

"Yes, that would be me," she says with an edge she can't keep out of her voice.

Dr. Warner sits on the Weeble love seat and crosses his legs, one clog dangling from the toes of his foot, the leg attached to that foot slowly and calmly moving up and down as he writes a few more words on the chart he has in his lap. He looks up from his chart and leans toward Gracie and says, "And what brings you here today, Mrs. Hollaman?"

The giggling stops. Gracie is silent as a stone.

"I guess I'll have to answer that," Ginger says. "Coats County Sheriff's Department brought her to the state line and Centertown officers picked her up there. It's all because of people knowing people. Ordinarily, she wouldn't have gotten here that way. My daddy knows people and the folks that had her and didn't know who she was know people. So that's how she got here. She ran away from home four months ago and she's been living with some black folks across the state line, up there in Coats County. They can't find her car anywhere. According to the Sheriff's Department, she was disoriented and noncommunicative when she was found. When they figured out who she was, they couldn't find my daddy, and they called me. I say she's gone crazy as a bat."

Dr. Warner writes something on the chart.

"I left a message for my daddy, and then came on over here to meet them when they brought her into the hospital." Ginger motions for Gracie to jump in anytime, but she stays quiet—like an object, not a mama.

"Has your mother been hospitalized for mental illness before?" Dr. Warner asks.

"No, never," Ginger says. But right then Gracie reaches over and taps Ginger hard on the arm and raises one finger in the air. "You have?" Ginger says, looking at the one finger sticking up in the air. She notices Gracie has a lovely manicure. Gracie closes her eyes and nods once. "Well," Ginger says, looking at Dr. Warner, "you'll have to ask my daddy." She crosses her arms and legs. "Damn if I know about any history of mental illness in this family."

Gracie's eyebrows lift as if she hears something and she begins to giggle all over again. She's giggling so hard the tears come back in her eyes. Ginger feels funny about this whole thing. Not funny *ha, ha*, but funny *weird*.

"What is she laughing at?" Dr. Warner asks.

"You tell me and we'll both know. I asked her earlier what was so funny and she wouldn't answer me."

Dr. Warner writes something down on the chart.

"I'm sorry," he says as he scribbles away. "I neglected to introduce myself. I'm Howard Warner. I am the psychiatric resident on duty at the moment. We have a full house you see, and I'll have to step out for a minute. I'll be back in a little bit. Would you like something to drink? Coffee? Sprite, perhaps?"

"No, thank you," Ginger says. Gracie doesn't say anything. *Surprise, surprise.*

Dr. Warner stands up and makes a little bow, then clomps off. Ginger notices that the backs of his socks are worn thin at the heels. He must be single. He must also have some shoes besides clogs. Gracie stops laughing.

Things are quiet for a quarter of an hour, fifteen silent minutes. A skinny strawberry blond nurse in purple scrubs and with a bad perm brings each of them a can of Sprite.

"I said I didn't care for anything," Ginger says.

"You better take it, sweetie. You two are going to be here awhile."

Ginger hates drinks in a can, but since there's no telling when she'll get a chance to have something else, she takes it. Gracie takes a few sips of hers and then starts in giggling again. She laughs so hard that she has to hand Ginger her Sprite. She laughs so hard that before Ginger realizes it, she's laughing too. Ginger doesn't have one single notion what she's laughing at, only that the giggling is contagious. A laughing disease. *Disease.*

"What are you laughing at?" Dr. Warner says from the doorway. Ginger looks around and sees he is talking to her.

"I don't have a clue," Ginger says, trying to stop, trying to regain composure. She reaches in her purse for a Kleenex. Her eyes are watering like her mama's.

"Have you ever been hospitalized for mental illness?" Dr. Warner asks. Nobody says anything and Ginger starts to say, *You've already asked her that,* when she happens to look up from her Kleenex and sees he is talking to her.

"I most certainly have not," she says, now utterly sober. "Just what do you mean by that?"

"I'm only trying to determine any family history, Miss Hollaman." Another man in a white coat steps into the Weeble room. "Miss Hollaman, this is Dr. Post. He is a student of psychiatry and we'd like to have him observe for the evening while we determine what to do with your mother. Is this acceptable to you?" Dr. Warner doesn't look at Ginger. He just keeps looking at that chart in his hands. *What could be so interesting in that chart,* she wonders, *since they haven't done a damn thing and we've been here in Weeble hell for over four hours.*

"I guess that's okay. Mama, is that okay with you?" Ginger asks, still trying to treat her mama like a normal person. Gracie closes her eyes and nods once. "Fine," Ginger says. "He can stay."

A chubby nurse with a stark white pageboy sticks her head in the door. "Dr. Warner, we have a problem with the gentleman in number eight."

"I'll be right there," Dr. Warner says to the nurse. He excuses himself, but first indicates with a look to Dr. Post that he should remain in the room with Ginger and Gracie. Before the door completely closes, Gracie starts giggling again. This time Ginger catches it right away. She can't help herself. It reminds her of her daddy tickling her when she was little. He would say her giggle box turned over.

Dr. Post leans closer. "Excuse me, what are you laughing at?"

He asks this question so sincerely, Ginger detects no pretense or condescension like she detected from clogman. It is comforting to see Dr. Post's black rubber-soled Rockports. Sensible shoes. A shrink should have sensible shoes. Ever since Ginger started dating Wally she's noticed everyone's shoes. Her mama, for instance, is wearing white Keds that have been polished with white shoe polish. She hasn't thought of polished canvas Keds since she was ten years old. Who polishes Keds anymore? Now she has something to laugh about. Tears roll down her face, her face is in her hands.

"Excuse me," Dr. Post persists, "what are you laughing at?"

In short breathless words Ginger manages to say, "I . . . have . . . no . . . idea." She looks up into Dr. Post's eyes and she sees it coming like a train rolling down a track. First his cheeks bunch toward his eyes and there's a little exhale through his nose, like he's laughing at her. But it isn't her. It isn't anything that either of them know about. Now he's in it, laughing, eyes watering. He angles around in his seat to get control of himself, but he can't, not with Ginger and Gracie going on ahead with it, riding it, letting it take them. In no time he doubles over, reaches under his glasses, and wipes tears from his eyes. He has caught the *dis-ease* and his giggle box is slam on its side when Dr. Warner walks into the observation room and looks hard at Dr. Post, who is trying his best to get serious.

"What is so funny, Dr. Post?" Dr. Warner asks with one eyebrow arched higher than the other. Ginger imagines him with a monocle. A German Weeble with a monocle. *He'll have to give up the clogs. Weebles don't have feet.*

"I have no idea, sir," Dr. Post is saying to Dr. Warner. Clearly Dr. Post wishes he wasn't laughing. Everyone starts to regain composure. They are almost there. But Gracie lets out a chain of giggles and then Ginger's laughing as hard as ever, and Dr. Post goes back to laughing full tilt in spite of himself. Only Dr. Warner isn't seeing the humor.

"Miss Hollaman, if you can compose yourself, please." He waits a minute until Ginger can sit up straight. "We will be keeping your mother for further observation, at least the next seventy-two hours. If you will, please wait with her while the room is made ready on Four North. Someone will be in to ask you some questions for the necessary paperwork. Please, Miss Hollaman, pull yourself together. Would you like something to calm your nerves?"

The impulse to laugh leaves Ginger as quickly as it came and she wonders where her daddy is, but she shakes her head and sits back in her Weeble chair. She pretends she's waiting for a massage, the nice slow massage Wally gives her when she's feeling stressed.

Dr. Warner makes a little bow before leaving and says curtly to Dr. Post, "If you have quite pulled yourself together, Post, may we proceed to the next patient?" Dr. Post winks at Ginger before he leaves, the wink of a conspirator. Ginger smiles back as he slides out the door.

How many crazy people come to the ER? How many mothers and daughters? How many husbands and wives? How many mothers and children? How many people adrift and separating, trying to hold on to each other, the distance between them all constantly growing wider and wider? How many of them laugh to the point of tears as the seam between them, the thing holding them together, rips open?

"How in the world did you get to Coats County?" Ginger fires at her mother once they are alone again, thinking she can jar them both out of it. Ginger thinks maybe she can scare her mama into answering a question. "That's what I want to know. And where is the car? Did they take the car from you? Did they take it and sell it or something?" Ginger looks at Gracie, but Gracie isn't looking at Ginger. After a couple of minutes, Gracie is laughing again, and looking past Ginger as if she is listening to someone else. But this time Ginger doesn't take the ride. She just sits here wishing she was home, with Wally, stoned.

Ginger meditates on the word *crazy* and wonders what, in the great scheme of things, that word really means. She is in a trance when the nurse comes to get them several hours later. The nurse seems at first unsure which one is the patient. "Mrs. Hollaman?" she says, looking back and forth.

"That would be *Mrs.* Hollaman," Ginger says, pointing an accusatory finger at her own mama. *Judas. I am a Judas. Where the hell is my daddy? Being Judas is his job.* "I am *Miss* Hollaman," Ginger says to the nurse. "I'm the *sane* one," she says, mustering what confidence she can.

Ed perches on a flat rock jutting out over the Smith River and looks at the reflection of the opposite bank that lolls on its surface, that play of light and dark and the translation of fact, everything just as it is—only upended and unstable. High trees undulate on the current, the root-rich banks on top, the full leafy canopy on bottom. That is exactly how Ed sees his life at this moment. Upside down and shifting. Everything looks normal, beautiful, rich, even through the filtering tint of the stream. But nothing is facing the right way. Nothing is looking in the right direction. Nothing fits comfortably in its place. And what should be solid is constantly changing, small changes on the surface because of stronger currents below.

First thing this morning, Ed was supposed to get up and head over to the hospital to meet Ginger and Gracie. He was supposed to see Gracie for the first time in months, talk to doctors, and probably have her committed for psychiatric observation. That much Ginger told him when she called last night. But instead of waking up at seven and taking a shower and showing up at Dixie Donuts at eight to ride to the hospital with Ginger the way he agreed to do before going to bed, Ed had gotten up at four in the morning and looked through the attic until he found his fishing rod with the Shimano open-faced reel. It felt strange in his hand. It had been so long since he'd cast a line, felt that sensation of hope, the flight of the baited hook and line through the air, the plunk of the sinker through the cool sheen of the water, the patient wait for the tug that brought butter-flies to his stomach. He flipped the rod in a casting motion a few times, loosening up his wrist, making up his mind there in the dim attic. He hunted his tackle box, wiped the dust from the lid, pulled and moved and shoved boxes until he spotted the big ice chest he used for the fish he caught.

After putting all the dusty equipment in the back of the truck, Ed made three ham sandwiches and put them and a jug of tea in a smaller cooler with some Blue Ice. He grabbed a pack of crackers, a tin each of potted meat, Vienna sausage, and Beanee Weenies (leftovers from his pre-cooking days), a Ziploc bag of homemade chocolate chip cookies, and a can of Niblets corn. He put all that in a paper sack and headed out the back door, leaving the kitchen Jesus praying at the rock in the harsh fluo-rescence of the overhead light. "Pray I catch something," Ed says over his shoulder. "Surely you've prayed for fish." He drove into the dark morning, headed over the state line into Virginia, hell-bent for Philpott Dam and the Smith River. Gracie wasn't the only one who could run away.

Now Ed sits over the river, not knowing what time the spillway will open, only knowing when it does, the water will rise quick and threaten-ing and he'll have to react. His reflexes will kick in and he will grab what he can and move to higher ground. But until the water begins its rapid rise, Ed sits on the flat rock and thinks about long ago, when the reflection in the water seemed more like a magic place he could reach for, when the image was not so fragile, when the reflection included Gracie. He remem-bers a day when he was twenty-one and his baited hook and sinker hit the stream and pierced the timeless flow of the old river. That day, Gracie had said the little thud of the hook and bait kerplunking into the water sounded like a hiccup of possibility—the possibility that something would bite, that it would be a keeper, that the day would be a good day for fishing and the supper would be the catch, rather than a cold tin of meat and beans and the dry crisp break of Premium Saltines.

All children think their mama is crazy sometimes, but Ginger's got the papers to prove it. Carbons anyway, right here in her hands. Yellow copies for insurance and pink copies for her daddy's records. Ginger's been in the hospital now for eight agonizingly slow hours, and doesn't understand why it's taking her daddy so long to get here. She knows he's gotten her page by now. *Where the hell is he? Where was he for all that time down in the emergency room?* That was forever. And now she's been here on the ward for over two hours.

The place gives her the heebeegeebees. The only thing that keeps her sane is meditating on the word *crazy*. Everyone in this world uses the word *crazy* quite loosely it occurs to her, sitting here in Four North, fourth floor, North wing, also known as the adult psychiatric wing, where she has just committed her own mama after her long absence to some black folks' farm up in Rockrun, Virginia. She vaguely remembers riding through Rockrun when she was a child, before so many four-lanes. She'd see it if she didn't blink.

We all do it, use that word. *Crazy.* Then we shake our heads. *So-and-so is just crazy*, or *That crazy so-and-so*, or *Have you heard the latest on crazy ole what's her name?* Then there's *Why, you crazy thing!* or the ever popular, *Are you crazy?* Ginger's said them all. But here in Four North, *crazy* is a real state of mind. Not just odd or slightly off-the-mark. A real bona fide state of being, sufficient to warrant somebody getting asked a few pointed questions and then receiving a few pointed injections.

Ginger is happy to see the dayroom doesn't look like it was made for Weebles. It's nicely furnished in padded blue tweed chairs and oak tables. If not for the wires in the windows and the locked door to the ward, you might think you were in the gate area of a small airport. But any flights out of here are strictly mind or drug propelled.

Take Clarence for instance, the young guy over by the window here in the dayroom. If Ginger had to guess, she'd say Clarence is close to her age.

He's also out of his gourd. Talking on a phone that doesn't exist, calling out numbers and vortexes and coordinates like he's Mr. Sulu on *Star Trek*. Flicking his long dark bony fingers like he's got water or something flying off the ends of them, Clarence is freaking Ginger out a little. And Violet, the old woman with almost no hair, it's cut so short, and no telling how many strings of beads draped around her neck, what is she in here for? Violet keeps walking around rearranging the furniture and sitting down and getting up and rearranging some more. Ginger's watched her move that one coffee cup ten times. And if Violet had one more scarf on her head or one more strand of beads around her neck, she might not keep herself upright. Somebody needs to tell her you wear bobby socks or panty hose, but you don't wear your panty hose over your bobby socks. But Ginger has to give it to her, Violet has a good tan. Of course, it's only when she's walking toward you. She's white as a sheet when she's going the other way. *Hawaii coming, Alaska going.* Ginger starts to laugh, but thinks better of it. *Where is my daddy?*

Oh no, here she comes. Violet is coming straight for Ginger. Violet moves the chair to Ginger's left away from her by a few inches. Ginger tries to ignore her. Violet moves the chair to Ginger's right and, *Oh Lord,* around and out in front of her. *Oh God.* She is sitting down in it. She crosses her legs and the top one bounces hard, with a vengeance actually, and Violet is staring a hole through Ginger. *Oh God. Be calm, be calm. Where the hell is my daddy? I know he's gotten my message by now. Do I say something? Where is the woman behind the desk? Where did she go? She was there a minute ago. She was talking to Violet and Clarence just a minute ago. Oh God. I'm here in this big room with Violet and Clarence and no health care professional! What are they thinking? I can sue! God, please take Violet away.*

"Just who *are* you?" Violet says.

"Ginger. I'm Ginger."

"Didn't God give you a last name?" Violet looks at Ginger in an evil way. Ginger definitely senses evil.

"Ginger Hollaman."

"Uh huh," Violet says, like she doubts the honesty of Ginger's answer. "You have persecuted someone and you will have to bear the consequences," she says to Ginger and gets up to put back the chair in just the right position. Ginger sees that Violet probably has all her clothes on at once. Her nightgown is over her pants and shirt. "I'm a Marine," Violet says as she walks off toward the refrigerator. "I know things about you."

"Violet, stay away from the Coke machine," a woman says from behind the wall of the empty nurses' station. Violet veers away from the Coke machine.

"Excuse me." Ginger is saying *Excuse me* out loud over and over to no one in hopes that the woman behind the desk will come back. Now she's up and over to that desk looking for somebody. The nurse is there behind the door, for Pete's sake, eating her lunch. "Excuse me, miss?" The nurse looks at Ginger like she's a pain in her ass. "Excuse me, but could you eat out here with me? I'm a little nervous. If my father doesn't get here soon, I'll have to leave and come back with him later."

"Honey," the nurse says as she tries to choke down a bite of her sandwich, "Violet and Clarence won't hurt you. But if you want me to, I'll sit out there with you. Betsy, the other nurse who should be out there, is giving out meds around the floor. I've been keeping an eye on you, honey. Don't you worry. Your mama ought to be back out here as soon as they get her settled into her room and check on all the doctors' orders for her." The nurse takes a bite of French fry. "Should be out here any minute."

"Thank you," Ginger says, wanting one of those fries. When did she eat last? This morning around ten o'clock. A plain glazed and hot tea. It's now half-past six.

"This your first time in the psych ward, honey?" the nurse says just before taking another bite.

"How'd you guess?"

She chews before answering. "First-time folks are a little jumpy. You'll get used to it."

Clarence makes an abrupt appearance at the desk. "I need to talk to the doctor about my planout, Mary. Very, very important that I speak with him to expedite my treatment, if you will. By the way, Violet keeps moving my natural seat. It's affecting my reception. I'm going to be forced to put a magnetic field around my chair if she doesn't refrain from relocating my position. Is this in your realm of expertise to assist me with this infraction? Or should I refer it to another commander?"

"Clarence, honey," Mary says, "when is the last time you had a shave?" She eyes his beard closely.

Clarence runs his hands over his jaw. "I believe it was day before yesterday at sixteen hundred hours. That seems correct to me."

"Clarence, honey, we need to shave some of that hair off your face." Mary shakes her finger at Clarence and then goes back to her sandwich.

Clarence pats his face. "They're whiskers, but not hair, definitely not hair."

Mary winks at Ginger like they have a secret, like they are sharing a joke that is Clarence. Ginger would rather share the sandwich. Ginger realizes now that hospitals are full of conspirators.

"I'm leaving now," Ginger is saying, thinking how all she wants to do is get to the Burger King drive-thru and order a chicken sandwich combo with extra-large fries and a Coke. Maybe an apple pie. She doesn't even like apple pie. "I'll come back with my father," Ginger says. "Please tell my mother that I'll be back." She's getting ready to explode. She needs to get out before they commit her. She feels *crazy* overtaking her. She has this urgent fear that the real *crazy*, not the loosely defined *crazy*, might be contagious. Ginger thinks about all that giggling in the Weeble room.

"Here, honey, let me buzz you out," Mary says as she licks mayonnaise from her finger. "When you hear the buzz, you just pull hard on that door and it'll come right open." Mary gets up and steps over to a button beneath a small window looking out onto the hallway by the elevators. "Clarence, you stand back now," she says. "Can't have you going home with Ms. Hollaman, now, can we?" Nurse Mary winks at Ginger again, like that is some kind of joke. Ginger doesn't have that good a sense of humor.

"And honey," Mary continues, as Ginger tries to find the door handle while looking at her with one eye and keeping Clarence in the corner of the other eye, "don't worry about your mama. She won't even know you probably till sometime tomorrow. She's got a good little cocktail going by now, if you know what I mean." Mary nods in the direction of Ginger's hands. "You pull hard on that door."

The buzzer is going and Ginger can't get her hand around the door handle. *Dammit, just pay attention.* She can't stop looking at Clarence, who is now several feet from the door. The heavy door is swinging open. It is swinging open and the buzzer has stopped. Ginger is moving, one foot in front of the other one. She is leaving the moon and returning to planet Earth, one small step at a time. The door is closing on Clarence's face while he holds his invisible phone to the side of his head. He asks for new coordinates. Ginger turns from the door as it shuts tight behind her. The click of the lock makes it official. She's returning to planet Earth and leaving her mama behind.

AFTER WAITING thirty minutes, Ed sees a short severely bucktoothed woman with a pencil behind her ear walking toward him. "Are you Mr. Hollaman?" she asks. He notices her wedding ring. *There really is somebody for everybody.* She takes him down a hallway and offers him a seat in a tiny office. It doesn't seem to belong to anyone in particular.

"Mr. Hollaman, how do you do?" Dr. Warner offers Ed his smooth delicate hand as he steps through the door. Ed offers the doctor his rough one. The handshake is a mixture of confidence and reluctance on both sides.

"How's my wife?" Ed takes a seat across the desk from Dr. Warner.

Dr. Warner searches through his pockets until he finds a ball, the kind they sell in convenience stores to relieve stress. Dr. Warner squeezes the ball in one hand and flips through Gracie's chart with the other. He talks to Ed without looking up.

"I have spoken to the Coats County sheriff about the circumstances under which she was found and what transpired while the Riley family had her in their care. I need to ask you some questions, if you don't mind, to help get a clearer picture of what's going on with Grace."

"Gracie," Ed corrects.

"I beg your pardon?"

"She always goes by Gracie."

"Not anymore. Actually, she seems to prefer the name Rachel at the moment."

Anxiety creeps up Ed's legs and tingles in a holding pattern at the top of his new blue socks, socks he bought for himself in Dillard's after buying Chef Bernard's full line of cookware.

"According to the information I received from the Coats County sheriff, the Rileys, the family your wife was living with, didn't know her name, so they gave her the name Rachel. It is evident through nonverbal communication with your wife that she prefers the new name the Rileys gave her to her legal name." Dr. Warner switches the spongy ball to the other hand.

"Tell me, Mr. Hollaman"—Dr. Warner looks up briefly—"has your wife been acting strange lately?"

"Well, she's at that age. I thought it was just *the change*. You know."

Dr. Warner finally focuses his attention on Ed. "This change is slightly more complicated than menopause, Mr. Hollaman."

"Yeah, I guess so."

"Behavior, Mr. Hollaman. Has she been behaving strangely?"

Ed leans forward putting his elbows on the chair arms. "Well, there's the Jesuses."

"Pardon?" Dr. Warner pushes up his wire rimmed glasses and leans toward Ed, just slightly.

"The Jesuses. Before she left, she drew these three Jesuses on the walls of the house. I thought it was odd, her asking me to paint those three walls white a few weeks before she left. Of course, I didn't know she was leaving. I just thought she'd gotten the idea for the white walls from *Country Living*, or one of those magazines she gets. It's just that we don't have a white wall in our house, except for the Jesus walls. She never liked white walls before."

"Interesting," says Dr. Warner. "Go on. What else?"

"Well, there's the music."

"Music?"

"She never liked that classical music, and then all of a sudden she got to where it was all she wanted to hear. If I put on some Johnny Cash or Glen Campbell, she'd come right in the den and turn off the record player and put on public radio. Said she didn't want to hear singing. She always liked to sing with the records before."

"Go on. What else?"

"There's big rocks under all the beds, some she's carted up from the creek behind our house. I'll be honest, I don't know how she carried some of those rocks so far. And they've been washed too. Clean as a whistle, except for the dust from under the bed. I'm not much of a housekeeper, and what I manage to do along those lines doesn't happen under the beds where nobody can see." Ed thinks of Parva up under the bed. Then he pictures her leaving, with that little wad of dust still stuck to the back of her pretty dress.

"Yes, well."

"She left her wedding ring on the bed when she drove away back in April. First time she's ever taken it off her finger, as far as I know. When I got home and saw that ring, I thought she'd just got mad and left me. Tossed the ring in the middle of the bed as a message."

"What did you think about that message?"

"I told you. I thought it was the change. Women do crazy things when they're going through the change. I've been hearing about it from the guys down at the Moose and reading about it some in *Reader's Digest*. I thought maybe she'd be back and maybe she wouldn't. But it never hit me she was sick."

"Your wife may have changed more than you know. Is there a history of mental illness in her family?"

"Her daddy shot hisself. I guess that requires a certain amount of crazy, wouldn't it?"

"What about Grace? Has she ever been hospitalized?"

"There was this one time when she was in college. She told me about it before we got married, but she never talked about it after that. I didn't know her till after she quit school. She's real smart, but she said college wasn't for her. Her grandaddy had her sent to a hospital for a while, after she dropped out. A few months maybe. That's all I know. I don't even know where it was. She said he was like that, sending people off when they didn't do what he thought they ought to do. She finally ran away from him. That's how we met. She was camping in the woods, hiding from him. I came up on her there on the riverbank."

"She was sitting on the riverbank?"

"More squatting. She was cooking some bream she'd caught. That woman can really fish."

"And Grace's mother?"

"I don't know if she could fish or not." Ed tries to joke with the doctor to get his legs to quit tingling at the top of his socks, but Dr. Warner doesn't seem to be a joking man. "I wasn't around her much," Ed says seriously. "She died some years back. A car accident."

"Hmm."

"Are you saying Gracie's crazy?"

"We don't use that term. And it is difficult to come to a definitive diagnosis of your wife's condition without further observation and medication. Right now she doesn't want to talk to anyone. But we get a little stronger response when we address her as Rachel. Medication may help with that. We want to keep her a little while longer, see if we can get her to talk. It is possible your wife has developed a form of schizophrenia. Does she have a history of mood swings? Depression then elation?"

"Dr. Warner, my wife has always listened to her own drummer. But she's never been what you'd call depressed. Just different. Always looking at things from a different angle. It used to be fun to be with her, see things through her eyes. But lately, she's been more angry about what doesn't suit her. That habit of looking for the silver lining, or seeing something in its most positive way, well, she seemed to be losing that."

"What do you know about schizophrenia, Mr. Hollaman?"

"People think they're more than one person?"

"No. Actually the movies promote that notion, but what you're describing is dissociative identity disorder. I don't know why they insist on calling it schizophrenia in the movies. Schizophrenia is a physical disease of the mind. The brain chemistry changes and the patient begins to have hallucinations and delusions. Schizophrenics are not thinking correctly, but they don't understand that. They think they are perfectly sane. Often this disorder is accompanied by some form of paranoia. But it is important to remember that the changes in behavior are a response to a very physical illness. Do you understand what I'm saying?"

"I think so. But what caused it?"

"We don't know much about what causes the chemical change in the brain. There are several theories. I'll see that you get a pamphlet that goes into more detail. Basically the disease lies dormant and erupts spontaneously, usually in teenagers or adults in their twenties. Late onset, like your wife appears to have, is rather rare."

"So, it's not the change of life?"

"Huge hormonal changes may cause things to unfold that are already present but dormant. But schizophrenia can exist totally independent of the patient's environment. It's interesting that you mention the father's suicide. There is a theory that some cases of the disease can be linked to childhood trauma."

"Can you cure Gracie? Can you cure this skitso whatever?"

"It can probably be controlled for the most part. Each case is so individual. Some patients respond to medications better than others. Some take their medications better than others. Treatment, in some ways, is a process of elimination. You should prepare yourself, Mr. Hollaman. It can take a while to get the balance of medicine just right for the best possible results. I'm sorry to say the disease cannot be cured, but it can oftentimes, in the best of circumstances, be controlled. And with a lot of support from family and a psychiatric team, many patients lead very full lives."

Ed leans back again in his chair. Dr. Warner leans back in his and moves the ball back to his left hand.

"Controlled doesn't sound much like cured, now, does it?" The anxiety crawls up past Ed's socks to just below his knees.

"No, it doesn't. I realize this is a lot to take in. Some families deal with this kind of illness better than others. It's like riding the high seas in some ways. Some people get their sea legs, and some stay disoriented. My advice at this point, Mr. Hollaman, is to educate yourself about the possibilities as we refine the diagnosis, and take advantage of some of the group sessions we have here at the hospital for family members of our psychiatric patients. You can learn a lot from experienced family members."

"I'm sure my daughter has found out about all the group meetings by now. She's very thorough."

"Then that is all I have for you right now, Mr. Hollaman," Dr. Warner says and stands behind his desk and offers Ed his soft hand again. "We will talk more later. I'm running late for the emergency room and I don't like to be late."

Ed shakes Dr. Warner's hand and wonders what bargain has been struck between them.

"The nurse at the front desk will have some information for you to read. If you, or your daughter, have any questions, you can refer them to Dr. Post. He had been assigned to Grace's case. The nurse will give you his card."

Ed stands beside the elevators, leans against the wall, and lets it all sink in. The elevators open and close and people get on and get off. Ed stands there, thinking about Dr. Warner's questions, thinking about this new ripple in the reflected picture of his life. Then Ed knows what he must have known deep down on the night Gracie left home. He had been expecting Gracie to run away for close to thirty years. And when she did, as disruptive as it was, it felt as natural as the day she'd come into his life. The strange has always felt normal when it comes to Gracie. That's how it has always been. Ed feels like he used to feel when he was a school kid in trouble waiting outside the principal's door. The same fact and the same question plague him now. The fact: Nothing is ever really finished. The question: What happens next?

"GRACIE, I UNDERSTAND you are a very talented artist." Sharon Underwood is Four North's art therapist, a holdover hippie—worn jeans, socks with sandals, long dark Cher-like hair that she constantly throws back over her shoulders, china doll skin—who once thought she'd illustrate children's books. But she never recovered from the decision to make practical use of her gifts. Sharon scans her new patient's chart. Grace Hollaman has just begun to talk after a week on the ward.

"Gracie?"

"My name is Rachel. Either call me Rachel or don't call me."

"All right, Rachel. Why don't you have a seat at the table?" Sharon turns to collect forms from a cabinet near her desk.

Gracie moves slowly toward the big round table in the center of the art therapy room. Violet and Clarence are seated there already with a third patient Gracie hasn't seen before, a sunburned man with a bald head. He has his eyes closed and is rocking back and forth.

Today Violet wears four outfits all at the same time, one polyester pantsuit plus three dresses of various kinds. The pants are rolled up to her knees and secured with rubber bands. Clarence touches the bottom of his black Converse high-tops to the tip of his nose, causing the bottom of his gray sweatpants to slide up above his chalky ankle. When he puts his foot down, he grabs the hem of his yellow T-shirt, stretches it out, and turns to Gracie for her to read, *To be or not to be*. Gracie nods and stretches her new white T-shirt with purple letters out over the zipper of her jeans so Clarence can read it. Ginger brought Gracie the jeans and the T-shirt that quotes Emily Dickinson, *I dwell in possibilities*. Ginger bought it for her because she thought the shirt reflected the hope of a cure. Gracie doesn't think about the shirt at all, other than to mirror Clarence's gesture, and she isn't aware she needs a cure. George, the third patient, just out of bed, nervously fingers the buttons of his blue-and-white-striped pajamas and the belt of his dark green flannel robe.

"You don't know George," Clarence says to Gracie. "This is George and he likes to hear his name said out loud. It makes him blink."

George keeps rocking, but opens and closes his eyes twice as Clarence speaks.

"Clarence, will you please get the crayons and the watercolors?" Sharon asks as she places a stack of paper in the middle of the table.

"Coordinates please." Clarence holds out his hands prepared to write on an invisible tablet.

"The blue cabinet," Sharon says, pointing across the room. Clarence scribbles something on his invisible tablet and makes invisible calculations. "Vector six," he concludes, and goes to the blue cabinet beside the windows, which span one entire wall of the art therapy room.

Sharon shares the room with Herb, the occupational therapist. Sometimes they work together, using woodworking skills and painting. His leather craft borders on art therapy. Most of what he does is adaptable. Sharon is single. Herb is single and straight. Sharon finds that a rare combination in these days of open closets. She collaborates with Herb as much as possible. But today she is on her own. Tuesdays and Thursdays are Herb's days to work in Fizdiz, hospital slang for physical disability. But he's back to Four North on Mondays, Wednesdays, and Fridays.

The windows look out over the visitor's parking lot. Beside the windows, multicolored cabinets line the adjacent wall. The other two walls are full of craft paper projects, drawings, and paintings. Some of the artwork is simple and childlike. Some is angry and fiery. Some is beyond articulation. A few pieces are competent renderings of something familiar. One construction paper mosaic of the Madonna and Child is stunning.

"Violet, will you get the paper from the orange cabinet?" Sharon uses a particularly gracious tone.

"Get it your damn self. I don't work here." Violet tries to adjust her bobby socks, which are plastered against her legs by the Sheer Energy support hose she has on over top of them. What little leg hair she has is dark and mashed flat beneath the nylon. "You don't tell me what to do. You're a hippie."

"Violet, remember, we had a talk about cooperation yesterday, and you promised to be more cooperative in art therapy."

Violet reaches into her outermost dress pocket and pulls out a purple scarf. She ties it around her head and looks at Sharon with a stern expression.

"I would rather eat peters than get paper out of that cabinet. I am your boss. I am the president of this company. I am the president of the United

States of America." While she talks, Violet takes one of many strands of beads from around her neck and begins winding it around her wrist in bracelet fashion. "I don't have to get anything out of that cabinet if I don't want to. And I don't. I'll report you if you don't stop giving me unauthorized orders." Violet stands and begins walking around the art therapy room. Her walk becomes an aggressive strut. Her beads and makeshift bracelet click together as each step hits the floor with force. Her hips swing from side to side to help convey her perceived authority. "I don't want to draw. I have passed all that."

Sharon opens the door and calmly calls, "Anthony."

Anthony is a six-foot-three-inch psychiatric nurse with a physique like the Incredible Hulk, only he's not green. He is olive brown, that beautiful Italian skin that Sharon loves.

"Violet doesn't want to draw today," Sharon says quietly to Anthony.

"Come on, Violet. How about a little *As the World Turns?*" Anthony asks. Violet takes his arm and smiles at him. She is a flirt. Sharon's only successes with Violet are on the days when Herb is in the room and Violet can flirt and draw at the same time. At the door Violet turns to Sharon and says with a haughty flourish, "You're fired." Anthony smiles and shrugs his shoulders as if to say, *Oh well, them's the breaks.* Then he and Violet go to the TV room.

"I'm sad to see you leave," Clarence tells Sharon as he comes back to the table, his arms full of old plastic sherbet containers with the lids on them.

"I'm not going anywhere, Clarence." Sharon peels back the plastic sherbet tub tops and pours crayons and pencils out across the table. "Violet can't fire me."

"Well, that's good," Clarence says. "I'll get the pastels. Can we use pastels today?"

"Absolutely. Grace, have you used pastels before? George, how about you?" Sharon is getting the paper and passing it around the table. George's eyes flicker open and shut.

"I told you already, my name is Rachel. And I don't use paper."

"What do you like to draw on?"

"Anything but paper." Gracie looks at the ceiling for a few seconds. *It's too temporary.*

Gracie redirects her attention to Sharon. "It's too temporary."

"Well, I can see your point there," Sharon says as she reaches for some sanded blocks of wood. "Try drawing on these."

Every place Mattie looks there are graveyards. On the dresser is a graveyard of men's cologne, each bottle a marker, a headstone. The wallet and change holder Sammy gave Arty for Christmas when he was ten years old, a monument. Sammy chopped wood every day after school to get the money for his Christmas presents that year. The wallet holder is wide, like it stands for two deaths in one. The picture frames all mark something that's gone. She can see the headboard of the bed in the mirror, but she can't bear to think of that. It's too obvious. Too deep. Too bottomless.

She looks out the window and sees the little field behind the garage full of old pieces of cars and rusted, broken farm equipment Arty meant to fix or sell for parts. Two and a half years have passed since Arty died and she still has it in her mind that he's going to sell those parts and clean up that field like he promised he would. Instead, Rachel paints one thing at a time, and Toot and Sammy move some of it, painted piece by painted piece, to the front yard. Mattie admits they're colorful and some of them funny. Some of the pictures of Jesus give you chills. So that graveyard of metal is disappearing by somebody's hand other than Arty's. If Rachel doesn't get it all, the field will take it one day. Then what will Mattie see when she looks out this window? She won't see Arty, she knows that.

Today is the day. Mattie gave in to Sammy last night and said she would clean out the closet. "Daddy's clothes can be of use to some poor soul who needs some," Sammy said. Even Toot agrees they aren't doing anybody any good hanging in this closet. But they do Mattie good. They make her feel something, if it's nothing but her heart still breaking. There isn't a sorrier sight in this world than self-pity, and she's got a bad case of it. Bad case.

One by one Mattie takes a suit or a shirt or a pair of coveralls and holds it to her. Imagines it filled out by the man she loved since she was nine-teen years old. She buries her face in each piece, smells a suit, rubs a shirt sleeve against her cheek, lets a tie slide over her arm, then takes the thing from its hanger and folds it neatly and places it in one of three cardboard boxes she's got sitting on the bed.

When Arty's clothes are gone from the rod, Mattie slowly spreads her clothes through the closet, careful to keep each hanger two fingers apart, the way Arty did in the Army. He laughed at how cramped his little bit of clothes were compared to all the space her dresses, skirts, and blouses took up. "And you say you don't have nothing to wear?" he'd say.

Mattie goes through the top shelf, Arty's hats and caps. There are fedo-ras from the days he traveled with the quartet, and the tan cap he wore when he used to plow the field behind big Sheba or her mama. He was twenty-three when they married and she can close her eyes and see him out in the field plowing row after row in that cap, him walking behind one of those big black Percheron. Mattie can see it as long as she holds this cap in her hands. She puts the cap on her head and closes her eyes. Then takes all the hats and the tan cap and puts them in the top of a box and folds one corner down and over the next and the next and the next and tucks the last one in under the first one. No use taping them. Sammy's truck has a shell on the back.

Other things hide on the back of the shelf. Her fingers touch the wall and she slides her hand until she finds them: his baseball glove, his drum-sticks, his saxophone, playbills from programs he performed in. The clothes are enough to give away. Maybe someday there'll be a grandson to take these other things. Maybe she can pass them on to Tyrone, if Sammy doesn't have any sons of his own. But they won't be put in a box to go to someplace Mattie's never seen to be given to somebody she doesn't know.

She looks down at the shoes. They are their own set of grave markers sitting around on the floor gathering dust. She puts the work boots in an empty box. She picks up a pair of dress shoes—brown wing tips, good shoes, expensive shoes, Florsheims—brushes her dust cloth across the leather and the shine comes back like they've just been polished. Mattie slides her hand down into the left shoe and feels the way it molded to

Arty's foot. The slick path his socks made every time he dressed up and slid his foot in past the shoehorn. The last time he wore these shoes he sang the Lord's Prayer. His recitation sounded better than Archie Brownlee ever thought about.

Arty and the Soul Searchers could have been big. They had big talent. But they were, every one of them, family men, except Leroy Pruitt. Leroy stayed in the business and sang bass with several groups out of Duke and Peacock and later Hummingbird. He came home about ten years back with a gold front tooth with two diamonds in it. Mattie and Arty got to laughing so hard about that tooth after he left. Mattie saw him when nobody else was looking and he just kept running his tongue over those diamonds to make sure they were still there. The other three, Bobby Agnew, Raymond Hester, and Arty, they made good lives for themselves and their families. As far as Mattie knows, Leroy is still singing, still smiling that diamond smile of his, only now he does it for R&B audiences. He has left several families behind. As far as she can tell, there was not a single regret among them. Not Bobby, not Raymond, not Arty, and not Leroy. The first three sang to praise God, not be famous. And Leroy, he wasn't so set on being famous as much as he just wanted to sing and get paid to do it.

Mattie runs her hand in and out of the shoe she holds. Pushes her palm flat against the insole. It is almost warm, like Arty just slipped it off his foot. She holds it to her face and smells his foot powder, draws a deep breath and tries to breathe more of him inside her. She did that right when he died too. Breathed in real deep so she could take his last breath.

At night when she's in bed, Mattie feels Arty's feet. If she tells anybody that, they'll think she's lost her mind sure enough. But she feels them like she did all those nights they slept together. Every night, even if they were mad at each other about something, she had her feet on top of his or he had his feet on top of hers. If not, they couldn't sleep a wink. And right to this day, when Mattie gets in the bed and turns out the light, she slides down in the covers and moves her feet over to his side of the bed and there his feet are, just as solid as her own. She always reaches for more, feels back behind her for a hip or a leg or an arm. But it's just his feet touching her feet. That's all she gets.

Mattie slides her foot into the brown wing tip. It has the weight of a man to it. She puts her foot where his foot has been, feels the shape of it, the warmth. She puts on the other wing tip and laces them both up real real tight so they'll stay on her feet. Then she clomps on over to the box and takes the work boots out and puts them back in the closet. Maybe she'll wear them tomorrow. Today she'll wear the wing tips. And maybe a fedora. She opens the box with the hats in it and takes back a fedora and the plowing cap and puts them on the shelf in the closet, at the edge where she can reach them easy.

Mattie will give up the clothes. She can do that. She'll let Sammy put them in some bin and let some other needy soul have them. But she needs to walk in Arty's shoes for a while. Feel her skin slide over the place where his feet have been. Just for a while longer. She's got to keep those feet.

Ed waits in the open area of Four North to see Gracie for the first time since that Thursday morning before Easter when he gave her a peck on the cheek and said good-bye for the day, what he thought was a *normal* day in his *normal* life, a day that stretched out almost half a year. Violet has marched around him twice, a kind of strut more than a march, but not pure march and not pure strut. Whatever it is, it is disconcerting. Clarence is nowhere to be seen today and Frank, the new patient, is sitting quietly watching CNN. Frank looks like any normal guy probably in his forties, except for the dark circles under his eyes, which Ed is told can come from medication. Violet makes another pass around Ed, then marches straight up in front of him, stops, and salutes.

"You know I have never had a marching lesson in my life?" she asks.

"No? You march pretty good." Ed tries to sound even, respectful, *normal*.

"God tells me how. Yesterday he told me to pull the fire alarm and teach the firemen how to march."

"That must have been exciting," Ed says.

"I marched forward and backward and in a circle. God taught me to do that. He wanted me to teach them. I'm really a Marine. They don't know it though."

"The firemen?"

"The Marines."

Violet does a rough about-face and marches—struts—away from Ed and up to Frank. She salutes Frank, who salutes her back, and returns his attention to CNN. Violet makes a right face and continues on out of sight.

If this is any indication of his future, *normal* has been permanently displaced.

Just visit with her, Dr. Post had said. *Just talk to her as if she isn't sick and see how she responds.* He made it sound so easy. Ed waits. Ed waits and watches Frank watch CNN. Ed is used to waiting, so much so that he has waited a week before coming to see Gracie.

The sun burns through the windows of the open area, blinding Ed. There aren't any shades to pull, only a large empty cornice across the top of the windows. The blaze strikes a perfect position and the entire open area is a ball of fire. Gracie enters from the same hallway Violet left by and walks over to stand in front of Ed, but to one side so that the glare remains in his eyes. She doesn't say anything. Ed can see her and not see her, as if she is a heavenly body partially eclipsing the sun. Ed knows that watching an eclipse is dangerous without the proper equipment, but he puts his hand up to shade his eyes and tries to make out her features. He tries to recognize her. *Just talk to her like she isn't sick and see how she responds.*

"Hi there!" He tries to sound excited to see her. "Sit down. I brought you some pound cake."

Gracie sits in the chair beside him. Ed turns to face her and changes hands in an effort to keep the light blocked. He wants to get a good look at her, see if she has dark circles under her eyes like the man watching TV. He hands her two pieces of pound cake wrapped in stretch-tite. Gracie takes the cake in cupped hands like she's trying to hold water, peels back the plastic wrap and sniffs, then gently sets the gift down on the table beside her. She flicks her fingers into the air and licks her lips. Ed notices then that her lips are dry and a little pasted up with something white and that her mouth stays a little open. He wonders what's happened to the tight line of a mouth he's been so used to.

"Try it. I made it myself."

Gracie looks at Ed as though he has said the oddest thing.

"I know, I couldn't cook before, but you'd be surprised what I can do now."

"That's what I'm afraid of."

"What are you afraid of, Gracie?"

"I'm not Gracie. I'm Rachel. I was Gracie, but now I'm Rachel."

"I see," says Ed.

"What do you see?" Gracie asks.

"I see. I heard from the doctors you changed your name."

"I didn't change it. God had Tootsie Mae change it."

"I see."

"What do you see?"

"Nothing." Ed closes his hands together and lets them rest between his knees.

"The drawings you made on the walls, the Jesuses, they're pretty good."

"I've moved on."

"Moved on from Jesuses?"

"No, walls. I've moved on to car parts. Do you think you can get me some car parts? I need big ones. Fenders would be good. Trunk lids and hoods would be better."

"Why do you want car parts?"

"The voices. They aren't talking to me, and it's because of the car parts. I ran out of car parts. They took me away from Tootsie Mae's and now I don't have any parts."

"They say in a few weeks you might can come home."

"Home is at Tootsie Mae's. I've disenchanted you."

"What are you talking about?"

"The spell by the river is over. I disenchant you. The circle is closing."

"What circle?"

"The story, our story, it's closing. I need to start a new circle."

"I don't understand. Won't you eat some cake?"

"No cake. I'm the queen, I have other circles to make. I have a lot to do, but I need the car parts."

"I'm not sure what you want me to do."

"Get me some car parts."

"I mean about us, about you being in here, about you getting well. And I don't think I can bring car parts into the hospital."

"You need to go back to being who you are and I need the car parts."

"I haven't changed, Gracie. You're the one doing all the changing. I'm just Ed. Just ole Ed trying to be here for you while you get well. That's all."

"I'm not Gracie, I'm Rachel."

Ed tries to quell his panic. He hears Dr. Post's calm voice. *Just talk to her.*

"What do the voices sound like?" Ed asks.

"Just voices. God mostly."

"Is it always God?"

"I can't tell you."

"Why not?"

The sun drops lower and the light changes. It is softer, more golden.

"Because if you were supposed to know, He'd talk to you."

Frank stands up across the room and goes down the hallway toward the patients' rooms. Clarence steps out of a door to the left of the open area. He rubs his head over and over. Gracie stands up and faces Ed. She takes the position of Jesus with the open hands. She closes her eyes and mumbles words Ed can't make out, then she lifts her arms to make a circle in the air.

"There, that should do it," she says. "I have to go now. They're going to give us pills and supper." Gracie takes the cake from the table and wraps it tightly in its plastic wrap. "Take this back with you. I can't risk it."

"Don't you want it? It's lemon pound cake. You like that, don't you?"

"Gracie did. But I don't. I'm not Gracie. I'm Rachel."

"I see."

"What do you see?"

"Nothing. Nothing."

"You could be casting a spell on me. I can't risk it. I have to stay Rachel. I'm queen of the fairies, and it's time for me to make other circles."

Ed thinks about giving Gracie a hug, but Rachel doesn't look like she wants one.

She turns and walks down the hallway that Violet and Frank and Clarence have already taken.

Ed picks up the pound cake and walks to the nurses' station. A nurse who looks Korean glances up at Ed and speaks with a Southern accent. "Did you have a good visit?"

"Yes, thank you." *Nothing is what it seems*, Ed thinks. "Will you please open the door? I'm ready to leave now." Ed almost offers her the cake.

"Sure, honey. Have a nice night." She pushes a button and the buzzer sounds. Ed walks through the door with the cake still in his hand and takes the elevator to the ground floor. He walks outside into the settling dusk and sits on a concrete bench that serves as a cab stand. A cabdriver sits at the other end of the bench reading the paper, waiting for a fare.

"You need a ride, mister?" he asks Ed. The cabdriver's hat is loaded with buttons and pins and a wiry black ponytail sticks straight out from beneath it, like a bushy fish's tail. He holds the paper between the tips of his dark arthritic fingers and his pale palms. His thumbs curl out like black question marks.

"No, I don't need a ride. Thanks though. My truck's in the parking lot." Ed unwraps the pound cake. "I'm just taking a load off."

"You got that right," says the cabdriver. "I need a customer, but I sure do enjoy the peacefulness of sitting here reading the paper and watching the sun go down."

"You want a piece of cake? I've got two."

The cabdriver looks at the cake.

"I made it for my wife. She's a patient here. But she didn't feel like eating it. Have some. It's lemon."

"I don't mind if I do. Thank you." The cabdriver takes the slightly mashed piece on the top and puts a bite in his mouth. "Mmm. You made this?" He sounds surprised.

"I did. I'm learning to cook."

"I'd say you've learned already. This is some good cake, man." The cabdriver takes another bite. "Mmm mmm mmm."

Ed eats a morsel from the piece left in his hand. It's buttery sweet and melts in his mouth. He'll make a pot of coffee when he gets home. He'll have some cake for supper. Maybe the whole cake. Then he'll take Ginger and Wally their dessert for the week. It's an experiment. Macadamia nut blondies with chocolate sauce. He calls them Million Dollar Bars.

A woman comes up to the cabdriver. "Is that your cab?" She tilts her head at the yellow Chevrolet with black lettering. Her hands are full of brown paper bags from Kroger, which are brimming over with clothes. She has a vase of three pink silk rosebuds tucked under her arm.

"Yes, ma'am." The cabdriver licks the cake crumbs from his fingers. "I'm just having a little cake with my friend here."

"Can you give me a ride to Motel 6?"

"Glad to. Glad to."

"Do you think it will be more than five dollars a trip?"

The cabdriver looks at the paper bags. "You are in luck. Today I'm running a motel ride special. Any motel in town, three dollars one way." The woman lets out a sigh of relief.

The cabdriver tips his hat to Ed. "Thanks for the cake, man. Hope your wife gets better soon." Then he takes one of the lady's brown bags, opens the back door of the cab for the woman, hands her the bag after she pulls her reedy dry legs up and into the cab, and closes the door behind her.

As the cab eases slowly around the pickup rotary in front of the hospital, Ed finishes his lemon pound cake and thinks about Parva Wilson. He remembers her broad bottom hanging in the air over the soles of her sensible shoes and her red glasses on the end of her nose and he laughs. He can't help it. He sits on the concrete bench, alone, eating cake, contemplating his troubles, but he feels lighthearted at the thought of Parva Wilson.

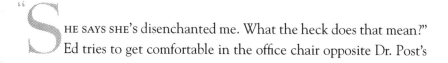

"SHE SAYS SHE's disenchanted me. What the heck does that mean?" Ed tries to get comfortable in the office chair opposite Dr. Post's temporary desk in his temporary office, but it's hopeless. Finally he leans forward and puts his elbows on his knees. "I tried talking to her like you said, but it's like trying to talk to someone who speaks a foreign language. I don't know what the heck she's talking about. She was afraid to eat the cake I made because she thinks I want to cast a spell on her—put a mojo on her with lemon pound cake! Jesus!"

"Ed, Gracie has a disease that keeps her from thinking correctly," Dr. Post says in that comforting voice that makes you feel like he's your best friend.

"That's for damn sure."

"Some schizophrenics have random ideas that pop into their minds with no apparent cohesiveness. Some patients, on the other hand, operate out of a cognitive structure based on a false body of knowledge, and therefore they behave based on a false logic. Some of these constructs can be quite interesting and intricate, almost believable, and very deeply rooted. The patients' behavior is logical and even predictable at times, but only if you consider the parameters of the world they have created in their psyche. Gracie's psychosis seems to be the latter. She reconciles Christianity with fairy lore. While she accepts the hallucinatory direction she believes comes from God or Jesus, she sees herself as queen of the fairies, believes you, in your youth, were the god of the hunt, and that you are now no longer useful to her purposes."

"No longer useful to her purposes? Because I'm not twenty-one? She sure as hell wants me to bring her some car parts to paint. I'm useful for that."

"Ed, try not to take anything personally." Dr. Post drums a pencil on his knee and tries to disguise his intense interest in the world Gracie is creating. "I know that's difficult to do, but Gracie isn't thinking like your wife, she's thinking like the queen of fairies.

"One of our team members presented her with ink blots"—Dr. Post raises his eyebrows and Ed nods that he knows what Dr. Post is referring to—"and Gracie saw fairy wings in every one of them. Not angels wings, mind you. All fairy wings."

"Well, she must think I'm king of the fairies now, since she's afraid I'm going to cast a spell on her with pound cake."

"Paranoia often accompanies schizophrenia. It's a common element of the disease, and it can take various forms. Better for her to be afraid you want to cast a spell with pound cake than for her be afraid you are a Communist spy. It's easy not to eat cake."

"It's all so much to get hold of."

"Ed, you may never get hold of it. Gracie's voices may subside with medication. Right now we're trying Zyprexa. If it doesn't stem the hallucinations and delusions, or she starts to exhibit extreme side effects, then we'll try her on Risperdal. There's a lot of drugs to try. The response to each drug is so individual with each patient. Our goal is to alleviate the symptoms to the point that the patient can have a somewhat normal life, and fit in as much as possible with mainstream society."

Ed gives Dr. Post a look that makes Post shrug. "That's our goal, Ed. Sometimes we hit closer to the mark than others. We just have to wait and see. It's early yet."

"What about the voices she hears?"

"Hallucinations. But it's important to understand that they aren't like the little voices we all carry in our heads. When a schizophrenic hears voices, like Gracie hears them, it is like you hearing my voice. Brain scans indicate that the same chemical reaction and brain activity take place in the schizophrenic's mind that are taking place right now in your brain as you hear and process what I'm saying to you. And that isn't the case if you have a little voice say to you in the grocery store, *Don't buy that coconut cake, your belt's getting too tight.*"

"So she can't tell the difference?"

"Nope."

"But she says they've quit talking to her. That's why she wants the car parts."

"That may be the Zyprexa, and it may be a temporary lull in the hallucinations. It's too early to tell."

"I'm a logical man, Doc. But I don't see this."

"If you are a logical man, think of Gracie's logic as the plot for a sci-fi movie. Things happen in that movie that are impossible in the physical world we're familiar with, but not impossible based on the physics and possibilities laid out for you by the scriptwriter and the special-effects man. That's the kind of world Gracie has stepped into. And while you can't be in the movie, as a viewer, you can understand the logic behind it. And as her meds take hold, some of that may change."

"Where does that leave me?"

"When Gracie's discharged, you'll have to make arrangements for someone to be with her. Your greatest challenge will be to see to it that she takes her medications. Many times, when patients stop hearing the voices, they go through a grieving process and they want to hear them again."

"Even if they understand they're crazy."

"Ed, if someone thinks he might be crazy, chances are very good he isn't. But when someone is suffering from a mental illness, he tends to think he's not. He's usually very sure he's not ill at all. Just a little more off-the-wall logic for you to contemplate. Any other questions?"

"About a million."

"Keep a list, and we'll take them a few at the time. If you have an urgent question, page me."

Later, as Ed's footsteps echo through the hospital parking garage and he mulls over Dr. Post's theory about who's crazy and who's not, Ed takes comfort in thinking he might be losing his mind.

"I SURE APPRECIATE you bringing by that coffee cake," Estelle says and takes a sip of Folgers decaf. "You're turning into a real gourmet cook. You know, if I stand up for more than fifteen minutes, this ankle gets to swelling on me." Estelle tries to find that fine line between needing a little help and being helpless. She never has thought much of women who acted totally helpless. But men don't like a woman to be too self-sufficient. "I haven't had much more than a sandwich in a week."

Ed is standing on a metal chair on Estelle's back porch—a covered deck really—making a screw hole in a crossbeam.

"I figured a little coffee cake would cheer you up. That broken ankle's got to hurt."

"When the boys started making over your cowboy cookies and those scones you brought in the other week, it got to me a little. They've never made over my chocolate chess pie like that."

"Well, it's probably the novelty of me doing the cooking," Ed says as he takes the hook out of his mouth and tucks a screwdriver in his back pocket. "Maybe it's their way of making fun of me. You ever thought about that? You know how they like to rib me."

"Maybe."

"I wouldn't take it so personal, Estelle. You make a mighty good chocolate chess pie. I'd like to get the recipe."

"And have them make more over your pie than mine? I don't think so."

"You can do like my Great-Aunt Rosie did, sabotage the recipe."

"What do you mean?"

"My mama used to say that Rosie would leave something important out of a recipe or add something that would make it taste bad or just not quite right. That way her version of something always tasted the best."

"Rosie sounds like an interesting woman."

"Think that if you want to, but everybody in my family, including my mama, called her an old bitch."

"Well, if you think she's a bitch, I'll just stick to my original plan and keep my recipes to myself," Estelle says playfully. This is the best conversation with Ed she has ever had. He is so relaxed and looks perfect doing her honey-do's out on the deck. She'll have to think of some other little fix-it jobs for him to do.

"I cook so much I can't eat it all. Taking food to folks gets me out of the house. If you like, I'll bring a casserole over tonight so you won't have to eat a sandwich for supper."

"You're just a doll. You'll stay and have supper with me, won't you?"

"I guess I can do that. I'll make a little run to the store and you can keep me company while I make you a few dishes you can eat off of for the week. I'm experimenting with some recipes that make the most of your larder."

"Your what?"

"Your pantry, what you've got on hand. We'll just have to get your pantry stocked with the right things. Easy meals for a game leg."

Estelle holds up her leg, "Does this look game, or gam?"

Ed fumbles with the screwdriver and almost drops it.

"How is Gracie these days?" Estelle has to ask this even though she knows the answer. She talks to Ginger regularly to get the latest on this *crazy* soap opera. That's how she refers to the situation to everyone but Ed and his family.

"She's doing as well as can be expected, according to Dr. Warner and Dr. Post. They're her psychiatrists. Nice fellows. Real down-to-earth, except for those clogs Dr. Warner wears."

"What?"

"Clogs. You know, them slip-on shoes like Dutch people wear."

"He's a man? Wearing clogs?"

"Yeah. But he's not funny or anything. Not ha-ha funny. You know." Ed flops his hand from his wrist. "He's not like that. He's trying a new medication this week to see if Gracie's voices will go away. They've told her she's queen of the fairies."

"Who has?"

"The voices." Ed reaches his hand down to Estelle. "Okay. Hand me that thing you want up here."

"Ed, it's a wind chime. Don't you know what that is?"

"I know what they are. I can't stand the blamed things."

"Are you sure that guy's not funny?" Estelle says.

"Well, I haven't asked him outright, but once you get past the clogs he seems normal to me. He's got an accent too. That might be why he wears clogs. I think he's German. Maybe I'll make him an apple strudel and take it to him on group night. I bet he gets homesick."

Estelle stares at Ed from her comfortable chaise longue. She takes a bite of coffee cake. It's so good. He never cooked before. Never cared if anybody was homesick before. But then, he never would have come over and done a little fix-it job like this before either, so maybe Estelle shouldn't look a gift horse in the mouth.

"Why in the world do you hate wind chimes? They're so soothing. Very oriental, I think. And New Age."

"All that tinkling gets on my nerves. That's all."

"I love the sound of them tinkling. Like having little angel voices whispering to you when the wind blows. What's wrong with that?"

"If you like them, that's fine for you. Have all of them you want, my dear. By the way, how did you break your ankle?"

Dear. Estelle closes in on that one word. He called her *dear.* Estelle will take down the wind chime in the bedroom window, just in case.

"Estelle, did you hear me?" Ed looks down at Estelle. "How'd you break your ankle?"

"What? Oh. Standing on a chair just like that trying to hang my wind chime."

GINGER KNOWS she should have waited to see her mama the day she was committed. She knows the nurse was sitting there watching the dayroom while Ginger was in there, seemingly alone, with Clarence and Violet. She knows that Clarence and Violet would probably not hurt her. But in defense of her instincts, she did hear from an orderly that before Violet was sufficiently medicated she hit another patient with a full, unopened Coke can from the drink machine beside the refrigerator that has all the free juice in it. So Ginger was justified in being uncomfortable in the dayroom without apparent supervision, even though she now knows that someone is always watching what is going on. If not the nurses, then interns or medical students or psychiatric residents or social workers. There is an army of watchers in Four North, hiding behind two-way mirrors or water fountains or patient charts or out in the open pretending to be distracted or occupied, but always watching. Ginger hopes she is never a patient in a psychiatric ward. She hopes she is never watched in that way. She doesn't even like being watched now as a visitor—a family member. *Are you a family member?* a disembodied voice says when she comes to the small window by the elevator and pushes the buzzer for them to let her in. "Yes," she says. But what she's thinking is, *Unfortunately, yes.*

"That word, schizophrenia, makes me think of plants, the Latin name for plants," Ginger says to Dr. Warner during her therapy session.

"And why is that, Ginger?" Dr. Warner says as he writes in his notebook. Ginger understands that the chart or the notebook or whatever Dr. Warner has in his hands at the moment he first meets someone is his barrier. He's not comfortable with initial contact, not comfortable with the intimate nature of his work.

"You can make a dandelion sound aristocratic, or you can make poison ivy sound poetic. But a dandelion is still a weed and poison ivy can still make you need shots and steroids and messy paste to stop the itch and heal the skin. Sitting here, thinking about Mama, I know that pretty word, schizophrenic, is nothing but a dressed-up way to say she is off her damn rocker. And where does that leave me?"

Since the family's introduction to Four North, Ginger has been offered psychiatric intervention and been invited to the family support group meetings. This has in some ways been helpful. She has been seeing Dr. Warner every Tuesday for the last four weeks, and he is drop-dead gorgeous. Ginger keeps having fantasies about him giving her off-site therapy. It took her a while to get over the clogs. But she understands the off-site sessions are just her fantasies. At this point, unlike her mama, she has a handle on what is real and what is just a little thought floating around in her head. She has fantasies about Chad Everett when she sees reruns of *Medical Center*, too. But she's not going to leave Wally and go off to California just to fulfill a fantasy. The question is, how long will she know the difference?

"Ginger, schizophrenia develops at an early age."

"I'm twenty-eight. Do I qualify?"

"Usually it's late adolescence or early twenties," Dr. Warner says, a little frustrated that he cannot get Ginger off this train of thought. "I think you would have shown signs of it by now."

"Hello. My mother didn't show signs of it until last Easter, the day she drew three Jesuses all over the house and ran away like a ten-year-old. By my count, she's fifty years old."

"I suspect she exhibited symptoms that went unnoticed."

"How can you miss schizophrenia? Tell me, how can you miss your mother thinking she's queen of the fucking fairies? Tell me that."

"Your father said that your mother was always a little different, correct?"

"There's different, and there's divergent. I think we would have noticed." Ginger crosses her arms and her legs and shifts to one side in her seat.

Dr. Warner crosses his legs and lets his clog dangle from the toes of his bouncing foot. "Admittedly, there have been some cases where the disorder appears later in life, but these are rare, and there may be an undocumented history of bipolar disorder that predates the onset of the schizophrenia."

"Is that supposed to make me feel better? What does that tell you, with or without your degree in psychiatry? It tells you that I could still be screwed. That's what it tells me." *That I could find myself one day being watched.* "And they could be asking Wally, 'Are you family?' And what will he say? We aren't married. And what if he isn't going to want to get married just in case I end up like Mama? What then? Will they let him in Four North based on a previous intention to marry me?"

"Anyone can visit someone on the ward unless there is a specific reason for him not to at the time, but I think we are getting ahead of ourselves here."

"Will Wally even want to see me if I go nutty as a loon? It sure took Daddy long enough to get here. And he's been late several times since. That's not like my daddy. He's always punctual."

"Your father must deal with the situation as best he can. Just like you must learn to deal with your mother's illness, find a place for it, a way to live with it and around it. It takes some people more time than others to accommodate the change that comes with this kind of traumatic family event."

"Do you have that paragraph memorized?"

"Why do you think you are being so hostile at this moment?"

Ginger refuses to answer and sits wondering how much effort it takes for her daddy to come to Four North. She hates it, hates coming to see her mama here. She doesn't really mind visiting with Clarence or Violet now. Clarence reads her vortexes and Violet gives her a new strand of beads every time she sees her. Violet believes they have magical powers. Ginger figures they can't hurt. But her mama, it's hard to come visit her, to look at that Rachel woman and wonder where her mama went. *Where's she hiding? Where has this new mama, this queen of the fairies, been lurking all my life? All her life?* Ginger wonders that a lot.

"I wonder what will keep me anchored to this world."

"This isn't about one's personal will, Ginger."

"How do you know? But I already know that answer."

"What do you mean?"

"Wally is solid as a rock. He can keep me from drifting away."

"A ballast," Dr. Warner calls him, with an insightful look on his face, his eyebrows up in high thick blond arches. His eyebrows are quite bushy for a man so young.

"A ballast? Is that a medical term like schizophrenia?"

"No, nautical or aerial maybe. I think of it in terms of balloons. Hot air balloons, but ships have them too."

That confuses Ginger because balloons drift off up into the sky and boats float, and that doesn't anchor anything to the earth. But she doesn't want to sound stupid, so she nods like he has said the most interesting thing.

On the drive home, Ginger thinks about the education she has gotten in just a few weeks. It's important when dealing with doctors of any kind that you seem interested in whatever they have to say. If you do, you might keep them talking to you long enough for them to say something you can use, or better yet, really understand. This skill is particularly important when working with psychiatrists, certainly the young ones. They are so enthusiastic about all the new words they learn and the new drugs they can prescribe. It makes them heady in ways that are not always transferable or translatable to those who are *family*.

As to Wally, she's always known he was good for her. My *ballast*, she now knows to call him. Even though when she met him, she thought he was a compromise.

Ginger always pictured her ideal man being tall, broad-shouldered, built like that baseball player Steve Garvey. Good forearms, tight butt. But Wally is skinny as can be. A strong wind could take him a mile down the road before she could look away and look back. We're talking spindly. And he wears thick glasses. But they are those round wire rims that look so GQ. He has the most beautiful long blond curls—like her daddy used to have, according to her mama—that fall down his back in a cascade like some ad out of *Hairstyle Magazine*. A woman would kill for Wally's hair. But the thing that did it for her was his socks and those black-and-white saddle oxfords. That's how she knows Wally will keep her sane. Because he is only *crazy* in one area of his life—his socks and shoes.

Wally has this amazing sense of rhythm that permeates everything he does, from selling tires at Tire Man, to walking in the door at five-thirty with his lunch box on his head, to dancing her back to the bedroom on Saturday afternoon after *The Million Dollar Movie*. He conveys way more than 150 pounds of lanky body and thick glasses. And after going to bed with him, she can honestly say that when that man isn't wearing his glasses, he finds other ways to witness what is in front of him. God knows how loud she would moan if he was totally blind.

In the afternoons, after he changes out of his Tire Man getup, he sits down to play drums while Ginger fixes supper. She peeks around the corner and sees him beat out some song on the drums, those long legs folded practically in half so he can sit on his little stool, bony knees sticking up like bent heads of bobby pins. Those crazy socks ride out from the legs of his jeans, whatever pattern of socks he has picked for the evening. Ginger can't help moving in a different way while she peels the potatoes or skins the chicken legs or layers the lasagna. She thinks about those ankles full of Winnie the Pooh or Sylvester and Tweety or cowboys on bucking broncos. Good Lord at the socks that man has.

He doesn't just hold her down, *ballast* her. He moves her, moves her past whatever could pull her under. His feet twist on the balls of his black-and-white saddle oxfords, his drumming shoes, and the heels of his feet pump up and down. He does it all at the same time, moves her, anchors her, and all the while his little purple-and-white-spotted socks, or maybe the ones with snowmen on them, or those fuchsia ones with streaks of lightning, those socks flashing like neon lights out from under the hem of his pants draw her like beacons, like homing signals. He dances while he sits on his little stool behind his big drums, dances with his hands and his sticks and his feet and his socks in the sexiest way.

Ginger never danced before she met Wally. But every night, now that they live together in this little house in the country, out far enough so that his drums don't incite the neighbors, he plays the drum part to "Pretty Woman," or "You Ain't Nothin but a Hound Dog," or "Run to Me," and Ginger is herself more than any other time of the day. With every beat her battery gets charged, her mind gets revived, her hips come alive, her arms feel electric, her cooking spoons start tapping. She cuts onions with the beat of the drums he plays. She opens herself up. She moves like she means it, not like she's lost it. She is the receiver for the message he sends out. It comes around the corner, across the breakfast bar, into the very vibration of her lungs and her heart and her potato peeler. When they finally watch the eleven o'clock news and then turn in, the beat of Wally, not just his drums, never stops moving her, even when her hips are still and her arms are under the pillows and she is asleep and dreaming. Even now, as she lies spooned with Wally, as she drifts off to sleep thinking about her therapy session with Dr. Warner, as she dreams of her mama and Clarence and Violet coming for her—she dreams about them all the time—she dreams they are coming for her like they mean to take her away.

ESTELLE SITS at the end of her green-and-navy Scotch plaid sofa. Her house is neat and spotless, even though she smokes a pack a day of Virginia Slims Menthols. She picks one room a month and washes it from top to bottom to make sure no nicotine residue lingers on the wallpaper or knickknacks. She washes every baseboard, door, picture frame, window, mirror. One room a month. If it can be washed, she washes it. If it can be aired out, she airs it. She steam cleans the carpet and any heavy fabrics—drapes, upholstery, and lampshades. If it's too heavy to do herself, she hires it out to Moss's Cleaners in spring and fall. Every Saturday morning, unless it rains, when Estelle gets up, her windows come up and the fan comes on, even in winter. The windows stay up until noon to let the fresh air in and the stale air out.

All items in Estelle's kitchen are sealed up. She has enough Tupperware to start her own warehouse, everything from a lettuce keeper to a cupcake saver. The thought of a mouse in her food makes her sick to her stomach, so she makes sure they have no reason to be in her house. She refuses to have any pets because she doesn't want to deal with cat hair, dog slobber, or bird do. Fish die too easy and a tank would just be one more thing to clean.

It is Saturday and Estelle has just closed the windows. The den is fresh with outside air and the smell of her roses. She is wearing jeans and a man's Fruit of the Loom T-shirt. Her white leather Reeboks are still as white as when they were new, and her tennis socks have little yellow balls on the backs. She should be wearing her elastic ankle brace, but her ankle doesn't hurt much and the brace is too tight. She wears only light makeup and lip balm. She stays away from lipstick when she's home by herself because she read once that lipstick fades your natural lip color.

Saturdays after she closes the windows, she reads, usually historical romances, occasionally a mystery. They are almost always from the library. Once in a blue moon she buys a book at the grocery or drugstore. After she buys a book and reads it, she takes it to Goodwill. She doesn't like to have too many books sitting around. They just collect dust or fill up the closet. Today she has a stack of three mysteries from the library, all women authors. She prefers women authors. She is about to pick the one on top. A cup of fresh black coffee sits beside the books, heat still rising from it. Two butter cookies, her daily limit, sit beside the coffee on a cocktail napkin. She settles in, takes a sip from her cup, and opens the book, an Agatha Raisin mystery about a woman who stumbles into adventure one book after another. So far Estelle has read three books about Agatha Raisin, in order of their publication. One thing she hates to do is backtrack.

Just as Estelle gets to the end of the first paragraph on page one, the phone rings. Estelle knows it's Ginger. She calls about this time each day to give Estelle a report on the situation. Ginger doesn't know she's giving a report exactly, she is just talking to Estelle because she doesn't have anyone else to talk to about what bothers her. Ed doesn't want to talk about anything personal. Never has. She won't talk to Wally because she is afraid he may get the idea that insanity is hereditary, which Ginger says it can be, and he may back out of their relationship before she goes *crazy*. Estelle eagerly takes on the role of Ginger's confidante. It gets her inside the loop and she is always hopeful that some piece of information will give her an edge with Ed. God knows she has loved him long enough. It is about time she got a chance.

It isn't like she hasn't had chances with other men. But from the first time she walked in Tire Man, Estelle could not get Ed out of her romantic sights. Every hero she reads about is Ed, every heroine is Estelle. Every touch, every kiss she reads about or sees in a movie is the one Estelle has waited on for twenty years. That's why all her dates end up platonic friends. Movie, dinner, a quick hug good night. She never hugs too long. At first it's Estelle who pushes them away at the count of two. After a while they know the count themselves and they seldom come inside after the evening out is over. If they do, it's to talk about some other woman they're interested in. Estelle is jealous, of course, but doesn't show it because, after all, it was initially her decision to pass up the offers of deeper affection.

Estelle has concluded that a single woman doesn't need a man. Not if you have a well developed Rolodex of skilled service providers. What skill you don't have you can pay for. And in the end, you save. A single woman may want a man, but all she needs is a darn good Rolodex. Estelle works hard to keep that subtle difference in mind, keep the phone numbers up-to-date.

Ginger starts in as usual. Tells Estelle the latest on Gracie's hospital activities, what Dr. Warner's said most recently. Talks about how bad Gracie wants to go back where she was, with those black people. Estelle hopes Gracie gets her way. Ginger moves on to Ed and how he's doing from her point of view. Estelle has her own take on that. She's mightily encouraged by his bringing over that coffee cake and staying to hang her chimes. He must be lonely and needing some attention for him to do that. Such tendencies are in Estelle's favor. The conversations with Ginger always end by Estelle reassuring Ginger that she has not noticed a single sign or symptom of mental instability in her for as long as she has known her, which has been almost all of Ginger's life. Ginger says good-bye and Estelle is hanging up when she hears Ginger's voice.

"Wait! Oh, I almost forgot! Estelle, are you still there?"

"What?" Estelle says as she puts the receiver back to her ear.

"Daddy has gone absolutely ape over wind chimes! I didn't tell you that, did I? He must have twenty of them hanging around the house. More out on the porches. Even one in his bathroom."

"What do you mean? He told me he hated wind chimes."

Estelle reaches for her cigarette case and pinches it open. It's red calfskin. She's partial to rich colors. But more than that, she loves the way the red case feels and the way it feels to inhale the Virginia Slim she draws from it.

"Well, he must like them now. I asked him what he was thinking of, hanging so many at one time. He said he was just trying them out. Mumbled something about another experiment. Don't you think that's weird? I mean, first this whole cooking gig, now the wind chimes. I'm starting to think Mama's not the only one losing a grip. Do you think this is a bad sign?"

"No." Estelle's mind is racing. "I wouldn't worry about it. It's just a little something to distract your daddy from what's really bothering him. He's never been one to deal with a problem head on, unless it was directly related to a machine, preferably with a gasoline engine."

"Well, if you're sure. I'd hate to have to commit both of my parents, especially at the same time. That's too much."

"If it will make you feel any better, I'll stop by his place and check on him when I go to the grocery store. He may just need a little company. How's that?"

"Thank you, Estelle. You're such a good person."

Estelle puts the Agatha Raisin mystery back on the top of the stack, kicks the ottoman out of her way, and picks up her coffee cup. She can drink her brew in the bathroom while she puts on a little more makeup. An experiment, huh? Maybe he's trying them out to see if he can get used to them for her sake. Maybe it's his way of trying Estelle out before he makes his move. Well then, the least she can do is meet him halfway. She'll stop by the drugstore for her Zoloft refill and pick up a set of wind chimes for a present. If he has a bunch of them in this short a time, he must have decided he likes them. And there's no sense in letting his experiment go to waste.

Estelle spritzes her hair, runs the tip of her new lipstick, Caramel Passion, around her lips and blots with a Kleenex. She squirts a mist of Amarige toward the door and walks through it, covering her coffee with her free hand. She won't change clothes. Her jeans and T-shirt make the visit seem impromptu. She's almost out the door when she thinks of something. She can't mention Ginger's call, so how else can she know about the chimes? Maybe she shouldn't take him any chimes. But what's her reason for dropping by? She can give him something he already wants.

She picks up the phone to make sure he's home. She gets the answering machine. "Hello, Ed. Estelle here. Just checking in to see how you are. Give me a call."

Well fine. She won't go by today. But she'll go at some point. And when the opportunity presents itself, she'll be ready. Estelle goes back to the kitchen, opens her recipe drawer, and pulls out a rubber-banded stack of index cards, all desserts. She finds a blank recipe card and a pen, sits at the kitchen table, and takes a sip of her warm coffee. She shuffles the now unbanded cards until she comes to the one she wants, chocolate chess pie. She looks at the card, bites at her pen, then quickly copies down the recipe in her most elegant penmanship. It's all there, repeated line for line and word for word—except for that one little change. Just a small adjustment. It won't make that big a difference. There's one thing Estelle knows, and Rosie knew it too. You have to hold something back for yourself. There are some cards you just never put on the table.

E D THROWS THE MAIL on the polyurethaned tabletop, fixes a glass of iced tea, and plunges his hand into a large bag of Lays. He's left the door open so the chimes will tinkle in the wind. Ed has taken to hanging them directly from the ceiling.

It's early October and this is likely the last warm spell of the year. The temperature is predicted to drop in the next twenty-four hours, but for now, a thunderstorm brews, probably because Ed washed and waxed the Adventurer that very morning. It felt good to slide the rag over her pretty lines, to polish her chrome, to feel the big wheel in his hands. What happened to cars and trucks? How did they get so boring, so artless? Ed misses chrome, big wheels, three-on-the-tree, taillights shaped like tits, the rich and shapely creases in metal bodies, the sheer weight of the things, and those little wing windows, like the ones on the Adventurer. He has kept her in mint condition since the day his father handed him the keys. Protected her paint job, safeguarded her upholstery, limited her mileage. But Wally's right. She's had no life. Maybe he'll drive her a little. Take her out for a spin once a week. Ed needs something to jolt him out of his slump. He needs more than cooking and scavenging car parts.

The wind whips at the many chiming tendrils above. There are ten in the kitchen alone. The ceramic frog chime has ten ceramic tadpoles that tinkle together. The whole thing is green, which bothers Ed because tadpoles are black. One chime is simply aluminum tubing hung from a circle of pine board. His favorite is the large chime with the copper butterfly at the top. It hangs down so long that Ed can brush it with the top of his head and make it whisper. A collection of painted balsa wood animals hang from an ark. They don't tinkle. They clack, a nice change from metal on metal. Ed is impressed by the creative variety represented in his collection. He thinks about going to Raleigh to see what chimes he can find there, but the truth is, he has more important business to deal with first.

He feels guilty about not going to the hospital that first day, about leaving it to Ginger. He made a flimsy excuse about the heater core in the Toyota leaking, but his heater core was fine. He's tried to be regular in his visits since he made that first try at giving Gracie the lemon pound cake. Yesterday, he tried cherry pie. She always loved cherry pie. Of course she didn't bite, didn't want to eat anything he offered her. The nursing staff on Four North was appreciative, though, and gave him the clean empty pie plate before he left the ward.

Ed decides to take a short nap before cooking supper and cracks the bedroom window to let the breeze blow through. A painted metal mermaid dangles from the ceiling over his bed, her smaller daughters gliding in the current directly beneath her. He stretches out and focuses on the mermaids swimming in circles, occasionally nudging each other like bumper boats, the mother mermaid's breast full and weighty, her wavy red hair flowing out behind her. She is only a molded tin half-woman swimming over his head, but she is all he can face. He doesn't want to look at Jesus. He's mad at Him. He doesn't want to think about Gracie because it is more complex than he knows what to do with. He doesn't want to think about Ginger because he's letting her down. He's afraid to think about Parva because his heart will break.

He wants to go to Parva, not Gracie. Explain everything. Make her understand how much he needs her. Take her a nice lasagna and a bottle of Chianti and talk things out. He's always avoided problems with Gracie, but he wants to face his problems with Parva. His eyelids grow heavy as he watches mermaids breaststroke around in the air. He wants to reach Parva. But as hard as he swims, harder than the big-bosomed fish women above him, stroke after stroke after stroke, he can't get through Gracie to get to Parva. But he will. He will take them in order. He is going to return Dr. Warner's call and set up another appointment. He will go with Ginger to a few family support meetings and wade through what they have to say. He will swim steadily into and through Gracie and eventually reach what he has lost on the other side. He strokes and strokes into sleep, each imagined sweep of his arms matching his throbbing sorrow.

When Ed wakes up a little while later, he stares at Jesus with open arms. "You started this. Now I'm asking You to help me fix it." Jesus looks back at Ed with the same poker face He's had for going on six months. He isn't revealing anything.

"Daggone it!" Ed says, getting up out of the bed. "I'm listening to blasted wind chimes and talking to the walls!"

Supper is not a beautiful presentation of gourmet fare. It's a bologna sandwich and tomato soup. More chips. Ed puts the tomato soup in a microwavable bowl and sets the timer. The whir begins at just the moment the first bolt of lightning divides the sky and a clap of thunder follows instantaneously. Ed's heart drops a few inches and springs up. The microwave keeps going. The wind picks up and the chimes sing and dance.

In the dim light of the storm, his heart calms and he reaches for the mail: electric bill, MasterCard bill, renewal for *Gourmet* magazine, a flyer for a missing child. For a moment, Ed wishes it is the child who has been found instead of Gracie. But shame overtakes selfishness. Ed has not prayed for much in recent years. But he stares out the window, afraid, the mail in his hands, and prays for that child. Then he prays for himself while the wind grows stronger and the chimes sing louder and louder, their swinging jumble becoming wilder and wilder, their plastic filaments and thin copper chains and polished cotton strings becoming more and more tangled. The wind dies down abruptly and the chimes slow to a clinking mumble.

In the relative quiet, Ed's attention returns to the mail. There, in the upper left hand corner of the last envelope, he sees the words Sinfully Chocolate Sweepstakes. Below that, *Cooking with Bernard*. Ed sits down at the table and holds up the cream-colored envelope with chocolate brown lettering, sees his own name and Chef Bernard's on the same piece of paper. His throat is tight, his palms are sweating. He lets the fluttering song of the wind chimes move through him, ease him into a lighter, more peaceful place. Then he tears open the narrow end of the envelope and blows into it. When he turns it up and shakes, a single piece of cream-colored paper falls out into his waiting hand. He unfolds it, reads it, and feels the knot grow in his throat. His eyes brim with tears, and for a moment he tries to blink them away, but they spill and run in two narrow streams down his cheeks. He cries so hard he pulls his handkerchief from his back pocket and holds it to his face with both hands. He cries because the chimes are all tangled and he'll have to untangle them, every last one of them. He cries for all the people he should pray for. He cries for the Jesuses on the walls throughout his house—for Jesus with the open arms, and Jesus knocking at the front door, and Jesus praying at the rock over the sideboard. Ed cries because his wife thinks she is queen of the fairies and the woman he loves is just beyond his reach. He cries because his Kahlúa Chocolate Cake with Pecans has won the Sinfully Chocolate Sweepstakes. He cries because, in his own personal note at the bottom of the letter, Chef Bernard wants to know what other original recipes Ed has to share, if there might be a cookbook lurking in his recipe box. He cries because Chef Bernard's assistant, Bonnie King, will call him to make arrangements for two round-trip tickets to New York City to be on Chef Bernard's show. And Ed cries because he knows he's going to have to go it alone.

SHARON UNDERWOOD hangs around the nurses' station waiting for Doris, at least she used to be Doris, Doris Bryan, first Sharon's college roommate at Cal Arts, then a struggling artist. But now Doris Bryan is Madam Bernadette Seniese. When Doris moved to New York after college, she decided to use her middle name and the last name of her first husband, a name she hasn't given up through two subsequent marriages. "The name is just too perfect for what I do," Doris told Sharon on the eve of her second wedding. "I'm hanging on to it."

Madam Bernadette Seniese is the successful owner of an outsider art gallery in Atlanta, Georgia. Once Sharon began to understand the level of Gracie's talent and its potential appeal, she called Bernadette, and asked if she wanted to get a look. Today turned out to be the perfect day. Madam Bernadette can see Gracie's work, and if she gets to the hospital on time, she can see Gracie in action.

At one o'clock sharp a woman in black tights, a leopard print tunic, and large hoop earrings passes the window. Sharon is looking at a chart and misses her, but she hears the door jiggle. Then a pixie appears in the visitor window, round face, big brown eyes framed in thick liner, a tiny turned-up nose, red lips, inch-long blue-black hair so popular with the avant-garde. Sharon envies Bernadette, who is perpetually cute. When Bernadette turns seventy-five she will still be cute, will still look good in Barbie clothes, and will still be successful.

"Sharon! I'm so glad to see you!" she screams in the shrill little voice she uses when she gets truly excited.

"I'll buzz you in," Sharon says, trying to match the excitement, but with a more quiet voice. "Pull the door when you hear it." Sharon hits the button and Bernadette Seniese bounces into the psychiatric ward looking like a cross between Jane of the jungle and Peter Pan. But beneath that sweet cheerleader personality beats the heart of a shrewd businesswoman. Sharon knows she will have to protect Gracie's interests, even from her friend.

"God, you look great! I'm so glad to see you!" Bernadette trills and throws her arms around Sharon, who returns the embrace. It's a love-hate relationship for Sharon, but mostly it's love.

"You are the one who looks great." Sharon pushes Bernadette back by the shoulders so she can get a better look. "You've cut off all your hair. You look like a sexy puck."

"Is there such a thing? Listen, before we go any farther, can we go to K&W for dinner? You didn't cook anything, did you?"

"Me, are you kidding? I knew you'd want to go to the cafeteria."

"Great!" When she can remove the Bernadette guise, she is still Doris Bryan through and through.

"Fine, but you can't go eat until you've seen my star patient," Sharon says.

"Fabulous. I'm so excited after talking with you. Where is she?"

"Right this way."

Sharon leads Bernadette to the door of the art therapy room. As they get closer to the heavy metal door with the thick wired-glass window in the center, the two women hear shouting. Several people are chanting *George! George! George!*

"Now when you meet her, I'm going to introduce her to you as Rachel. Part of her psychotic construct includes a name change."

"Do you think that's my problem?"

"Probably."

Sharon opens the door and the chanting gets significantly louder. *George! George! George!*

A petite woman stands at the wall, her long red hair in a knot at the nape of her neck. A rainbow of pastels lies on the little table behind her. She is halfway across the long wall, drawing a mural as she goes. She finishes a drawing of George Washington and then turns to the crowd with her arms extended, as if to say *Come unto me.* Or maybe, *What now?*

"George Jones!" cries Nurse Mary. Immediately the small woman turns back to the wall and begins sketching a caricature of the country western singer, complete with rhinestone jacket and molded hair and sideburns. It is amazing. Before George Jones, Rachel has drawn George Washington, Babe (George) Ruth, King George III, George Harrison, George Brett, and Boy George. In a few minutes George Jones is on the wall, frozen in mournful, lonesome song. A few people from CCU and neonatal ICU have come by on their lunch break to see Gracie draw. Rumors of the mural event have spread like wildfire through the snack room and smoking area. Some of the hospital administrators stand around the room. All are chiming in. *George! George! George!*

"George Washington Carver!" yells Clarence. Rachel sketches out George Washington Carver holding a jar of Jif peanut butter.

"George Hamilton!" yells Herb. Rachel colors in a suntanned man with sunglasses, full lips spread into a toothy grin, and lots of gold jewelry.

"George Burns!" shouts Dr. Post. In minutes Rachel has drawn George Burns smoking his cigar. All the drawings are colorful, and each naively drawn character is fully recognizable in a funny way. Gracie's use of color is excellent for the market Bernadette deals in.

"Curious George," Frank says in his usual understated way. Up goes Curious George *and* the man in the yellow hat—who looks a little bit like Frank.

"George Wallace," says Nurse Valerie, from cardiac ICU. Everyone in the room turns to look at her. "Well," she shrugs, "he's the only other George I could think of. No, wait, George Clooney." By the time everyone turns back around to face Rachel, she has drawn the outline of George Wallace in his wheelchair. In a seamless motion she goes from an emasculated George Wallace to a debonair George Clooney with his signature impish smile.

"George Jetson," sings out Dr. Post again.

"George of the Jungle," calls Heather. Rachel draws George Jetson in his flying-saucer car, then she moves on to tall trees and draping vines and a cartoon hunk of a man in a loincloth flinging himself into the wall that is now her canvas.

"Sweet Georgia Brown!" calls Herb. From a handful of pastels, Rachel creates a beautiful buxom woman filling and spilling out of a low-cut dress.

"George Foreman!" yells Dr. Warner, uncharacteristically spellbound by the spectacle of it all. Without pausing, Rachel begins drawing a fine young boxer, gloves up.

"Blinking George Johnston!" says Anthony. At this, Madame Seniese witnesses what she does not know is akin to a miracle. She sees everyone stop shouting and turn to look at a young man in a wheelchair. He is bald. He wears blue-and-white-striped pajamas and a dark green flannel robe. He is bouncing up and down in his wheelchair, his one-sided smile wrapping around and pushing out the clumsy words. He is shouting in his now lone voice, "George! George! George!" His eyes are blinking wildly.

When Bernadette turns back to the wall, Rachel is sketching the same young man, only in the drawing, he has dark-rimmed glasses and his eyes are wide open.

"I'm sold. What else do you have?"

"I hear she paints car parts."

"Fabulous," Bernadette whispers. "Absolutely fabulous."

SUFFICIENT GRACE

There is no such way to attain to greater measure of grace as for a man to live up to the little grace he has.

—Phillip Brooks

E D SHIFTS in his seat and fiddles with a napkin holder. The chimes whisper across the kitchen and throughout the house.

"I'm out of coffee. Would you like some iced tea, or hot tea? I can make hot tea."

Parva rubs her hands together. "Hot tea sounds very nice. I've got a chill today, what with this rain. It's so wet." *Of course it's wet, you idiot! But it isn't just the rain.* She realizes there's no heat in the house. "I wondered if I would even get here. There may be flooding. That's what they're saying on the radio."

Her sweater's embroidered with fall leaves. She's wearing hiking boots. It occurs to Ed he's never seen her in jeans before. He can't picture her hiking.

Parva stares up at the dozens of wind chimes. They hang from the ceiling, the window frames, the doorways. They rattle on from the kitchen into the hall and dining room and beyond, whirling and fluttering softly, their movement connected by a slight draft.

"So, do you like to hike?" Ed says, grabbing at any source of conversation.

"Do I look like I hike?" She pats her ample thighs and smiles. "I'd like to if I could find someone who walked slow enough for me to keep up, and who would stop every now and again so I could just stand and breathe for a while. Do you know any hikers like that?"

"I'm sure you can find someone to do that," Ed says. Then he feels awful because Parva looks up at the ceiling and around the room without responding. She has taken his comment the wrong way and he doesn't know how to repair the damage.

"I imagine you have a concert when the wind blows," she says.

"What? Oh, the chimes. Yeah. It gets pretty noisy. Sometimes I can hardly think." Ed wishes that were true as he fills the yellow teakettle with water and sets it on the range. "I made some macaroons yesterday. You want a few macaroons with your tea?"

"I love anything with coconut in it." Parva looks at Jesus in the garden and wonders what he and his brother Jesuses have to do with the wind chimes.

Ed places the cookies on a small platter. He likes the sound of the word. He listens to it over and over in his head. *Macaroon. Macaroon. Macaroon.* He has been thinking more and more about the sound of words. About what it means to hear. He'll pick a word out of the dictionary and say it over and over and over until it doesn't sound like it means anything anymore. Even with the dictionary's definition staring back at him, the word means nothing. He repeats the word until it doesn't even sound like a word at all. Just hard and soft utterances made by a moving valve with air flowing through it. *Wife. Wife. Wife. Wife.* He says the word over and over in his head until it sounds like the noise a fan makes when it whips at summer air coming through the window at Ginger and Wally's.

"I'm sorry about the way things ended the last time we saw each other," Ed says as he puts a small platter of macaroons on the table. He knows he's stumbling. "I feel terrible." He doesn't look at Parva, only at the platter.

"I thought I would hear from you."

"I didn't think you'd want to. I told you I lived alone, and then my wife shows up."

Parva smooths her hands across the woven place mat in front of her. "You never said you were divorced or widowed, Ed. I chose to interpret your vague statement about living alone in a way that pleased me. Single women have a way of doing that, making vague statements mean what they would like them to mean." Parva shivers and rubs her hands up and down her arms.

"You're cold. Let me turn on the heat." Ed goes into the hallway for a moment and returns to the table. "I have a little woodstove in the den." The furnace kicks on and Ed glances at the teakettle. "When the water boils we can fix tea and go in there by the stove if you want to."

"That sounds nice. It is a little chilly. Of course if you'd rather I didn't stay, I could . . ."

"No," Ed is intensely aware of his arms and legs and the pit of his stomach. "Please stay. I want to explain the situation. I owe you that much." Ed rubs his face with his hands. "God, it sounds like I'm going to tell you why you didn't get a bank loan."

"Nonsense." Parva waves her hand at something invisible. "When I didn't hear from you, I assumed you wanted to be with your wife. That your life was, you know, back to normal." *Is that why you called to see if there was a good time to give him his birthday present almost six months early?* "I assumed what wasn't working before was working again." *Then why are you here ready to drink hot tea and eat macaroons?*

"First of all, I don't have the foggiest idea of what normal is anymore," Ed says. He puts his hands in his pants pockets and jiggles the contents. Some change. A pocketknife. Some fishing sinkers.

"Well, I mean I assumed you and your wife are together again."

"I don't know what that means either," Ed says. *Marriage. Marriage. Marriage.* He repeats the word over and over in his head until it sounds more like *mirage. Mirage. Mirage. Mirage.* Then even *mirage* loses its meaning.

Ed looks out the window as he waits for the kettle to whistle and sees that the side yard is now a big water hole. The grass is submerged and the water in the street is rushing almost level with the curb. "God, it really is flooding."

"They've canceled school today because of it. The weatherman says not to expect it to let up until tomorrow afternoon."

"You shouldn't be out in this mess." Ed tries not to sound fatherly. He tries to sound grateful. He sounds neither.

Parva looks down at the macaroons and is reminded of her reason for visiting, at least the one she mentioned to Ed on the phone.

"Here, I have a little something for you. It is your birthday present. A little early, I know, but I've had it since before we last saw each other. I was waiting for your birthday to roll around, and with all that's happened, well, I figured I might as well go ahead and give it to you. It has your name in it and it should be yours. When I saw in the paper that you won the Sinfully Chocolate Sweepstakes, I realized it was a good reason to give you a gift. To celebrate your good fortune. So here you go. It already had the birthday paper on it." *And I was afraid I'd lose my nerve if I waited to rewrap it.*

Parva forces herself to stop babbling and scoots the package across the table toward Ed. It's wrapped in navy gift wrap with "Happy Birthday" written over and over on a diagonal in gold script.

Happyhappyhappy, Ed thinks. A strip of gold ribbon almost hides a white spot on the paper, the spot where a card had been taped. "You didn't have to do that," Ed says. *Happybirthday, happybirthday, happybirthday.* It sounds like a freight train. Ed is afraid to take the gift. Afraid he'll pull Parva into some churned-up version of reality, one that he can't trust or judge from one day to the next. His '63 Dodge Adventurer flashes into his mind. For an instant, he is in the sea-foam and white truck, he is young, the chrome shines all around him. The window is down, the vent pushed out, his left hand rises and falls with the current of air blowing past, his right hand rests on the top of the steering wheel. He is driving through the desert. A long straight road stretches out before him. The wind swirls in the windows and he moves forward at an awesome speed.

"I know I didn't have to get you anything. I wanted to. I just got a little ahead of things," Parva says. "Edgar. Ed?"

Ed comes back from the desert and looks at Parva.

"It was your gift even before your wife came back." Parva pauses. "What is your wife's name, Edgar?"

Ed looks at the package sitting in front of him. "I'll open it when we have our tea," he says, pushing the package back toward Parva. "Gracie. My wife's name is Gracie."

The steam from the teapot finally builds to a whistle. "Just plain tea okay? Lipton?"

"Fine. Lipton is fine. Where is she, Edgar?"

Ed makes the tea without answering, and puts the cups on a tray along with the dish of macaroons. *Macaroonmacaroon*. He tries not to look at Parva while he works. When he has napkins, sugar, milk, lemon, and spoons on the tray, he walks into the den without a word. Parva gets up, takes the present from the table, and follows him. The den walls are golden knotty pine. Bookcases full of pictures and trophies border each end of the room. Dead stuffed fish and a gun rack hang on the walls along with the head of a twelve-point buck. The couch and chair have a deep blue stripe in the mostly green background and the recliner is solid blue corduroy. A basket full of the week's newspapers sits on the floor beside the recliner. The end table is cluttered with cups and glasses.

"It certainly is warm in here," Parva says with relief, choosing to sit in the rocking chair on the opposite side of the stove from the recliner.

Ed sets the tray on a metal TV table by the kitchen door and then picks up the table and tray together and carries them to the front of the little Swedish green enameled cast-iron stove, embossed with deer and trees. A picture window looks out onto a screen porch and over the now flooded backyard. What few roses remain at the tops of the bushes ride high above the water line near the privacy fence. The blossoms droop in the weight of the rain, and slowly each head loses its fragile browning petals, unable to hold up against the pelting water. An iron table and chairs on the lawn near the roses are more than ankle-deep, as is a concrete birdbath.

Ed sits down, and Parva plops the present in his lap, then proceeds to put lemon and sugar in her tea.

"I don't want to have to give you that present again. Open it."

Ed pulls at the tape gently, trying to save both the bow and the paper. Then he remembers there is no one to tell him to save it for next time, and he slides his thumb under the tape and tears it open. From beneath the ragged paper Ed sees Barney looking back at him with a big smile on his face and a crispy fried chicken leg raised in each hand. Above the chef's head arch the words, *Cooking with Bernard*. Ed opens the book and on the first page, written in large open script, are the words, *To Ed, from one gourmet to another. All the best, Chef Bernard, 2000*.

"That," says Parva with pride, "was written before you won the prize.

There's no telling what he'll want to write in a book for you now. I bet he signs the next one just *Barney*. That's how he signed mine after we spent the day together. Just, *Barney."* Parva nibbles on a macaroon to keep from prattling again.

"Thank you," Ed says. "I don't know what to say."

"Thank you will do nicely," Parva says, covering her mouth as she speaks through the coconut.

Ed squeezes a wedge of lemon into his cup of tea then says, "My wife is *crazy."*

"Well, Ed, I'm sure you have your differences, but . . ."

"No. I mean she's mentally ill. I didn't know it when she left. I thought she was just going through the change. You always hear about women getting a little weird when they're at the change of life. And she's always been just a little weird anyway. But come to find out, she's out and out *crazy*. I can't quite make it all fit together in my mind."

Ed reaches for a macaroon. He's been eating cookies like crazy for weeks now. His pants are getting tight at the waist. A gust of wind blows the back door open, and the wind chimes begin beating and clacking and tinkling all through the house.

"Good Lord!" Ed says and jumps up to shut the door.

Parva leans forward to take in the chaos. Then it hits her that the den doesn't have a single wind chime, and that it doesn't have a Jesus drawn on the wall. Ed comes back. What little bit of hair he has left on the sides of his head looks wild.

"I didn't know you liked wind chimes so much. I don't recall seeing or hearing any on my last visit." *Of course you had something else on your mind, didn't you?* her little voice says.

"They're my voices," Ed says.

"I beg your pardon?"

"Gracie hears voices. That's what the doctors said."

"We all hear little voices," Parva says defensively.

"These voices told her to leave. The voices told her to draw the Jesuses. I expect the voices tell her not to eat what I cook for her. The doctor says sometimes, when we try to talk to her, she can't hear us because the voices are talking to her, drowning us out. I asked her to just tell me what they sound like. But she won't talk to me. It's like she can't hear me anymore."

"Huh," Parva says and leans forward, sensing Ed's rising panic.

"I hung a set of chimes a month ago for Estelle, my secretary. She'd broken her ankle, so I did a few things she needed to have done around her house. I hung the chimes on her porch. When I said I didn't like the darn things, Estelle said she did because it was like a voice whispering to her. I started thinking," Ed says, gesturing as he talks, "about the chimes and the voices and I wanted to know what it's like for Gracie. What would make her so willing to give up her family for the voices she hears, voices that aren't real. So I started hanging chimes. Started letting them cover up the sounds of my life. I even hung a couple at my office. But there's no breeze in my office. I have to keep a fan going for them to talk to me." Ed looks out the window at the falling rain. "Every time I go see Gracie, she seems farther away from me. So I come home and hang some more chimes, thinking her voices are getting louder, so my voices need to be louder. I just leave the windows and doors open to let them speak to me. That's why I keep the heat off. I have the windows open all night. The only reason they're closed now is because everything was getting wet."

Ed hears the panic now in his own voice. Hears it building in his throat.

"It's as if I don't exist," he says, "or I'm some stranger asking her questions. I took her lemon pound cake and cherry pie and she wouldn't eat a bite. I thought she'd be surprised that I could cook. Even crazy, that should've shocked the daylights out of her. I couldn't boil water when she left. She didn't say a word. She didn't even take a bite."

Ed starts to come up out of his seat, but then sits back down on the edge of his recliner, his hands hanging between his legs. The panic rises to the top of his throat. It's at the back of his tongue. *Macaroonmacaroon*. It moves forward, forcing his mouth open, spewing out with his words. The real words. "Everything has changed," he begins. He tries to hold back. He makes himself stop. He drinks his tea and fills his mouth with a cookie.

Macaroonmacarron. He slows it down. *Macaroon. Macaroon.* Lets the word take back its shape, its sound, its meaning.

Sometimes he wakes up and finds himself like the birdbath and the yard furniture in the backyard, knee-deep in a flood, threatening to cover him up. "I wake up and can't breathe," he says to Parva. "It's like I'm drowning and I need to get to some higher ground. I feel myself changing. Like I'm learning to breathe under water, breathe in some new way. Not a good way really. Just a way that helps me get through one day, and then another day. The doctors say they can help me, you know, give me a little something, give me somebody to talk to, but they can't help me. I'm not sick. I'm just trying to find my place in it, in all this new life I've got, that's all." *I need to grow some gills so I can breathe. Doctors can't help me do that.* "I have good days and bad days, and when I can't find my place in it, I throw open the windows and let the chimes do the talking. Sometimes I just want to drown in all that tinkling." They clank and spin and fly around above him like fish. What he doesn't say to Parva is that he moves beneath them like a bottom feeder trying to survive on what's left, what mental nourishment might fall his way and settle below. Above him is that lolling reflection on the river of what he thought his life was—even upside down, but he is below that reflection now, down where the current moves faster and the light isn't as strong, and where he doesn't know what's right, where he doesn't know what to do with Gracie and he doesn't know what to do with Parva. And when he can't take it anymore, not the river of voices he's hung above, or the possibilities that reel through his mind, he goes to the garage and sits in the Dodge and thinks about riding through the desert or over the mountains, or he comes in the warm den and sits in his recliner and sleeps.

Now, he looks at Parva. She needs to know. She needs to understand the danger of such a deep world, the world that lives right beside the other one. She needs to know why he is afraid to invite her in, because the deep world changes the shape of everything you always thought you'd recognize.

"Tell me about your wife," Parva says. "Just breathe in and out and tell me about Gracie. Think about this warm den," she reassures, "and the fire, and my hands. Just breathe." She takes his hands in hers and squeezes his fingers.

"I'm telling you about her," he says quietly, his mind still moving in the deep briny place he struggles to free himself from.

Parva lets go of his hands and leans back in the rocker. "Breathe, Edgar. Breathe with me." He takes a deep breath. She takes one herself. "Breathe again." Parva bites into another cookie. The rain continues to fall, lightly but steadily pelting the picture window. The water in the street is now above the curb. Parva takes a sip of tea. She's not sure how dangerous it is to stay, but she knows it isn't safe to leave.

"Just tell me about her before, what she was like before. Then you can tell me about how she is now, and what the doctors say. But start with the old Gracie, the Gracie you knew."

Ed takes his tea and sits back, rests his head against the sculpted corduroy pillow at the back of the recliner. His eyes close and he hears his own breathing. He forgets about the deep water and the fact that Parva has come out on such a bad day. The chimes are quiet and it is only his breath that he hears and the cracking and popping of the fire and the creaking of Parva's chair rocking back and forth and the sound of Parva's cooing voice. A picture takes shape in his mind, a college girl run away from home. She's twenty-one. She has on a white T-shirt with the sleeves rolled up and he sees the tight muscles in her arms, her red hair tied in a knot at the nape of her neck. A hut rises up behind her, made of woven saplings and vines. She reaches into a bucket. A young Ed slides down the path and lands in front of her, his fishing pole and tackle box in one hand and a can of corn in the other.

"The first time I saw her," he begins, "she was down on the riverbank scaling bream with the back of a spoon." *I am queen of the fairies*, he hears Gracie saying in the psych ward's multipurpose room. But that is now. *What did she say then?* Ed breathes and shapes his own sentence in his mind and the words ease out of his mouth and float across the room. He goes back to the beginning and looks for pieces. He gathers them one by one. For the first time in his life, he feels like he might really tell someone everything. He might tell Parva Wilson all he knows.

Toot and Tyrone walk to the barn in the rain. Their spirits are soaked to the bone despite the fact they are dry under their rain gear. It has been raining steadily for three days. Everything is heavy with rain. The landscape is soppy, the furniture is damp, the fire in the wood-stove back in the family room seems to be more steam than flame.

"Goodness me, I think we fixing to have another flood. Three days down and thirty-seven more to go." Toot hunkers in her coat as if defending herself against the weather.

"You mean like Noah and the Ark? That kind of flood?" Tyrone peeps out from under the hood of his yellow slicker.

"Naw. I just joking. God promised not to send no other flood like that one. That's why we got rainbows, to remind us and Him of that."

"I thought they were refracted light."

"Everything always more than one thing. Don't you know that?"

Their feet sink into the red clay mush and every few steps it is like quicksand, sucking a foot down, requiring effort to pull it back out and put it down again. Together they try for more solid ground.

"I shoulda left you in the house. It's bad out here."

"But it's my job to feed Sheba. You said so."

"True enough. And you do good work. That ole Sheba likes you. Course it could be all the peppermints missing out of my candy dish that she like. You reckon?" Toot sounds stern and Tyrone looks up at her. The raindrops peck at his face. But Toot smiles and Tyrone smiles back, then drops his head to keep the rain from running down his neck.

Once inside the barn, Toot turns on the lights and hangs her coat on an empty nail beside a row of tack. Tyrone stands on a crate to reach his nail and does the same.

"You get the grain while I get the wheelbarrow and the fork," Toot says.

Tyrone goes into the room off the main hall of the barn and opens a fifty-gallon steel drum. He scoops feed into a five-gallon bucket that once held bathroom cleaner. All the barrels and buckets are recycled. *Every-*

thing is always more than one thing, Tyrone thinks. The grain scoop is a two-pound Maxwell House can and the water trough that Tyrone will fill is cut from a plastic barrel Toot got from the junkyard. Tyrone closes the gallon drum and walks to Sheba's stall. The black Percheron's bulk would frighten most grown folk unaccustomed to horses, but to Tyrone, the blaze-faced mare is a friendly giant. Sheba sticks her big head into the bucket for a sample.

"Don't let her crowd you, Tyrone. She got to respect you to love you."

"Back, Sheba," Tyrone says in a firm voice, pushing at her huge head. The mare looks up and nudges Tyrone toward her feed trough. He swings the bucket slightly back in her direction to back her up a few steps and pours the grain in the trough. As Sheba nibbles, Tyrone gets the manure fork from Toot and mucks out the stall, scooping the fork in and out around Sheba's feet, which are the size of salad plates. Meanwhile, Toot gets feed in a bucket for her chickens.

"You a good worker," Toot says to Tyrone when they have finished their chores and are reaching for their coats. "You gon' be something someday if you keep working hard."

"Thank you," Tyrone says, proud now of any compliment Toot gives him.

"And because of that I'm gon' help save your soul."

"Ma'am?"

"You can give that mare one peppermint a day with my say-so. So that way you won't be stealing. 'Cause I can't stand no thief. But you stick with one, 'cause she's old and that's all she need and that's all I'm willing to give for your one little soul."

"Now?" Tyrone asks.

"I reckon so."

Tyrone reaches beneath his slicker, into his jeans and produces two pieces of hard candy wrapped in cellophane. He puts one in Toot's open hand, unwraps the other and offers it from his flattened palm to Sheba.

"You be good to that horse, and she be good to you. But remember this. Don't let her think she the boss. You a little boy and you got to make up for your size with attitude. That don't mean you got to be mean, but it mean you got to be strong in your mind. It's good you ain't afraid of that big horse, so you always let her know you ain't afraid. That way of thinking works for about anything, not just horses. You remember what I tell you."

"Yes, ma'am. I'll remember."

"What you gon' be for Halloween?"

"A cowboy."

"Sammy got a book on black cowboys."

"I saw it. That's what gave me the idea. That and Sheba . . . Speaking of trick or treat," Tyrone says and turns to face Toot directly, "Mama Toot, can I still have one peppermint for me?"

Toot looks hard at Tyrone then returns the peppermint in her hand. "I reckon so," Toot says, "since you took the trouble to ask like a honest person."

"Thank you," he says as she swings the door wide and lets in the blowing rain.

"Uh huh," she answers. And together they step back out into the weather.

Estelle takes two-sided tape and sticks the black cat up on the front window of Tire Man. She has already sprayed the words BLACK CAT TIRE SALE on the window with black and orange spray paint. With Ed out of the office so much, she's making some headway. Wally isn't as rigid as Ed. Wally allows room for a little creativity. With Wally running things most of the time, Estelle is trying things she's been wanting to do for years, like take advantage of the seasons and the holidays more. Halloween is just around the corner, and what better way to take advantage of that than a Black Cat Tire Sale. Ed is too smitten with what's-her-name or too preoccupied with crazy Gracie to notice if Estelle pushes a few ideas through when he's not around.

Estelle goes outside to see how it all looks. She's quite talented when it comes to marketing. She's particularly invested in this campaign because Halloween is her favorite holiday. She loves to dress up and give out candy. She makes her house look like a witch's cottage. She puts a big cauldron in the front yard with dry ice in it so it looks like it is bubbling up a potion. She cackles like something right out of Macbeth. But Estelle has never read Macbeth. She always says she has when people hear her cackle and make the comparison, but she hasn't. She doesn't have a lot of formal education. What Estelle has learned has come from a keen instinct, paying attention, knowing when to make a move, and when to keep quiet and nod knowingly. She skirts the issue of education when it comes up.

Ed is clearly becoming a Casanova, now that his poor wife is in a mental institution, or ward, or whatever. First he came on to Estelle by bringing her that coffee cake and hanging her chimes. Then, when she drove over to take him the recipe, she finds a woman leaving his house. But she had been there before. Estelle could feel it. Ed and the woman were quite familiar.

Estelle had pulled up right as Parva Wilson was walking to her car. *What kind of weird name is that anyway?* Ed introduced them like it was every day he had two women in his front yard and neither of them his wife. As if it isn't enough that Estelle has been competing with Gracie for twenty years, and is now proven to be the better woman, since she is still sane and Gracie is off her rocker. Estelle has no intention of competing with yet another woman for Ed's attention. She can take a hint. The two, no, three-timer. At least he's distracted, and she'll use that to vindicate herself as a creative businesswoman, a side of her Ed has chosen to ignore all these years.

There he stood in the front yard, that hussy looking at him like he was her hero, and poor Gracie's mums blooming everywhere. Ed started telling Estelle about his cookbook. How he's going to write a cookbook and Parvo's going to help him. *Well, isn't that cute?*

"How about you, Estelle? You want to share some recipes?" Ed said, smiling like he was completely ignorant of what he'd done.

"Well, as a matter of fact, that's why I'm here," Estelle had said. She looked over at Parvo and smiled. Then she said, "When you were over at my house the other day working on my honey-do list, you asked for the recipe to that chocolate chess pie you like so much. I decided to share after all." Estelle had smiled again at that fat thing in her schoolteacher sweater standing there beside Ed. And then Miss Fatso starts telling her that she's heard all about her delicious chocolate chess pie and that she couldn't wait to try it sometime. *Imagine.*

Well, Estelle just pulled that little recipe card out of her purse and handed it to Ed and said, "I can't stay. I have some important things to do today. But here is your recipe for chocolate chess pie. Feel free to share it with Parvo here."

"Parva," he corrected. *Let her correct me herself*, Estelle thought, *I know what her name is.* But Estelle smiled and got back in her red convertible Camaro and drove off, leaving Ed and Parvo with a recipe for chocolate chess pie that called for just a little too much salt.

In honor of Ed and Parvo and Halloween, Estelle has decided to go to Big Dog Books over by the community college and find a book on casting spells. Next weekend, instead of wasting her time on men who don't appreciate her, she's going to work a little magic of her own. After all, she already has the cauldron. *Bubble, bubble, toil and trouble.* Isn't that what witches say? Seems like she heard a witch on TV say that sometime or other.

Estelle stands outside Tire Man and looks at her handiwork. She loves Halloween. She loves it for all sorts of reasons. The decorations. The mystery. Remembering the little chill that went up her spine as a child, feeling her way through the dark, trying to get a little something for her trouble. *Trick or treat!* Now, she likes to watch the children traipse through the neighborhood in their disguises. She loves to see their eager hands extended, their masked faces. No matter what kind of mask appears at the door, the hands come toward her holding bright orange bags or plastic jack-o'-lanterns. On Halloween everyone wants what she has to offer. All those empty hands waiting to be filled, and her there, ready for them, in her witch's hat, her black garb.

As Estelle stands there in front of Tire Man admiring her marketing strategy, the broad, toothy grin of the black cat, the big fat letters painted on the window, the best reason she can think of for Halloween being her favorite holiday comes to her. When it's October and that time of the month, like now, all she has to do is go home and rip open all those plastic bags of chocolate. Milky Ways, Three Musketeers, Kit Kats, Hershey Bars, Reese's Peanut Butter Cups, Baby Ruths. She can surround herself with brand-name miniatures, piles and piles of them. She can sit on her sofa, waiting for the doorbell to ring, and in between giving away what she has, she can reach out for a chocolate, one sweet rich bite after another, and eat her heart out.

"WHY ARE YOU DRIVING the Dodge?" Ginger asks as she helps Ed unload Thanksgiving dinner and carry it into her dining room. It's as if her mama's leaving has freed her daddy in some way. For the first time in his life, Ed has cooked Thanksgiving dinner.

"Wally got me to thinking it's a waste to keep her locked up in the dark."

It was supposed to be Ed, Gracie, Ginger, and Wally, but Gracie refused to leave the hospital for the day unless she was going back to Rockrun.

Ed has prepared the entire meal, allowing Ginger to contribute only green beans and the pumpkin pie. Pumpkin Ginger Chiffon she's named it. He has set the bar so high lately with his gourmet cooking that she's actually intimidated.

"How's the cookbook manuscript coming, Ed?" Wally asks as he plates up some sliced turkey.

"So far so good."

"Have you thought much about the tire business lately?"

Ed has never liked to discuss business at the table, but this is the perfect opportunity to lay out his new plan.

"How'd that Black Cat Tire Sale turn out?"

"Oh, you saw that?"

"I ride by."

Ginger is deciding if she wants garlic mushroom mashed potatoes or pecan-crusted sweet potato soufflé. She opts for both.

"Estelle has some good ideas, Ed. The sale was pretty darn successful."

"How would you like to be general manager of Tire Man?"

Ginger's forkful of sweet potato soufflé stops just short of her lips. "What?"

"I think Wally's been doing a fine job." Ed sits poised at the head of the table with a fork in one hand and knife in the other. "What do you think of Estelle as sales manager?"

Wally pensively fills his plate with an array of vegetables, deep-fried turkey, and homemade crescent rolls, then drizzles everything on his plate with gravy.

"Aren't you going to say anything?" Ed asks.

"I'm thinking," Wally says.

"I'm thinking, too," Ginger says, putting down her fork and wiping a dab of sweet potato from the corner of her mouth. "I'm thinking both of my parents are out of their gourds. What are you going to do?"

"Cook. I've got a few ideas in the fire, not just the cookbook. And I'm thinking that I could become a silent partner with Wally, let Wally and Estelle keep handling things in the fine way they have been while I make a few adjustments here and there, and I can go into what you might call semiretirement."

"You're going to retire at fifty? Have those wind chimes been talking to you for real?"

"Why not?" I've got a good little bit set aside, and all this with your mother has made me take a look at what I do and how I do it. Gracie may not be queen of the fairies, but she's right about one thing. I need to pay attention. I'm just paying more attention. That's all." Ed looks at Wally. "So?"

Wally looks at Ginger who shrugs her shoulders.

"All righty then," Wally says and puts down his fork only long enough to shake hands with his new partner.

"One thing," Ed says before tasting his Thanksgiving dinner.

"What?"

"You tell Estelle, and you take all the credit for her promotion."

As it turns out, Ginger is a chip off the old block. Out of two pies, the three of them eat all but two pieces of Pumpkin Ginger Chiffon. The pie-feeding frenzy takes place over several hours, starting right after the formal meal at noon and then continuing through returns for leftovers and snacks on through NFL football. For a few hours Ed allows himself to be pulled back into his favorite armchair sport, but before dark he makes his excuses and heads for home to catch what's left of Food Network's Thanksgiving lineup and a little Discovery Channel. He's recently subscribed to *Scientific American* and *Natural History,* and during a special about the Old West, Ed donated a hundred dollars to Public Television. He's getting good at *Jeopardy.* He was never good at *Jeopardy* before. He never watched *Jeopardy* before.

Alone in their house, the table cleared, Ginger washes dishes and Wally dries them. They make a good team.

"Are you ready for all this?"

"What, general manager?"

Ginger nods.

"I think so."

"I guess Estelle will start chasing you, now."

"You know, Estelle can be a bitch and a little sneaky, but she's not a bad businesswoman. She'll be so busy fulfilling her potential as a tire diva, she won't even think about flirting."

"Are you afraid I'll go crazy like my mother?" Ginger hands Wally the wet turkey platter, counts slowly in her head until he answers. *One, two, three, four.*

"Where did that come from?"

"You're being evasive. You must think it's possible."

"I don't believe it will happen. No one can say it's impossible. I don't think your father would have predicted your mother's illness. Do you?" Wally takes a handful of silverware from Ginger's hand.

"I was driving home a couple of weeks ago," Ginger says as she passes Wally a Pyrex pie plate, "and a bunch of starlings were flying off in the distance. A flock of them. They were coming over the treetops and swinging out parallel with the highway. They just kept coming. I've never seen so many birds. I finally pulled off the road and watched until the last of them came out from behind the trees. The black band of birds seemed endless." Ginger hands Wally the pot they cooked the green beans in. "Then, when I was almost home, I noticed starlings covering the power lines to the left of my car. They moved along with me. They swooped up from one line and landed on the next until they had escorted me home." She hands Wally the other pie plate. "I thought of that movie *The Birds*. For a minute I believed the starlings were following me. That they had been following me since I watched them come up over the trees out at the highway. I thought they had a malevolent purpose. That maybe they were angels or devils, and not birds. And then I was afraid I was going nutty. Like her. Like I was crossing some line that I might not be able to step back over. I thought about you and how you wouldn't stay with me if you knew I was having such crazy notions." She reaches into the water and adjusts the drain so the water begins to swirl and funnel out of the sink.

Wally puts the pie plate down and pulls Ginger to him, looks her in the eye. "I love you. Everyone has weird thoughts like that sometimes. Alfred Hitchcock counted on it. Lots of creative people count on it. It's what sells books and movie tickets. We all have those thoughts or something like them. That's not going *crazy*. That's having an imagination. You aren't any crazier than you've ever been, and that's why I love you. If you weren't a little crazy, I wouldn't be here in the first place. And besides, you like my socks."

Ginger lets out a little laugh, part sigh of relief. She kisses his lips and holds his face in her wet hands. Wally takes her right hand in his and raises it into their favorite dance position and pulls her more tightly to him. Their cheeks are touching, their mirrored arms fully extended. Together they step out of the kitchen and tango toward the bedroom. They never make it past the woodstove. The flame burns too hot.

The yellow Formica table is covered with a plain white tablecloth, which is in turn covered with a white lace tablecloth. There's three place settings of green and white china. Toot and Mattie and DuRon hold hands as Mattie says grace.

"Bless this food, oh Lord, to the nourishment of our bodies. We love you, Jesus. We ask you to keep Sammy and Tyrone safe on their journey, and may Doristeen appreciate that she has my men at her table today." Toot cuts her eyes up at DuRon, who cuts his eyes down to her. Then they both look back at their plates. "And bless Rachel, or Gracie, or whatever you call her now, and bless her family with your consolation in their time of need. Bless the three of us at this table, and keep us close, as Arty would want us to be. May you and Arty be at this feast with us today and share in our bounty and our Thanksgiving. Amen."

"Amen."

"Amen."

Amen.

"Pass the turkey, please."

"DuRon, you always in a rush to eat," Toot says. "I'll give you turkey when I'm ready for you to have turkey. Now you be polite and pass Mattie those deviled eggs in front of you."

"Yes, ma'am." DuRon passes Mattie the deviled eggs.

"That's better."

"Have you heard any news about Rachel, I mean, Gracie?" DuRon asks as he reaches to take the eggs back.

"She's still in the hospital," Mattie says.

"They gon' put her on so many drugs for being crazy she won't know none of her names," Toot says as she hands DuRon the rolls and takes the eggs.

"You think they can keep her at home when she gets out?" DuRon sprinkles salt and pepper on his potatoes and passes the shakers to Mattie.

"Mmm," Mattie says as she takes a bite of Toot's sweet potato casserole. "This is different. What'd you do?"

"Put ginger snaps on top."

"What magazine did you see that in?" Mattie asks.

"Wont no magazine. Gracie's husband sent me a little book of recipes when he wrote that thank-you note for us taking such good care of Gracie and asked us to send her paints and brushes. I guess he heard we like to cook."

"Well," DuRon says with his mouth full, "she's pretty good at making pictures on car parts. I got to give her that. You know, there's rich people that would call that art. She might could make some money doing that."

"Lord, Lord," Mattie says. "Lord, Lord."

"By the way, Harvey and Clyde Rodey found Gracie's car," DuRon says, deciding to tuck his napkin in at his collar.

"Where?" Toot and Mattie say together.

"It had slid down an embankment into some trees below the highway about three miles from Harvey's house, at the edge of some of his woods. They were tracking a deer and found it."

"Well, I sure hope Clyde brings by some good venison tenderloin like he usually do this winter. Ed Holloman give me what looks to be a fine recipe for that. Smothered Venison."

Mattie passes Toot the green beans. "You didn't tell me about no recipes."

"I didn't think to tell you about it. I got busy getting the brushes and things ready to mail. They look pretty good. I'm gon' try one every now and then and see how they do. I got me a feeling this ain't done, this thing with Gracie." Toot forks up some green beans for her plate and passes them on to DuRon. "They gon' be able to drive that car again?"

"I'd say so. What kind of pies did you bake for today, Mattie?" DuRon asks right after he puts a fork full of potatoes and gravy in his mouth.

"She made several," says Toot before Mattie can get a word out. "And if you stop talking with your mouth full, we'll let you take one home with you."

"Lord, Lord," Mattie says.

DuRon looks up from his food like an innocent child.

MATTIE SITS UP in bed. The knocking at the door is still half in her dream and half in the real world. It is getting louder. Mattie makes it into the hall about the same time Toot rounds the corner into the living room. Tyrone peeps from behind his door. Sammy is still out with a pregnant mare in distress.

"Get back in bed, sweetie," Mattie says to Tyrone. "I'll come tell you what it's all about in a little bit."

Tyrone skitters across the floor, jumps back into his bed, and pulls the covers up to his chin. He strains to hear what's said when the door opens.

Toot waits for Mattie to get in position behind the door with the baseball bat before she hollers through the door into the night, "What you want?"

A man's voice says, "I got a fare here for this address."

"You got a what?" Toot says. She thinks she misunderstood him.

"I got a fare for this address. Right here she is."

"Do you know it's one o'clock in the morning?"

"Oh, I know exactly what time it is, ma'am. And sure hope you're who we're looking for."

About that time a familiar voice comes through the door. "Open up, Tootsie Mae. It's me."

"For Pete's sake," Mattie says and drops the bat from her shoulder.

"Keep that bat ready till we see what's what," Toot whispers. Mattie lifts the bat over her shoulder again, this time halfheartedly. Toot steps forward, unhooks the latch and eases open the door.

There stands Rachel in her jeans and T-shirt and an old red sweater. Her hospital wristband is still on her wrist. A black man stands beside her. He's probably close to sixty years old. Nice-looking man except for that fishing hat covered in buttons and pins. The metal and plastic coating of the pins makes his hat sparkle in the front porch light.

"I hope somebody here's got a hundred and seventy-five dollars," the man says, "because that is this lady's fare and she doesn't appear to have any money, now that I have driven all night and ended up in the middle of nowhere." He has a gentle hold on Rachel's arm.

"And just who might you be?" Toot asks, wrapping her blue chenille housecoat tighter around her and cinching the tie of her belt.

"I'm a cabdriver trying to do a good deed. Name's Norvis Dibner. I picked this woman up in Centertown. She said she needed a ride up above

Martinsville and it was too late to catch a bus. Said her mama was dying. Said her family would pay."

"Humph. Her mama been dead fifteen years. Do we look like her family?"

"I admit, you're not what I expected."

"Uh-huh. I bet you surprised all right. And you must not be in your right mind neither, to bring a cab fare across state lines." Toot squints at the man in the hat. "I don't even know if what you done legal."

Toot opens the door a little farther and Mattie steps around to see Rachel and the cabdriver.

When Norvis sees Mattie, his stern face opens into a broad smile that pushes his cheeks up into his eyes, barely visible below the rim of his hat. Mattie steps back and pushes up her hair before she can stop herself.

"I sure hope you not planning to bean me with that bat," Norvis says. Mattie lets the bat drop to her side. "I picked this here woman up at eleven o'clock and been driving for two and a half hours. It is lovely to meet you pretty ladies, and all," he directs this statement to Mattie, "but if you know her, I sure would appreciate you taking her and paying me so I can get on back home. I'm sleepy enough already."

Toot sees he is saying this more to Mattie than to her.

"We know her, all right," Toot says, "but I don't know that we got money to pay a hundred seventy-five dollars to ransom her. If you willing to reduce your price over a cup of coffee, come on in. If you not, then both of you can stay out there."

Norvis sees what he is up against. "I'd appreciate a cup of coffee, ma'am. I'd like that for sure. Why, that would drop ten dollars off the balance right quick." He grins at Toot now. "I'm sure we can work something out."

Mattie goes into the kitchen to make coffee.

"I want to go paint," Gracie says. "I got pictures in my head I need to paint."

"You go get yourself in your bed and go to sleep," Mattie says from the kitchen before Toot can answer. "You got us all up in the middle of the night, scared little Tyrone half to death, and brought this poor man out for a steep fare he won't get and you want to be up carousing? I don't think so." Mattie comes back through the door with a wooden spoon in her hand. "You get your butt to bed. You can paint your pictures tomorrow."

Gracie goes to her room, waving at Tyrone, now standing in the doorway of his room. Tyrone smiles and waves back, then jumps back in his bed satisfied that all is well. Gracie climbs in her bed with her clothes on. Everyone but Norvis Dibner knows she will be out in the garage painting before they can get back to dreaming good. No telling what she will have painted by morning. But for now, Mattie wants her in the bed. She wants to concentrate on how Mama Toot is going to get out of paying a hundred and seventy-five dollars to this man. And she wants to see what kind of man is dumb enough to bring a crazy woman two hours into the country without payment in advance.

Mattie pours three cups of coffee and puts some fried cherry pies on a plate and sets them on the table. "How much you going to take off that bill for some fried pies?"

"Oh, I'd say ten apiece. How's that?"

"That's good. And I hope you real hungry. I got all the pies you can eat."

It's going on two in the morning so Mattie doesn't see much point in using a pitcher. She sets the Pet Evaporated Milk can on the table and puts some spoons out in case the man wants some sugar with his coffee. Then Mattie goes to her room and combs her hair.

Toot puts some milk in her coffee and three spoons of sugar, then stirs it good and pours a little in her saucer. She eyes Norvis Dibner as she blows across the saucer and then she takes a sip.

"My mama used to drink her coffee like that," Norvis says, trying to be friendly.

"How I drink my coffee ain't none of your business. And how your mama drank it ain't none of mine. Eat your pie and take off that ten dollars while we figure this all out."

Mattie comes back in the room with her face washed, her hair combed, and a little color on her lips. She has changed into her traveling housecoat too, the one she saves for trips and possible visits to the hospital.

"Mattie, you call DuRon. He needs to be in on this," Toot says between slurps of coffee from her saucer.

"It's almost two in the morning. DuRon is snoring his head off about now."

"He the sheriff. He don't need to run for office if he don't want to be woke up in the middle of the night."

"All right. But I think you just trying to aggravate the man." Mattie reaches for the phone on the wall by the back door.

"That's just gravy," Toot says as she looks up at Mattie, then trains her eye back on Norvis. "That's just a little gravy." Then to Norvis, "I don't expect you gon' be getting back anywhere tonight. Best I can tell, you got an escapee from the mental hospital you done brought back here. I hope you don't mind sleeping on a pile of hay in a barn, 'cause you probably rather do that than drive back when the sheriff finish with this."

"Hay sounds good to me. How much that gon' cost?" Norvis asks, getting settled into the barter that is obviously going to whittle his fare down to gas money, if he's lucky.

"A soft bed with continental breakfast," Mattie chimes in, "I'd say twenty-five dollars."

"Based on these pies, I'd say it'll likely be a good breakfast. Okay, twenty-five." Norvis takes a sip of coffee. "You two try to leave me with enough money to get home on, if you don't mind." He takes off his hat and puts it on his knee.

Mattie sees the gray hair spread through the black and sees it is pulled tight into a bushy ponytail sticking out at the back of his neck. A man as old as that with a ponytail. He holds his pie daintylike, but his other hand, the one that holds the coffee cup, is stiff. Arthritis, she thinks.

It isn't often Mattie eats her own baked goods. She'd be big as a house if she did. But she reaches across in front of Norvis Dibner and takes a cherry pie and a napkin. "No sense letting a good cherry pie go to waste in the middle of the night," she says, and takes a bite.

TOOT, WRAPPED in three sweaters, sits in the front porch glider thinking about Rachel, the grown woman, and Gracie, the little girl. The glider slides forward and back, forward and back, through the brisk December air.

It was the only time she ever saw a man shot, and he'd gone and done it to himself. Toot heard it while she was washing up the lunch dishes. She stood at the top of the steps to the basement for a long time, just calling Mr. Price's name over and over, and the whole while Mrs. Price was screaming her fool head off upstairs in the bedroom. She never even opened the door to come see what happened. Toot never once went to her door and asked her to come see, either. Mrs. Price knew. They both knew what that shot meant the minute it sounded through the house.

Toot stood and called his name over and over until she tasted the salty tears that had run down her young face and found the edges of her mouth. She was twenty-eight years old and scared to death. Scared of what she'd find in the basement and scared of death itself. Now she fears neither. When she finally made it to the foot of the basement stairs, she could see it all in the glow of the bare bulb. Mr. Price. The gun. The red spray across the concrete wall behind him. She saw the blood and other parts of his head on the dirt floor. His eyeball dangled from its empty hole. It was such a sight that she sat down on the steps and couldn't look away. No telling how long she sat there. After a time, the thought of little Gracie coming home from school brought her out of it, brought her back to herself.

She called the sheriff and called the doctor and went to Mrs. Price's door.

"Mrs. Price," she said as firm as she dared, "I need the name of some of your people." Toot stood at the closed door, willing that woman in the bedroom to do what she said do. She stood there at the bedroom door for the longest time until she heard something moving. A little piece of paper came swishing out from under the door and stopped at the toe of Toot's shoe. It was a pink note card, Mrs. Price's nicest embossed stationery. It had her daddy's name and address written on it in fine penmanship. And that's what Toot gave to the sheriff when he came.

What'd be your life, little Gracie, if I never asked for nothing, if I'd left it to that woman to come out that room for her child? Toot pushes the glider forward and back, forward and back.

The second pot of coffee is perking on this cold day. Mattie left early to go Christmas shopping with DuRon in Roanoke. They've gone to the art store to buy all kinds of nice paints and brushes and a real easel for Santa Claus to bring to Tyrone. Mattie told Toot over her morning coffee that she didn't want to make a habit watching Gracie leave.

Toot's going to make bacon and eggs and biscuits, Mr. Price's favorite breakfast. That man used to come to the kitchen and sneak bacon the whole time Toot was cooking it. Sneaking because Mrs. Price didn't believe in being in the kitchen with the help anymore than she could manage. It was the way she was raised. Mr. Price was a good man though. Toot has prayed for his soul more times than she can count. Today she's going to fix him his favorite breakfast and, all these years later, feed it to the people trying to clean up after the mess he left behind.

Toot hears Ed before she sees him. He's coming down the gravel road in an old green and-white pickup. She'd have figured him to be driving a newer vehicle than that. Then she gets a good look at it, and she knows that truck. Toot has seen it before.

."I need to know your people this time, little Gracie," Toot says softly to herself. "This time, it ain't enough to just know they names." The only response is the sound of the truck easing around the mailbox and pulling up into the frosted yard.

Ed unloads his basket onto Toot's kitchen table. Oven-baked chicken legs in Parmesan breading, crab-stuffed tomatoes, smoked oysters, crisp green beans in garlic-and-lemon butter, black-eyed pea salad over baby greens, carrot cake, and rhubarb pie.

"You cook all this?" Toot asks.

Ed nods. "I couldn't boil water when Gracie ran away. I've gotten pretty good at cooking since she's been gone, but I can't get her to eat anything I make."

"I ain't much used to folks bringing food with 'em when they come. It's usually the other way round."

"I just want to thank you for taking such good care of Gracie. I'm sorry

I wasn't able to come get her the last time, once we found out where she was."

"Um-hum. She go by Rachel around here."

"Yes, ma'am. I'm trying to get used to that, but I called her Gracie for thirty years. It slips my mind, that new name."

"You wait here," Toot says and goes back to the laundry room.

In a few minutes, she has coaxed Gracie into the kitchen. "Tootsie Mae, I'm not going to eat a thing that man cooks. Do you hear me?" She addresses the last part of her statement to Ed.

"That's fine. I got leftovers for you to eat if you don't want some of this nice food. But first, I'm gon' start us out with some breakfast. Tyrone and Sammy gon' be coming in soon with a Christmas tree and wanting something hot to eat. Y'all sit down." Toot points to the kitchen chairs and Ed and Gracie take seats.

"Mr. Hollaman, you seen any of Rachel's artwork?" Toot asks as she lays thick strips of smoked bacon across the bottom of a large iron skillet.

"Only a mural in the hospital and some blocks of wood," Ed answers. "And of course the Jesuses."

"Jesuses?"

"Three Jesuses she left on the walls of our house before she ran away."

"Yeah, she started with Sheetrock, didn't you, baby? Now she into car parts. But she paint a nice mural of Bible stories over at the church social hall last night, didn't you, Rachel?"

Gracie nods.

"Yeah, after she and that cabdriver wake us up in the middle of the night 'bout scaring us to death, she snuck out and went to the church and did a fine job of Jonah and the whale, Daniel in the lion's den, David and Goliath. She got five or six stories in 'fore I come looking for her. The colors bear a strong likeness to some birdhouses I got." Toot gives Gracie a look as she puts the bacon on paper towels to drain and starts breaking eggs into the pan. "We'll take a little tour after breakfast, Mr. Hollaman. Let you see what your girl been up to while she here."

"Please, just call me Ed."

"I disenchanted him," Gracie corrects. "I'm not his girl."

"You ain't no ex-wife neither," Toot corrects back. "So you his girl as much as anybody's."

Gracie thinks about what Toot has just said. "I want to be an ex-wife."

"Not till after breakfast," Toot says. "Not till after breakfast. And then I'm gon' show Ed all the work you been doing while you get ready to ride on home with your husband."

Gracie pouts while Toot pours Ed some coffee. As if on cue, Sammy and Tyrone bustle into the kitchen smelling of evergreens.

"We got a big tree," Tyrone says as he pulls off his work gloves. "Big and fat, and I cut it down all by myself."

"Ain't you something?" Toot says.

After breakfast, Toot takes Ed to the field out by the garage to show him some of Gracie's paintings. They round the corner of the outbuilding and face a battery of car and tractor members emblazoned with images of Jesus, biblical characters, and what first appears to be gnats, but upon closer inspection turns out to be tiny fairies.

"I'll confess, Mrs. Riley. We haven't had much to do with church most of our life, so I don't know which is more surprising. Jesus or the fairies. I don't know what to do about all this." Ed extends his hands toward the metal menagerie.

"You ain't got to do nothing 'bout this. That woman from Atlanta 'pose to come see all this and more next month. You know 'bout that?"

"Dr. Post mentioned it. You think somebody's going to pay money for this? I thought art was more, more, realistic."

"Ed, you be surprised what somebody pay for. Besides, this 'bout her vision. What's inside her. They plenty of people don't have nothing inside and they see something like this and think it's gon' fill 'em up. I get tickled myself seeing what she gon' come up with next."

Ed walks up to an old Chevy truck tailgate. He can see the embossed word Chevrolet through the painted figures partaking of the Last Supper.

"I can pay you for the parts she's used."

"I don't want no money. You just keep getting her car parts. If you don't have no place to put 'em, you bring 'em out here. She can come paint for a few days whenever it suits you."

Ed wanders from one metal canvas to another, studying each one.

"You feel guilty 'bout something?" Toot asks.

"Why do you say that?"

"'Cause you didn't come get her the first time, for one thing, and you don't really want to take her back this time. Am I right?"

"I don't know what's right, Mrs. Riley. I don't know what to do with her, being like she is right now. I just don't know. But Rachel, or Gracie, or whoever she turns out to be when she leaves the hospital, is my wife and my responsibility. And I don't aim to shrink from it."

"People sick in the head can be hard to deal with."

"I'm finding that out."

"But they's more there than just her sickness. They's still a little bit of Grace left. You got to know where to look for it. That's something you gon' have to learn for yourself. But it's there. Maybe they's a mask on it, but it's there."

"Yes, ma'am."

"Where you two meet up?"

"On the river. She was fishing and living in a house made from little trees."

"A butterbean tent?"

Ed looks up in amazement.

"We used to make them when she a little girl." Toot points to the tree line. "Tyrone and me got one in the woods down past the cornfield. He go there sometimes when it's warm enough to read his books outside.

"I was expecting you to be driving a fancy vehicle. Not some old jalopy truck," Toot says, eyeing the Dodge in the driveway, "you owning your own business like you do."

Ed laughs, comfortable for the first time all morning. "I've got a new Toyota pickup in the driveway back home, but that jalopy was a gift from my daddy when I turned twenty. I like to drive it now and then."

"Like the day you met her on the river?" Ed looks at Toot, again astonished. "Come with me. I want to show you something."

Tyrone, Sammy, and Gracie are busy in the living room putting up the tree. Toot motions for Ed to come follow her into the laundry room.

"This where she stay. Look here." Toot pulls the bed away from the wall and there in a three-foot high band above the baseboard is the fully painted Garden of Eden. The blond Adam is taking the blue fish from the red-headed Eve. They stand under the tree of knowledge, with a harmless chicken snake asleep at their feet. There are no elephants or giraffes in the garden. Just mountain lions, wild pigs, deer, coyotes, foxes, birds of various kinds, and a Bluetick Coonhound. All the heads are big and the bodies boxy. Along most of the wall, tiny fairies buzz the garden like gnats, as if the Garden of Eden is below the gnat line. But they keep their distance from the couple in the center of the painting. Eve has a crown of flowers and translucent wings and Adam's hair curls around his arms and down his back like yellow vines. Ed recognizes the tableau, so much so that he feels it more than he sees it. "And look here," says Toot, as she pulls back the clothes hamper at the end of the bed. There in a beautiful pale blue-green-and-white wash of color is the Dodge Adventurer, right down to the little yellow blinker indicators on the hood and the wing vents in the front corners of the windows.

Ed is starting a very bad habit for a man who used to run a tire store. He sits on the little bed in Toot's laundry room and weeps. Toot sits down beside him and pats his hand. "It's gon' be all right, now. It's gon' be all right."

Later in the day, just before Ed takes Gracie away, Toot asks for Ed's recipes for Parmesan chicken legs and green beans in garlic-and-lemon butter. In exchange she gives him her recipe for chicken and dumplings and one of her many seasoned cast-iron skillets just the right size for her recipe for crackling corn bread. "You say you learn to cook like this on television?" Toot says, suspicious of such a claim.

Out by the Dodge, Toot takes Gracie's face in her hands. "You be good," Toot says. "You be real good and you gon' get to come back. We done talked about it."

"I'm not eating a thing he cooks," Gracie says through the truck's open window.

"That's all right. I'll eat his cooking and you eat mine."

Ed waves, drops the gearshift down into first, and eases out onto the gravel road.

When Toot gets back into the living room, Sammy and Tyrone are putting holly in the windows and running cedar on the mantel. She makes them some hot chocolate and gives them a plate of sugar cookies to go with it. Then she leaves them to their work and goes back to the laundry room, where she sits on the edge of the bed and stares at what used to be an ordinary wall.

GINGER AND ED stand at the den window and look out onto the back lawn. Ed's arm is around Ginger's shoulders, and Ginger is trying to decide whether to scream or cry. It could go either way.

Gracie has carried a heavy metal lawn chair across the yard and placed it in front of the dormant rosebushes. She is dressed in her sweatpants and sweatshirt and some red tennis shoes she insisted on buying when she went to Wal-Mart with Ginger to pick up her medicine and do some last-minute Christmas shopping. Four rosaries hang around her neck, the crucifixes nestle together at the center of her small bosom. Gracie has kept three rosaries—the pink glass one, the mother of pearl, and the one made of small brown stones—in her jewelry box for as long as Ed has known her. He doesn't know where she got them. He knows the heavy black one belonged to her grandfather.

Ginger thinks Gracie needs to put on a coat, but Gracie refuses to wear one. Gracie has a cardboard box beside her, one she brought down from the attic. Just one of her many strange activities since her release from the hospital. First there was the broken glass in the silverware drawer. Ginger suspects Gracie may want to do her father harm. Then there was the refusal to eat anything Ed cooked. Her refusal was so steadfast that she didn't eat for two days. So, Ginger bought ten TV dinners to last most of the week, and Gracie ate three, one right after the other, as soon as Ginger got them cooked. Gracie also set fire to most of her clothes, leaving the clothes ruined and a black smudge on the patio pavers. Ginger and Ed took her back to the doctor and he adjusted the Haldol, the latest attempt at drug therapy. Now Ed and Ginger are watchful, hopeful, grateful that Gracie is focused on strange things that seem to be less dangerous.

Ginger and Ed were talking in the den earlier in the afternoon, planning who would look after Gracie on what day at what time and drawing up a schedule to post on Ed's fridge and Ginger's, when all of a sudden there was a loud rumbling from the attic. They heard boxes sliding across the floor, heavy things dropping and rolling from one end of the attic to the other. Ed took the stairs two at a time, with Ginger right behind him. In the dim light that filled the eaves from windows in the dormers, they could make out Gracie hunched over boxes of her mother's things in the far corner. One by one, she peeled open a box and looked inside, then she slung it aside and looked in the next box in the same hurried way.

"What are you doing, honey?" Ed said, trying to sound calm.

"Looking for pictures of the baby."

"We don't keep photos up here. Remember? They're in photograph books on the shelf in the den." Ed heard the patronizing tone in his voice. He hated it.

"Not those pictures. Pictures of the baby," Gracie insisted.

"Mama, there are lots of pictures of me in the den. I don't know of a single picture of me up in this old attic."

"Not you," Gracie said, as if Ginger should have known this, "the baby."

"What baby?" Ginger said.

"The one before you," Gracie said.

Ginger looked at Ed who motioned for her to go back downstairs.

"What baby?" Ginger whispered at Ed in a raspy voice.

"I'll explain later," Ed said. "Go on downstairs and let me talk to her." He had a feeling he knew what Gracie was referring to, but there couldn't be any pictures. He knew that was impossible.

Ginger threw her hands in the air and let them fall to her side. It reminded Ed of a move she used to do when she was a cheerleader in high school. She stomped down the steps, mumbling cuss words all the way.

Ed approached Gracie slowly. Gracie looked up at Ed fearful and teary-eyed.

"Help me," Gracie said. "They have to be here someplace."

"Help you what?"

"Help me find the books."

"What books?"

"The red books with all the pictures."

"I don't know what books you want."

"The red books, Number One and Number Two. I can't find them. I know they're here." Gracie looked up and pleaded with Ed. "Help me."

Ed didn't know what else to do. This was the first time since she left that Gracie had wanted him to do anything except get her old car parts and otherwise leave her alone. He began opening boxes, going through the motions, acting as if he were looking for photograph albums. He opened box after box in tandem with Gracie. He moved things around and lifted things out. Then, in the fifth box of what looked like a hundred old pasteboard boxes stacked at the edge of the attic floor near the strips of pink, fluffy fiberglass insulation, Ed found a row of red books with numbers on the spines.

"Is this what you're looking for?"

Gracie climbed over the pile of boxes between them. She stood beside Ed and peered in the carton as he tilted it toward the window light.

"Yes," she whispered. Relief came in the quiet sounds that escaped her mouth. "Yes," she whispered again. She rifled through the books until she found Number One and Number Two. They were Childcraft books, from her childhood. How often her father and Tootsie Mae had read to her from those books. How she loved the illustrations, the cherubic faces of children water-colored happy and healthy and loved.

"I thought you were looking for photograph albums," Ed said.

"I never said photographs." She quickly flipped the pages of one of the books she had lifted from the box. "I said pictures. You're the ones who said photographs. I can't have a photograph. You know that."

"I don't understand," Ed said, taking a seat on Mr. Price's old steamer trunk. "What picture of what baby?"

"Here," Gracie said, flipping through Number One and stopping at page one hundred seventy-four. "Look here. Isn't she beautiful?"

Gracie pointed to an illustration of a fairy sitting on a toadstool. Ed was struck by the resemblance to Gracie as a young girl. The long thick red curls, the pale skin, the rosy cheeks, the dainty feet. At the bottom of the page, the same fairy lay beside the river as she threw a fish into the water. "You see how beautiful she became?"

"Who?" Ed said, as encouragingly as he could muster, trying hard to see some shred of logic in what Gracie was doing.

"The one they took from me. I held her in my heart and then I let her slide back into the water. And all this time she's lived in the world next to ours. That's what fairies do. Their world is right next to ours, but mortals can't see it. And she's there. She's a fairy now. And that's her picture. And that one, too." Gracie's finger moved to the picture of the fairy and the fish. "Her name is Fay and she talks to me sometimes." Gracie pulls up her shirt and then lifts her breast and points to the tiny birth mark. "This is her hand. This is her fairy's hand."

Ed looked in the direction of Gracie's midriff, but he saw only what he remembered. In the beginning he found the little hand erotic. Then there were times he would stare at the birthmark while Gracie slept naked beside him and think it looked like one of Ginger's Barbie dolls had left a muddy hand print on Gracie's rib. He came to cover the mark with his finger and pretend it wasn't there, as if it held a troubling portent.

Gracie pulled down her shirt and reached into her pocket for her sewing shears. She began cutting the pictures out of the book.

"What are you doing?" Ed asked.

"I want her pictures."

Gracie pulled a pen and a small notebook from her pocket and wrote down all the fairy poems she could find in books one and two, then she flipped through them again and cut out more pictures of fairies.

Ed stayed there with her until she was done. Then she rummaged through some more boxes looking for other things, Christmas ornaments, her mother's old jewelry, a box of pink stationery embossed with her mother's initials. She collected the items in a box with the fairy poems and the fairy pictures. Then she went downstairs. Ed closed the attic door behind them and followed her. When they got to the kitchen, Gracie kept going. She went out to the yard alone and dragged a lawn chair to the roses and refused the coat Ginger insisted she wear.

Now, Ed and Ginger look out the den window into the yard. They have become watchers. Gracie lifts a red felt Christmas tree skirt from the box and places it around her shoulders. Ginger feels like a mother dealing with a stubborn child. *Just do it. Wear a coat. Just do what you are supposed to do. How hard is that? How hard is that?*

Ed doesn't see Gracie as Gracie, or the yard as the yard. He imagines that he's looking at a painting of his yard and Gracie is in it, along with the chair, the rose bed, the winter-brown grass, the charred bricks of the patio. Just a few brushstrokes could change everything, but what would he change? Would he put Gracie back in her right mind? Would he change her to Parva? Would he put himself out there? Would he make it summer and the roses blooming? Then Gracie wouldn't need a coat. *What does Gracie need?* He cannot abandon her, no matter how much she may reject him or refuse to eat his cooking for fear it's bewitched. The medication has helped, but not enough. The doctors are debating on more hospitalization. They say there is a bipolar element to her condition. They say she may be depressed. Ed can't understand how going to the hospital can help depression. Based on what he's seen, it looks like it would make depression worse. *Onset.* That is the word they use at the hospital. *Late-onset schizophrenia.* Ed thinks about painting the yard as it is, but empty of people. No people at all. *So sad.* Just the roses, sleeping their wintry sleep, and the empty chair. Maybe he would paint two empty chairs instead of one. Maybe he will go *crazy* and see what happens then.

"What baby was she talking about?" Ginger asks, not taking her eyes off her mother.

"Her first year of college your mother got pregnant. She married the young man. But your great-grandfather was convinced the boy had gotten her pregnant and married her for her money. So he paid the boy off and had the doctor abort the baby before your mother understood what was happening. He was a hateful old son-of-a-bitch, her grandfather."

"How do you know all this?"

"Gracie told me about it just before you were born. I guess she's found a way to get that other baby back."

"What are we going to do?" Ginger says. She's leaning toward screaming, but still hasn't committed either way. "Just what are we going to do with her like this?"

"The best we can," Ed says, and decides he would paint the picture with Toot in the other chair, talking calmly to Gracie. In his painting, Gracie would be happy and talking back. Ed realizes with inspired clarity that Gracie has always been happiest when she was escaping something. After all, what was her marriage to Ed but an escape from her grandfather? And now Ed is the thing she longs to escape. Ed paints and paints in his mind until he paints away his own backyard and paints Gracie and Toot in the Garden of Eden, like the painting behind the little bed in Toot's laundry room. Ed sees that Gracie wants to go back and begin again, but without him. She wants to pick up where she left off all those years ago by the river. Ed feels a twinge of regret mixed with an overwhelming sense of relief and understanding. He will never send her away, never ask her to leave. But the Gracie that remains is a child longing for what's lost. The Gracie he married is gone.

———

WHEN SISTER REBA began traveling for God, she took for granted the roadside attractions she passed day after day as she winterpreached up and down the state of Florida: Six-Gun Territory, Florida Wonderland, the Walking Catfish, the Citrus Tower, Presidents Hall of Fame, Alligator Joe's, Tiki Gardens, Storyland. Today the Citrus Tower, once surrounded by orange groves, is surrounded by concrete and asphalt and overlooks Kmart. Alligator Joe's is no more. But Sister Reba still spends her winter navigating the old highways and finds the hard-core holdouts, the part of Florida that isn't Disney. On this New Year's Day she cruises Highway 54, making her way from Odessa to the Epiphany celebration in Tarpon Springs, where hundreds of Greek Orthodox boys dive for the cross on January 6. Sister Reba is not one to draw lines between denominations—or even religions. When she gets down to the root of her belief in God, God has many faces, many paths lead to Him, and she preaches about the face He shows to her, the place He has set for her at his table.

The sun is straight up in the sky when she spies a favorite spot between Gatorland Putt-Putt and Uncle Sam's Shell Shack. Before long three elderly gentlemen and an older lady are sitting under Reba's tent, waiting their turn to talk to her about salvation. Florida is a rich territory for Sister Reba, lots of folk thinking about their past life and the afterlife, contemplating all the decisions they've made and how it's too late to change what's been done, too late to take things back, too late to take a different path.

As the tent fills with everything from street people to retirees in golf attire, Sister Reba gets the crowd singing, "I'll Fly Away" and "What Wondrous Love Is This?" "And when from death I'm free, I'll sing on, I'll sing on . . ." She leads them in a second round of "Wondrous Love" because of its drive, its momentum. It primes those gathered to be moved in unison.

"Who here toDAY has reGRETS?" Sister Reba asks. "Who here toDAY thinks they should have had a LIFE DIFFrent from what they HAD?" A few honest members of her congregation tentatively raise their hands. Others trickle in from the sides and back of the tent to fill the benches, where seats are still available.

"Well, MAYbe you didn't get the life you WANTed. But GOD gives us the life we NEED. You got the life you NEEded. Are you WITH me, brothers and sisters?"

A weak *Amen* comes back to the pulpit.

"Did brother JOB get the life he WANTed from START to FINish?"

A slightly weaker *No* comes back to Reba.

"But what did GOD give JOB in the END? He GAVE him EVERYthing. Give me a good amen on that one."

A little bit stronger *Amen*.

" 'How HAPpy is the one whom God rePROVES; THEREfore do not despise the DIScipline of the Almighty. For he WOUNDS, but he BINDS UP; he STRIKES, but his hands HEAL.' Job 5. Who today wants to be HEALed?"

The *Amen* grows a bit more.

"How many of you are good at using LEFTovers? How MANY of you can take what's LEFT and makes something GOOD to eat? Can I HEAR it from you?"

The *Amen* is loud, it's growing. Sister Reba feels the chain catch on the sprocket, feels them pulling into line, moving with one mind. She feels it come up into her stomach then her chest.

"Regret is the LEFTover. You got to TURN that LEFTover into WISdom. Don't be reGRETful! Get WISE! Can you get WISE toDAY?" She's putting it where they are, where they can reach out and touch salvation.

Yes! Amen!

"God gives you hardship so you apPREciate the GOOD he DOES give you! God gives you hardship so you KNOW what your neighbor GOES through when their time of TRIAL is upon THEM. He gives you the life you NEED so you can have the WISdom to know how to LIVE!"

Amen, and Amen. Praise Jesus. Even the golfers in the plaid pants and white hats are waving their hands, jumping in their seats.

" 'Does not wisdom CALL, and does not UNderSTANDing raise her voice?' Let me HEAR your voice!"

Amen!

" 'On the HEIGHTS, beside the WAY,' we got the road right HERE, the highway, Highway 54, 'at the CROSSroads she TAKES her STAND.' Can I hear you?"

Amen!

" 'Beside the GATES in FRONT of the TOWN, at the entrance of the portals she CRIES out: 'To YOU, O PEople I call,' that's what she says, 'and my CRY is to ALL that LIVE.' "

At this instant, and moments like it, Sister Reba doesn't feel a drop of remorse for her choices, doesn't long for what she's left behind, doesn't think about the family she could have had. She has had the life she needed, and those who have lived without her have had the life they needed. "Yeah!" *Yeah!* The congregation echoes. She jumps up and down in the pulpit. Her own small regrets are jarred from her. "Yeah!" *Yeah!* She jumps down into the aisle clapping her hands. Her big regrets fall from her shoulders. "Yeah!" *Yeah!* She jumps and claps until the whole tent is jumping with release, jumping with redemption. It's a new day. "Yeah!" *Yeah!* The sprocket is spinning. It's a new year. "Yeah!" *Amen!* The chain is rolling forward. It's a new life. "Yeah!" Sister Reba's eyes are closed, her hands are over her head. She is jumping like she is trying to touch the top of the tent. "Yeah! Let me HEAR you!" *Amen! Amen!* The pilgrims under the used funeral tent whirl headlong into the heart of Heaven. "Let me HEAR you!" *Hallelujah! Hallelujah!*

A HAMMERING NOISE comes from the garage. The garage doors are closed to hold in heat from the electric space heater Toot uses to warm her workroom on cold days. Toot stands at the worktable nailing a small pine box onto the back of a flat pine circle. She wears two pairs of sweatpants and a heavy wool sweater to keep warm because much of the heat escapes through the gaps in the uninsulated walls. The garage is, if nothing else, well ventilated. Mattie sits in an old rocking chair in the corner away from the electric heater. She wears a short-sleeved T-shirt, jeans, and Arty's work boots. She also wears heavy leather gloves to handle the small squares of roofing tin she's cutting with tin snips.

"Lord, can't we turn down that heater?" Mattie asks as she runs her hand across her forehead. "I am burning up. It feels more like June than January."

"Get you some hormones if you want, but leave that heater alone."

"How many of these zigzag pieces you want me to cut?" Mattie asks.

"Start with five or six. I want to make some look like the sun and some look like angels. The smooth ones, they look like halos."

Mattie counts out the jagged-edged semicircles she has already cut. Three.

Toot turns the wooden circle over and reveals a painted face with a hole for a mouth. She picks up two pieces of whittled wood she already painted red. Using a thick washcloth to keep the hammer from marring the paint, Toot nails the small red pieces around the hole in the circle that leads to the interior of the small box. She takes up a brush and begins painting big wild eyes on the bright yellow face.

"What made you decide to do faces for birdhouses?"

"Can't do just the same thing forever. You got to do something a little different," Toot says around the two-penny finishing nails she holds between her lips. "Before long, everybody gon' have the kind I been making. If I make something new, the same people gon' buy that too. That, and I have faces in my head now. All the time I see faces. I'm just trying to get some of 'em out."

Toot picks up another circle, a woman's pink face already painted there, the eyes completely blue with black pupils in the centers. Toot nails on a pink whittled nose, then one by one glues tiny blue whittled teardrops down the pink face. Instead of a piece of tin for a halo, the pink woman is crowned with a wild head of broom-straw hair.

"You seeing faces like that?" Mattie asks, looking up from her cutting.

"You can't begin to know the faces I see in my head these days."

"If I was a bird, I'd be scared to fly in her puss and make it my home."

"Speaking of which, what you think of that Norvis Dibner and his face?"

"I don't think nothing about his face. Why you ask me that?"

"Well, he been by to check on you several times lately. I was just thinking that he was a nice-looking man."

"That don't have nothing to do with me." Mattie pushes the scraps of tin off her lap and onto the floor. She picks up another square and slaps it on her lap. "I didn't ask him to come around here. You know me better than that. I got no use for him." Mattie cuts at the tin without the pattern.

"I know you, too good. You got hold of a rope, and if you ain't careful, that rope gon' pull you in a dark hole you can't get out of. I know that."

"What hole is that?"

"The grave. You letting yourself be pulled into the grave and you not dead."

"And what do you mean by that?"

"Look at your feet, girl. You wearing a dead man's shoes that's about five sizes too big for you. You think that's good for your soul? You gon' put some of these nails in there and walk around on them too? So you can punish yourself for being alive?"

"I don't know what you're talking about. These boots are comfortable. I'll give the boots and shoes away when I'm ready."

"All I'm saying is, you living. They ain't no getting around that. You ain't the first one to lose a husband. I lost one myself. And the man you grieving over's my own son. I know the loss of him too. But you got to let go. Arty don't want this for you. Nobody does. I know Sammy been plaguing you, but I got to say, I worry about you too. You need to walk in your own shoes. And I don't mean just the shoes you got on your feet. I mean you got to live, even if Arty can't."

"I don't see how you, of all people, can say that to me." Mattie stops cutting. Puts the snips in her lap on top of the metal square. "Let's just talk about something else if you want me to help with this tin." Mattie starts cutting the tin again, roughly forcing the snips over a rib in the metal.

"All right. As long as I'm talking about faces, what about Doristeen? You know Sammy gon' marry Doristeen."

"Can't we talk about last Sunday's sermon or what kind of flowers you want to plant in that old bathtub Rachel painted and you put in the yard?"

"You don't like Doristeen, now do you?"

"She isn't the one I would have picked."

"I wouldn't have picked you neither. At least not when you first come here." Toot smiles at Mattie.

"What? What did you have against me? You sure did keep me a long time for somebody you didn't want." Mattie doesn't smile, but her temper eases.

"The first time you come here, I thought you was too citified to live out here and be satisfied. I was afraid you'd take Arty away from what he loved, this farm. I also thought you might get yourself killed."

"What are you talking about?"

"That bull!" Toot says and turns to look her daughter-in-law full in the face. Toot's lips are in a knot, but not a tight knot.

Mattie puts the snips in her lap again and laughs in spite of her effort to stay somber.

"Here we couldn't find you and looking all over for you. And where did I finally come across you? In the pasture with a Limousine bull, you standing right in front of him rubbing his face like he was a tired old mare. Petting the front of his head and saying how pretty he was. Looking him in the eye! I knew for sure we was gon' have a funeral before we had a wedding."

"Well, the bull never was nothing but nice to me." Mattie takes off one of her gloves and covers her face with her bare hand. She hasn't thought of that bull in years. When Arty told her later what could have happened, what likely would have happened, why you don't stand in front of a bull and look him in the eye, why you don't rub his head, why Toot had been mad as a wet hen, then Mattie's knees had gone to jelly. But there in the garage she shakes at the shoulders. At first Toot thinks she's crying, but when Mattie takes her hand down, she is laughing, laughing so hard she can't speak.

"There I was," Toot goes on, seeing Mattie's mood lightening, "telling you soft like to step back to the fence nice and slow and you just kept rubbing that bull's nose. I thought to myself, *Lord, you done brought my boy home with a fool for sure.*"

All the while Toot and Mattie laugh at the memory of Mattie's first day on the farm, the pink-faced woman looks on through her watery eyes.

"I guess we can put Doristeen in front of a bull and see how she do," Toot says and slaps her leg. Then they both bend over laughing. Toot keeps laughing at the thought of Mattie and that bull while she nails a pine box onto the back of another circle.

"It's not easy," Toot goes on, "to let a son go to his own woman. Not one that might keep him. I'm telling you, I was afraid of you when you come here. Afraid you'd take Arty from me. But you didn't. Not anymore than should happen when a man takes a wife. And you been a good friend to me and a good daughter I never had. I'm glad now that he brought you, and I'm glad the bull didn't kill you, I reckon. And maybe you need to give Doristeen a chance to be a friend to you."

"How can I do that if she's never here?"

"She will be."

"Maybe."

Toot lifts the next circle. It is a brown-faced man with black yarn for hair. Above the perfect inner circle of the birdhouse door Toot has painted an upper lip and a top row of teeth, one with a gold star and a diamond in the center of it.

"Lord ham mercy. Is that supposed to be Leroy?"

"Um-hum."

"You not gon' make a birdhouse out of Arty, are you?"

"I'm making faces. That's all I know."

Mattie stares at the new, round Leroy. "Well," she finally says, "Doristeen or not, Sammy is getting might attached to that boy."

"You can't tell me you don't love that boy, too. He grown on you like he grown on me. I might just let him call me Granny. But you remember," Toot points a finger at Mattie, "he was a good little thing when we got him. He good because she good to him. She independent. A woman need to be independent. Even when she marry a man, she need to be independent of him some. We don't know what the sun gon' bring with it when it come up. You know as well as me, we don't know what's gon' be here and what's gon' be gone. And my point about that nice Norvis Dibner is sometimes we don't know what's gon' show up, but we need to pay attention."

"Is the sermon over?" Mattie asks, then counts the misshapen halos she cut while she was mad.

"It's probably just getting started, but that'll do for today. It's time for supper."

"Let me ask you one thing, before we go to the house," Mattie says.

"Where did you get the idea for painting those houses you did last week?" Mattie points to the second shelf from the bottom. Bright birdhouses lined up in a row, a purple house with white lightning bolts, a green house with pink polka dots, a red house with pink and blue wavy lines, each house more bright and busy than the next.

"That Wally's socks, when he and Ginger bring Gracie out here to paint. I asked him to tell me about some more of his socks. They wild ain't they?" Toot shakes her head.

"They're wild, all right. What about the girl?"

"She ain't no girl. She nearly thirty, if she a day. I hope she don't ever have no children."

"Why in the world would you say a thing like that?"

"'Cause, she remind me too much of one them faces I have in my head. Now, let's go check on the roast. Ain't you hungry?"

Mattie stands up, straightens the tin, and puts the cut pieces on Toot's worktable while Toot closes up her paints and puts her brushes in turpentine. Toot turns off the heater.

"Thank the Lord," Mattie says.

"You gon' catch pneumonia," Toot says, as she latches the garage doors. Toot wraps her sweater around her to keep warm in the cold wind. Mattie opens herself up to the air, her bare arms spread, then she uses her handkerchief to mop at her neck and dab at the sweat pouring down her face.

Since the night Norvis lost his large fare to Toot's and Mattie's bargaining acumen, he has come to visit Rockrun two or three times a week. He says he's checking in on *the family*, but it's clear to everyone, even Tyrone, that Norvis is checking on Mattie.

Mattie could have run Norvis off any number of times, if he could be run off, but she hasn't tried too hard to discourage him. Just fussed a little bit for show. She takes a step forward and a step back, like a horse that's been stalled too long. Except, in Mattie's case, each step forward's a little longer, each step back's a little shorter. Toot has been where Mattie is now, feeling like part of her life has been amputated. Toot feels for Norvis Dibner, making that long drive up from North Carolina every chance he gets and not getting a thing but a little food for his trouble.

"She ain't home," Toot says this afternoon when he shows up. "Mattie gon' to the store."

"Well, if it's all right, I'll visit with you, Mrs. Riley."

"Come on in. I been crocheting an afghan all morning. I'm fixing to eat lunch. You want some?"

"Don't mind if I do," Norvis says. "Can I help you?" Toot sees that Norvis is just trying to be polite. He's not as anxious to help her as Ed was the day he came after Gracie. Norvis won't be asking Toot for her recipes.

Toot sets out two plates of pintos, collards, warmed-over cream potatoes, and a dab of cream corn. Then she comes back again with chopped onions, chow chow, and beet pickles in little glass dishes Tyrone gave her for Christmas. Then she thinks to get out some stewed tomatoes in case Norvis likes them on his beans. Finally, she puts some buttermilk in glasses and brings that to the table with silverware and a little plate of warmed-over corn bread.

"Thank you, ma'am. This looks mighty good."

Norvis reaches for his fork and Toot says, "You want to say grace?"

Norvis looks up and clears his throat, then moves his hand away from his fork like he wasn't going to pick it up anyway. He bows his head.

After he says the blessing, he reaches for his napkin this time and doesn't look at Toot until he's got a mouth full of beans. He reaches for the tomatoes. Toot smiles, satisfied. *I knew it. He look like a man would want stewed tomatoes in his beans.*

"You best call me Mama Toot like the rest, if you gon' be eating here regular. *Mrs. Riley* coming from somebody eating at my table regular make me sound like I run a boardinghouse. I don't do that."

"Call me Norvis."

"I already do."

Toot admires Norvis's nice looks, despite his ponytail and arthritis.

That can be good, because nobody wants to look on an ugly man all the time, but it can be bad if he doesn't have a good heart. Toot doesn't know yet what kind of heart he's got.

"Mattie, she may not like you inviting me to eat with you regular, you know," Norvis says. "I been coming here for a while now, and she don't seem to be warming up to me none. You got any insight into that, Mama Toot?"

"I know what it is to see safety in grief. I know what it is to fear life, to wrap your hand around a rope that ties you to death," Toot says. She knows why he's here same as him. No use in beating around the bush about it. "Mattie has done that, tied herself to that rope." Toot sees her wanting to look back to the light, but she doesn't say that to Norvis.

"You're talking about your son. Two years is a long time in some ways and short in others," he says and takes a big mouthful of warmed-over creamed potatoes. Toot thinks Norvis probably hasn't had a good meal since Sunday when she fed him after church. He eats good though when the food presents itself. That's a good sign all by itself. A drinking man doesn't eat good like that. Toot thinks about it and decides to talk some more about Mattie.

"You lose somebody, it's like hanging off a cliff," she says. "You hang there by a rope, and the dead, they try to pull you up and over the edge. And you thinking all the time they pulling you up and keeping you safe. But the tug of life pulls you down to the ground. Your hand slips little by little. But you work to stay with death. Your hand becomes used to the strain of holding on. You think death got you, but really you got death."

Toot leans over her plate and says, "You see what I'm saying?"

"Yes, ma'am," he says. Toot sees that he starts listening good because he knows she isn't just chatting. He knows she's decided to give what he's asking for. He's still eating, but he's slowed up.

"Now me," Toot says, "I held on so long that when my hand finally let go, well the rope held onto me. The rope and my hand become one in the same. I still wait. Death like the hand of a friend to me now. You get what I'm saying?"

"Yes, ma'am." She can see maybe he does understand.

"But Mattie," Toot says, "it's not too late for her. She can still let go of the rope. She can still fall back to the land of the living. Now if you was going to let go of a rope and fall, wouldn't you want to know what you was falling into?" He nods his head. "Would you want to look and see rocks, or grass, underneath you? Would you want to fall on rocks or grass?"

"Grass," he says.

"That's right," Toot says. "And it's up to you what she sees. It's up to you, Norvis Dibner. You see what I'm saying?"

"Yes, ma'am."

Toot looks in his eyes and sees that he knows exactly what she's saying. At first he doesn't say anything. Then he surprises Toot, and she doesn't surprise easy.

"I'm not a stranger to the rope you speak of," Norvis confesses, and puts his fork on the table. "The truth is, I've been twice widowed. I've felt grief squeeze the breath out of me." Norvis puts his hands flat on the table, as flat as they go. "The first time it squeezed, it squeezed me down into a bottle. I was young and had no faith in time or anything else. The second go-round, grief just took my ambition, that's all. But each time I've come back to a place just beyond misery's touch. I'd like to help Mattie do that. But I know I can't. I can wait around, though, and see if she comes back to that place on her own. Forgive me, Mama Toot, but I also know that what starts out being grief can become self-pity. What starts out being about someone else ends up being about you. And the more folks you have offering you a push, the less likely a grieving person is to let self-pity become everything." Toot just listens, sees how far he's going to go. "Sometimes a face, a face from out of the blue, can call you into another stage of living. Like a woman's face in the middle of the night, a woman holding a baseball bat in one hand and pushing up her hair with the other." He takes a piece of corn bread and butters it and doesn't look at Toot until he's taken a bite and swallowed it down with a little buttermilk.

Toot eats and lets him eat, until they start talking about the snow that's coming. But Toot knows he's thinking about what she's said, and she's thinking about what he's said. *What do you want to be? You think I'm gon' to help her let go of the rope to fall on rocks? If you think that, you don't know the power of death.*

"You want some sweet potato pie?" Toot offers.

"Oh my," Norvis says, loud like he's full. "I think I have just enough room for one piece."

He smiles a good smile, and Toot says to herself, *That's a good sign.*

Just then Mattie comes in the back door. "I might have known you'd be here," she says to Norvis. "When is it you drive your cab? And what town—excuse me—what state is it you live in?"

"Good afternoon to you too, Mrs. Riley."

Mattie looks hard at Norvis Dibner. Then her face softens a bit.

"Just call me Mattie," she says. Mattie sets down two paper sacks on the kitchen counter. "If you're going be here all the time and help DuRon eat all our food, you might as well help me carry it in." She turns to go back outside to Sammy's truck for more sacks. Norvis Dibner winks at Toot, gets up from the table, and follows Mattie out the door, leaving his pie for a little later.

TOOT SITS IN the third pew on the right, near the aisle, where she always sits. She and Homer sat together years before, then she and Homer and Arty, then she and Homer and Arty and Mattie and Sammy. When Homer passed, it was Toot and Mattie and Arty and Sammy. Then Toot and Mattie and Sammy and Gracie and Tyrone. Today it is down to Toot and Norvis Dibner.

Toot starts to pray softly to herself. The pew looks empty and feels full. Homer, Arty, Mattie, Sammy, Gracie, Tyrone, Norvis. Toot even pictures Doristeen fitting in there someplace. She feels them all praying.

Toot's fingers slide up and down against the smooth pale wood of her pew. It is her pew. Arty donated five hundred dollars to the Jezereel Holiness Church and told them to put his mama's name on her own bench.

This morning Mattie is in the nursery taking care of babies. Tyrone is helping her. Reverend Love is fixing to close out his most recent revival with a Sunday morning service. He has been preaching and preaching for two solid weeks. Norvis shifts around in his seat.

Toot's left hand flattens into and smooths over the empty space beside her that Gracie has taken up for weeks. Gracie. Rachel. It doesn't matter what name she goes by. With her hand on the bench, Toot feels Gracie vibrate out of the wood and into the sanctuary. They are sad vibrations. Toot becomes restless. She places her purse in her lap and taps her fingers lightly against the navy leather. Rubs her thumb over the gold-plated clasp and the blue leather handle. She smooths her dress and smooths her fingers over her purse again. She puts it down on the floor under the pew in front of her where it was before and draws her Bible to her lap instead.

"Brothers and Sisters, can I get an aMEN this MORNing?" Deacon Alston stands at the pulpit, tapping the microphone only to get a flat tip-tip-tip. From the milling congregation making their collective way to seats in the two rows of short pews and greeting and hugging friends and relatives all along the way, Deacon Alston gets a faint but cohesive aMEN. With this signal from him, everyone begins moving with more purpose to their seats and the focus of the morning shifts from greeting each other to greeting God.

Deacon Alston looks back to Deacon Regina Childs to assist him with the microphone. A lanky woman, with bone structure so sharp she might cut you if you get too close, glides across the altar stage. She has a way of standing and moving in her red suit with broad shoulder pads that lets you know it is her space she travels in—wherever she goes. Deacon Childs walks to the panel box in the choir loft just behind the pulpit and switches buttons on and off until Deacon Alston's finger makes a loud TAP-TAP on the microphone. He nods and she gives a nod in return, then glides back to her seat behind Deacon Alston.

"God is good," he says into the round head of the microphone.

God is GOOD to ME, answers the congregation a little louder than before.

"I SAID, GOD—IS—GOOD."

God is GOOD to ME.

"AMEN!"

AMEN! *Praise JESUS! GLORY hallelujah!*

Deacon Alston continues to warm up the congregation. This is a talent. Deacon Alston knows it and the preachers he works with know it. It is important to get the spirit moving among the people, get them focused on their prayerful purpose of praise. But it is equally important to know when to hold back. Not let your ego take you too far. An inexperienced deacon or preacher can shoot a revival right in the foot by taking the congregation too far too fast. The whole room will peak quickly and then be flat for the rest of the night.

"Are you here to praise JEsus?" Deacon Alston asks. His gaze sails out over the full church, one hundred and fifty members. It grazes the tops of all their heads. He speaks to the back walls and the double doors being closed by those members who'll sit in the rear. The church is packed today. The collection may pay for the rewiring necessary to keep the church safe—that part of the collection that doesn't go to Reverend Love. He takes fifty percent.

Some members of the crowd are regulars at Jezereel Holiness Church. This is their spiritual home. This church was their family's church before them. Some people in the pews are from neighboring churches. Some come from far off. They come to hear Reverend Love wherever he preaches, mostly women, middle-aged women.

"Do you love JEsus?" Deacon Alston asks in a lower voice. He doesn't want them jumping off the cliff yet. Just to come closer to the edge.

"We all know JEsus. JEsus at the door. JEsus praying in the garden. JEsus and the little children. JEsus at the Last Supper."

AMEN! AMEN!

Deacon Alston looks for Sister Mattie Riley in the congregation. He's been keeping his eye on her. He noticed her more regular use of the fan in church. Last Sunday she was taking big sweeping strokes at air with Jesus in the garden. It must be near her time. If it's one thing Deacon Alston has learned in his sixty-eight years on this Earth, it is to stay clear of women in that kind of way. Yes, sir, women in their time are dangerous. Deacon Alston is tugged away from his thoughts of Mattie Riley by the hum in the front row. Lillian Harris is beginning the guttural drone that will shortly send her into the hands of the Holy Spirit.

"Would someone like to get us started this morning?" Deacon Alston calls. "Give thanks to GOD for working in their LIFE this week? Start us out with a SONG? AMEN."

A heavy woman in her thirties halfway down toward the pulpit stands and adjusts her jacket. "I give thanks to the Lord," she says strongly, "for my children, and my husband, and my little house. I want to thank GOD for each day that I WAKE UP healthy in the MORNing. I want to THANK GOD for keeping me STRONG in the face of things that would WEAKEN me. AMEN."

AMEN AND AMEN!

The visiting woman, Thelma Pace's cousin from Maryland, begins to hold her hands over her head and mumble to herself, "Walk with me, Jesus. Bless me, Lord. Sanctify and shield my family." On and on she prays half to herself.

As Thelma's cousin sits down, another voice comes from the far corner of the church. Loud. Sweet. Clear. Mellow-smooth. Embellishing. "Ho-o-o-oLY i-i-i-is THY na-a-ame."

"Can I get a witNESS?" Deacon Alston calls, throwing his shoulders from side to side as he punctuates his request with kinesthetic enthusiasm.

Praise God! Praise JEsus! Amen and AMEN!

The sound of prayerful voices begins to fill the sanctuary as people take themselves to a higher spiritual mindset. Momentum builds until finally Sister Mary Heart stands, another long body with graceful arms and neck and dark fingerwaves carefully outlining the beautiful shape of her head.

"God is good," she begins. "God is good." Her graceful fingers point in little jabs around the room to signify that God is good to everyone around her. "God is good to you, and you, and you."

Yes. Yes, He is. Hallelujah! Have mercy.

"And we are here today to thank JEsus for keeping us safe ONE more WEEK, for some of us, ONE more DAY." Her hands hang gracefully in the air.

AMEN! Amen! Amen! Say it, sister.

Sister Mary begins to sway her long reedlike body and clap her hands, sliding her fingers down across her palm to circle back up and slap and slide again.

"I am here to tell you."

Yes, yes, yes. You tell it.

"I am here to tell you that GOD works in MY life EVERY day."

Amen. Sing it, Sister.

"He has HELD me."

Oh yeah.

"STROKED me."

Oh yeah.

"SAVED me."

Tell it! Tell it!

"ForGAVE me."

Amen!

"LED me,"

Pray it, Sister!

"THROUGH the Valley of the SHADOW of Death."

Ungh. Praise JEsus!

"And I made it through beCAUSE GOD got to me in time."

Oh yeah!

"IN time, ON time, time AFTER time."

Yes! Praise God! Praise the Lord Sister.

"My God is an ON TIME God. He didn't come too soon."

No, sir.

"He didn't come too late."

No, sir.

"He came ON time."

On time!

"And I THANK you, Lord, THANK you, JEsus."

Amen and AMEN! Praise God! Praise Him. Jesus!

Sister Heart sits down until the hymn starts. Then she is back up and swaying like a reed again. Ready to jump with the Spirit. She periodically wipes at the tears streaking her face.

Toot closes her eyes and rocks gently to the rhythm of prayer and song.

The men's choir takes to the choir loft and begins to rock into "Walk with Jesus." The congregation is singing and walking in place. The people are slapping and sliding their hands to the beat of the music. Toot keeps her eyes closed and concentrates on her own walk with Jesus. Norvis watches and hears. He sways to the men's voices, his own voice deep and foundational and mixed in with the church's united voice. But Norvis's eyes are open. He appears a detached witness. Toot begins to hum. She hums and rocks until Deacon Alston takes quick charge of the pulpit again to welcome Reverend Love.

As the Spirit builds around her, Toot begins to rock back and forth a little stronger and her fingers clamp around the lip of the bench to anchor her motion and her soft song. *Wade in the water,* she sings. *Wade in the water, children. Wade in the water. God's gon' trouble the water.* She tries to pray, but as she asks the Spirit to fill her with light, she sees in her mind the scenes that have haunted her in her sleep since Gracie was first hauled away by those two deputies that came with DuRon. But this isn't a woman in Toot's head. It is a young white girl, eight or so years old. She has bright red hair, wispy curls. Her eyes are hidden by long bangs that nobody trims. She wears a pale blue dress and red tennis shoes. She carries a doll with a cracked forehead and a dirty white dress.

The first night she dreamed about the girl, she had seen her outside the store. RAINBOW IS GOOD BREAD was written in bright colors on the metal sign attached to the screen doors, what little screen was left. The store was sad and dirty, but two pretty white wicker chairs sat on the wooden walkway before it. In spite of all the colors, everything looked yellow. Like everything had been Cloroxed a few times too many.

Toot goes on rocking and humming up stream, *Wade in the water, children,* while the congregation drowns her out with its *Walk with Jesus.* Norvis Dibner hears the difference, but knows better than to trouble Toot when she is taken with the Spirit.

The second night the girl had come to Toot in her dream, she was in a graveyard. Not the one at Mount Jezereel, but some other place. In the distance was a hip-roofed house with the windows boarded up. A big oak tree shaded one corner and weeds and kudzu grew up into cracks in the window seals and cracks in the walls. The house was up on blocks. Some trash house. The electric box looked bigger than usual. The sky was black and the clouds were white. And yet, the clouds feathered out at the edges into gray and then smokelike smudges. It was daytime. The redhead peeked out from behind the oak tree. The tip of a red shoe edged out from behind a big root. Again everything is bleached out yellow except for the sky and the child and the toe of the red shoe.

Reverend Love keeps everyone singing and Deacon Childs stands beside him marching in place and singing, looking into his eyes every so often.

The third night Toot's dream was about a hallway, big, with waxed oak floors and a polished cherry table in the center. Sun came streaming through the twin screens at the end of the hallway. A man stood in the center of the hall behind the round table. He had boots on and a long coat. But the man himself was hidden in the sun's light, or maybe it was the light reflected from the polished cherry table. A banister looped around to the left and out of her dream. Toot had opened her eyes the next morning knowing the little girl had been on the steps, hiding, getting smaller and smaller, trying to be invisible.

Reverend Love's body movement is changing. When he took the pulpit he was cool, deliberate. Now he is moving in a way not of his own making. A jump here. Raised hands there. The Spirit is moving in him. Toot rocks on and hums, lost for the moment in the memory of her recent visions.

The fourth dream was of a big brick house, like a plantation house, with columns and big oak trees all around the house, but not up the drive. This house had no tree-lined road. This was a ghost house. Empty and dark but with bright white columns, as if somebody had let the house decompose, except for the white columns and the triangle of white wood under the front porch roof. Weeds grew everywhere and there were dark patches in the weeds that showed when the wind blew. Toot was tired the next morning because she had spent all her sleeping time trying to find the little redheaded girl with the blue dress and the red shoes.

As Toot rocks back and forth, she still searches for the redheaded girl among the weeds and in the patches of darkness. As she rocks and hums, Reverend Love takes the pulpit fully and calls the congregation to turn to

First Samuel 30 and 31. Toot hears Reverend Love tell the tale of David and Ziklag and David's two wives, Ahinoam and Abigail, and his daughters—all taken by the Amalekites. Ziklag was burned and David was beside himself.

"David was DIStressed. He was DIStressed," Reverend Love repeats in his sweet Philly preaching voice. Toot sings softly as he preaches, "I am distressed. Why am I distressed? Where is the child?" And as Toot asks the questions she sees that old house is on fire. Only the white columns are not burning.

Reverend Love is in the throes of his own preaching. He is a fine preacher too. He is hopping and jumping, and in the most subtle and powerful way. "DAvid said to the priest Abiathar son of Ahimelech, 'BRING me the EEphod.' And what my good BROTHers and SISTers is an EEphod? Can you TELL me what IS an EEphod?"

From the back of the sanctuary, Sister Thelma in a deep voice coming close to passion says, "PRAISE garment! Praise Jesus!"

"A PRAISE garment!" Reverend Love echoes. "DAvid asked for his PRAISE garment. In the midst of ALL he lost, he knew to praise GOD. And when DAvid asked GOD what should he do, what did GOD say to DAvid?"

Pursue! AMEN.

"PurSUE; for you shall SUREly overTAKE and shall SUREly REScue."

In her trance, Toot turns from the burning house and she sees the little redheaded girl being taken away. Dragged by the arms, one of her red shoes dangling from her foot about to be caught and devoured by the weeds and the roots rising up out of the ground. Two deputies are taking the child away. She hangs from their hands, not hollering but crying. Crying to Toot. *Tootsie Mae, please. Tootsie Mae, please be my mama.*

Toot opens her eyes and turns to Norvis Dibner, who is mesmerized, watching only her. She pinches him to snap out of his own trance and pay attention. She whispers so low he barely hears her, "We got to GO. We got to take the cab to North Carolina. We got to FETCH the ephod." She stands up and walks up the aisle and through the church doors, Norvis Dibner close on her heels.

SECOND OFFERING

What is fidelity? To what does it hold?
The point of departure, or the turning road that is departure and
absence and the way home?

—Wendell Berry

"I JUST WANT what's best for my wife, Dr. Bradigan. I just want what's best for Gracie."

"My name is Rachel. I want to be the ex-wife and live with Tootsie Mae. That's what I'm supposed to do."

"I'm sorry, honey. I'm trying to remember to call you Rachel, but *Gracie's* a hard habit to break after thirty years. I'm trying though. I'm really trying."

He is trying, a voice says to Gracie.

"Yes . . . well . . . I think we'll . . . get to that," says Dr. Bradigan. "We have a lot of . . . items to discuss, according to Miss Hollaman's . . . list."

Dr. Bradigan is a beautiful man, tall and fair-skinned, sprinkled with freckles, a gleaming white beard and close-cropped hair, starched white coat that he leaves open. He looks like he just stepped off a tractor and put on that white coat so he can play doctor. His halting speech is annoying at first, but then it becomes somewhat soothing, except to Ginger who today can't be soothed.

With Coats County's small budget for its Day Treatment Program, Bradigan, unlike many psychiatrists, directs the program, conducts therapy sessions with the patients, and monitors their medications. The facilities are small, so the group sits around the round laminated maple table in the break area of the county offices, the table a donation from someone's kitchen. A box of assorted Dixie Donuts rests in the center of the round table, and everyone has a small white Styrofoam cup of coffee with powdered creamer.

The refrigerator kicks in and out of a loud hum, and when it kicks in, they all talk louder. "You get used to it," Bradigan says, reaching for a powdered doughnut. Then everyone reaches for a doughnut except Gracie. Bradigan has put a sign on the break room doorknob that says, *In use*, and closed the door. Around the table in clockwise order are Ed, Gracie, Toot, and Ginger. Mattie is back at the farm and leaving the business of it all to Toot.

"If you can take her in your program, I think we got most of it worked out," says Toot.

"I just want to be sure we're all on the same page. That's all," says Ginger. "That's why I made the list. Anyone's welcome to add anything I've left off."

"When is . . . Rachel"—Dr. Bradigan gives a nod toward Gracie—"planning to . . . move to Rockrun?"

"She moved," says Toot. "We got her stuff this morning and she all settled in, ain't that right, Ed? We gon' build a bigger room for her onto the back of the house, ain't that right?"

Ed nods confirmation.

"And you will be in charge of her care, Mrs. Riley?"

"Yes, sir. Ed still be helping, but she gon' live with me and do her paintings and my daughter-in-law and me be giving her the medicines and keeping an eye on her. We got a big family, we all keep an eye on her. Ed, he gon' make sure she supplied in car parts and paints and all the other things she need. You got to come see her paintings on the car parts. Some woman in Atlanta wants to sell 'em."

"I'd . . . love to see Rachel's . . . artwork . . . Well then . . . we can get the . . . paperwork filled out . . . today and you can start the program . . . next week, Rachel. How's that? We'll start getting . . . to know each other a . . . little better then."

Gracie doesn't say anything, she only looks at Toot.

"Now . . . let's have a look at this . . . list," says Bradigan.

"I put divorce at the top because I think it warrants the most discussion, since it appears many of the other decisions have already been made." Ginger gives Ed and Toot a stern look. She is pissed off that the arrangements were decided on before she was brought into the conversation, and she has no intention of letting them forget it.

"My circle's closing. I need to be the ex-wife," says Gracie emphatically. She taps her index finger hard on the tabletop. "And Frank, at the other hospital, said I can get my name changed legally for two dollars, if I do it when I get divorced."

Good memory. I'd forgotten that, says a voice.

"Rachel," says Bradigan, "do you want a divorce because you want to change your name? You can do that without a divorce."

Tell him, says a voice. *Tell him what you want.*

"I want to be the ex-wife," says Rachel, tapping her finger hard with each item on her list, "and I want to be Rachel Price, and I want to paint car parts, and I want to live with Tootsie Mae, and I want to close this old circle. That's my list."

Good. You got the whole list. Very good.

"I see," says Bradigan.

"What do you see?" asks Gracie.

"I see . . . that you have a very . . . well-thought-out . . . list of your own," says Bradigan, smiling.

Gracie smiles back.

"Are we going to let a crazy woman make her own decisions? Sorry, Mama."

"Miss Hollaman . . ." Bradigan says patiently but not condescendingly, "We're simply . . . discussing . . . possibilities for Rachel's future today, and Mr. Hollaman . . . and Mrs. Riley . . . have asked me to be included in the . . . discussion, since I'll be treating Rachel for an . . . undetermined time. The decisions are not . . . written in stone, and I have no . . . final say. The logistics of a divorce . . . are a family . . . legal matter that . . . if I understand correctly . . . have been discussed with legal . . . counsel. It's my understanding that Rachel still has her own . . . power of attorney . . . and if she seems to be of sound . . . *enough* . . . mind . . . to make a . . . *somewhat* rational . . . choice, and the other parties involved . . . agree to that choice . . . and arrangements have been made for her . . . care and support . . . I can't see that her . . . wishes wouldn't weigh in . . . rather largely . . . on the decisions at hand." Bradigan turns to Ed and Ginger pushes back from the table. "What about you . . . Mr. Hollaman? How do you . . . feel . . . about a . . . divorce?"

"Not so good, exactly. We've been married for almost thirty years. I don't want it to look like I'm divorcing Rachel because she's sick. I wouldn't ever do that. It's not her fault she's sick." Ed shifts around in his seat, looks Ginger in the eye for a couple of seconds, then at the table. "But she seems hell-bent on being the *ex-wife*, so I'm willing to do what she wants, as long as it's clear I am still a responsible man and have her best interests at the front of it all. I'll be honest." Ed looks up at Dr. Bradigan. "I got used to being on my own when she ran away and I didn't know where in the world she was. And I got pretty angry because I thought she'd run off and left me, maybe for another man. But now I know she just wants to close that daggone circle, and I'm willing to do what's best for her. Hell, she's been home from the hospital for two weeks, and I can't get her to eat a blamed thing at our house. And she won't eat if we go out because I'm paying for it, even if I give her the money. She'll starve to death if she stays with me."

"I've disenchanted him." Gracie leans into the conversation. "I can't risk eating anything that man offers. It's the rules. I've told him that. I don't think it's poison, it may be good, but I can't risk it."

"I see," says Dr. Bradigan.

"See what?" says Gracie.

"That you've . . . disenchanted him."

Everyone in the room looks at Bradigan.

"A fairy can . . . enchant a person . . . if the person . . . accepts food from the fairy's . . . hand. I'm part . . . Irish. . . . We tend to . . . know these things."

Ah! A smart one, says a voice. *He's good*, says another.

Gracie smiles.

"Mr. Hollaman . . . there's no legal . . . reason why you and Rachel can't . . . get divorced if you both . . . agree that's the thing to . . . do . . . particularly if you're . . . willing to still be . . . responsible for her welfare. I'm not a lawyer, mind you. But . . . based on my . . . time in the business, I'd say this can all be . . . worked out to everyone's . . . satisfaction. And if Mrs. Riley is in agreement about . . . all the arrangements . . . what else would you . . . like to discuss, Miss Hollaman?" Bradigan turns to Ginger, who crosses her arms in front of her.

"That's it? You're just going to let the queen of the fairies call her own shots?"

"Within . . . reason," Bradigan says to Ginger. Then to the group, as he rubs his hands together, "Now . . . we have a two-day . . . program for the . . . older clients. They're called . . . clients now . . . not patients. And a . . . two-day . . . program for the younger clients. Then everyone comes in on . . . Fridays, and we have a little . . . fund-raiser . . . where the clients run a . . . biscuit sale to the state . . . employees in the mornings. The clients . . . enjoy it, and it . . . helps us pay for some of our . . . field trips and other . . . extracurricular activities." To Gracie, "Rachel . . . would you like to come for the whole . . . week next week and . . . see which group . . . you prefer? At your . . . age . . . you are right in the . . . middle."

Gracie smiles and nods.

"You are all welcome . . . to visit the . . . program or volunteer at any . . . time, and I'll be in touch with each of you as I get to . . . know Rachel a little better. Dr. Post and Dr. Warner and I have had a . . . conference call about Rachel's . . . current treatment, and their . . . outpatient instructions, and for now we'll . . . stick pretty close to that. Now, it's almost break . . . time. We better open the door. I don't want to make any . . . enemies among the . . . budget makers or the . . . check signers." Bradigan laughs.

"What about the rest of my list?" says Ginger.

"Most of what's on your . . . list, Miss. Hollaman, will be better . . . discussed with the . . . lawyer handling the separation . . . agreement. You are clearly a . . . strong . . . advocate for your mother. I suggest you express your . . . concerns as that . . . process . . . unfolds. Now . . . shall we?"

They all rise.

When Ed gets back from Rockrun, he goes to the guest room to straighten things up. He strips Gracie's bed and washes the sheets. He dusts and vacuums and waters the plants she refused to take with her, the ones the guys at the shop and Estelle sent when she was in the hospital. He gets the dust mop and runs it under the bed. The rocks are gone, but the mop head strikes something more substantial than dust motes. Ed gets down lower and swings the mop across the floor in the other direction, from head to foot. Out from under the bed comes Number One and Number Two of the red books, the ones Gracie searched for in the attic.

He sits at the kitchen table and takes a drink of Viennese cinnamon coffee. Parva had coffee toddies on sale last week, and Ed has taken to cold brew. He opens Number Two and thumbs through the first few pages. Many of them look like a two-year-old got hold of them with a pair of scissors, but it was only Gracie looking for her baby. He spots a fairy Gracie missed. One she didn't cut up and put in her pasteboard box. Then he sees there are several on the page. They are blowing long toothpicklike trumpets and waving toothpicklike wands. Ed's eyes fall to the left-hand page and he reads the poem there.

SOMETIMES

Some days are fairy days.
   The minute that you wake
You have a magic feeling
   that you never could mistake;
You may not see the fairies,
   but you know that they're about,
And any single minute they
   might all come popping out;
You want to laugh, you want to sing,
   you want to dance and run,
Everything is different,
   everything is fun;
The sky is full of fairy clouds,
   the streets are fairy ways—
Anything can happen
on truly fairy days.

Some nights are fairy nights.
   Before you go to bed

You hear their darling music
  go chiming in your head;
You look into the garden,
  and through the misty grey
You see the trees all waiting
  in a breathless kind of way.
All the stars are smiling;
  they know that very soon
The fairies will come singing
  from the land behind the moon.
If only you could keep awake
  when Nurse puts out the light . . .
Anything can happen
  on a truly fairy night.

The house is still and quiet. The chimes hang mute from their many fixtures. Emptiness echoes from one wall to the other, but its lonely movement makes no breeze, no shift in anything, least of all the chimes. Ed sits at the table long after his coffee cup is empty. He opens Number One and turns the pages. As if some fairy whispered in his ear, he knows there is another poem in there, one meant for him to read. He feels it in his fingers as he lifts the browning pages. The book feels heavier as he moves closer, page by turning page. Then he sees it. Page eighty-one, "The Butter-Bean Tent." The title calls to him with that familiar term from long ago. It makes everything fall apart, makes everything come together, makes it clear that nothing in life is what it seems. He reads the words he knows are left behind for him to see.

Such a good day it was when I spent
A long, long while in the butter-bean tent.

Ed knows when he goes to his room to go to bed that the Jesus with the open arms will no longer have a poker face. He will have a satisfied face, a contented face. Ed reads the poem one last time and lets Number One fall closed in his hands.

"THIS HAS GOT to be one of the dumbest ideas I have ever heard of," Ginger says.

"Not really, Miss Hollaman . . . Action is . . . everything. The subconscious understands visual . . . cues, so to give an action is to give a . . . visual cue, you see."

"You want me to go defile graves with a shovel so she can mail letters to dead people?"

"Well . . . when you put it that way . . . yes. I don't think you need a . . . shovel. I imagine you can get the job . . . done . . . with a little . . . garden trowel. And I think this will . . . help her resolve . . . issues with family members and . . . others . . . who are . . . passed away. You just said you would do anything to . . . help your mother."

"Except this. I could get arrested. Defiling graves is a crime."

"Well, if you took the smaller . . . implement, and were very . . . subtle, I think you could manage it. You seem . . . quite . . . capable when . . . determined."

"But I don't know why I should risk going to jail for a mama that only talks about some baby she never had. I mean, what about me?"

"Miss Hollaman . . ."

"Look, if I'm going to be coming out here as part of her family support, call me Ginger. That Miss Hollaman stuff gets on my nerves."

"Ginger . . . have you ever seen the pictures of the . . . *fairy child?* The ones your mother . . . cut out of the . . . Childcraft volume?"

"No."

"You see, your mother is . . . very sick and . . . her brain isn't working . . . properly. But her subconscious mind is still a very . . . strong . . . aspect of who she is. I sense a very . . . powerful . . . subtext in Rachel's psychotic . . . construct. There is a part of Gracie that still . . . wants very much to be . . . your mother. The fairies in question bear a striking . . . resemblance to you."

"What?" asks Ginger, half curious and half peeved.

"By . . . creating this . . . fairy child, she can . . . possibly . . . be your mother . . . even in her new persona. Gracie knows you aren't the type of personality to . . . play along. So she . . . makes you a fairy she can . . . take with her."

"Are you sure about this?"

"Not at all. It's just a . . . hunch."

Ginger sits silently for a couple of minutes. Bradigan gives her the time she needs. Silence never bothers him. Ginger pulls her down coat from the empty half of the love seat she sits on and hugs it to her.

"Okay, I'll buy the garden trowel."

The timer on Dr. Bradigan's cluttered desk goes off and their session is done for the day.

Bernadette Seniese's silver all-wheel-drive Volvo station wagon bumps along the gravel road. She glances down at the directions Ed Hollaman gave her. Everything looks right so far. He said there would be a big curve on the gravel road and then the view would open up and the Riley farm would be in front of her. She sees a sharp curve coming up. Something white is visible through the bare trees. As she rounds the curve, the trees stop and the fields begin. The white house sits to the right of the road. "As soon as you see it, you'll know it," Hollaman said.

The yard is full of painted objects, mostly automotive parts. Fenders, trunks, hoods, some framed in the chrome grills or bumpers of other cars. A brown, V-shaped car hood hangs by yellow nylon rope from a pin oak. The crucifixion is painted on it, the size of Christ's hands and feet exaggerated, calling attention to the nails buried there. A few feet away, a trunk lid is painted with Jesus sitting on a rock, apparently laughing with small children who all have gossamer wings. He is laughing hard enough to be bent over. And the children are laughing too. Giggling, it looks like.

Bernadette pulls the Volvo up in front of the house and gets out. She walks up to each painted car part and snaps a photograph.

"May I help you?" a small voice asks. Bernadette turns to see a boy in a quilted nylon jacket and a hat with flaps down over his ears standing on the porch. The chin strap for his hat blows out from his face in the light wind that crosses the yard. "Are you the gallery lady?"

"Yes, that would be me. I'm Bernadette Seniese. And you are?"

"Tyrone."

"Is Rachel Price around?"

"She's at the mental health center. It's Tuesday."

"Does she go there every Tuesday?"

"Yes, ma'am. Tuesday and Thursday. She won't be home until about three-thirty. Granny Toot isn't here, either. Do you want me to get Sammy or Mama Mattie?"

"Yes, I'd like to talk to someone about these wonderful paintings. What's this one? Do you know?" Bernadette refers to a painting of a tree that goes around the sides of a large metal drum. The leaves intertwine over the top.

"That's a bower. Have you ever heard of the Australian Bowerbird?"

"Can't say as I have."

"The other name for it is a butterbean tent. It's a house made out of trees."

"You're a very smart young man."

"Thank you. I'm an artist too."

"How fortunate for me," Bernadette says, and smiles.

Tyrone smiles back and leaves Bernadette in the yard taking photographs. She is already intently deciding how to best exhibit them. What price will she set for them? Will Gracie care? Who will she call first about them? She will have five of them sold by tomorrow, keeping them on loan for the exhibit, of course. What a find! The mural at the hospital pales when compared to the visionary images on the various metal shapes scattered throughout the yard. The paintings are more passionate, more narrative, more intense. Bernadette can see Gracie's talent growing, deepening. *These things are so hot with color, they sizzle!* "God, what a find," she whispers.

Something moves to her left, just at the edge of her vision. When she glances over, there's nothing there. Then she looks down and sees a yellow dog dancing as if she's with someone. The dog is eager and ready and wanting something thrown her way. Suddenly she lunges and then hops like a deer through the grass toward the fence row at the edge of the yard, as if she is running after something, fetching an invisible stick.

PARVA HAS A GALLEY kitchen at the back of her apartment with a window that looks out onto the landing of a back stairway. The trash cans are under the stairs and her recycling bins are on the landing. She has a smidgen of green grass she calls her backyard. In the summer, she puts pink geraniums on the steps, big full pots. Two lawn chairs are folded up under the steps beside the trash cans. She pulls those out on pretty days, sits in one and puts her feet on the other. She used to hope maybe someone would come sit in the other chair. Now that it's happened, she wonders what she will do with her feet.

The dinette set is at the kitchen end of the long living room and a couch, a chair, and a TV are at the other end, by the door. There is a little hallway beside the table that leads to the bathroom and the bedroom, just big enough for Parva's double bed and dresser and a comfortable reading chair with ottoman. Lace curtains sift the light in every room, light in, prying eyes out. Parva has never liked feeling watched.

Lamps are everywhere. Parva doesn't use the overhead. She prefers the soft, indirect light. It makes everything look richer than it is. It allows for more shadows, and possibility dwells in the shadows. The quilt her mother made when Parva graduated high school hangs behind a basic cream-colored sleeper sofa bed. She's only pulled it out once for a cousin who came to visit when Parva had surgery on her foot. Parva's mother doesn't drive. The quilt on her bed is the one her mother made for Parva's hope chest. But Parva reached a point without hope a few years ago and put the quilt on the bed and made the chest a coffee table. She puts several heavy books on the coffee table–hope chest, otherwise the lid pops up.

This isn't how she thought it would be. She's saved herself, the way her mother told her to. She had a few heated dates in the backseat of a GTO in high school, but never more than a little petting, and she felt guilty about that. But it turns out she didn't save herself for a husband. Not a husband anytime soon, anyway. But he's coming to her apartment for the first time. It's Valentine's Day, and he is coming over for dinner. First he's going to Rockrun to see his wife this afternoon, take her a heart-shaped box of candy like he has every year they've been married, even though she won't eat it. He accepts that.

Edgar is getting divorced because his wife wants that. And lucky for Parva, because Ed isn't the kind of man to divorce his wife because she's sick. Parva can only say what she knows: Edgar is the one, the one she's waited for. She'll take him however she can get him, whatever the timetable. That's really all she knows. She's almost too old, but she's going to scoot under the wire and act like a young woman.

She's been reading books and looking at pictures and deciding how she wants the evening to go. There are red candles on the table, long tapers in glass candlesticks. She's sprinkled red glitter over the white tablecloth. She's using her best china—Spode. And in the bedroom, there are twenty glass votive holders with red unscented candles in each one, the wicks pulled up for easy lighting. Books of matches are placed in several strategic places. People light votive candles to keep a prayer going long after they have gotten up off their knees. Parva believes these candles will be praying with her tonight. She thought about scented candles, aromatherapy. Aphrodisiacs perhaps. But the truth is, the smell of those scented candles gives her a headache. And the last thing she wants tonight is a headache.

They are having sirloin medallions in a burgundy gravy, a salad, and a small sweet potato. Supper should be light. She read that in a book. Men get sleepy when they've had too much to eat. She doesn't want him to be sleepy. Not tonight. Dessert is raspberry sorbet, if they get to dessert. Breath mints are hidden in various places throughout the apartment.

Her dress is black crepe with buttons up the front, and she's wearing black sheer stockings, deciding against the seam up the back. She wants to look elegant, not slutty. She did opt for a garter belt and real stockings.

They feel funny, but nice. Her bra matches the garter belt—black silk from Victoria's Secret. The sales clerk said large women shop there all the time. Parva was surprised. Goodness knows what made her walk in there in the first place. She was on her way to lunch. The sales clerk sold her on tap pants too. Her hairdresser kept her in the chair from seven this morning until right before Dillard's opened the doors at ten. She always likes a new hairdo better when she has a chance to fix it herself. Everything she did today makes her feel sexy. She hasn't felt sexy in years. And the garters are a kick. It may be sexy or funny—this evening ahead of them. Either way will be fine. As long as they are clear, honest.

Parva invited Edgar to her apartment because she didn't want the Jesuses watching. Theoretically He is always watching, but she doesn't want to think about it. Even so, she can't get the Jesus in the foyer out of her head. The one knocking on the door. Knocking on a door that's almost never used. *What did she mean by that? What was her purpose in that?*

There it is. She hears it. The knock at the door. Parva walks quietly across the carpet in her black sling backs with French heels, also new. She can hear the soft swish of her stockings as they rub together with each step. The door swings open and there stands Edgar in a suit and tie, holding red roses. She sees he's nervous, it's there in his shoulders. But they'll get through it without a hitch this time. She can't get under the bed here. For one thing, it isn't high enough. For another, there are too many boxes under there. Not much storage in this apartment. She doesn't have any Jesuses to stare them down. Gracie is with Toot, where she wants to be. Ginger doesn't know where Parva lives. There is nothing between them here in this little apartment except what they place there.

"Good evening," Parva says, as she invites Edgar across the threshold.

"Good evening," he says. "You look beautiful."

He steps in and hands her the roses and bends to kiss her. It's almost like a romance novel, but not quite. They are both too old and those plots are never this complicated.

"Did you see Gracie?" Parva asks as matter-of-factly as she can.

"No. She wasn't there. I left the candy with Tyrone. I'm sure it will be his before the night's over."

Parva sniffs the roses. "And what else are you sure of before the night's over?" she asks.

Ed closes the door with his foot and takes back the flowers and lays them on the table by the door, the place where Parva keeps her keys and her purse and her collapsible umbrella. He kisses her again, this time harder, deeper, and it occurs to her that they may not eat right away, that she's glad she turned off the oven and covered the sirloin medallions with Reynolds Wrap, that she may not get a chance to light the votives the way she intended. He pulls her close and takes her breath and makes her knees bend in that way she's only seen in movies. Life doesn't always go the way you think it will. You have to change course sometimes, recalculate your destination and pray for the best. Pray that in the end, when the dust settles, despite your sins, you are blessed.

———————

I STILL THINK this is the dumbest thing I've ever heard of," says Ginger.

"What?" says Gracie.

"Spending a cold, but beautiful, Saturday mailing letters to dead people."

Ginger is behind the wheel of the semirepaired Oldsmobile. Since its recovery from the woods beside the highway, the Olds is making a loud, whop-whop noise. Ed has been too busy with some mysterious project to fix it, but Ginger's car is at Tire Man getting a new radiator and she wants this job over with. The slower the car moves, the slower the whop-whops, and Ginger is moving more and more slowly, cresting the small rises and descending into the shallow hollows of Pine's Rest Funeral Garden. The whole idea is creepy to her.

"And why," Ginger continues, "we can't just take these letters you've written to a regular mailbox is beyond me. Kids mail letters to God and to Santa Claus all the time. I don't see much difference."

"I know I'm supposed to be crazy, but I see the difference between Angela and Santa Claus," says Gracie. "And I surely see the difference between Albert Webb and God."

"So do I, Mama. But Angela and this Albert Webb are dead. So what would be the difference in mailing them a letter and mailing a Christmas list to Santa Claus? That's all I'm saying."

"Don't you want to help me?"

You just want to humor that cute Dr. Bradigan, a voice says to Gracie. Gracie smiles.

"I have the garden trowel in my purse, don't I?" Ginger whop-whops through an archway that separates the oldest section of the cemetery from the newer property acquired in the 1960s.

"There!" Gracie jumps in her seat and points up the hill. "Up there near that white oak. He's somewhere up there. Angela's back in the other section. We can mail her letter on the way out."

By the time she reaches the tree, Ginger has already scanned all the gravestones. "I don't see any grave marked Albert Webb," Ginger says. Outside, the March wind whips around Ginger's bare ears and she contemplates how little she knows her mother, and how hard the ground will be when she finally tries to pierce it with the hand trowel.

"Well, it should be right over here somewhere," Gracie says. "It was a little marker. I know Albert is somewhere near this tree."

"How did he die?"

"His brakes failed. Went over a cliff. Happened right after Granddaddy paid him off. I don't think he got a chance to spend a dime of it."

"How did Aunt Angela die? Pine away? Didn't you steal Albert from her?"

"Ovarian cancer. Just plain ole cancer. I don't think she ever pined for anything."

Ginger walks back and forth across graves and reads headstones. "Are you sure you're remembering this," Ginger says, stopping to look at her mother, "or is one of your little voices telling you where his grave is?"

Gracie looks at Ginger.

"Take me back to the Day Treatment Center. Maybe Dr. Bradigan will help me."

"Mama, a medical professional is not going to help you dig holes on top of graves. A medical professional is just going to ask me to do it. Look, I am trying—trying—to be a supportive daughter here. But you must admit I have had a real ride these last few months." Ginger waves her garden-gloved hands in the air as she talks. "My mama disappears. No one knows where she is. Then she turns up over four months later crazy as a bedbug, no offense. Then my daddy starts cooking all the time and being late and not going to work and acting weird and sleeping in the guest room. Then I find out my mama had a first husband, who turns out to be some man named Albert Webb, and there was an almost baby I never heard of, and blackmail."

He's sleeping in the guest room. What do you think that means? a voice says to Gracie.

I bet I know, another one says.

"You don't have to know everything," Gracie says, apparently to Ginger.

"Wait, I'm not finished. Then I find out you stole this Albert Webb from Great-Aunt Angela. And now, you have a new doctor, a new place to live, a new name, and you want a divorce. I don't have any say in any of it. Well, it's all a little much. Okay? It is just a little much." Ginger wipes a gardening glove across her face and under her eyes.

"I'm not as crazy as people think," Gracie says in a calm, faraway voice. "I just know things. Even if I'm your mother, I still have my own business. Albert Webb was my business, not yours."

He was a young man with a taste for wealthy virgins, a voice says to Gracie. *What do you think Ed's doing in the guest room that he doesn't want Jesus to see?*

"And Angela's quarrel with me is my business."

You closed several circles with that one. Were you satisfied? Were you mean enough? Were you ever mean enough, Rachel?

"I don't know why you wouldn't write your own letters to bury like Dr. Bradigan told you to."

You didn't write about the annulment. Why don't you tell her about that? About why you left college. Why the old man had you hospitalized? Why you were living in the woods.

"Because I'm not crazy and he's not my shrink," Ginger says through clenched teeth.

"Does Dr. Bradigan talk slow," Gracie says, changing the subject, "or is it just my medicine?"

Ginger takes a deep breath and lets it out. "No, Mama. He talks slow so you'll understand him."

Ginger scans the even, dead grass dimpled with occasional concrete, brass-plated rectangles. "How many of these letters do we have to do in all?"

"Five."

"I don't understand it. That's all. I don't understand the purpose of this exercise."

You're getting things in order.

"I'm trying to get things in order," Gracie says.

"For what?"

Because you need to close the circle.

"So I can move on. And I have a long list of things to take care of."

Beginning with Albert.

"Beginning with Albert. You're going to have to go ask where Albert is. Go on down and ask." Gracie points toward a squat brick building at the bottom of the hill. "They'll have a map with him on it. I could have sworn he was near this tree."

"Great. Now I have to go make sure everyone sees me and knows my name and my face before I defile a grave."

"Maybe not," Gracie says. "You know you've always been so melodramatic."

"Uh!" Ginger takes long, deliberate strides toward the office, then looks back and calls, "What about Angela? Should I ask about her, too?"

"No," Gracie hollers back. "She has a big ole statue. You can't miss her."

"*This* is crazy," Ginger says softly in the last space between the cold quiet of the funeral garden and the pulsing sound of the photocopy machine in the cemetery's overheated office.

Three hours later, with two letters down and three to go, Ginger crouches over top of her grandfather's grave, a small pick in her hand, which she purchased at the local hardware. She makes rapid birdlike pecks at the hard March ground until she has pecked around an eight-inch circle of sod. Then, with a single hard blow, she pierces the dirt and pulls back a grassy clump of red clay. It rained a little the day before, so her digging is easier. "By the time we get all these letters buried, I'll be pretty good at it. I could be a grave robber. Mama, move a little bit to the right, please."

Gracie stands at the head of her father's grave, seventy-five miles from Albert Webb. The headstone is a pink marble pedestal topped with a warrior angel whose wings are spread for flight or attack, one sandaled foot lunging in front of the other.

I'm sorry, little girl, her father says to her from the angel's mouth.

Gracie's tilts her head and listens. *I'm painting you pictures.* She pushes the silent airy cloud of words out of her mouth. Her hands are in her skirt pockets and she holds her skirt out as far as seems natural in an attempt to conceal Ginger at work.

Ginger ignores Gracie's funny breathing. After Ginger picks enough dirt loose, she smooths the hole with the gardening trowel.

"All right, Mama. Give me the letter."

"I'm supposed to put it in by myself."

"Well, hurry up. I don't want to get caught. They put people in jail for this shit."

"Don't use that word."

"I always use that word."

"Well, I wish you wouldn't."

"Mama, don't even get me started on what I wish you wouldn't do. Besides, you say shit. Are you going to mail that letter?"

"I'm supposed to have a little ceremony with these last three."

"Fine, I'll come stand where you are and you come over where I am and have whatever ceremony you want, as long as it's short and invisible. You never know when some guy with a WeedEater's going to step out from be-hind a mausoleum and ask what we're doing."

"Just tell them."

"Right. Then we'll both be carted off to Weeble hell, and I might not get out as easily as I did last time."

Everybody has their time.

"Everybody has their time."

"Not if I can help it."

Gracie changes places with Ginger and, clutching a pink envelope in her left hand, stares up at the angel's face, then at the place her father's face would be. Her lips move, but only a jumble of indistinguishable sylla-bles spill from her mouth. Periodically, Gracie makes the sign of the cross. After two full minutes of signifying, Gracie places a pink envelope in the hole as delicately as one would plant a fragile seedling. Ginger sees a draw-ing on the outside of the envelope: Jesus praying at the rock. Gracie pulls the rosary of polished stone beads from her skirt pocket and places it on top of the letter, then pulls the dirt in on top of it. She takes the cut turf in both hands and settles it back in place as best she can, then stands and stomps on it, mashing it flat into the grave while hollering the words, "Mazel tov!"

"What was that for?" Ginger glances around the cemetery to see if Gracie's abrupt and rather loud ceremonial climax has drawn attention to them. She sees no one.

"I saw it on TV," Gracie says. "It formally ends a ceremony."

"Fine. Three down, two to go," Ginger says as she bends down to gather her tools.

"Why don't you like Dr. Bradigan? Why didn't you write the letters like he asked you to."

"Dr. Bradigan is too fucking earnest. And I don't have any thoughts to bury. I don't know these people. Don't bring it up again."

"*Shit* is bad enough, but please don't say *fucking*. I can't stand that word."

"Have you ever said it?"

"That doesn't matter."

"Actually, you just said it. Just now."

"That doesn't count."

"Sure it does."

No, it doesn't.

"No, it doesn't."

An hour later they stand side by side in another cemetery.

"What do you want to do with his?" Ginger looks at the marble mausoleum and the letters of her great-grandfather's name etched into it, a name that means nothing to her. Just some dead relative her mother and father never talked about.

"I guess we dig a hole right here in front of it."

Difficult even after death, isn't he?

"I'm not talking to you," Gracie says.

"Why not? I'm doing exactly what you asked me to do," Ginger looks up at Gracie.

"I wasn't talking to you."

"Who were you talking to then?"

"I can't tell you."

"Fine. Did you take your medicine this morning?"

"Yes, I took my fucking medicine."

"I knew you used that word."

"I picked it up from you. That's how bad habits work. Words are powerful things. You can cast a spell with words, you know. You better be careful what you say."

Ginger pecks at the ground in front of the mausoleum.

"Who do you talk to?"

"Why do you want to know?"

"I guess because I'm jealous."

Tell her who talks to you.

"God."

"You talk to God? So you just told God you didn't want to talk to Him?"

"That wasn't God."

How do you know?

"I just know," Gracie says, pulling out a second pink envelope, the one with the picture of Jesus with the open hands drawn on the front.

"Why do you want a divorce? What has he done to you? It seems to me," Ginger says as she gets to her feet, "if anyone should be asking for a divorce it should be him."

But he never will.

"But he never will."

"What has gotten into you?"

Bury his letter now. Give him his letter.

"Are you ready for me to do the ceremony?"

"Have at it."

Gracie mumbles words, but this time there is no sign of the cross, no graceful hand motions. She places the envelope in the hole and covers it, then stands and stomps the dirt flat without the benefit of a final utterance.

"Let's go," Gracie says, and walks away.

The Olds whop-whops back out to the highway, and both women ride in silence for a long time. At least Ginger is silent. Gracie has her listening face on. Ginger is learning to distinguish between Gracie's real silence and the silence of her listening. Her eyes are different. The way she holds her head is different. It is almost as if Ginger can hear the voices herself, faint, very faint, but there, hanging in the apparent quiet, like a car radio turned down so low you forget it's on until suddenly you wonder where the noise is coming from.

"What are all those rocks for?" Ginger asks, knowing she's interrupting. "The ones you hid under the bed?"

"They're giant fairy stones. I thought I might need money, and you can sell fairy stones. I wasn't sure how I would live. But my back hurt too bad to put any of them in the car when I left."

"Those aren't fairy stones, Mama, they're just big creek rocks. And you left your credit cards cut up on the table. You could have had money."

"That's not the kind of currency I need."

"Un-huh."

Once again, the illusion of silence falls until they reach a spot at the bottom of Philpott Dam. Ginger takes the galvanized bucket and puts it on the ground near the river. She takes out the matches, some from the Starlight Lounge where she and Wally went to hear Benny Walker play blues guitar last week. The matchbook is dark blue with silver stars all over it. It seemed appropriate when she was gathering all her equipment for the dead letter tour.

Gracie pulls the third and last pink envelope from her skirt pocket. Jesus knocking at the door is drawn on the front.

You burn it. Don't let her burn it. You should burn it.

"I'll burn it," Gracie says.

"I wouldn't have it any other way," Ginger says, handing Gracie the matchbook. Gracie holds the match in the air for a minute while she mumbles a few words. Ginger holds the letter. This is as close as Ginger will get to a ceremony. This is for her fairy sister, even though she doesn't really exist. But somehow the idea of her makes Ginger willing to participate. Gracie lights the corner of the envelope with the match, and then takes hold of the envelope with Ginger, who holds it until it's clear it will burn clean. Ginger lets go as the heat climbs the paper. Gracie hangs on to it until the last minute, just before her fingers burn. Then she lets the pink letter fall into the bucket and be consumed by the fire. When there is nothing left but black brittle ashes, Gracie takes the bucket and wades into the water at the edge of the river near the picnic tables. She reaches in and crumbles the black pieces to dust and casts them out onto the waters. Then she tosses the pink plastic rosary that she has kept in her jewelry box for all these many years into the current. It floats when first swept away, and then it snags on a rock just below the surface. The water's foam plays over the rosary. With each pulse of current, the rosary knocks and knocks against the slick stone.

NORVIS AND MATTIE are riding in the cab up 220 North toward Roanoke. They are planning to have a nice dinner at the Tailgate Restaurant, courtesy of the owner—a bonus since Mattie agreed to try out some suggested dessert recipes for the restaurant's new spring menu. Her cream-filled pastries and berry tarts are so popular, they have been reviewed in the *Roanoke Times*.

Norvis has taken off his fishing hat and cab-driving clothes and put on a nice blue suit and tie. Mattie has taken off Arty's work boots and put on some black high-heeled pumps. Her feet feel naked. She crosses her legs and pulls her skirt down well below her knees.

"So you bake desserts for this place we're going to?" Norvis asks to launch a conversation.

"Um-hm."

"That makes you a pastry chef, then, doesn't it?"

"It makes me a woman with a cottage industry." Mattie feels the heat rising from the pit of her womb up to her throat.

"I see."

"Norvis, I need you to be straight on something. This is not a date. Sammy's out sewing up some stallion that tried to go through barbed wire, and I got to get to Roanoke. You keep showing up in a cab, so I'm taking advantage of it. The cab, not you. I'll pay you for taking me."

"I don't want you to pay me. Consider me a family friend and leave it at that."

Mattie looks sideways at Norvis.

"I didn't buy this suit for you. I already owned it. Now just relax. You had someplace to go and I am a transportation professional."

"So we're straight?" Mattie says.

"Straight."

Mattie and Norvis continue in silence until Mattie sees the sign. Rocky Mount, ten miles.

"Norvis, turn this thing around and take me home. I can't do this. I want to go home." Mattie wipes at her throat with her hand.

"Are you sure? We're almost there."

"We're only halfway there. This is a mistake. Please, just take me back home."

Norvis turns the cab around before they reach Rocky Mount. He never gets angry. Never appears disappointed. Mattie thinks surely he will give her a hard time, but he doesn't. When he walks her to the door, he comes in uninvited, knowing Toot and Tyrone will give him a warm reception. He stays for a little while, sits in the den, and watches *Emeril Live* with Toot. She has a satellite dish, now that Ed has told her about Food Network. When Emeril says, "This is Emeril Lagasse! Good night, everybody!" Norvis Dibner politely tells Toot, Tyrone, and Mattie good evening. Tyrone goes to the window and watches the big yellow cab lumber out the driveway and up the gravel road until the taillights disappear. No one says anything to Mattie after Norvis drives away.

Not long after Norvis leaves, Mattie takes a cup of tea into the living room and turns on the stereo. Sam Cooke sings from the speakers, and she holds up her hands as if Arty is holding her, moving there with her, dancing. Sam sings "You Send Me." The weight of her hips moves back and forth like a pendulum. Her fingers bend and straighten as if they are touching the back of Arty's neck, her head bends as if it rests on Arty's chest. The motion makes her heavy. She changes from the swimmy-headedness she felt when Norvis left to feeling solid. She feels like moving and moving in the living room until she can't move, until she turns into rock. When Sam finishes singing, Mattie sits on the sofa and puts her head on the round corduroy pillow, pretends it's Arty's thigh.

By the time Mattie wakes up it is late, almost bedtime. Her full teacup is stone cold. Toot flicks on the lamp in the living room and picks up the teacup to take it to the kitchen sink. Mattie forces her eyes to stay open. Squinting toward the light, she sees Toot leaving the room, bent over with a small afghan around her shoulders, blue and gold shell stitches curving around her narrow frame. Toot's hair is thin and pinned in a small bun at the back of her head. She looks like an old woman because she is an old woman. Mattie feels like an old woman because it is all she can manage. Her neck hurts from sleeping on the hard sofa pillow. Her back hurts from some funny way she picked up a grocery sack earlier in the day. Her ankles are swollen from eating barbecue the night before. Her face is swollen from crying too much. The skin around her eyes puffs out and itches from hard sleep. She knows she has no more crying in her. Toot is right. She is drying up. She feels her liver evaporating at the edges, her bones growing brittle with every breath, and her heart getting tough and stringy as old beef. She is heavy and hard and older than she is supposed to be.

Mattie goes to her room and slips off her pumps. She slowly slides her silk stockings down each of her recently shaven legs, slips her bare feet into Arty's slick black dress shoes, ties them as tight as she can, and takes his picture in her hands.

The light filters through Sister Reba's small blue tent. She fell asleep last night to edgy calls of screech owls and hoot owls and coyotes, while this late March morning she wakes to a variety of melodious twitters and warbles amid the more poignant cry of mourning doves. She stretches and yawns and is so grateful for that nice Sister Frances in Odessa, who gave her a queen-size air mattress and bicycle pump. Reba has been sleeping like a rock ever since Odessa.

Her tent is a safe bubble, a seed pod from which to germinate. At least she prays the right ideas will germinate. This is her annual retreat—no preaching, no soul-saving, no jumping and shouting. Instead, she spends a week or more chopping wood, carrying water, keeping quiet, and immersed in contemplative prayer. During this annual time alone, Sister Reba is led to the theme of her sacred discourse for the coming year, and the broad strokes of her route throughout the southeastern United States.

She avoids the early spring vacationers and lake enthusiasts by backcountry camping between Fairy Stone Lake and the tailwaters of Philpott Reservoir. During her break from driving and preaching, she wanders the trails of Fairy Stone State Park, at the edge of the Virginia Blue Ridge, and she sometimes takes her dime-store rod and reel to the banks of the closest tributary to cast her line. Sister Reba has never caught a fish, doesn't even like fish, but it is the quiet occupation of waiting for fish that allows her mind to wander, allows her thoughts to percolate. She is angling for ideas rather than trout. Without a catch of the day, she lives on grilled hamburgers and hot dogs, canned beans, and sandwiches, raw fruits and vegetables. Each afternoon she ventures out to buy milk and ice at a country store, where she smiles and tries to say as little as possible, safeguarding her monastic experience. As in her on-road life, Sister Reba prefers to deal with the small operations, family businesses, independents. She believes the supernatural is estranged from the modern world because of its mega chains, blockbusters, supersizes, and staggering proportions. The divine prefers to occupy the natural world and the intimate society at its borders—the small, the intimate, the bantam.

On her third day of silence, the word *miracle* comes to Reba as she lays wood for a fire. She dwells on that word and writes on a yellow legal pad about miracles for two days. Not a narrative, rather, random thoughts and notes and lots of lines connecting one thing to another. Sister Reba likes both the structured nature of her annual ritual and the chaos she allows herself to process its purpose, a rhythmic liberation before dedication.

Now, people will tell you that miracles are a thing of the past, but Reba knows better. Without miracles, there would be no surprises. Sometimes miracles go by the name coincidence. Sometimes they go by the name accident. Sometimes they go by the names unexpected, longshot, curveball, miscalculation. Those who misconstrue the miraculous mistakenly assume the sacred to be awesome, overwhelming, exaggerated because they are too close to see the simple paths daily miracles make. It can be more difficult to see a miracle than to spot transparent slug trails on a busy carpet. But Reba knows the sacred to be as daily as loaf bread and iceberg lettuce. *The little things accumulate in such familiar and sometimes troubling ways,* Reba writes on her pad, *that we only see those small pieces and can't step back and see the miracle that is there. Like the blind men feeling parts of the elephant, we humans separate ourselves from the full picture of our own divinity.* Reba lists all the daily ways her people can see their miracles. Her mind moves faster than her hand. She will take her message to the road from this quiet woods.

Sister Reba's year ends with Good Friday and begins with Easter Sunday. She may attend sunrise service at Natural Bridge, watching the sun come up like a resurrection, hearing someone else preach to her. Then she'll turn her Rand McNally Road Atlas to the map of Virginia and make her way over the blue and gray highways, the places where people are still holding on to the side of the road.

TYRONE HOLDS the door for Toot to go into the chicken house. Three cinder blocks serve as steps to the old gray building. Inside it smells brown and warm, like the mix of earth and heat. Dust motes float in the streaks of sunlight slicing through the empty space between the wallboards. The right and back walls of the small outbuilding are lined with two rows of planks holding straw-filled crates. Every nest has a hen and each hen has eggs to be gathered. Tyrone carries a basket and Toot carries a basket. Tyrone carefully takes the eggs from the lower level while Toot extracts the ones from the row above.

"Tyrone," Toot says as she pulls two brown eggs from a bed of straw, "you ever think about going into business?"

"What kind of business?"

"The egg business."

"No."

"Well, you might think about it."

"Why?"

"'Cause, as your soon-to-be great-granny, I'm going to pass this egg business right here on to you, if you want it that is."

"So we wouldn't do it together anymore?"

"I expect I'll keep on helping, but the responsibility and the money gon' be yours. I be your highly unpaid helper seeing as how I'm really retired anyway."

"What does that mean exactly, that I'm in the egg business?"

"It means these hens and rooster is in your charge, they feed and water, the gathering up and counting and crating and selling of the eggs. Can you handle that? You want to take it on? It might give you a little spending and saving money and teach you about business. Everybody ought to know a little bit about that and the younger the better."

"All right."

"I figure you coming up on Palm Sunday and Easter weekend. That's a good time to go into the egg business 'cause it's all kinds of people wanting eggs to buy. It's always good to start out strong, then learn the ups and downs while you got a little change set aside. You see what I'm saying?"

"Yes, ma'am."

"Good. You learn to try different things and then you hit on one that will be your life's work, like Sammy doctoring animals. That's that boy's life's work. And he come by it honest, right from his daddy, only his daddy didn't have no money to be a veterinarian. He was a mechanic who loved horses and cows. He had a gift."

"How did they find out what their gift was?"

"Arty, he marked by a horse before he's born. Sammy just got it from his daddy, I'd say."

"How was Arty marked?"

Toot and Tyrone climb down the cinder blocks with full baskets and walk toward the swept yard.

"You go put these baskets in the egg refrigerator and bring me some lemonade, and I'll tell you." Toot sits down in the metal chair near the back door. Tyrone takes the baskets onto the screen porch one at a time and sets them in the refrigerator used just for Toot's eggs, now Tyrone's eggs. It's Monday, so there's room to set the eggs in, baskets and all. Tyrone goes in and asks Mama Mattie for two lemonades. When he comes out of the house, Toot is lightly bouncing her metal chair and smiling with her eyes closed.

"Here's your lemonade." Tyrone sits in the chair next to hers; his feet dangle above the swept dirt. "Now will you tell me the story?"

Toot commences the story with her eyes still closed, like she can see the movie of what she says in her mind.

"Homer and me worked for a man name of King Ed, and his wife, they call her Queenie on account of her being married to a man who real name was King. He was a nice enough man all right, and he owned a big Percheron mare name of Venus that Homer used to plow the man's fields. We was young, been married two years, and I was carrying a baby. Every Saturday, King Ed, he let us take that horse out the barn and saddle it up, and me and Homer, we go for a ride. Now Homer, he good with horses too, and that big horse like an old dog. Just do whatever you tell it. We rode that horse every Saturday, I tell you, less it was raining. Go have us a picnic by the river.

"Well this here one Saturday I was right heavy and over my time to be having the baby, but we decided I'd climb up the ladder, which is what I'd been doing for weeks to get on ole Venus, and Homer, he get on behind me and we'd take our ride anyway. Sometime riding a horse can make you go ahead and have a baby, and I sure was ready to have that one. But don't you know, every time that day I'd get up close to that horse, she'd step away. And Homer, who was right up behind me to keep me balanced, he have to move Venus back over next to me again and again. And I go try to get on again and again and she'd step away. She won't gon' have me on her back that day. And after some time of that, I felt a big rush of water come from me while I was still standing on the ladder. That's what happens to the mama when a baby coming. And I started to hurt so bad in my back. And the next thing you know, little Arty, he born. That horse knew what was coming, and she marked my baby with the gift of animals. Sure did.

"And you know what?" Toot asks.

"What?" Tyrone answers, enthralled and expectant.

"Arty saved King Ed's youngest girl from drowning in the river, and King Ed so happy he gave Arty a filly out of Venus. And so many fillies from that is standing over there in the pasture, and her name Sheba."

"Sheba is Venus's grandbaby?"

"Gran, gran, gran."

Tyrone looks down at his feet as they swing just above the powdered dirt. "Do you think anything has marked me?" Tyrone asks, almost afraid of an answer.

Toot considers his question. "I'd say your mama working with a pencil doing arithmetic while you was in her marked you to use a pencil. Whatever it was marked you had to have something to do with reading and drawing, 'cause you the readingest, drawingest child I ever did see."

"What marked you?" Tyrone asks.

Toot's mind goes to the basement the day Mr. Price died. But she makes herself see another vision, one of Homer kissing her for the first time behind the tobacco barn on King Ed's farm.

"My mama ate strawberries by the bucketful when she gon' have me," she says instead. "Everybody say she gon' give me a birthmark by doing it. But all that happened was I can't eat more than three strawberries and I'm full."

"I thought you liked strawberries."

"I do. I love them things just like my mama. But I guess she ate so many, I'll always be just about full of them too."

"Is that all that marked you?" Tyrone says, sounding a little disappointed.

"Child, I'm an old old woman. Almost old as God. You can be marked after you born as easy as before, and I been marked so many times in my life I can't make no sense of all the scratches it's made. We all marked. You'll see. We all got something that shapes us, and we got to decide is it going to shape us for good or bad, 'cause we can make it go either way. One day, you gon' know what I'm tell you. One day you gon' look around the world and see marks everywhere, on everybody. You got lots of gifts in you. And I see you already can see what can't be seen. One day, you gon' know just what I'm tell you."

Toot takes Tyrone's hand and squeezes it, and he squeezes her hand in return.

"You can call me Granny Toot if you want to," she says, and they both close their eyes.

BENEDICTION

*The lightning and the thunder require time, the light of stars requires
time, deeds require time even after they are done, before they
can be seen and heard.*

—Friedrich Nietzsche

"GRANNY TOOT, why do we eat fish every Friday?"

Tyrone stands on his stool and mashes together the canned salmon, saltine crackers, chopped onion, lets it squish between his fingers, while Toot sprinkles salt, pepper, and some fresh dill into the bowl.

"I used to work for a Catholic woman, and back then they had to eat fish on Friday 'cause it was the day Jesus died. They couldn't eat no meat. Some things Catholics believe don't make no sense to me, but I thought that was a good thing. So I started fixing fish on Friday, too."

"But you're not Catholic?"

"Lord, no. I'm Holiness."

"What's that green stuff?"

"Dill. I'm gon' try some in the salmon patties. Chef Bernard say dill and salmon make the best marriage of meat and herbs, so I'm gon' try it. You mash those little back bones up good in there now. They good for you, but nobody wants to think they eating bones."

"I thought you said fish wasn't meat?"

"Best I can tell, just for Catholics and vegetarians. You excited about your mama and Sammy getting married next Sunday?"

"Yes, ma'am."

"Sammy gon' make you a good daddy."

"And Miss Mattie and you are going to make good grandmothers too."

"You think so?"

"I know so."

Tyrone is not surprised that Granny Toot is Holiness. He thinks he sees a halo around her head most days.

"What's wrong with these salmon patties?" Sammy asks later at the dinner table.

"Ain't nothing wrong with the salmon patties," Granny Toot says. "What's wrong with you? You been grumpy all day."

"Nothing's wrong with me. There's something funny about these salmon patties."

"Mmm. They taste good to me," Mattie says, trying to signal Sammy to be quiet and eat his food.

Tyrone loves Sammy, and Sammy is the smartest man he knows, but he likes everybody to listen to him, and he isn't always good at listening to someone else. So Mattie's signals go unheeded.

"Did you put something new in these things, because if you did, I like the old ones," Sammy says and makes a funny face as he takes another bite.

"I know why they taste funny," says Tyrone. "It's dill. I helped make them. Chef Bernard says dill and salmon are a perfect marriage of meat and herbs. Right, Granny Toot?"

"Hush up, Tyrone," Toot says. "If you don't quit telling everything goes on in my kitchen, you not gon' help me."

"I like the dill just fine," Tyrone says.

"Me, too," says Mattie.

"Me, too," says Gracie, who hasn't said much today at all.

"I wish we hadn't gotten that satellite if you're going to change the way you cook," says Sammy and puts his fork down and wipes his mouth.

"Something's bothering you," says Mattie, "and it's not dill in the salmon patties. What's the problem? Spit it out."

"I think Doristeen and I should elope."

"What?" everyone at the table says together, including Gracie.

"You most certainly will not elope," Mattie says and takes a drink of buttermilk.

"It would just be so much easier. Doristeen has gotten it in her head she wants a woman preacher. She said she wants to be married at Jezereel, but she doesn't want Reverend Love to marry us. She wants him invited to watch a woman do it."

"When did she decide that?"

"I guess it's been in her mind since they got in that argument back in the fall. And I guess she's been thinking about her mother being a preacher and all and how she can't come to the wedding. I don't know. I just know she's acting nuts about the whole thing."

"She just got the wedding jitters," says Toot. "You just plan the wedding. Everything be all right. If she don't like Reverend Love, we find somebody else. I don't know no women preachers, but I know plenty of other preachers."

"Fine, then you talk to her about it. Tyrone, are you done? There's a special on the Science Channel about star nurseries." Sammy obviously wants to change the subject.

"I'm here to tell you," Mattie says, "I don't like TV, but that was a good show about that Hubble telescope and those exploding stars last week."

"I liked the one that looks like a big blue eye," says Tyrone.

"That was nuclear waste," says Sammy.

"I prefer to call it stardust," says Mattie.

"Looked like the eye of God to me," says Toot.

Gracie doesn't say anything, her head is a little to one side.

Toot clears her throat, always a sign for everyone to pay attention.

"I got an announcement to make. We gon' have a wedding in nine days, and I'm gon' be gone this weekend. So we got to plant the garden on Good Friday, like we usually do, which is good, 'cause that's when it's 'pose to be planted anyway."

"Where are you going?" Sammy asks and pops the last bit of roll into his mouth.

"You'll see."

Toot leaves the table, and the others are left to finish their food and think about how they are going to have a wedding and plant seeds too.

———————————

Toot and Ed get out of the taxi on Fifty-second Street. Toot is wearing a dark wig and a new lavender pantsuit from Dillard's. Ed pretends he doesn't notice other than to tell her she looks lovely.

"Lord ham mercy, they make tall buildings in this city."

"Nothing like this in Centertown, Rockrun, or anywhere in between, I'd say." Ed pays the cabdriver and gets his receipt. Bonnie said to keep all receipts for transportation to and from the airport and the studio and they would be reimbursed. The show had offered to send a car, but both Ed and Toot wanted to do some sightseeing on their way to the studio. When they checked into the hotel, they each found a fruit basket and flowers waiting for them in their rooms. The flowers were compliments of Chef Bernard. The fruit baskets were from Norvis Dibner. Norvis had volunteered to take them to the airport in Greensboro, and, with some hard work on Toot's part, Mattie had agreed to stay in Greensboro and go to dinner and take in a movie with Norvis. Mattie had wanted to get special permission to escort Toot and Ed to the gate, but Toot sent them away saying if she and Ed couldn't find the gate at the airport, she didn't expect they'd find their way back from New York City.

"I want them off to theyself," Toot told Ed as the two of them stood in line for the metal detector. "Norvis Dibner has his work cut out for him. That's all I got to say. They 'posed to go to a nice restaurant for dinner and then to a show. I made Mattie promise not to turn chicken until after the movie let out. But I know Norvis gon' take her to a restaurant where they's dancing."

"Bonnie said to call her from the lobby," Ed tells Toot as they enter the tall building and look at the reception desk. Ed thinks about Parva and how he'll have to take her dancing. She can wear that pretty black dress. He didn't get to see much of it on Valentine's Day.

"Did you see about us getting on *Emeril Live?* You know I like that Chef Bernard fine, but Emeril, he's my man. I want to get to sit up there at his countertop. He feed folks some good-looking cooking up there."

"Bonnie said they have a lottery for Emeril's tickets. But she promised she'd look into it. Sometimes they can get complimentary passes."

"I sure hate the thought of coming all this way to miss seeing Emeril. Tyrone looked it up. They tape his show in this same studio. This here studio right here."

"Bonnie knows he's in town. You know how he travels all over the place. Las Vegas or New Orleans or Chicago. But he's here in New York this week, she knows that much. So we've got a shot at it."

"We got to be excited about Chef Bernard, too. I know that. He the one paid for the trip and all. I just want to see Emeril. Get him to sign my book."

"What about Chef Bernard? Did you bring any of his books?"

"He always giving away books. I figure he give us some books, and signed too. You see him hit that woman in the head with a champagne cork last Tuesday? I bet he giving her a whole library of his books." Toot laughs and Ed shakes his head. He did see that show, and the woman was clearly not a devoted fan. There are lots of classy ways to handle oneself on live television when something unexpected happens, but she didn't consider any of them.

"We're suppose to go to the publisher's office at two o'clock, so we should try to get a snack or a sandwich sometime before then."

"Ed, honey, we at the Food Network. Food's everywhere."

"You've got your manuscript with you, right?"

"Right here." Toot reaches into the tote bag Doristeen gave her for Christmas and pulls a manuscript out far enough for Ed to read *Sophisticated Soul* on the cover sheet. "I'm not leaving this thing in the hotel to burn up while we gone."

Ed is nervous. The mall was hard enough for him to warm up to, but skyscrapers, and publishing people, and television celebrities, are a whole new ball of wax. He keeps his tire gauge in his inside breast pocket to remind him of what's real. At the bottom line he knows he is still Tire Man.

Barney was as good as his note, getting Toot and Ed appointments with Charlie Higgs, his editor, to discuss their cookbook manuscripts. Ed has already submitted his first cookbook to Charlie, who called last week to say his house was very interested in publishing *Redneck Gourmet*. Parva came up with the title. If they pay a nice advance, Ed had another idea to pitch to them today. Ed is confident Charlie will be eating out of Toot's hand once they meet, particularly since Toot is taking him some sweet potato tarts as a sample. Bernadette asked Ed to mention to Charlie that Rachel's art would be perfect for her cover, since she's started painting tables full of food, Toot's food. Bernadette, like Toot, knows how to work her market.

Ed asks the receptionist to call Bonnie's office, and he and Toot wait near the elevator. When the doors nearest the reception area open, a small, intense young woman in her early twenties steps out to greet them. Her hair is black as ink and so are her clothes.

"You must be Ed Hollaman and you must be Mrs. Riley." Bonnie extends her hand first to Toot and then to Ed. Despite the severity of all that black, she puts them at ease immediately. "Chef Bernard is waiting for you. He's very anxious to meet you."

"Did you get us any Emeril tickets?" Toot asks.

"Not yet, but I'm hopeful."

"Honey, you and me both. I just love Emeril. I like Chef Bernard too, but I love that Emeril."

"Yes, well, you're not alone, Mrs. Riley. And I am hopeful."

"So . . . how long have you . . . known you were a . . . fairy?" Dr. Bradigan asks Gracie, then takes a sip of coffee from his white Styrofoam cup.

"I've always known it."

"Are you . . . familiar with . . . Bruno Bettelheim and his . . . book . . . *Uses of Enchantment?*" asks Dr. Bradigan.

Gracie shakes her head. "Enchantment has many uses, all right." She places a peppermint on her tongue. "Mint?" She peels away the cellophane and holds the bare candy out to Dr. Bradigan.

"Oh . . . thank you."

"You're welcome." Gracie reaches back and twists her long red hair into a knot at the nape of her neck.

"Bettelheim's theory . . . and of course others have . . . written about this . . . as well, is that fairy tales . . . portray growth through . . . conflict, and prepare . . . children in particular for life's . . . changes." Dr. Bradigan pops the peppermint in his mouth and maneuvers it to the side of his cheek. "He feels fairy . . . tales work on a much . . . deeper level than most people . . . realize."

"We all have larger stories than we know."

Except you know yours, don't you, Rachel?

"Sadly, people's . . . propensity to put children in . . . therapy . . . displaces the need for . . . fairy tales. And of course, those . . . politically correct versions are . . . utterly . . . useless. They miss the whole . . . point. I'm not even . . . sure they're good . . . stories."

"A good story closes."

"What do you . . . mean by that, Rachel. That the story . . . ends?"

Tell him how it works. He wants to know.

"A story has to travel its circumference. Straight lines are dangerous stories."

"Dangerous?"

And sequels are useless. Tell him about sequels.

"Sequels are very bad. They keep a story open. They keep a story in a straight line and the story dies. People are glad it's over. A story closes and then it lives on inside its circle, and the next story is a new circle."

"I see."

"What do you see?"

"The circle."

Gracie smiles. "You have to start a new circle or you're stuck in a straight line. That's very very bad. No matter what they tell you, there shouldn't be remakes, or sequels. You have to avoid them. Only new circles."

"If only . . . Hollywood conformed to this . . . principle." Dr. Bradigan chuckles as he moves the peppermint to the other cheek.

The trick is to know when the circle is complete, isn't it, Rachel?

"Are you familiar with . . . Elie Wiesel?" Dr. Bradigan asks.

Gracie shakes her head.

"Well . . . doesn't matter. In one of his . . . writings . . . he drew on an old . . . Jewish tale. A man asks why . . . God . . . created Man. A man answers him . . . 'Because he loves stories.' I've always liked that thought. What do you think?"

"Are you Jewish or Catholic?"

"Neither. I'm just curious. Curiosity is my religion. And I suppose work is my church."

Good man. Ask him how he likes the peppermint. That was very slick, the way you got him to take the bait.

"How's your peppermint," Gracie asks.

"Hits the spot, thank you. Hits the spot." Dr. Bradigan momentarily contemplates Wiesel's statement as he lets the hot disk slide around on his tongue.

"Tell me, Rachel . . . what happens to the . . . people in a story when their . . . circle closes?"

"Everything else."

E D HAS CALLED Parva to come over right away. It's her day off from Dillard's and Ed is planning for her to have a lot of days off in the future. He has a new job in mind for her, one that will let her capital people skills and imagination shine. He can barely restrain his enthusiasm.

He carefully unfolds the old map he came across some months ago when he was cleaning up the mess in the attic. He spreads it out across the kitchen table. The big red circle is as good a place to begin as any. He hears her car and stands where he is to get her reaction when she comes in the door.

"Edgar, what on earth is that big silver bullet in the driveway?" She gives him a tight hug and a peck on the lips.

"It's a 1967 vintage Airstream Outlander, mint condition just like the Dodge."

"Are you taking a trip?" There is a hint of concern in Parva's question.

"Well, I was thinking we could take a trip. A really long trip." Ed takes her hand and leads her out to the driveway, opens the door to the land coach, and invites her inside.

"Oh my. It has turquoise appliances. It kind of matches your Dodge."

"Exactly."

Parva takes a seat on the white vinyl sofa. "Wasn't it expensive? It's in such good shape."

"Well, it's a tax write-off."

"How is that?"

"My new cookbook proposal depends on it. *Highway Gourmet*. A partner and myself will travel around the country, living in and entertaining out of the Outlander."

"Partner? Are you taking Gracie?"

"No! I'm taking you, if you'll go. We take the Dodge and the Outlander and travel around meeting a lot of other RV travelers, sticking mostly to the smaller roads, not relying much on the interstates. We can write chapters on stocking the pantry, economics of space, fall-back food for when grocery store options are limited. I've got a rough outline I used to pitch the idea, and Charlie Higgs went for it. Together we can beef it up. What do you think?"

Parva runs her hand over the clean white vinyl, looks at the bright turquoise appliances, the gas range, the dishwasher. "I think it's wonderful. But isn't the Dodge too old for such labor?"

"Honey, that truck is in better shape than my Toyota. And anything that goes wrong with it, I can fix or replace. What do you think? Are you in?"

Parva clasps her hands in front of her face, then spreads them wide. "Yes! Yes, I'm in!"

Ed pulls her up close to him and kisses her.

"Have you told your family?"

"I expect I will when they see this mammoth tin can sitting in the driveway." Ed laughs. He's ready to tell Ginger about Parva. And he has a strong suspicion Gracie won't be surprised at all.

"One question: Where do we sleep?" asks Parva.

"You were just sitting on it." Ed pulls out the sleeper sofa.

"Perfect," Parva says. "Perfect."

Sammy is driving Doristeen down the road toward home. What is going to be their home. He has house plans to surprise her with on their wedding night. Toot has given him a choice section of property on the other side of the pasture and the woods, near the church, so they can be close and have some privacy at the same time. Sammy is full of so much he can't talk about it. He sits behind the wheel thinking. He holds Doristeen's fingers with one hand and steers the truck with the other. Doristeen is disappointed that she hasn't found a woman preacher to officiate at the wedding. Sammy reluctantly, but at his mother's urgings, offered to postpone the wedding until Doristeen could find a woman to perform the ceremony, but she refused. Doristeen is thankful to have such a good man in her life, such a good father for Tyrone. She wants him enough to go ahead and have Reverend Love do the job. Reverend Love isn't a bad fellow. He's just stuck in some old ways that fret Doristeen. It's fretful for someone to throw the reasons for your life into question. The important thing is that she's marrying a good man and marrying into a good family.

Sammy is passing by Rodey's Store when he notices Norvis Dibner's taxi at the gas tanks. Sammy toots the horn and Doristeen, who has been daydreaming about her life as a married woman, looks to the roadside just in time.

"Stop!" she hollers. "Stop!" she hollers again, turning around and looking back over her shoulder as they pass. "Oh, my God! Stop!"

"What? You need to stop? We're almost home."

"Stop! Go back! Oh my God!" Doristeen jumps in her seat, beats her hand on Sammy's headrest. "Baby, turn this thing around. Go back to the store. Hurry."

Sammy pulls up beside Rodey's Store and Doristeen is out of the truck before he can come to a complete stop. She doesn't go in the station. Instead, she takes long strides toward a little funeral tent set up in the gravel lot beside Rodey's Store. There's an empty bench in the back, and Doristeen sits on it. Sammy is still trying to figure out what is going on when Norvis walks over and puts his hand on Sammy's shoulder.

"Your bride-to-be have a sudden fit of religion, my man?" Norvis asks.

"She just started hollering to stop and carrying on, so I brought her back. I thought she had to pee. Who's that in the tent?"

"Sister Reba Renfro. Powerful preacher. Good-looking too. Not as pretty as your mother, of course."

Sammy grins at Norvis. He knows Norvis is in love with his mother, but Sammy isn't sure where Mattie stands. He has been too distracted by his own life in the last few weeks to worry about hers. She has come a long way this year. A long way. Then it hits Sammy. "I know what this is about."

"What's that, young Samuel?" Norvis says as he admires the pretty woman preaching beneath the tent in the distance.

"A woman preacher. She's been wanting a woman preacher to marry us. She doesn't care much for Reverend Love, and Pastor Alston is out of town this weekend. It was going to be Reverend Love or nobody, but I guess she's going to ask this Sister Renfro."

"You want some advice from a twice happily married man?"

"It couldn't hurt," Sammy says.

"Go over there and sit with your woman and act like this matters to you. The effort is small, and when you're married, it's those small efforts that give you the big payoffs." Norvis offers Sammy his hand. "Brother, I must get on down the road."

Sammy shakes hands with Norvis and goes to sit beside Doristeen on the folding sinners' bench at the back of the tent. The white awning flaps and flaps over his head.

Dr. Bradigan sits behind a metal desk in his small office to one side of the activity room. A few of the interns are transcribing notes in the other office. Gracie sits opposite him in a wing-back chair discarded from the library during renovation. The room is filled with odds and ends: old stained coffee mugs, a bulletin board filled with photographs, mostly of patients. Diplomas hang on the wall. Books are stacked in tall columns on the floor around the baseboards.

Dr. Bradigan always likes the people he meets, regardless of their various degrees of mental stability. Gracie has quickly become one of his favorites. She has an interesting background and her onset is unusual. He has lots of questions about what is really happening here. Dr. Bradigan loves that the unique qualities of her case are couched in such a compelling logic, as Post told him. In his line of work, there is always more than meets the eye.

Good Friday moves forward with a momentum of its own. Other clients are in the hallway selling coffee cake and sausage and bacon biscuits and leftover cupcakes from Gracie's Last Supper anniversary reenactment to the hundreds of county workers who took their required fifteen-minute break at the same time to attend. They are taking longer and more frequent breaks today and coasting into their long Easter weekend. Easter Monday is a holiday for all county workers.

The clients are raising money to go on a field trip to Monticello in May. They need to sell a lot of biscuits between now and then. Bradigan faces budget cuts for the center every time he turns around, so this biscuit money becomes more important every year.

Today, both young and old clients are busy keeping the biscuits and coffee cake moving. The center's routine works well. Young people come on Mondays and Wednesdays. Older people come on Tuesdays and Thursdays. And Fun Fridays are multigenerational. Interns from the university are on site to help manage the larger population, and the small staff takes advantage of their presence to catch up on paperwork. The clients have fun with the interns and with their biscuit business. The county workers get to feel good about helping the mentally ill. Everyone gets to start their weekend on a redemptive note.

Away from the hustle and bustle, midway through his weekly session with Gracie, Dr. Bradigan sits quietly for a moment. He is a contemplative person. This drives people around him crazy, if they aren't already *crazy*. He thinks about each sentence before he says it, and then often thinks about what he is saying mid-sentence. His voice is calm and easy. The combination, for some, works like cat claws on a chalkboard. But his patients get used to it. Clients with schizophrenia and schizoaffective disorder are used to mental gymnastics, and the interplay of thought and speech intrigues them. In truth, they love him.

Gracie has come to appreciate this rhythm of Dr. Bradigan's language. His personality is soothing, a tranquilizer. Her crush on Dr. Bradigan makes her happy. She is happier than she has ever been. Dr. Bradigan's voice interrupts the momentary quiet.

"Rachel . . . whose voice do you hear . . . when the voices . . . speak to you?"

Tell him. You can tell him.

"Sometimes it's my daughter, the fairy. The one who was never born. Sometimes it's voices that are familiar, but I don't recognize them. But mostly it's God. He sounds like different people, and yet I always know it's Him."

"Who . . . for instance? Who . . . does God . . . sound like?" Dr. Bradigan swivels away from his desk a few degrees and props his feet on a cardboard box behind his desk. He has no idea what's in it.

"Jack Benny, my Great-Aunt Wynona, Louis XVI, the man that used to run the Sinclair station on Chestnut Street in Martinsville. Blackie, I think his name was."

"Are they all . . . dead?"

Pretty much.

"Pretty much."

"Does Louis XVI speak French or English?"

"French."

"How do you . . . know . . . they're God?"

Who else would it be?

"He tells me. I have my own ways of knowing things without words, too."

"Does God ever . . . sound . . . like a woman?"

"Yesterday He sounded like Patsy Cline. One day He sounded like Eleanor Roosevelt. I know what you're thinking."

"You do?"

"Why does God sound mostly like famous people? Isn't that what you're thinking?"

They always ask this question and they are never satisfied with the truth.

"Well . . ."

"I thought so. The reason is because He talks like all kinds of unfamous people, but I don't know who they are to call them by name. There's a lot of voices He can use. They all belong to Him, even my voice and your voice. They all belong to Him and He has to use them because He can't use his own."

"Why not?" Dr. Bradigan says without pausing, engaged in the idea of knowing, a philosopher as well as a psychiatrist.

"Because we couldn't stand to hear it. It would be so powerful it would turn us to ashes, like a nuclear bomb. When an atom splits, that is God talking. The dust of His word can melt the world. And we can't survive it, any more than we can survive looking at Him the way He really is. We can't take Him in. He just has to be in us. That's the mystery. He is hotter than a red sun. There are some things we're never meant to experience."

"What was it . . . like . . . when you first . . . heard the voices?"

"It was like that old song my daddy used to sing. 'I Come to the Garden Alone.' Have you ever heard it?"

"I think . . . perhaps I have."

Gracie sings what she half remembers, the lines confused, in alto.

"'I come to the garden alone, while the dew is still on roses. The voice I hear, falling on my ear, is the sweetest I've ever known.'" Gracie is quiet for a moment. "We won't know if I'm right or wrong until it's all over," she says. "You don't know anymore than I do."

Dr. Bradigan thinks about what she has just said. That's why his patients love him. Because he listens to them.

Gracie begins the chorus. "'And He walks with me . . .'"

Dr. Bradigan harmonizes in a halting tenor, using words he dredges up from childhood memories of Sunday mornings visiting churches with his parents. Neither of them was ever satisfied with their religious heritage. " ' . . . and He talks with me . . . ' "

In the narrow space between what is real and what is not, what is of this world and what is not, a resonant baritone disguised as Elvis Presley and heard only by Gracie joins the harmony.

. . . and He tells me I am His own.

In Gracie's mind, the voices blend to such a beautiful sound that tears pool above her lower lashes.

" 'And the joy we share, as we tarry there, none other has ever known.' "

Meanwhile, in what is aeons and seconds and hours rolled into nothing near our consciousness, nothing remotely resembling our time, a sun explodes and a dusty sapphire eye of a cooling star opens and looks out on all of heaven and on the waters and the firmament. It sees all light, all darkness, all substance, all emptiness. It grows and grows until it is much more than itself, much more than dust, much more than any eye we can understand.

Dr. Bradigan and Gracie and the voice as resonant as music itself sing in the safety of an office set aside for those who can see beyond the visible.

At the same time, back at the farm, Toot and Mattie and Norvis Dibner plant their delicate beans and lettuce seeds and onion slips and tomato plants.

Tyrone carefully gathers his day's eggs.

Down the road, next to Rodey's Store, Sister Reba Renfro preaches for the last time this year about how God uses leftovers. Her next sermon, on Easter Sunday, will be about miracles.

"He don't throw away no LEFT overs. If you cloth, He gonna MAKE you a QUILT. If you down to being nothing but a dab of peas and carrots, He gonna MAKE you a SOUP. If you leftover JUNK, He gonna MAKE you into ART and set you in some place and SHOW you OFF."

The small congregation under the tattered tent beside Rodey's Store laughs, and Sister Reba decides to stay here through Sunday, decides to miss Natural Bridge and the sunrise service there, invites everyone to Sunday service right here in Rockrun. "We gonna be DOWN by the river. And when the sun RISES, we gonna celebrate the RISING with a bapTIZING. We gonna celebrate the resurRECtion with the RIVer water."

Sister Reba preaches on, full of the Spirit. A little wind whirls dust around her feet. The men in the congregation lean forward to hear the words coming from her lovely lips. Doristeen, her only daughter, who holds tightly to the hand of the man she's about to marry, sits unrecognized and longing at the back of the tent. She sees her mother reach out to all these strangers and sees how they respond to her, feels her channel the love back to them. For once in her life, Doristeen feels her mother's love, feels all the good she does in her life without family. She is so pleased to see her mother, after all this time, on such a perfect day.

Gracie and Dr. Bradigan and the voice disguised as Elvis sing verse two of "In the Garden."

Ed, back in his bedroom, listens one final time for some word and hears nothing, so he spackles the last of the holes left from the chimes before he rolls a pleasant Martha Stewart green over the eyes of Jesus with the open hands. Then it will be a grayish mauve over Jesus at the front door. But Jesus over the sideboard is safe for now. Ed has grown attached to Him. Ed accepts that everything changes.

Estelle sits behind her desk at Tire Man and makes plastic packages of cream-filled chocolate eggs to go along with the Easter Bunny Monday Sale.

At Dixie Donuts, Wally and Ginger fill box after box of plain, glazed, and white powdered doughnuts for Easter Sunday church orders from Burlington to Centertown. Wally had to borrow the Tire Man van so he can deliver them all on time.

Parva Wilson, called into work because of the busy day at Dillard's, fills a clearance table full of Easter paraphernalia: egg dyeing kits, bunny cookie cutters, Russell Stover Easter egg candies.

Soon, Mattie and Toot will work on Sammy and Doristeen's wedding cake, and Tyrone will pick tiny wild roses to go on the top.

Gracie and Dr. Bradigan hum the last notes of their hymn while the others busy themselves preparing for sunrise services and a small wedding that will be presided over by a woman preacher. The chorus begins one last time in the small office at the Day Treatment Center as Good Friday eases toward Easter Sunday, and Gracie and Ed's circle eases toward its close.

ACKNOWLEDGMENTS

I am indebted to so many people who have assisted in some way with the creation and honing of this novel. Thank you . . .

Joe and Juanita Arnoult, for the love, the eccentric childhood, and the magic in the madness.

Stella Connell, Leslie Meredith, Martha Levin, and Kit Frick, for your patience, guidance, astute observations, and your hard work in so many areas on behalf of novel and novelist. And to Carisa Hays, Jill Siegel, Carleigh Brower, Amanda Walker, Eleni Caminis, Andrew Paulson, and everyone at Free Press who has had a hand in this novel's publication.

Lee Smith and Isabel Zuber, without you, I might have given up years ago. And thank you for helping *Sufficient Grace* find the right shepherd. Other friends, family, and colleagues who have read and reread all or part of this book and some who have provided valuable technical information, including: Johnny Banes, Virginia Boyd, William Brock, Bill Brown, Joni Caldwell, Donna Campbell, Susan Campbell, Barbara Collins, Linda Dumat, Pamela Duncan, Clyde Edgerton, Georgann Eubanks, Rebecca Flippen, Kaye Gibbons, Judy Goldman, Phyllis Grayson, Sharon Haley, William Henderson, Iris Tillman Hill, Lucinda MacKethan, Emily Masters, Debbie McClanahan, Jill McCorkle, Alyson McGee, Sharon Meginnis, Patti Meredith, Linda Page, Catherine Peck, John Price, Tom Rankin, Bruce and Vivian Sevier, Carol Spear Stewart, Beth Stone, Jody Stone, Kory Wells, Michael Lee West, Lisa Whitehead, Annelle Williams, Gary Williams, Lynn York, and Ginger Young. To Parks Lanier and the SELU Sisters (male and female), to other members of the Roger Flourish Writers Group, wherever you are, and to my good friends at the Center for Documentary Studies at Duke University, now and back when, to the Grey Mule Writers Circle, and the Southern Amen Revelation Sisterhood. To Amy and Dave Wilder, Darryl and Kim Brock, and Emily and Lauren Brock, for your encouragement and for making me feel a part of the family. To my exceedingly good friends who have been there for me all along the way, you know who you are and you are always in my heart.

I am particularly grateful to . . .

My children, Chad and Beth Stone, for your love, encouragement, pride in my successes, and for more than I have words to say, but you *know*. To my daughter-in-law, Jody Stone, for being there and encouraging always. To little Ella Stone, whose presence keeps everything in perspective.

More than anyone, I give thanks for and to my beloved husband William Brock, who believed I could write a novel and gave me the opportunity to do it. Because of his love and faith in my purpose, his priceless sense of humor, his ability to endure a range of circumstances, his occasional kick to my rear, and his paycheck, this book is a reality. William, always.

Sufficient Grace

A NOVEL

DARNELL ARNOULT

Reading Group Guide

A Conversation with the Author

Author Profile

ABOUT THIS GUIDE

The following questions, author interview, and author profile in *Nashville Scene* are intended to help you find interesting and rewarding approaches to your reading of Darnell Arnoult's *Sufficient Grace*. We hope these elements enhance your enjoyment and appreciation of the book.

READING GROUP
DISCUSSION GUIDE FOR
SUFFICIENT GRACE

Introduction

Description

One quiet spring day, Gracie Hollaman hears voices in her head that tell her to get in her car and leave her entire life behind—her home, her husband, her daughter, her very identity. Gracie's subsequent journey will effect profound changes in the lives of everyone around her. Ultimately, her quest leads her into the home of Mama Toot and Mattie, two strong, accomplished women going through life changes of their own. As the bonds between these women grow stronger and the family Gracie left behind comes to terms with their loss, both worlds slowly and inevitably collide.

Discussion Questions

1. How would you characterize the voices that Gracie Hollaman hears as she prepares to leave her home forever? What do these voices suggest about Gracie's mental state, and in what ways do they connect to a religious framework?
2. "People say men have midlife crises, but it's the women." Why does Ed Hollaman initially interpret Gracie's disappearance as her abandonment of him? What does his reaction to her absence suggest about the nature of their marriage and their feelings for each other?
3. When Mattie Riley discovers Gracie Hollaman lying on Arty's grave,

why does she see it as some kind of divine signal? How does Mattie's grief over her husband's untimely death affect her decision to take Gracie into her home?

4. How does Gracie's disappearance from their home improve Ed's life? What changes in his character and day-to-day existence seem especially dramatic or interesting? Given the uncertain circumstances of his marriage, to what extent are his feelings for Parva Wilson understandable?

5. In what ways is Mama Toot the "glue" that holds her family together? What explains Toot's delay in recognizing "Rachel" as the grown-up little girl, Gracie, whom she took care of so many years before? How does she make sense of Gracie's reappearance in her life?

6. How would you describe Ginger's reaction to her mother's schizophrenia? Why do you think that she fears for her own mental instability? What do you think of her boyfriend, Wally, and the prospects for their relationship?

7. In what ways do the characters experience the presence of Arty in the novel? Do you think he is really present? Why or why not?

8. Do you feel Mattie must choose between her grief over Arty's death and her burgeoning feelings for Norvis Dibner? Why or why not? Why do you think the author chose to conclude the novel before Mattie reaches closure with Arty's death and fully embraces her romantic interest in Norvis?

9. Why are Ed Hollaman and Mama Toot content with Gracie's desire to change her name to Rachel, divorce Ed, and return to live with the Riley family? How does Gracie's decision have an impact on both families?

10. Besides the close look at Ed and Gracie's relationship, in what other ways does the novel seem to address the idea of love and marriage?

11. How does the novel explore the concept of mothering? What about mother-daughter relationships in particular? What about the definition of family?

12. What is the significance of Tyrone's great-grandmother's prediction for his future? In what ways does the prediction come true?

13. We know Gracie becomes obsessed with closing the circle of her story with Ed. Where else do you see circles at play in the novel?

14. "They have been raised up to believe anything of God, to believe He can say your time is out no matter who loves you or how much." What role does faith play in the Riley family? To what extent does it play an important role for the Hollaman family?

15. Sister Reba and Gracie both feel "called" to make some of the same decisions. They both leave their families for a different, nontraditional life, a life with a focus they believe is defined by something beyond their own desires, even by God. They both retreat to the woods at times. Can you think of other common ground shared by Reba and Gracie? Why are these similarities viewed differently from one character to the other?

16. On a larger scale, how do you interpret the issues of faith and fate in the novel? Of miracles and coincidence? Of the thin gray line between a passionate, inspired calling and bona fide illness?

17. Why is food so important in *Sufficient Grace*? What does cooking represent to Mattie Riley? What does it symbolize for Ed Hollaman? What significance does it hold for the time frame of the novel? How does Sister Reba's sermon on leftovers apply throughout the book? How did the sensory descriptions of cooking and eating in *Sufficient Grace* affect your reading experience?

18. How did you interpret the title of the novel? In what way does the religious concept sufficient grace relate to events in the book?

19. Which character(s) in *Sufficient Grace* did you most identify with and why? Who is your favorite character and why? Do you think that there is a single "hero" or "heroine" in this novel? Why or why not?

A CONVERSATION WITH
DARNELL ARNOULT

Sufficient Grace **explores many of the uncertainties involved in marriage. What drew you to this theme as a writer?**

I suppose it has something to do with the fact that both of my parents were divorced before they married each other (that was my mother's third marriage), their marriage was permanently disrupted by her illness and other factors, and my first husband and I divorced when I was twenty-five. I was single for almost twenty years before I remarried. During that time, I paid attention to what seemed to make a good and lasting marriage, what seemed to constitute the disillusionment of marriage, what made people think they wanted to be married in the first place. Having remarried at forty-six, I am interested in the ways romance and commitment work at middle age, both for people who are coming at it from previous experience and those who are still inexperienced, like Parva.

What kind of research did you do on the medical condition of schizophrenia with which Gracie/Rachel is diagnosed?

My mother was diagnosed with chronic paranoid schizophrenia when she was forty years old and I was eight. Before that time, my mother had been a resourceful businesswoman and a popular person in the community. Her late onset of the disease probably started in her late thirties, but the symptoms became undeniable when she was forty. So I have grown up with this disease, seen treatment and diagnosis of my mother change over time, and talked at length with some of her doctors and caregivers. And, until I moved to Tennessee in 2000, I've always spent a great deal of time with my mother and she has lived with me and my children on a few occasions. Along with that close personal experience of the disease, I have talked with psychiatrists, psychologists, and psychiatric nurses about the changes in treatment and the different perspectives on the disease and its variations, and about the evolution of treatment. And, of course, I've read about it all.

You have an undergraduate degree in American Studies with a concentration in Southern folklore. To what extent did this background influence your portrayal of Gracie Hollaman, a character who undergoes a "rebirth" of sorts?

My undergraduate studies included folk art, anthropology, religion, and material culture, among other things. I dipped into each of these disciplines while writing *Sufficient Grace*.

The most obvious link is with Gracie's art. Nowadays the definition of the term "folk art" extends beyond utilitarian decorative arts to include a wide range of work and terminology, and sometimes controversy: outsider art, visionary art, untrained artists, self-taught artists, and so on. I know authors, gallery owners, exhibit curators, and collectors who specialize or have experience in this field. In the last fifteen years there has been an explosion of interest in outsider and self-taught art, and the number of traditional and online venues for viewing and purchasing this work continues to grow. While many outsider and visionary artists are *not* mentally ill, some artists in this broad category do experience mental illness, and their art therapists are often early witnesses as that artistic vision manifests and develops.

While this novel is not autobiographical, I have borrowed certain things from my own experience and given those things to my characters in places. The scene where Gracie draws the Jesus at the foot of Ed's bed comes from my mother drawing a Jesus at the foot of my bed when I was eight years old. She had a feeling something wasn't right with her, or that others thought so, and that she might be forced to leave me. She wanted me to know that Jesus was always with me and looking out for me, even if she couldn't be there. My mother isn't a visual artist, but that act, coupled with exposure to outsider and visionary art from my studies in college and later work at the Center for Documentary Studies at Duke University, has fed into the character development of Gracie and the art-related themes in *Sufficient Grace*.

The history of mythology and religion play a huge role in the novel in both obvious and subtle ways. Gracie's religious point of view is widely inclusive. She believes in both angels and fairies, figures from both a Judeo-Christian-Islamic tradition and pagan tradition. Our modern visual concept of angels is heavily influenced by Egyptian, Greek, and Roman ideas of goddesses, with some later influence from Celtic traditions. So, on some level, the angels and fairies have become intertwined. The Celtic influence is evident in the fairy stone myth, a myth I didn't make up. Those fairy stones and their legend really exist.

Sufficient Grace is full of the borrowing from one cultural tradition to another. Even Toot admits her knowledge and acceptance of "the old ways" even though she is washed in the blood of the Lamb, and Tyrone is the subject of prophecy that some might consider outside the strictest interpretation of Christianity. Yet, others might reconcile and absorb these phenomena to be the work of a larger godly design.

Sufficient Grace is suffused (both structurally and thematically) with references to faith. How do you see faith operating for the characters in your novel?

The short answer is "A variety of ways!" The long answer is [that] I am the child of a jackleg Catholic father and a schizophrenic, formerly Protestant, currently Catholic mother with religious cornerstones in the psychotic ways she sees the world. As an older child, I lived with my grandmother, who was a Baptist, then a Methodist, who was suspicious of Papists. I've studied mythology, religion, and religious practice, and I'm married to the well-educated son of a Pentecostal Church of God preacher. To say the least, I have an eclectic personal spiritual position and vision. Basically, I am a seeker full of questions and constantly formulating shifting answers. That probably has a lot to do with why I write.

I try to make facets of my religious history and education come through in my characters. I want my characters to explore their spiritual lives and personal relationship with something both inside and beyond themselves, some characters stretching the confines of a traditional belief system and some openly challenging the same. While some of my characters are churchly people, and I respect that, I want them to, on some level, either proactively or reactively, step beyond Man's attempt to define and confine God by rules and fragile reason, to be less occupied with defining God by limiting him with doctrine and dogma, much of which has and always will be politically defined and motivated.

Alongside evangelical Protestantism in the novel, Catholicism is present in cameos and in the underlying structure of the novel and the story. Historically, Catholicism is the root of modern Christianity. And Catholicism has always borrowed from pagan cultures to create its rituals and calendar. Toot and Gracie borrow and absorb beliefs and practices from Catholicism. The sections of the novel come from a loose interpretation of the Mass and other religious worship services, but the Mass in particular. In the Mass, transubstantiation occurs and the food *becomes* the body; the wine *becomes* the blood. The participants eat the body and become one with Christ. They become part of the death and rebirth, the Resurrection. The novel begins with "invitation," the invitation of the voices to Gracie, but it is also meant to reflect the call to worship at the onset of a religious service. The other sections have similar double meanings as in commitment to faith, the offertories—the second being more defined in purpose, the Eucharist, and the close with a benediction, a prayer to carry participants out of the sacred ritual and into the secular world prepared to maintain a spiritual existence.

All of this is of course playing with ideas, not certainty. In my mind, my novel is not about divine intervention so much as the *possibility* of divine intervention. What implication does that possibility have for Gracie as well as all the other characters in the novel, whether they are believers or not?

The bottom line is that my religious perspective doesn't have to matter to readers. How they interpret *Sufficient Grace* and judge its characters and events will be as personal and individual as their own beliefs and questions, and their own points of view on faith, religion, charity, and possibility.

You introduce some wonderful comedic moments into the relationship that develops between Parva Wilson and Ed Hollaman. Why does their intimacy lend itself to such moments of humor?

My first answer to that question is "That's just how it came out." But giving the question more thought, I believe it has something to do with my own marriage and the courtship that started when I was in my mid-forties and my husband had just turned fifty. We had both been divorced for years before we met, and our accumulated experience taught us that one of the most important elements of a relationship can be a compatible sense of humor, that a shared sense of humor is one of the most intimate connections between people. While Ed and Parva don't laugh so much at themselves, and do experience from the beginning a kind of electric attraction, they have a lighter, more slapstick approach to love and romance, despite the serious circumstances that surround their relationship. That vision of love and my attraction to the evolution of their midlife relationship surely come from my own marriage on some level.

Descriptions of food, cooking, and recipes abound in *Sufficient Grace*. How did this culinary theme emerge in your work?

At some point I realized that Ed was really hungry and, in more ways than one, he needed to learn to feed himself. Later I thought there was too much food and cooking and eating going on in the book. I tried to stop writing so much about it, but it wouldn't go away. Then, one day it hit me like a ton of bricks that my novel started on Holy Thursday, the day of the Last Supper. Then I knew my subconscious was trying to tell me something, trying to help me write my novel. I realized that everyone in the novel is indeed hungry for something.

As for the food, the truth is, I'm not a great cook. I'm a passable cook. But I love to eat, and I have been exposed to a variety of food cultures and the Southern propensity to heal and nurture with food. All that experience was helpful as this particular theme became apparent during the novel-writing process.

Annelle Williams, a friend and food columnist from my hometown (who is a much better cook than I am) has helped me come up with some of the recipes mentioned in the book. Despite all this self-effacing humility, I will go on record by saying that I make a darn good salmon patty and killer deviled eggs.

You are both a published poet and a novelist. For you, how does the composition of poetry and of fiction differ? Is there any overlap?

I began writing poetry when I didn't have time to write anything longer. A poem is small, compact, travels well. I could write and revise in short moments in the bleachers of a Babe Ruth League baseball practice, or while waiting for middle school to let out, or in those last few tired minutes before I turned out the light. Much of my poetry is character-driven narrative poetry because I had all these characters in my head when I was a young single mother and no time to put them in a longer story. But as I began to take poetry more seriously as a genre, line length, rhythm, language, form, and the value of just the right word took on more and more importance. Being a poet makes me a better fiction writer than I might be otherwise.

Short fiction is much more like a poem than a novel. But in each case, the increased elbow room of a longer type of story gives you space to explore and make side trips, to add characters and geography, to develop backstory and subplot, and let things develop in layers. The poem is looking through a keyhole and imagining what is beyond the boundaries of what you see, the short story is sticking your head in a window and seeing that one room pretty well and maybe being able to see into another room slightly, and the novel is walking through the door into a life, a whole world. With a novel, I have to live with my characters. I work hard to get them solidly planted in my head, and then they don't want to leave while I'm having dinner or going for a ride with my husband. They are *there* for the duration, or I lose them and have to work like hell to get them back.

For me, separating that act of writing poetry from fiction is like combing out a badly tangled head of hair. It is important to explore poetry as a writer, even if you never show your poems to anyone. I read a lot of good fiction before and while I'm writing fiction, but I read lots of poetry as I revise because it makes me mindful of my most precious tool, words and the way they work individually and together to build a narrative. And poetry is a wonderful exercise in distilling ideas in relatively few words using the concrete, not the abstract. That same approach makes the novel more real to me.

I'm always writing poetry, good and bad, as part of my writing practice. But reading other poets' work often gives me ideas for something other than poetry. Despite the apparent differences, separating the writing of poetry from the writing of fiction is almost impossible for me.

Sufficient Grace is your first novel. How long did you work on it, and what were some of the challenges and delights you encountered along the way?

This novel started years and years ago as a short story about Ed and Gracie that wouldn't stay a short story. After a couple of years, I gave up on the story and gave in to the novel. I was so stretched for time in those days that I carried notes on characters and scenes and fifty pages of the novel around for several years before I was able to focus on it in a big way. That time came about ten years after the conception of the novel and the two families. When I married my husband back in 2000, he gave me the gift of time and encouragement to work on the novel full time. Oh, and he paid the bills! Once I got down to business, it took me about a year to write the first draft and about another eight months to revise it to a point I was ready to send it out to agents. I worked all this in around revising my poetry collection, because I decided to make it my master's thesis, and LSU Press had expressed interest in publishing a shorter version of the thesis. It was like having two babies at once, only not twins.

Do you consider _Sufficient Grace_ a novel in the tradition of contemporary Southern fiction?

I am a Southerner. I grew up in the South, a part of the South heavily influenced by Southern Appalachian culture. I love and appreciate the beauty and complexity of the South. And my longtime friends and mentors are considered some of the South's finest contemporary writers. So it would be hard for me to write a book that wasn't considered Southern. But like so many other writers whose work comes out of that experience steeped in place and artful storytelling, I hope the novel has a universal appeal because, while it addresses themes commonly thought of as regional, those themes have significant implications far beyond the Mason-Dixon line and Gulf of Mexico.

What's your next project?

I am working on a novel about a woman who has seven husbands—not all at the same time. The working title is *The Nine Lives of Loody Tibet*. Of her nine lives, one is defined by her father, seven by her husbands, and the ninth life she shapes for herself alongside, in spite of, and in the space in between the men in her life. This is another story I began years ago. After I married my husband, I found out his grandmother had been married seven times. This is where the *Twilight Zone* theme starts playing in the background.

Enhance Your Book Club

1. To read more about the inspired art Gracie Hollaman creates from everyday objects, visit http://www.outsiderart.info/.
2. Have you ever been tempted, like Ed Hollaman, to enter some of your best recipes into a cooking contest? Visit http://www.foodreference.com/html/recipecontests.html to learn more about ongoing contests and how you can show off your finest foods!
3. Gracie Hollaman is diagnosed with schizophrenia in *Sufficient Grace*. To understand more about the symptoms and treatments of this medical condition, visit this comprehensive website: http://www.schizophrenia.com/.

LONGSHOT MIRACLES

*How a writer managed to survive teen pregnancy, ADD,
Internet dating, and a house fire—and still publish
two acclaimed books in six months*

MARIA BROWNING

Back in rural Virginia, Darnell Arnoult was one of those sensitive young girls who dreams of growing up to be a writer. It's a classic adolescent female phase, like being crazy for horses, and thanks to role models like Harper Lee and Flannery O'Connor, Southern girls are especially prone to the fantasy. Besides, there's something wonderfully attainable about it: you don't have to be rich, or beautiful, or popular. In fact, it's better if you're not. Misfortune is a writer's primary material.

Darnell Arnoult first latched onto the dream during her senior year of high school, when she was newlywed and pregnant. A teacher's praise for a story she wrote planted the idea, but she's had to wait a long time for that seed to bear fruit. In 2005, as she was about to turn 50, Louisiana State University Press, one of the premier poetry publishers in the country, brought out her first volume of poems, *What Travels With Us*. In 2006, Free Press, a prestigious imprint of Simon & Schuster, released her first novel, *Sufficient Grace*, with glowing blurbs from the likes of Kaye Gibbons and Clyde Edgerton. The story of how she managed to keep her ambition alive for three decades is a tale of perseverance, talent, and good luck. It's also an object lesson in the way all good things come at a price.

*   *   *

Arnoult doesn't project the slightest air of either struggling artist or literary diva. She's a grandmother who commutes from her rural home to Nashville several days a week for babysitting duty, but you'd never peg her for a grandma either. A petite, zaftig blonde with a pretty smile and a lively manner, she could easily pass for a decade younger. When she mentions that she was once a cheerleader, you can instantly picture her at 17, a wholesome Aphrodite of the sidelines.

Arnoult is quick to get to the heart of her approach to both writing and life: "I have this idea that whatever happens to you, no matter how bad it is, you have to find a way to laugh"—a philosophy she developed very early. At eight, she was packed off to a Catholic boarding school after her mother developed schizophrenia. The next year her father went bankrupt, and she and her mother were sent to live with her grandmother and great-aunt in the mill town of Fieldale, Virginia. Teen marriage and motherhood were followed by an early divorce and the challenges of single parenting.

She relates her story with frankness and humor, and not a whiff of self-pity. If anything, she revels in the richness of it, and the general absurdity of life. Her tale of how her first husband pushed her to enroll at the University of North Carolina—Chapel Hill, even filling out the application for her, because it meant he'd be able to get basketball tickets while she got an education, isn't a complaint about marital bullying, but a comic portrait of what it's like to be young and clueless.

Arnoult's upbeat attitude about her troubled history is echoed in her work. *Sufficient Grace* is the seriocomic story of a white, middle-aged Southern housewife, Gracie Hollaman, who one day begins hearing voices and drawing outsized Jesuses on the walls of her tasteful home. In a psychotic fog, she abandons her husband and grown daughter, who fear she's been kidnapped or run away with a lover, and finds refuge with a loving but troubled black family headed by the venerable Mama Toot. Mattie, Toot's grief-stricken daughter-in-law, believes the catatonic Gracie is some kind of messenger from God, sent to connect her with her dead husband. Eventually Gracie is found and enters the world of hospitals and psychiatrists, but her creative vision cannot be stifled. Medication breaks through her speechless trance, but she refuses to return to "real" life and her former identity.

Though we get a sense of her childhood trauma and her helplessness in the face of her visions, the novel only hints at Gracie's inner turmoil. It focuses instead on the way her madness uncovers the mundane suffering of all the healthy, responsible people around her. Every one of them, it seems, is lonely, or mourning, or just looking for some purpose in life. Gracie's determination to step outside the bounds of normality allows them—actually, forces them—to question their accepted roles. The process is not painless, but ultimately it's all to the good. By the end of the novel, everyone finds love and gets a few steps closer to understanding his or her true calling—which, for a remarkable number of them, seems to involve cooking. Writer and longtime friend Lee Smith calls the book "a parable of art," but it's also an extended paean to baked goods. "I think I gained 30 pounds writing this novel," Arnoult says with a laugh.

This is a remarkably sunny view of mental illness, and when you consider that it was written by the daughter of a schizophrenic mother, you begin to understand that making lemons into lemonade is Arnoult's specialty. "I learned to laugh in difficult situations from my mother. She can tell a story about trying to hang herself, and she'll be laughing, and we'll be laughing and crying at the same time." *Sufficient Grace* is all about embracing the chaos of life with an open heart—about trusting your own vision, about having faith that there is logic in the most random, baffling impulses. It's about understanding that hard times are never as bleak as they seem.

Mama Toot sums up the novel's broad wisdom as she tries to help a child reconcile spiritual truths with physical reality. "Everything is always more than one thing," she tells him. Gracie may be afflicted, but that doesn't mean she's not inspired. She can be a helpless woman having a psychotic episode, *and* a messenger from God. The trick is to keep your faith in the limitless potential for good, while dealing honestly with the harsh realities life can throw your way. As another character, an itinerant preacher, puts it, "Sometimes miracles go by the name coincidence. Sometimes they go by the name accident. Sometimes they go by the names unexpected, longshot, curveball, miscalculation."

*   *   *

This is an insight Arnoult applies rigorously to her own life. "I don't even have a circular life," she says." I have a curlicue life." She loves to tell stories about how bad things become good things. Shortly after she enrolled at UNC, she and her husband split, and she was on her own with two small kids (bad thing). With only enough money for one more semester's tuition, she decided she might as well take a creative writing class (good thing). The professor thought her first assignment was so hopeless she was asked to withdraw from the class (bad thing). Lee Smith, already one of Arnoult's favorite writers, had just begun teaching a writing class in the university's evening degree program. Arnoult, as a day student, would normally have been barred from taking it, but a friend in the class dragged Arnoult along one night and insisted that Smith let her enroll. Smith agreed (*very* good thing).

"She was extraordinary as a student," says Smith, who has remained a mentor for more than two decades. "Everything she wrote was just golden . . . It was clear that she was a major talent." Smith, along with Isabel Zuber and poet Kathryn Stripling Byer, is part of a large community of Chapel Hill writers that has provided invaluable support to Arnoult over the years, critiquing her work and helping her make contacts in the publishing world. It was Smith and Zuber who eventually helped Arnoult find an agent to place her novel. In time, Arnoult herself began offering support to beginning writers, teaching workshops and continuing ed classes.

But friends and colleagues can help only so much. Ultimately, every writer has to struggle to get the words on paper. Arnoult wrote when she had time, between cleaning houses for a living, trying to finish her college degree, and caring for her two children. "My kids always came first," she says. She switched from fiction to poetry because she couldn't summon the focus necessary for full-length stories in her brief opportunities to work. (Arnoult has been diagnosed with attention deficit disorder. While she sometimes uses medication to help her stay focused and organized, she finds it interferes with the creative process.) She never stopped writing, but it wasn't clear if life would ever give her the time and mental space she needed to produce the fully formed work that was in her head.

By November 1998 she had settled into an interesting administrative job at the Duke Center for Documentary Studies. She was working on a master's degree in creative writing at North Carolina State, her children were grown, and she had published a handful of poems and stories. Most people, past 40 and living a comfortable life, would not be looking to take big risks. Without resorting to some notion of fate that only Mama Toot could explain, it's hard to understand why one night, on a whim, Arnoult answered an Internet personal ad placed by a retired Atlanta contractor named William Brock.

A few years earlier, Brock had decided to leave hectic Atlanta for a small farm in a remote corner of Smith County, Tennessee. He planned to continue working as a private contractor, but a subsequent brush with death in the form of double-bypass surgery left him determined to devote himself to doing only what he enjoyed—and for Brock that was finishing sheet rock and riding horses. "Life's too short to compromise," he says. The venture into Internet personals was as much a whim for him as for Arnoult. After a little good-natured sparring via email, the couple commenced a long-distance courtship, and married on April Fool's Day 2000.

Brock was no well-off retiree, and his medical history made him uninsurable. But he respected Arnoult's literary ambition and didn't see any reason why she shouldn't devote herself to what was important to her, as he had. So they agreed that she would give full-time writing a shot. Maybe, if all went well, the novel would sell, and their bet would pay off. William, at least, says he was content to accept whatever fate delivered. "When it happens, it'll happen. If it don't happen, it won't happen."

It was a leap of faith that a lot of people half their age would find daunting. They lived on Brock's income as sheet rock finisher, in a small, rundown farmhouse built around a 150-year-old log cabin. No credit. No insurance on themselves or the house. No prospect of a book deal—for a long while, no finished book. Lee Smith says of Arnoult, "She has no sense of 'I can't do this.' She will try anything."

When Arnoult talks about her early years in Tennessee, there's a definite sense that she felt challenged. "But we were both optimistic that eventually we'd be able to bounce back." Arnoult earned some money teaching writing classes, first through Middle Tennessee State University's continuing education program, and then on her own, gaining students through word of mouth and meeting with them at whatever site was available. "I was the Mary Kay of creative writing," she says.

True to form, Arnoult made her gamble work. For an emerging writer to have two publications simultaneously issued by prestigious presses is almost unprecedented. Her determination to follow her vision was redeemed, to say the least. (Not without some ADD challenges. She laughs about the time Brock literally taped her to her chair so she'd stay in front of the computer and make necessary revisions to the novel.) Of course, selling a literary book doesn't make you Dan Brown rich, but it does greatly increase the odds that you'll sell your next one, and it puts you in the running for lucrative teaching gigs, the kind of job Arnoult feels she could manage and still be able to write.

Sufficient Grace has seemed marked for success from its first appearance. It won a starred review in *Publishers Weekly*, a bible of the publishing industry: "Arnoult's rhythmic prose beautifully reveals the human potential for unconditional love and faith." Arnoult's agent, Stella Connell, believes it has the potential to appeal to a broad audience: "It's a book that beautifully straddles the line between literary and commercial fiction."

Leslie Meredith, Arnoult's editor at Free Press, agrees, pointing out that Arnoult's work fills a new niche in the fiction landscape. "We saw Darnell's voice as representing a new generation of Southern literary/commercial writers in the post–Civil Rights South." She notes that the novel presents blacks and whites on an equal footing, and emphasizes human relationships over the redemptive violence found in the work of Southerners like Larry Brown and Pat Conroy. "We saw *Sufficient Grace* appealing to readers of Ann Tyler as well as Jan Karon, to readers of Lee Smith as well as Sue Monk Kidd," she says.

And just as Gracie's inspiration rippled out to those around her, there has been positive fallout from Arnoult's literary success. She used her advance to buy Brock a welder, a big boy toy he'd been wanting. Brock has a degree in structural engineering and devoted his Atlanta career to supervising the construction of high-rise buildings. He's not a guy who's spent his life nursing secret artistic aspirations. But Arnoult's suggestion that she'd like some yard art got him experimenting with his welder and cast-off roofing tin, and the result is a collection of remarkably beautiful metal bird sculptures. The love of nature that led him to flee the city 10 years ago is expressed in these elegant, lifelike structures. The birds now grace a number of their friends' homes, and will soon be sold by an upscale home décor catalog.

All of which would make for a lovely happy ending if this were a novel, but the twists and turns of a curlicue life never resolve themselves quite that neatly. Arnoult was looking forward to the publication of her novel on Christmas morning in 2005 when hard luck came calling again. While she was treating herself to a quiet day reading and Brock was out working on his sculptures, an electrical fire broke out in their ancient house. They rescued Arnoult's computer, a few of their belongings, and Gus the dog. The house was a total loss.

So now, as Arnoult tries to work on her second novel while juggling the promotional tasks for *Sufficient Grace*, Brock is single-handedly constructing a small new house for them on the site of their old one, as money and time become available. They're living in a borrowed trailer a few miles away, taking turns trekking to the farm each day to feed their horses, goats, and outside dogs. They've accepted a little help from friends, but they're largely determined to get through this on their own. In fact, they seem to enjoy the challenge. Optimists by nature, they carry each other along. "We both have our down days, but they're never at the same time," Arnoult says.

As she and her husband show off the house-in-progress, she seems genuinely excited by all the possibilities—where she'll put a garden, what the floor will be made of, how they'll both find room to work in the limited space. Since Brock currently has no secure place to store his welder, it's been temporarily left with a friend. He's taken up painting to replace the sculpture, and hopes to continue working in both forms. Arnoult beams as she describes the tiny sunlit studio they have planned for him.

Standing on the concrete slab, looking around at the bare frame structure that will one day be her home, Arnoult laughs a little ruefully. She always hoped that someday they'd have a better house on this idyllic property. "I just didn't think it would happen like this," she says. There's a touch of exasperation in her voice, but there's a glimmer in her eye, too—the pleasure of a writer with one more story to tell, one more opportunity to find the good thing hiding inside the bad.

ABOUT THE AUTHOR

DARNELL ARNOULT was born and raised in Henry County, Virginia. She lived for twenty years in Chapel Hill and Durham, North Carolina, where she received a BA in American Studies from the University of North Carolina at Chapel Hill and an MA in English and Creative Writing from North Carolina State University and worked at the Center for Documentary Studies at Duke University. She is also the author of *What Travels With Us: Poems*, published by Louisiana State University Press and winner of the Appalachian Studies Association's Weatherford Award. Her fiction and poetry have been published in a variety of journals, and she has taught creative writing to adults for over fifteen years. She and her husband live on a small farm near Nashville, Tennessee.

Visit the author at www.darnellarnoult.com